Belfast, with Dinosaurs, 1979
– a Prehysteric Farce

by Martin Connolly

Published in 2022 by Shanway Press,
15 Crumlin Road, Belfast BT14 6AA

ISBN: 978-1-910044-42-1

for those who dig the past
and those
stuck
in
it

Contents

BOOK ONE

Chapter One: Northern Irish Dinosaurs, pt.1, April, between 20-25, 1979

The dinosaur story all started as a bit of a joke -a bit of a 'geg', as it might be translated in Belfast-talk. It might also have been a wee rumour that started the ball rolling -the 'wee' being a freely floating and much over-used diminutive which wasn't necessarily, or always, a diminutive. Or, like any gigantic snowball, it would start out 'wee' and then just balloon as it ran. 'Geg' or 'wee rumour', it was difficult to say which was first or most pertinent. But start it most certainly did.

Whatever the story was, it threatened to sabotage some serious research into good Antrim soil and rock. Professor Janek Heinkle, of the Palaeontology Department of Heidelberg University, now visiting Prof at Queen's University, certainly felt so. He was nothing less than livid, if 'livid' is expressive enough, when he found out. He called his minions before him, to the stage area of a rather antiquated lecture room where he'd hurriedly arranged to meet them. His team comprised of one of Queen's archaeologists, Professor Tweedy (who actually often wore Tweed, even in summer), together with twelve under- and post-graduate helpers and researchers ('apostles' they called themselves), all of whom now wondered what was going on with their boss (or 'Führer' to some). Professor Heinkle wondered, too, and out loud: 'VAT is dis?', holding out a newspaper, which some could see was *The Belfast News Letter*. His voice boomed through them, and beyond, around the rickety nineteenth century auditorium. The silver threads of his usually well-behaved – abundant but orderly – hair shook, dislodging a renegade clump or two which then fell disconcertingly behind his glasses. Beads of sweat dappled his well-creased forehead, helping to amplify the image of a man in raging consternation. 'Duelling Dinos Discovery!' he trumpeted -just as the headline trumpeted, in robust alliteration, albeit as a fairly small headline on a fairly small article on page four...

[It might be noted here that the Editor of the paper in question had hoped – against hope – that this dip into alliteration wouldn't come across as too-tabloidy, or even if it did... 'What the odds!' he'd exclaimed, as only newspaper editors can. 'Just what we need!' This was the first smile anyone had seen on the Editor's face in weeks, murder and mayhem in Belfast and environs having taken centre stage for so long. 'This'll take their minds off things!' This blinding positivism was given an edge by virtue of the fact that the reporter responsible for the story was no less a figure than his own dear nephew, Ivan Stacks, neophyte in the journalism business, whose own positivism convinced Uncle not to have the story checked. 'I have it here in black and white!' thrusting his notebook under Uncle's nose. Nepotism blinds, too.]

'Vat is DIS?' Prof Heinkle screamed again, with even greater intensity, the boom making an echo of sorts, if only within the minds of his astonished audience. 'Duelling facking Dinos Discovery? I'll be made a laughingstock off. Dis cud destroy my reputation! Obliterate za mission! Vat is somevon doing to me?' His normally well-pronounced and functionally civilized English had succumbed to a fury which put the usual delicacies through the ringer, so to speak. It had Tweedy doing a bit of a double take, never having imagined he would hear his eminent superior formulate such indelicacies, even if he had sometimes bristled at his style. He straightened the lapels of his Tweed jacket, even though said lapels didn't actually need straightening.

It soon became clear from the reactions of the assembled team members which one, or ones, were likely to blame. The faces of Tracey Williamson (local lass) and Manny Jal (from Birmingham, England) were exhibiting a wider range of expressions than those of anyone else in the room, gauged in depth of frown and micro-twitches, realization why they'd all been summoned so precipitously dawning at last. Their body language also spoke reams, be it in the dog-like tilting of the head (made more noticeable by their respectively distinctive coiffures) or the sudden need to fold arms, and then unfold them again, with the odd scratch at the back of the head thrown in for good measure.

Heinkle had them right away. 'Du!' he exclaimed, his 'du' imaginable as a sonic projectile launched beyond the reach of his suddenly out-flung right arm, hand, and gun-barrel-like index finger. It helped that he was six-foot tall and stood as straight as a die. 'Are you the…' and he then brought the paper up to his eyes, eager to pinpoint the offending article. This entailed both hands, and no little exasperation as he soon realized he had to tear off his pince-nez glasses (which he didn't need for reading). At last, he had it, and read: '… *"sources close to Professor… Hanek Jeinkle"*?' He stopped. You could almost say he smiled. 'Thank Moder Mary Jesus unt all ze saintz, at least they spelt mine name wrong!' he roared with what you might term the coldest of cold comforts. Tracey and Manny looked up in unison, doubt, shame and/or fear coursing through their neural networks, making whatever differences they possessed as individuals physiognomically unimportant. They were just two frightened kids. 'Yes,' they said chorally, if weakly, tremulously, pathetically. 'Da!' exclaimed the Professor in a startling release of exasperation, 'Da!' -startling as it concerned the possible ruination of all, all his research and planning, and all those weeks spent in calm and methodical study of the secrets of the distant past, even as a bloody -both uses- war raged on all around. (Not to mention 'ze damned weater'!) Heinkle thereupon strode toward the offending two, twisted the newspaper into a baton and set about beating them on the head with it, slowly and methodically (as was his way in palaeontology), more in mock-blows than ones with any physical force, but fit for purpose. What he was doing was dealing out public punishment for private betrayal. In return, Tracey and Manny uttered suitably anguish-filled mock 'Ow!s' and 'Ah!s' and other utterances that defied transcription, lending to the scene a decided touch of the surreal, or the farcically surreal, even the Dada-esque.

The others looked on disbelief, not so much because they felt these students had let the side down, as Tracey and Manny were well known as 'loafers' and 'spoofers', never taking things as seriously as they should, but because their eminent Professor had been reduced to this. It was a case of tut, tut, tut all round. This went on for several seconds, until poor Professor Janek Heinkle (not Hanek Jeinkle), of the Palaeontology Department of Heidelberg University, sixty-five years old, and now suddenly feeling each and every one of them, desisted, dropped the paper baton, and, like a broken man, exited the auditorium in what were discerned to be actual tears…

Alas, here we see what 'loose talk' can mean, or could mean back in the late '70s when this all happened, in Northern Ireland, land of conflict, clash and contumacy. Had it been a case of some silly rumour floating about, a rumour generated by a bit of spoofing, perhaps? Is that what had sparked this Greek tragedy? Sure, everybody knew they had to be careful what they said in certain company in ole Norn Iron… All eyes fell on Manny and Tracey, but they weren't saying boo. 'Whatever you say, say nothing', the mantra of the day, was usually only about politics and religion -not dinosaurs. You could always chance your arm, of course, if you were fishing (and not for fish). You'd either catch something or get pulled in. Disaster or glory, there was a very fine line between the two, and, bejeepers, glory had a shine to it. There were fearless ones about who'd plough through all the barriers, just to get a decent morsel – and bugger the consequences if it all blew up in their face.

Ivan Stacks was the man for all this, the man to uncover the tightest-held secret, or, if need be, unearth a story completely devoid of truth, but pungent with all the juice he imagined his readers, and his Editor uncle, would willingly lap up. That, and he had always been partial to anything to do with dinosaurs, having never gotten over the happiest time of his life, starting at the age of ten -a mere thirteen years ago-, playing with his plastic dino kit in the front parlour of the family house on the Shankill Road. He'd done his best to develop things by trips to the local library, but it was the images of these fabulous beasts stalking the plains with erupting volcanoes in the background that he lived for, not the difficult-to-pronounce or hard-to-remember terms and descriptions. Dinosaurs had lived in his mind as safely scary playmates, and inhabited a place where he could always go, when the going got rough, so to speak. Like when he'd be smacked for making a mess, be it a poorly balanced glass of milk, standing in for a volcano, on the parlour settee, undergoing an... 'Earthquake!' So, when he got his job as 'Junior Reporter' at the *News Letter*, and was given 'free rein', not realizing that in fact he'd just been shunted off into a place where he couldn't possibly touch any story of worth, he leapt at the chance to follow his heart whenever he could. And with a heart such as his, and his wallet stuffed with cash, Ivan felt he was on a mission to loosen tongues and shake the treetops for all the precious coconuts he could have rain down on his head. Wherever it took him and into whatever nook and cranny he had to squeeze (and with even the largest nook or cranny he'd likely have to squeeze quite a bit, having grown slightly porcine since the age of the dinosaurs), he would gladly go.

He was pals with a bloke who knew a gal who worked with another bloke who knew a gal who, he was told, was a 'vital member of the team of Professor Janek Heinkle of the Palaeontology Department of Heidelberg University', digging for dino bones in the ground near Carrickfergus. And that bloke, the first one, the one who was pals with Ivan, knew that Ivan was into all that kind of thing, so he started in: 'I know this gal who works with this bloke…' 'Yeah?' replied Ivan, 'I know this other gal who works with this other bloke...' 'Aye, but wait'll ye hear…' Ivan's eyes narrowed in expectation. 'Aye, well, this bloke…' 'The one who works with the gal?' 'Aye. The same. Well, he knows this other gal…' Now Ivan was looking confused. Abe had him where he wanted him: '…who is a flippin' dinosaur hunter!' Ivan, in mid-sup, blew some of the head of the new pint he was raising to his lips onto the face of his drinking interlocutor. 'Watcha!' said a slightly splattered Abe, but then resumed his tale. 'Apparently, there's this team up in Carrick, and, well,' confided 'Abe', as he was known (for his conspicuous Abraham Lincoln-like overgrown goatee, but plain 'Davy' to his Ma and Da), 'it's all very hush-hush, ye understand…' He'd gotten Ivan's attention, and, with a little tap of the glass, accompanied by a look which plead the poor mouth, he'd also gotten Ivan's acquiescence to get the next round in, even though it was Abe's turn. 'Don't fuckin' go away!' blurted a deadly serious Ivan, as he rushed to the bar and hurriedly petitioned the barman for two stiff ones (and a shining new pint of Harp for Abe).

He could feel his journalistic juices rise – there was a story here to be had. Three rounds later there was a story: that Ivan Stacks was as gullible as a toddler watching *Romper Room*. Strictly speaking, however, this dino story was a mixture of Abe 'codding him on', not to mention 'drilling him for drink', combined with actual rumours Abe had heard down through that chain of blokes and gals. Abe/Davy/bloke/Ivan's friend and latest source hadn't taken these seriously (or cared tuppence either), but now he saw a use for them. Ivan swallowed every word (just as Abe swallowed every golden drop) and all he had to do now was 'get on it', in the best traditions of investigative journalism. They'd discovered evidence of a world's first, Abe insisted, almost believing it himself, of 'actual signs, in the fossils, that two fuckin' dinos had been four-square in battle together, millions and millions of years ago! Bitemarks, torn-off limbs, broken teeth, you name it, beating the fuckin' shite outta each other!' Ivan sank a sizeable slurp of his own pint, Tennent's ('less chemicals than thon'), followed by a drag of his White Horse, briefly contemplating the ancient scene: 'Fuck!' he exhaled. 'A scoop ready to be had, Ivan!' Abe stoutly slapped his friend's shoulder, and asked, 'Are you the man for the job?' In Abe's defence, he was pretty 'snattered' by this stage, having imbibed copious amounts of Harp and even a few Carlsbergs, too (a speciality here). That *and* he loved to rib his friend. 'Remember, Ivan', slurred Abe, one whole hour later, as they were leaving the Rex Bar, on the Shankill Road, the one carrying the other, 'fuckin' hush, hush... don't let them know you're onto the bastards...' 'Gotcha, Abraham,' slurred back Ivan, 'they won't know what hit them...'

Ivan woke up the next morning in his wee house off the Woodvale Road with two things weighing on his mind, his Goliath Crane scale hangover and the distant memory of a glory that was his for the taking. Wolfing down an Ulster fry the size of a large frying pan, he worked on both. As he forked into his second piece of 'tatie bread' (ominously, Belfast rhyming slang for 'dead'), satisfyingly coated with Heinz beans in tomato sauce, and sprinkled liberally with salt, he started on his plan. Sure, it was 'hush-hush', but it would have to start with a simple inquiry, a phone call. Or, would it be a trip into work to peruse the files on recent activity in science-related stories? (With all this roadworks going on inside his noggin, he winced.) A few bites of salted black pudding and runny-egg-soused soda bread later, he realized it would have to be a bit of both, and before he knew it, he was dressed and out the door. To cut a long story short, Ivan rifled through whatever files he could get his hands on in the offices of the *News Letter* on Donegall Street, to the bemusement of many, found this and that, phoned Queen's, and put it together that he'd need to get to Carrickfergus, and slightly beyond, to a spot called 'Eden', to attack this thing properly, even get an interview. His hangover had long dissipated. The lunchtime pint in The Morning Star made sure of that.

The Carrickfergus Investigation, undertaken early Saturday, began as a bit of a wash-out. Yes, because it bucketed out of the heavens, but also because his attempts to make contact with the dig team came to nothing. After 'tholing' the hour-long ('stuffy') Ulsterbus ride, Ivan hailed a cab with this delightful petition, 'Eden, please! Tree of Knowledge here I come', to which the cabbie, disappointingly, merely grunted in response. 'That joke was wasted on ye,' muttered Ivan. Yet, as though decreed by a still-angry God of the Old Testament, there would be no joy in Eden. While it looked very *post*-diluvial, very neglected-wasteland-like, in greys and whatever colour mud is, Eden was also *presently* under sustained attack from the Heavens, with or without a capital 'h'. Being so close to the shore, there was also more than a bit of a chill about the place, which Ivan's hand-me-down Mac did little to blunt. To Ivan, the place looked like a construction site, and as with most construction sites, it was well-cordoned off, with not even a buzzer on the corrugated wall. With the rain falling in sheets you could write graffiti on, he felt like he was in the wrong place at the wrong time. 'Let me see,' he muttered to himself – which was Ivan-code for 'I need a drink.' Thankfully having asked the taximan to stay awhile, it wasn't his worst decision ever to give up for the time-being ('strategy, strategy' he consoled himself, in Churchillian mode) and head back to Carrick proper. And, with the fickleness of Northern Irish weather being what it often is, within the short space of the ride, the rain dried up *en masse* and the sun came out to play.

Now, however, Ivan found himself at a loose end, wandering around the town as he wondered what to do (wandering and wondering…), visiting the harbour and the Castle, or at least its entrance, which was, rudely, CLOSED. There was nothing for it, he decided, but to retire to The Central for a compensatory libation. 'Only Abe can help now,' said a down-but-not-beaten Ivan, as he started in on his second Tennent's, and rifled through his pockets for the phone number at the furniture store where his friend was 'sub-manager' (one time prompting the witticism: 'Watch out for the Blue Meanies!' He further recalled that no penny had dropped in Abe-world.). An hour later, things were looking up. He was simply in the wrong bar.

The Dobbins Inn it would be, he'd gotten the nod. That's where 'the leakers' drank. 'Could you repeat that, Abe? That's very funny, you know!' Abe, struggling to catch what Ivan was 'on about', didn't know what he thought was funny until Ivan tried to explain it, by which time Abe thought maybe he'd better tell him it was all a joke anyway. Before he could, though, Ivan was calling time on their chat, as he had to 'get cracking!' Abe signed off, wondering if their friendship would ever get over this major leg pull. 'Ah, sure, we all need a laugh…' thought Abe back in Belfast, suddenly mindful of the backdrop of hell that life was in Northern Ireland these days, murder, bombs and bullets a-go-go. 'And they say Easter is a time of Christian love… It's nice some people have a hobby to take their minds off such things….'

The Dobbins was a fine establishment, where you could even spend the night (if you'd had a few too many?). With no windows and the walls done in whitewash, the lounge Ivan had made his way to -many hours, more wandering around and a leisurely dinner hence- had the touch of a cave about it, a very cozy one, of course, with wooden beams overhead, brass fittings and fine grain wooden tables and chairs all round. A few maritime bits and pieces on the walls, too. Ivan stationed himself next to the couple he'd been told about ('he's a bit brown, like, and sporting an Afro and she's got long hippy hair, you couldn't miss 'em, especially in Carrick…'). Very devious this journalistic business, Ivan had to admit, as he did his best to eavesdrop on their conversation amidst the chatter of other nattering punters. After -no less than- two pints of Tennent's, a single Teacher's, and an earful of endless chatter about 'femurs', 'fossils', 'scales', 'bitemarks', 'footprints', and someone or something called 'Pangea', he could hold himself in no longer and arched over toward his targets. (He'd come up with a 'wee plan'.) 'Excuse me,' he said, in his best polite-gentleman's voice, making eye contact with the girl, 'my table doesn't seem to have a menu on it, would you mind reaching me *thon*?' At '*thon*' he nodded his head, and the girl (gal, young woman, hippy-ette) and the boy ('not quite a local lad' Ivan pegged him) who'd been locked in chat stopped and followed his nod. 'Oh, this, is it?' said the girl, and plucked it off the holder on the side of their table. She looked at it. 'Actually, it's a wee ad for this place, not a menu. Do you still want it?' Ivan had to think about that but thought a positive response would be better than a negative one and said, 'Well, sure… I could always educate myself about this place. It's a great wee hidey-hole, this.'

This, with the handing over of said item, was enough to instigate a chat. It helped when the boy asked, 'This your first time here, then?' From this point, Ivan was in. Within minutes, he'd introduced himself, apologizing for having 'ears on me like an elephant', having heard that they seemed to be 'terribly interested in fossils and the like if you don't mind me saying so.' 'Not at all!' they piped back, chorally, with the boy adding, in his non-local, maybe English accent, 'We're dinosaur-hunters, we are!' Ivan, giving his best look of mock astonishment, divulged his own love of the subject, to their eager expressions of delight and wonder. 'Oh aye,' he continued, after learning he was 'Manny' and she was 'Tracey'. 'There's nothing I like more than contemplating the eating habits of the ole Diplodocus or the Brachiosaurus.' After lecturing them on the 'incredible' use of 'swallowed rocks in their stomachs to grind up all their veggies', Ivan then dismissed his learning with a well-timed: 'But I know nathin'!' (The heavy intonation on the final word added a special Northern Irish note designed to get a laugh; Ivan had a way with words.)

This was Stage One in his strategy, to broach the subject and have them dive in. Stage Two was to get himself invited to their table. He did this by letting it slip that he was a humble reporter for a big paper in the city and if he had to answer their casual half-rhetorical questions on the troubles of late, it'd be hard to let them in on what he'd seen unless he could join them and speak with the low tones of a man who didn't wish to blab it all around. Ivan had a stock of stories to tell, none of them first-hand, but that didn't stop him from putting himself right into the midst of the action. Bombs, shootings, beatings-up, tarrings-and-featherings, Ivan was always the first on the scene. 'Sure, and here I am,' almost tearful as he said so, 'just trying to get a wee bit o' solace and human company after a week the likes of which...' That had been Stage Three, to get them to talk about something lighter, even if it entailed death, gore and brutality, as long as it was death, gore and brutality happening a hundred million years ago.

Stage Four was to treat them to drinks and thereby loosen their tongues. ('I've this reporter thing down rightly', Ivan thought to himself, 'Sure, cunning isn't the word for me.') 'Ah, sure, you're poor students, and don't be saying no, it's perfectly my treat, have a wee pint o' cider, or a wee Teacher's here with me and a few of whatever takes your fancy...' And so they did,

Tracey unsure, but Manny glad of the chance to kick back after a day (and a week) of what had been, for him, terribly uninteresting side-work on the dig, the labelling of empty canisters and specimen boxes, shunted off with Tracey into the margins for their apparent lack of obedience to Herr Heinkle.

The rest of the night's conversation went like clockwork, from Ivan's point of view, even if he did have to fight against the flow of alcohol in his bloodstream to make sure he got all they were saying, with regular trips to the jacks where he'd pull out his notebook and pen before pulling anything else out, and jot down all he could remember. He would scribble down items he'd heard but couldn't quite grasp, and upon returning, surprise them by returning to the pre-exit chat, which was always about the details of what they'd turned up in their dig. (He was digging, too. Or was it fishing?) Ivan had no idea sometimes what they were saying at all, and toward the end of the night, with the three of them now rightly rightly, he would even bring out his notebook and pen right in front of them, brazenly, and ask them to repeat what they'd said, or to spell out a term, even asking them once, 'Could ye draw a picture of that, love?' To which Tracey happily acceded, and when she was done, they all had a laugh about the woefully inadequate depiction of the Megalosaurus' head she'd done. 'Looks like the Reverend Ian!' exclaimed Manny, louder than Tracey would have liked, but no-one looked over. Ivan thought it was 'brilliant' though, so that was enough. Tracey, now on the verge of bursting into giggles, queried, with her Northern accent having become more pronounced as the night wore on: 'Are ye gonna write this up as a wee story, then, Ivan?' 'Aye,' said the suddenly green-faced-looking Ace Reporter, then forgot what he'd been asked, excused himself with a non-intelligible burble, and ran out of the lounge, in the general direction of the toilets. He didn't return for ten minutes, by which time Tracey and Manny had taken the notebook he'd left on the table and drawn other bits of dino here and there, and scribbled in a note or two, Tracey finishing with, after consultation with her well-soused companion: 'Discovery confirmed of a fight between two dinosaurs, a Scelidosaur and a Megalosaur, at Eden site, Carrickfergus, April 1, 1979'. 'Wait'll he sees this one in the morning!' she exploded, now quite inebriated herself, and feeling the hiccups coming on.

The two waited until Ivan came back and told him to be sure not to lose his precious notebook, to tuck it away 'right now! Before ye forget it!' They made no remark on Ivan's appearance, his prematurely balding head doused with sweat, and his cream tie, against his cream shirt, and powder-blue overly creased (was that polyester?) casual jacket, the tie daubed with something unmentionable. His eyes protruded, as did his cheeks, but, sure, it was late. They all grabbed their bits and pieces (which included Ivan's bag, in under the handle of which he had stuffed his Mac hours earlier) and made their way out, back through the passageway they'd come through so many hours previous. ''Tis lovely!' exclaimed a well-plastered Ivan, now experimenting with various facial expressions, and who sometimes had to be physically helped to keep upright by his two companions, 'Like a wee smuggler's cave in here, a wee smuggler's cave…'

Sure, wee smuggler's caves are great places to find treasure in, and upon waking the next morning back in Belfast, courtesy of a long and pricey taxi ride home (during which he threw up only once, happily with the door open as it idled at a red light), Ivan found his own little piece of treasure, his notebook, their drawings, and that particular final pencilled-in note. He stared at it for a full two minutes, wracking his brains to try and pinpoint when they'd discussed this actual dinosaur fight discovery (when he wasn't being wracked by his hangover). Try as he might, he couldn't quite recall, but, as is often the way, the words on the page forced him to imagine that they had indeed talked about it.

Sure, that's what he'd been looking for. 'That's right,' he admitted, 'a "Scelidosser" I'd said… and a "Megadosser"… something like that…' And thereafter, with the meticulousness of a future Pulitzer-prize winning journalist (or whatever the equivalent was here) Ivan Stacks reconstructed the whole conversation on the remaining blank pages of his palm-sized and slightly worse-for-wear notebook, making stabs at the coherence he knew he needed to attain to get this whole thing into printable (and believable) shape. 'In a wee hideyhole near Carrick there's this bunch of people digging into the rock for dino bones…' morphed into 'In a quiet corner of a suburb of Carrickfergus, a team of researchers is delving into the mysteries of the distant past, uncovering evidence for what may be a unique discovery…' Et cetera, et cetera. 'University *ed*ucation, university *ed*ucation,' Ivan hummed as he typed, to the tune of some mish-mash of Elvis with high intonation on the 'ed' and a few 'ah ha ha's thrown in for good measure. He'd graduated a year ago and now he was the big man.

Manny and Tracey woke up the next morning in bed together at the digs they shared back in picturesque Carrickfergus (when it wasn't raining), and, after coffee, and a joint, laughed hysterically about the evening previous. 'That poor wee man,' said Tracey, 'that poor wee man. Unless he gets the joke…' 'Aye,' replied Manny, 'we're terrible! We really are…' 'I can just see it…' spoke Tracey, employing her hands like ever-widening frames of a TV screen, '… Yes, folks, a world exclusive… and here's the man who broke the story, Ivan Cream-Puff Stacks, Ace Reporter for *The Times of Belfast*.' At this point, the two of them broke into uncontrollable giggles, so intense they seemed to induce headaches. Or was that just the hangover?

Chapter Two: Northern Irish Dinosaurs, pt.2, April 26-30 (and beyond...and back)

In terms of the grand flow of history, this story would be over before it started, the merest of tiny blips in the vast spacetime continuum. It couldn't, of course, compete with the Troubles, which raged on and consumed the attention of everyone, even those living in the -some would say, Elysium-like-Malone Road. Correction: in terms of the most meagre and whimsical flow of history, or even the slightest trickle of the most insignificant ephemera, this story was over before it started. Or... – correction again – that was what some of the main players in the drama desperately and fervently desired. The Editor of *The News Letter*, uncle to the hapless Ivan Stacks, wanted nothing more than for this discredited story -which he had allowed to be published – to just disappear, just like Paul Daniels had made that bunny vanish on TV last week. Talking of funny little creatures, Ivan had gotten off with a flea in his ear (there's two), and a forced exile into the Notices section. He had to learn the intricate details of font sizes, appropriate wording, and location within paper and page, and spent many an excruciating afternoon having to transcribe the tearful words of bereaved family members wishing to place an obituary. He would himself die for a drink at the end of the week, but for the moment avoided Abe: the one time they did meet, Ivan found himself using not very Presidential language. Tracey and Manny wanted the story to bury itself like an obedient corpse and never crawl out to see the light of day, or dark of night, again. They had done the decent thing and quietly retired from the team. Tracey wondered whether she'd follow Manny back to Birmingham, and if she did, what of her studies at Queen's, not yet finished? It was one of the first times she had become serious in her student life.

Professor Janek Heinkle, of the Palaeontology Department of Heidelberg University, now visiting Prof at Queen's University, perhaps more than anyone, wanted to see the back of this story, and with the kind of finality one finds only when ancient geological forces conspire to erase all trace of what has gone before on the surface of the earth, the kind of forces he usually worked against, but now longed for. Of course, you wouldn't be able to discern such longing in him if you were lucky to have seen him on the extended UTV news item about this 'kerfuffle' (a new word for him, which he took to and used extensively) that aired on the Monday evening of April 30, from 9.30. It was a piece of programming that owed something to the concerted behind-doors effort by upper figures at Queen's, who had assailed other upper figures in the *News Letter* and various other media outlets with supplications which began with grand statements like these: 'The reputation of our beloved institution is at stake', 'This is a matter of pressing public importance', 'Society may begin to lose respect for the pillars of education', and 'Integrity of research is the cornerstone of our society!' – when, in fact, the cornerstone of society was peace and quiet and the ability to just sit down and have a cup of tea without getting shot in the head.

On the TV, Prof Heinkle came across as disarmingly unruffled and as affable as a familiar uncle, laughing it all off as a 'silly mistake, a… "kerfooffle", you might say!' He also had science on his side, and when pressed, took the opportunity to detonate the story with the confidence of a true veteran: 'Lord, no,' he guffawed charmingly, 'I'm afraid the Scelidosaurus and the Megalosaurus could never have "battled it out", so to speak, "mano a mano", ha ha.' Apparently enjoying himself, he then went on to explain that they belonged to two distinct periods, the *Early* Jurassic and the *Middle* Jurassic, which were separated by *millions* of years. 'The Scelidosaur was long gone before our friend Megalosaurus came along... it would be like thinking that...' and here he paused, wondering who to choose, '...your Vinston Churchill had punched Alexander ze Great on ze nose and...' not satisfied he had drilled the image home, '...they had then both collapsed onto ze ground and were punching and kicking and biting eachother, ha ha ha!' At this point, the camera turned to the TV reporter, who looked embarrassedly at his unseen audience and said something, but most of said unseen audience were focused on the sound of the professor in the background, audibly laughing vigorously to himself, as he indulged in gestures of air-punching and mock facial grimaces.

Despite Professor Heinkle's best efforts to appear unruffled by the affair on screen, it was clear to his disciples he had succumbed to nervous exhaustion, with his mood swinging between the two poles of airy positivism and dark pessimism (or embarrassment). This indisposition was short-lived, however, and just days after the 'ordeal', as he would later term it (dispensing with 'kerfuffle' as one might a used tissue), emotional and intellectual control began to return to the eminent scholar, who wanted nothing more than to – rather like any Antrim farmer – plough ahead with the field work, and damn the rain (and the 'mad violence' of 'ze Province'). He, and his remaining team, did their level best to endure the difficult few days immediately following the release of the baseless story in the *News Letter*, and its subsequent adoption by *The Belfast Telegraph*, which devoted not an article to the supposed discovery but just a few lines in a column of regular commentary. The column, penned by Alf McCreary just two days after, was not about dinosaurs at all, but about the recent troubles suffered in Northern Ireland, which were many, and 'heinous' (a favoured and much-employed adjective at that time).

Alf had taken aim at the perpetrators of the recent carnage, on *both* sides, although the just-finished Easter had seen the

Republicans deal out death 'with a clinical brutality that defied all concept of civil society.' Four RUC [Royal Ulster Constabulary] Officers had been blown to kingdom come by a van bomb in Bessbrook, Armagh, the IRA claiming a kind of extra cachet in the disclosure that this, at one thousand pounds, had been their largest bomb ever. Two Prison Officers were gunned down, in separate incidents, one a forty-year-old woman, a wife and a mother of young children, the other a Catholic man in his early thirties, gunned down by the IRA (who would have seen him as a traitor) as he left the church where his sister had just gotten married. He was shot dead in front of his wife and children. As Alf put it, 'Cold hearted brutality doesn't come much crueller or more vicious than that.' He had a point, and then another to make about the twenty-five old Catholic man, who'd been abducted almost a month previous, his body only found on Sunday in the River Bann, beaten to death by unspecified 'Loyalists', bringing memories of the Shankill Butchers into the minds of many... Hyperbole, however, Alf realized, could never adequately fulfil the expectations of a language that could never hope to express the truly ugly reality of the Northern Ireland 'Troubles'. And so, he turned philosophical, and... to dinosaurs. Yes, it might be simplistic, he began, but, reacting to and making casual but explicit mention of the dino story, he argued surely there was something to be learned from it. These ancient beings knew only hunger and killing and territorialism. The dinosaurs didn't kill for religion or for ideals, however, 'or any warped notions of such'. No, 'they killed because they were hungry animals and they lacked compassion, conscience and awareness of others' suffering.' 'We might learn in school to view these creatures as stupid because of that', he wrote, 'when compared to us with our civilized sensibilities, but, oh, just look at the news', he suggested. 'Are those with murder in their hearts any better, any more evolved?'

This passage, albeit dependent on a story that was about to be deflated like an oversized balloon, struck a chord. It elevated what had been a page-four minor article of interest to natural history lovers (not to forget Belfast wags of all ages) into a talking point, a theme, a narrative, when narratives or ways of understanding present circumstances were few and far between. There were a few, of course, who chaffed against the very premise, a hardcore few (comprised of many) who dismissed Darwin and believed dinosaurs had palled around with humans, Noah filling his Ark not only with giraffes, hippos, goats and monkeys, but also with Mr & Mrs T. Rex and a pair of giant lovestruck sixty-foot and sixty-ton Brachiosaurs. Talk of dinosaurs annoyed them because they had to fit these enormously awkward creatures into a timeline that only went back four thousand years. But, as a casual way to describe 'the scum that plagued the Province', it opened up a way to condemn 'the other side', be it between punters at some pub in East Belfast or callers to radio discussion programmes (more anon). 'They' - and 'They' for these were 'Republicans'- were 'savages who should go back to the Dark Ages where they came from'. They were 'predatory animals' who were only happy when they were killing 'us'. Lastly, they were 'lizards'.

To others, though, it was simpler than that and more in line with what Alf had been saying: the murderers on both sides and those who supported their campaigns (or at least their 'ideals') were 'all bloody dinosaurs'. It was that simple, and, like a catchy pop song, it caught on and soon everyone was using this idea, at least for a few days -or until the next atrocity knocked the smile off everyone's face (which was either the next murder or the election of Margaret Thatcher the following week). The narrative was helped the following morning, Friday, by none other than Ivan Stacks, invited by the recently established Downtown Radio (much flashier than old-hat Radio Ulster) to give the backstory on his scoop. 'I'm not the one to comment to that, mind. I'm just a journalist,' he said in answer to how his story had struck a philosophical nerve. 'But,' he continued, to the surprise of the host who thought he had finished, 'fighting and killing, it's been going on for millions of years. It's about time we threw in the towel and embraced our fellow man.' This moment of eloquence drew praise from said host, Candy Devine, who lamented: 'We can learn from this, Ivan, I really think we can…' With such high-mindedness, no-one minded that her journalist guest was particularly flubby about the details of how he'd made his marvellous scoop. He got away with the suspiciously non-specific 'sources close to Prof Heinkle', calling them only 'committed experts', whom he had met on numerous occasions and from whom he taken copious notes of 'a highly technical nature'. 'I had to edit things down a little for publication, Candy, or the Editor would have had my guts for garters.' He chortled. Ivan was also forgiven his occasional technical slip, as when he described the Scelidosaurus as 'horny' rather than 'horned' and suggested that the Megalosaur only killed because 'of his upbringing'. By the end of the session, despite the effervescent Ms Devine having to field a few callers who insisted that Republicans or just Catholics were 'animals', and 'gloried in savagery' ('and you can call them bloody dinosaurs if ye like'), everyone could feel good about themselves. There was something to learn after all from the behaviour of the behemoths: love and understanding was the only way to create a better world and, Ivan again, 'that was probably what Charles Darwin hoped for, God bless him.' Ivan spent the afternoon at the Garrick and other fine establishments in the city, praising 'Charlie D' and toasting the Scelidosser and Megadosser and having a right ole laugh and bit o' craic with whoever came up to him and slapped him on the back. Pressed at one point on his knowledge of the creatures by a fellow tippler, he responded, 'I know one's a "herbivore" and the other a "carnivore", but I'm a bloody "beer & whiskey-vore!"'

It didn't take much time either for some wag to tweak things a little and assign the particular dinosaurs at the centre of all this their own religion and political persuasion. It happened during Ivan's session at the Garrick, and at pubs elsewhere. Or it began soon after the piece appeared on Wednesday. By general assent, and some mysterious force which aligned everyone with the same notion -a rare thing in those days!- if for very different reasons, the Scelidosaurus became a Taig (or Catholic) and the Megalosaurus a Prod. (Of course, it couldn't be denied that the drawing of the Megalosaurus' head, which was reproduced in Ivan's article, did bear an uncanny resemblance to the Right Reverend Ian Paisley, and this no doubt had an influence.) The assignation travelled like jokes sometimes do, or did, jokes which happened to catch the right note about things, drinker to drinker, punter to punter, street wit to street wit, school kid to school kid, sweeping through the city and environs as the latest and best thing you had to hear. The latest bit of fun.

On the Taigs' side, it was because they saw themselves as underdogs, and the 'wee Scelidosser', as he was often termed – *après* Ivan? – was much the smaller. People were obviously reading Ivan's article in detail. He was no less plucky for that, however, as, being quadrupedal -and this description was well liked- he was the 'more down-to-earth' of the two. The same people would cast the Megalosaur as, negatively, the 'superior type', looking down on the lowly, and lording it over the indigenous Irish with high-handed contempt. Interestingly, the Protestant wags saw things very similarly, but from a different angle, that they were rightly in the ascendance, and held a grander claim to the territory and to destiny in general. And, sure, they might argue: 'Who'd want a pathetic weed-eating four-legged piece of shite when you could have a thirty-foot-long beast

29

weighing ten tons that'd put the jeepers up a T-Rex?'

This, at least, was how the precocious Sammy Lyttle, ten-years-old, termed it in fierce chat with his classmate, Billy Stewart, the pair loving the school's-out moment on this bright spring day, as they ambled about Ormeau Park, after a hard day's learnin' at Nettlefield Primary School. The chat soon descended into vigorous play-acting and before you could say 'Brontosaurus' five times, they had flung off their satchels and were taking on the roles of the mighty Scelidosaurus and the -on-paper- even mightier Megalosaurus. 'Take that, ya Fenian bastard!' said Sammy in as mock-guttural and mock-monster a voice as he could summon, swooping down his right hand/claw Megalosaurus-like and mock-assailing Billy, who was on his hands and knees, and, not to be outdone, then flicked out his left foot/horned tail and sent his opponent crashing to the ground, with a doughty 'Feck you, ya Prod fecker… Gotcha!', as niftily Scelidosaurus-like as he could manage it. Earlier that day, their pal wee Pete Ferguson had brought a copy of the relevant *News Letter* to school and shown everyone the dino story, inciting much distraction from that day's serious business. After all the chat, now was their chance to act things out in style. A nearby woman pushing her pram and her thankfully quiet baby-passenger looked daggers at the two of them, whispering to herself: 'The language of them! Bloody scuts!' The boys went at it, flailing in the dirt and grass and loving every moment.

Drinkers in dens throughout the land (or just the truncated land of the Six Counties of Ulster) re-enacted their own less physically demanding versions of the fight to great hilarity and general cheer. It helped if you had a few pints in you and didn't go so far as to invoke the annoyance of the bartender. It was liberating to be able to mimic and make fun of the conflict in their midst with such abandon and good spirit, in a city where you normally spoke politics in public only at your peril, unless you were happily ensconced in your own ghetto. So with two veteran tipplers in The Rock Bar, on the Falls Road, whose discussion of the story began with mention of the Downtown Radio broadcast of the day before. Discussion developed -after the third round- when one of them asked which dinosaur they'd rather be. Assuming, on a whim, the role of the 'Protestant' Megalosaurus (thanks to its Paisley looks), Rabbie announced: 'I can drink ye under the table, ya Papist bastard!' (This was probably the first and only time anyone had ever uttered such an epithet in this hallowed den). The fellow's drinking partner, Paulsy, threw him a querulous look. Rabbie did his best to clarify things: 'Scelidossers couldn't hold a pint! Ha!' And to back up his teaching point, Rabbie unfolded a copy of *The News Letter*, also a first at this establishment. 'Where in Jesus Mary Christ did you get a hold o' that?' his shocked-looking partner exclaimed (and received a dirty look from the barman for his profanity), never having actually seen a copy of the 'Protestant rag' up close. 'Oh, never mind that, laddie, just take a wee read of this…' So, Paulsy, gingerly, took physical possession of the publication he had grown up to despise (because everyone he knew despised it), and read the indicated section: '…the Scelidosaurus was quadrupedal…' He looked up at his friend, none the wiser: 'I don't get it. And what the fuck is "quad-rupee-dal" when it's at home?' 'Bejeepers, did you not get an education? It means he had four bloody legs!' 'I still don't get it,' said Paulsy, his querulous look deteriorating into a look of irritation. 'Try holding a pint of Guinness with your feet and you'll know all about it. I knew you Taig Scelidossers were as thick as shite!' After a pause which saw Paulsy's jaw drop even further than it had earlier on, the penny finally dropped. The two tipplers then erupted in raucous laughter. The barman shook his head and got on with washing the glasses.

Hard to believe how a tiny story like this could spread so quickly and so far, but Belfast had interlocking networks within interlocking networks, and you'd not want to be the last to hear the latest bit of fluff. And on top of that, this one had an angle to it you couldn't help but laugh at or comment on round these parts, the narrative of prehistoric beasts fighting to the death finding echoes in the daily news of shootings, bombings and general civic mayhem.

How the story elements were used was far from fixed, however. You'd have Proddy Scelidossers and Taig Mega-'dossers', too, especially when the chat was about the living off the dole. Or there'd be versions with no religion in the mix at all. Two aul fellas whacking away at each other outside Lavery's, for example, were categorized by one passing wit as exhibiting 'frightfully prehistoric behaviour', and the near-nightly marital rows at 84 Atlantic Avenue had the neighbours commenting: 'They're bloody going at it like dinosaurs in there. They'll knock the friggin' walls down!' In the administration offices of Anderson & McAuley's Ltd., Donegall Place, the Managing Director was accused -of course, behind his back- of being 'a right bloody Megalosaurus' for issuing some edict thought to be 'high-handed'. Whether or not the staff thought of themselves as Scelidosaurian in their opposition of mumbled groans and shared sense of victimhood is anyone's guess. All this, and yet the 'buzz', as any trend would be termed, was more or less buzzed-out only a week later, some say, with the election of Margaret Thatcher, and the Conservatives, description of whom as dinosaurs no-one thought particularly funny (because it was true). It was a Belfast thing, after all. Ideas linger, however, or only appear to die out. They become submerged for long periods of time and then re-emerge, like Nessie, or an unexpected bout of the flu, or sectarian prejudice, when people least expect it. As an example, such a thing happened many months later, towards end of the year when, of all things, poetry-lovers got their hands on Seamus Heaney's latest tome, *Field Work*. It would take one particularly inquisitive student of Anglo-Irish Literature at Queen's to process what she had seen in its dense pages, and weeks to build up the courage to ask her professor about it, a month shy of Christmas.

Up until then they had been studying the 1975 collection *North*, Heaney's stylistic re-imagining of contemporary Irish violence and the plight of victims, derived from his perusal of ancient bog bodies from Scandinavia (or 'something like that', a phrase she found herself using often when studying 'Famous Seamus'), so Grace McLarnon didn't think it too out of place to throw out a question about a line in his latest masterpiece which seemed equally stylized. 'Professor, what do you make of this wee phrase in part two of "Triptych"' [a tripartite poetic meditation on the 'Troubles', part two relating the words of an ancient sibyl], she said, bringing out her already dog-eared copy of *Field Work*, and showing him the page, pointing with a long pink index fingernail, '"I think our very form is… bound to change… Dogs in a siege…" ah…here, *"Saurian relapses"*?' She'd injected much into her delivery of the latter two words, making it sound almost accusatory. 'Is Heaney saying we…' she hoped he'd throw her a lifeline, '…we used to be, like, you know, reptiles, and now we're, I suppose, turning back into them, or something like that…?' Grace smiled a hopeful, worried smile, a smile that acknowledged she'd thrown something into the session that might just mark her out as laughingstock material. She winced until Professor Fitzsimons broke his silence, with a smile of his own. 'Good question, Grace,' he responded in his finest diplomatic tones, and then: 'Would anyone else like to have a go at answering that?'

Grace interpreted this to mean 'What a silly question!' She'd just been thrown to the wolves – her fellow students would sink her now, being, as she'd gathered during the course, 'mad Heaney-ites', and nothing less than Fitz's 'yes-men'. She would have to endure the inevitable slings and arrows, the first of which came from Barry, from Glenone, only half-suppressing his tittering: 'Well, of course, Heaney's phrase has to be seen in its context, proffered as it is by a mythical ancient figure, the Sybil, used to seeing the world in heavily metaphorical terms herself...' And, then William, from the Malone Road, launched his own stinger, sounding as studious as he could possibly muster: 'Well, I'd say that Heaney is employing a series of shock images from a nether-world, a world which only appears to intersect with our own, to challenge the reader and to shake up preconceptions...' Et cetera, et cetera, until Grace herself had heard enough, and still nothing from Professor Fitzsimons, who all the time had sat impassive, smiling, and admiring. Grace blurted out: 'But "saurian" does mean "reptile" or "lizard" and "relapse" means *"returning back to", so what's the bloody meaning of that if not going back to being dinobloodysaurs!* Don't you remember that story about the discovery up in Carrick?'

The Professor held out a conciliatory hand, and, in his sweetest, dulcet tones pronounced: 'Of course, of course, Grace, but that narrative about the two dinosaurs turned out to be bogus. I doubt Mr Heaney gave it a moment's notice... Rather, I think what he's telling us here is that wisdom sometimes speaks to us in strange voices...' A general murmur of assent rose from the others in the room, as Grace stood up precipitously, pushed her chair back awkwardly into a shelf of books, fixed a stare of anger at Professor 'Fitz', and shouted, 'Shite on you, you only listen to your effing yes-men!' She then marched out, slamming the door behind her, the noise not terribly dissimilar to how a three-ton standing behemoth might sound if flipped backwards onto unforgiving rock.

Grace had a point, although it would likely never be proven, that Seamus Heaney *was* referencing the mad few days in mid-April 1979 when Belfast had become obsessed about their apparent dinosaur past with his otherwise perplexing 'Saurian relapses'. It was possibly just as some had initially reacted, after Alf McCreary's telling and heartfelt words of wisdom: we (or for some just 'they') were 'lizards' after all. Evolution dictated that us humans had evolved upwardly from 'lower life forms', yet contemporary activity suggested that some had chosen to *return* to that lower life, and revel in a stage of bloody gore and unimaginable grief. It took a lot, for some, and just a step, for others, to take up a gun or a bomb and ruin someone's day. But once you did so, you could rightly be accused of abandoning civilization, and embracing animalism, either ancient and prehistoric or the kind you'd find pretty quickly if you entered the cage of the Bengal Tiger at Bellevue Zoo for a quick pet.

There was one little problem which this heavily moral/moralized view failed to address, however: Northern Ireland was an artificial state founded on religious and political schismatic thinking, a societal fix for the blundering hoofprints of a pretty ancient Imperialism, advantaging some but severely disadvantaging others. Whether right or wrong, it was never going to be a pleasure park of fun and love, with everyone sitting around the campfire, holding hands and singing 'Kum Ba Yah'. In the chasm of a complete historical mess, whether or not you chose to look, it was more or less inevitable that victims of that historical mess would begin to thump their feet and shake the ground on which they stood, screaming loud and long to not insult them with non-contextual moralizing. 'Look around,' they'd shout, 'it's not us who live in the past. And it is not us who are ultimately responsible for wreaking havoc. It is an ancient creaking societal structure which has wrought this daily hell.' And, they'd conclude, with shuddering earth-quaking finality, 'we live in a vicious, archaic, unjust, and desperately dangerous Dinosaur State.'

Chapter Three: Dinosaur State, pt.1,
Friday, April 27

Whether Northern Ireland was a Dinosaur State or not, the battle-green (and not very Irish-green) British Army Saracen, as svelte and sporty as a brick outhouse, trundling down Donegall Place, looked remarkably Triceratopsian – *if* that was an adjective. So wondered young Christopher Maguire, who didn't know very much about dinosaurs but had started to think about them, influenced by all the news or jokey gossip about the so-called 'earth-shaking discovery' near Carrick. He'd only heard others in his class mention the story – in jokes – yesterday, but he possessed a bent of mind that made him gravitate toward anything new, or anything redolent of a world beyond this. And dinosaurs were certainly that. A Saracen (a large bulky heavily armoured British Army vehicle) as a Triceratops was a neat transformation of the ugly present into a highly exotic past, a past so remote it constituted an entirely different world, a different universe. Imagine, he mused, beneath my very feet, giant monsters had had it out on a regular basis right here in what would be Belfast, vicious claw-swipes being met with thwacks from thumping great mace-like tails, studded with horny bits. Or was that 'horned'?

There was much to want to transform, he felt, in this 'hole', as his friends sometimes termed Belfast, and as often he did, too, following them, even if the word summoned up something he'd rather not picture in his mind. He knew it wasn't just a matter of aesthetics, of lumbering brick outhouse-like beasts trundling down streets flanked by ruined buildings and streets littered with broken paving stones, but of politics. It was a 'hole' because it was (counter-intuitively) 'shat upon', and 'fucked', a place no-one gave 'a shit' about, and where 'the Brits' had no right to be. But aesthetics (and linguistics) came into it, too. Christopher wasn't sure which one tugged at his consciousness more, the look of the place, or why it was like that in the first place. And, why, he also thought, the need for all the cloacal vocabulary? 'Cloacal' was the most interesting word he'd come across recently, via, and strangely via, H. G. Wells. (He had been reading a lot of late, when, that is, he wasn't 'swotting' for the up-coming 'O'-levels.) Donegall Place, was, of course, a little more presentable than the Lower Falls or Sandy Row, being host to some of the finest ('Imperialist!') architecture, large and elegant nineteenth century buildings on either side of the wide street, but it was also host to… the 'Ring of Steel'. Somehow, for Christopher, 'Ring of Steel' didn't quite have the ring of the exotic about it, and it certainly didn't qualify as exotic-looking either, or redolent of worlds past or faraway, unless it suggested, with extreme squinting, the stockade from Robert Louis Stevenson's *Treasure Island*, erected to keep out the renegade pirates. And here *he* was, the next best thing, a renegade Catholic in a city which was stamped PROTESTANT all over. The Protestant City Hall at his back (Christopher made a mental list), Protestant and Imperialist Robinson & Cleavers building to his right, with its imperious turrets looking down, Protestant RUC men waiting to process him as he would pass through their stockade, aided by their inevitably Protestant flak-jacketed helpers from across the water.

There was a Protestant man just ahead of him as he began to queue up, a slight queue forming because of the large number of pedestrians, decked in duffle coats, trench coats, Afghans, furs (fake? he wondered) – a few sunny days fooling no-one. Christopher didn't 'know' the man in front was Protestant, and, he quipped to himself, 'considering he doesn't have two heads, maybe he isn't.' Christopher just had a hunch about him which he reckoned was probably correct. The definition of racism, he then admitted to himself is to classify your fellow man, and make sure you know where he is in relation to you: *different*. He mused on: 'Catholics have fair hair, Prods are dark (and greasy...?). ... Prods are taller, and definitely more confident in the way they walk about, which comes from being the masters of this wee chunk of the island of Ireland. Did I say "Ireland"? Ha! For the eighth letter of the alphabet they say "Aich" and we say "Haich"'. All the shibboleths – another recent linguistic steal – were set in stone, and yet, the man in front was short, had a very meagre head of hair, which was fairly fair, or as his own had once been unhappily described to him, 'dirty fair', and had none of the strut of an Overlord. In fact, he seemed to be tilting left and right a few times, consistent with the behaviour of someone who's had a few too many. No Northern Presbyterian sobriety in that! All these background-playing autonomic observations, Christopher concluded, were just what happens when living here: wondering what religion another human being subscribed to was part of Northern Irish consciousness. Differentiation would be easier, he cringed as he thought it, in South Africa. And yet, on a roll, as he followed this line, 'Why did us Taigs call Protestants "black"? And then why did Northern Prods have an affinity with the white Afrikaners?' It was all a bit confusing, juggling racist, bigoted thoughts in a head which knew better.

They weren't moving. Something was up. Things usually went pretty smoothly. Christopher wondered why he had even come here. Just a few minutes ago, he'd been standing at the bus stop in Donegall Square, waiting for his bus to take him home. He'd been looking into the middle distance with the occasional sideways glance at the City Hall through its few spindly surrounding trees, when it struck him: his mind was as blank as a well-licked dinner plate. That, or he was still wondering how he could ever prove that the internal bisector of the angle of a triangle divides the opposite ratio of one whose sides consist of well-intentioned sines and cosines -which swung back and forth all day long on their summery vectors. Then there was the knotty problem of that metal rod of uniform thickness and the indeterminate mass indicated by points A Y X and Z and how it would behave if placed in a bowl of mercury with a circumference the size of Jupiter – or, was it, something slightly smaller, like the boundaries of Ballymena? Or, how to 'calculate the speed of the wind' based on some bloke flying his aerybuzzer 900 miles from A to B at 250 mp.h., if X and Y are in cahoots with the local airforce and are de-gravitizing the entire area with exotic material from Z. Et cetera.

With the 'O's approaching like the Four Horsemen of the Apocalypse – the four scary ones being Science, Mathematics, Geography and, embarrassingly, Irish – Christopher was beginning to panic. It was a panic which took temporary refuge in mad extrapolations of the incomprehensible, and more sustained refuge in the act of at least appearing to do the right thing and sit down for extended periods poring over a page inscribed with hieroglyphics, filling his notebook with plenteous notes, and only the occasional doodle. This latter idea was one of the reasons which forced Christopher to break out of his mindlessness, his Beckettian waiting for some bus that might never come, and to gravitate toward the Central Library by simply ambling down the main thoroughfare of central Belfast. He also fancied a 'chip' from Victor's, and what the odds -his internal quipper quipped- if today was Friday and he'd get chips when he got home, too? He loved chips! He loved chips much more than metal rods of uniform thicknesses and triangles uselessly adorned with letters balanced precariously on their knife-sharp points. And so, succumbing to that love, and to the slightly more artificial desire to assume the mantle of the serious student, he had taken steps toward the achievement of this double goal. It was early yet, anyhow. He could study an hour and a half, jump on the same bus outside the library and get home in time for a bit of that day's action from the World Snooker Championship, and… tuck into the Ma's chips.

This had brought him to where he was now, at the top of Donegall Place (which, in his blissful ignorance of even the basic geography of his own city, he thought of as 'Royal Avenue') and to a sudden realization that he would have to pass through the security barrier to get back into the centre, a prospect which was starting to give him second thoughts about the whole enterprise. All that patting your pockets and opening your bag and trying to look serious when they made eye-contact. And yet, just as he thought of turning back, the man in front, the tilting one, turned back instead, in his general direction, to impart: 'Another day in paradise, eh!'

'Aye,' he replied. He'd been spoken to, and now that he could see the man's face, became firmer in his conviction that he was indeed a Protestant: ruddy face, big smile, protuberant cheeks and eyes (not that any of these corresponded to the usual checklist). He was intuiting, and now wondering if girth played a role. Catholics were supposed to be all wiry, after all, and this guy was no beanpole. He'll react if he turns round further and sees my school badge (which was not as easily disposed of as the tie which he had torn off and stuffed in his bag), thought young Christopher then. And he did. 'A CBS man!' the man exclaimed cheerfully, and uncomplicatedly. (You'd have to be dead, reflected Christopher, not to know CBS, the – Catholic – Christian Brothers School; all the big schools had their symbols branded into general consciousness.) Now the man had turned round more properly, and it was clear to Christopher, from his generous smile, that he had taken a drop, but whatever it was that had been in his glass had led to a very pleasant demeanour, the kind that would make a person feel like the free flow of communication between humans of any persuasion was the only way for things to be. Christopher knew this to be true and was happy to respond in kind. 'Oh aye, like me Da before me and his…'

'Had enough schooling for the day, then?' the man asked jocularly, with a brief open glance at his watch. It was early, just gone two, but in light of the cancellation of some afternoon class, the Brothers had given a special dispensation to anyone with reason to lope off before the bell. Christopher was impressed; Belfast people always got right to the point. 'Aye, well,' he burbled, 'French was cancelled,' throwing in, to hopefully spice that up, 'thank God -our French teacher's a bit mad, like!' 'So was ours, a real headcase! Must be something they drink every night,' shot back the 'Protestant' man. 'Aye, too much red wine, likely…' countered Christopher. 'Le vin rouge!' pronounced the man in his best accent, which was heavily Belfast-sounding, and not something you'd hear on the streets of gay Paree. Christopher stopped himself from, falsely, uttering some words of praise, as his mind raced for a reply. As ever, Belfast intercommunication had the answer, with a throwaway, if overused, 'Oh, aye.' 'Oh aye' in a Northern accent was a badge both Prods and Taigs or anyone could utter at the drop of a hat, anywhere, proudly, and with great gusto, announcing precisely where they were from: firmly north of the border. You could live a whole life in Dublin and never hear it uttered once down there. Christopher, however, if he thought about his interaction so far, had now used the utterance 'aye' no less than four times. This from a Grammar School student preparing to sit his 'O'-levels and who, when he could ever find the time, was reading his way through Herman Melville's *Billy Budd and Other Stories*. To wit, he was beginning to feel a bit Bartleby-ish.

Belfast people notice these things, even – or especially – if they're drunk, and wonder, as the man seemed to be wondering, if this Grammar School student would be able to open his mouth and say something of worth to the conversation, if it was a 'conversation' and not just a bit of chit-chat between strangers as they queued up to get through the security barrier (…in a city where you could have a real conversation with the cash register lady and a monosyllabic one with your Ma and Da). Somehow, perhaps because – he told himself – he was sensitive to the wafts and warps of the slightest disturbance of the atmosphere, Christopher picked up on this and wondered how he could bring something to the table that would be worthy of a fine Catholic youth educated at one of the finest institutions in the 'country' ('Province', 'region', he never knew how to describe Northern Ireland in shorthand). Something other, at least, than 'aye' or 'Oh aye'. But, though he tried dredging his mind for something half decent to impart, like 'Sure, doesn't the Pope like a drop?' (no, that'd open up a box better left shut) or a 'I'm more of a Guinness man, myself' (no, as this would only incur shock and surprise as he was obviously underage, even if his interlocutor was 'half-cut'), or, in confessional mode, 'I'm just making my way to the Central for a spot of reading' (no, boring), *he couldn't think of anything to say.*

Had he arrived at the moment described by Seamus Heaney in that poem about encountering his Protestant neighbour and not knowing what to say to him, if not something about the price of grass-seed? Until, by some innate force, some tiny spark within his cavernous brain, like a match flame in a cave etched by Gustav Doré, young Christopher Maguire, taking sudden stock of the man's appearance, a powder-blue suit, with cream shirt and cream, slightly creased, tie, which passed for flamboyance in these parts, had a brainwave, blurting out: 'You're not famous are you, an actor, or… a reporter, maybe? You have the look of one.'

It was as though Christopher had unlocked the Great Gates of Kiev. The man's face lit up, and beamed him a wondrous smile, exclaiming: 'I didn't know this was the uniform they all used, but, hey, good guess! Spot on! Reporter I am! Ivan Stacks, at your service!' The man thrust out his right hand and Christopher grabbed it, feeling relief and something like success. It was all too brief a moment, however, as the queue had suddenly jolted into movement once again, forcing Ivan to break the shake and turn and face the music of the expected frisk. Christopher followed on and they both entered under the scaffolding-like tunnel, with its mysterious signs above for women, or women with prams, but not for men... (Christopher always wondered why, but never asked.) It became clear why there had been a delay, as one tall pedestrian could be seen remonstrating with a policeman. Christopher noticed two soldiers, who had likely until then stayed well in the background, take steps toward the apparent altercation. It was a small space under this makeshift tunnel contraption, but it was a place which was darker than outside and certainly had its own atmosphere. Christopher could hear the tall man, who seemed to be in his early twenties – as, he realized, was his most recent acquaintance – 'effing and blinding' as the euphemism went. And Christopher could tell, with even greater precision than he had labelled Mr Stacks, that this fellow in the altercation was Catholic and definitely Republican leaning. Christopher wondered how he had such courage to express himself so eloquently and freely in the centre of town, and in the charged space of this Ring of Steel security tunnel. 'Fuckin' Brits, aye, they'll have yer back, eh? Can ye not fight yer own [unintelligible].' Not only could Christopher know his religion and his political persuasion from what he heard and saw, he could have a pretty good idea that he was from West Belfast, or North Belfast, the two most fervently anti-establishment and Republican leaning places in the city. Christopher lived in the comparative bubble of a quiet and fairly 'respectable' housing estate safely *beyond* North Belfast but went to school right next to Divis Flats, at point Y in the vector of a staunchly Republican area. He knew how this might end – badly, with a crack across the mouth from an Army service rifle, but, then again, he realized, no, not here, not in the city centre, and not in front of these nice folk.

Words had been said, but the RUC officer in charge, employing his best de-escalation tactics wouldn't be drawn. It was all over before it could develop into anything, and during the time it took for his new 'friend' to be frisked, and himself, and for the lady police officer to take a (meaningful) look in his bag (at Melville's stories and the, hopefully uncontroversial, *Collected Poems of Thomas Hardy, Deaths and Entrances* by Dylan Thomas and a few textbooks), the tall man had been allowed to pass on. It might have ended differently a few years ago, thought Christopher. By the time he had been allowed to pass he'd almost forgotten all about Ivan Stacks, reporter, and, because they had only chatted briefly to pass the time, he thought it best not to throw out a 'See ya' or whatever. He actually felt quite nervous and disturbed by the altercation (his general sensitivity coming into play). It was Ivan who took a different tack. Drink can do that, or maybe it was his natural demeanour. Whichever it was, Christopher was gladdened to have the man turn round one last time and call to him, in beautiful demotic Belfast English: 'Be seeing ya, pal!'

And, even more surprising, and pleasing for the sixteen-year-old student, was that the man called Ivan Stacks turned round one more time and this time thrust out not his hand but something in his hand, which was obviously a newspaper. Autonomically, Christopher reached out to take it, muttering 'thanks' when he actually wanted to shout the word out, as he had felt a little tiny bit of random friendliness when he had least expected it, hands across the barriers and all that. 'Page Four, circled in red. Enjoy! It's big news, fella, big news!' Christopher smiled as simple and honest a smile as he was capable of producing and again uttered 'thanks', watching as his random and new Protestant friend turned round and boldly strode down the street. He looked down at the paper in his hands, turning it around to see what it was. He didn't know whether to feel elated or shocked or whatever the opposite of those feelings would be when he noticed the banner: NEWS LETTER, with what looked like a fat turkey to the right and an ad for SAWERS (the fish & deli shop) on the left. He opted for the former. He was feeling good. Accepting difference felt good to him. He'd rarely held a copy of this newspaper in his life. Now he had the gift of one, specially presented to him, Christopher Maguire, Christian Brothers Catholic Grammar School boy, by Ace Reporter and roundly (in two senses) Protestant Ivan Stacks of the venerable Belfast NEWS LETTER, here in Donegall Place (not Royal Avenue), April twenty seventh, nineteen seventy-nine, year of our Lord, whichever boot you thought He kicked with.

Chapter Four: Dinosaur State, pt.2, same day

As Christopher Maguire stood there, just past the security gate, outside of Boots ('the Chemist'), initially looking at the disappearing figure of Ivan Stacks, he then looked down onto what he was holding, a copy of the *News Letter*, and, before beginning his own walk down the street, he located the article he'd been told about, on page four, halfway down the page, squeezed in between a piece about 'Disgruntled Antrim Pig Farmers' on the left and, on the right, an ad for 555 cigs: 'Mild. But Not Meek'. The headline in question, with its slightly wince-inducing alliteration, virtually trumpeted its presence to Christopher: 'Duelling Dinos Discovery'. Assembling folds of the paper so that this article was face up and the whole manageably small enough to be held in his left hand, Christopher started to amble, eyes half on what he was ambling past - pedestrians and the occasional street post- and half on the article. He savoured the printed name of the author, thinking to himself (in his best Hiberno-English grammar): 'I'm only after seeing Ivan Stacks... Must tell the Da about this.'

He soon realized this was not an ideal arrangement, especially after bumping into a lady shopper carrying full plastic bags in both hands, who said: 'For eff's sake, look where yer going.' Ideal or not, he persevered, snatching pieces of the story on the page as he did his best to navigate the pavement, ignoring Smyth's for Records, against his normal instincts... He'd actually been hoping to noodle around the record shops a little, like Harrisons and Makin' Tracks, and he was sure he would, but for the moment, he was in a different world... A Scelidosaurus, he learned, was a rather small dinosaur, not much bigger than a large dog. The Megalosaurus, however, (whose head and mouth, in the inserted drawn illustration, somehow looked like someone he felt he knew, someone famous...) was 'almost the size of a

T. Rex'. And the article suggested that 'palaeontologists' (Christopher had to look up from the paper after encountering that word, and back down again, in a concerted effort to be able to pronounce it properly, while dodging a fast-walking bloke wearing a not-very-well-preserved Rory Gallagher T-shirt) had discovered fossils in a site near Carrickfergus which indicated that some sort of battle between the two had been uncovered 'through painstaking work'. Christopher loved that the site was located in 'Eden', a detail which set him off on a series of playful associations which saw him imagining Adam and Eve playing hide and seek as hungry dinosaurs stalked them. The God of the Old Testament would have kept them safe, he guessed, zapping any of the giant beasts who got too close. After a brief vision, which was actually a memory, of Hieronymus Bosch's *Garden of Earthly Delight* (from a booklet from the Prado Museum his brothers had brought back from sunny Spain the previous year) in which strange creatures cajoled within the same space as the earth's first nubile lovers, Christopher's shoulder made painful contact with a hard thing jutting out of a street post. It was a sign, possibly from the same God he had just been thinking about, he mused, telling him to desist with the reading-while-walking thing, and just walk. And so, somewhat reluctantly, he did just that, opening the flap of his dark leather school bag and consigning the paper into darkness and invisibility, to make friends with Herman and the two Thomases. He then started walking on, eyes up and ready for any moving, or unmoving, obstacle.

Apart from the occasional red and cream-coloured Citybus making its way down the street, perhaps even the one he could have been on, he noticed a police Land Rover pass by -how could he not, with its gravelly high-gear whine and sudden expulsion of noxious gas. It reminded him of seeing the Saracen a few minutes previously, which then prompted him to wonder why it had been there at all. You usually saw Saracens in 'trouble spots', he reflected, not in the centre, mucking up the tarmacadam and spoiling the image of what was supposed to be one of Belfast's premier shopping streets. Like the Saracen, this Land Rover was armoured and as ugly as sin, grilles on the front and headlights, over the windscreen and up top, a little circular grille round the spotlight (or was it a camera?) at the top. Drab green and a little battle-scarred, too, it was a reminder, if you needed one, of what normality was like in 1979 Belfast. The vehicle passed but its exhaust smoke lingered a moment like a ghost, a ghost that needed a good scrub. Welcome to Belfast, city of dinosaurs on wheels.

It was time to bid farewell to the big thoroughfare, though. His stomach had been sending him messages for the longest time. He turned left up into Castle Street past the doughty brown of Anderson & McAuley, with the image of fried potato chips etched onto his mind and the contours of his stomach. And yet, life is funny, as they say, and the unexpected happened: SAWERS happened, again. The banner draped above the long window display, 'Celebrating 100 Years of Good Food Service', helped to open up a narrative, but Christopher had visited this famous delicatessen many times before, and was always 'gobsmacked' by the various arrays. It wouldn't hurt to take another 'butchers', he told himself punningly, as though needing to assure himself that his loyalty in Victor's hadn't wavered.

Well, inside the shop it did. The sight of an enormous white flat fish, and accompanying full-body dappled fishy partners, beached on a bed of ice did not excite his taste buds, but, aesthetically-speaking, it did slap him up the face. This was fleshy glistening modern art, clamouring for attention, and punctuated with wooden staves near the heads of each telling us the price they had died for. It did the trick, opening Christopher's eyes just that little bit extra as he surveyed the shelves and counters with their various crammed jars or fresh-cut slices of cheese and ham and veg and cured and smoked bits of this animal's leg and that animal's breast. Somewhere within the murk of a jar of mixed pickles and another of curled anchovies, and then the chance sight of 'Today's Special Offer', Victor's 'chip' dissolved like the sound of a solitary passing bee might on a summer's afternoon. Today's Special Offer was a palm-sized paper bowl of Fresh Ardglass Mussels, 29p. Christopher almost dropped his coins on the floor in anticipation of just getting his hands on this most delectable prize. It was compensation for his decision not to have a chip after all, and for not being able to afford to purchase one particularly sexy wedge of Stilton, which had called to him plaintively as he spent an inordinate amount of time looking into the cheese counter, obviously bothering others. These mussels would provide plenty of gastronomic relief, and, as he exited the shop, past the cured hanging hams, and left that atmosphere which was also a cloying smell of the recently cut or killed, he plunged in the provided plastic toothpick to the first -of about twenty- and, closing his eyes for the maximum effect, just bunged it in his gob (which had become once again rightly smacked).

Whether it brought him back to his family outings to Carnlough, up the Antrim Coast, and the phase of winkle collecting they'd all enjoyed so long ago, or maybe not so long ago, it satisfied enough for him to keep his eyes closed just that little smidge longer, drinking in the brine, and/or reeling in the years. And in that murk of his own making, he could hear Belfast all around him, feet clodding the pavement he was on, punters passing by, snatches of chat ('Any odds on ye?... Well, yer odd enough lookin'!', 'Sure his head's a marley!' and 'Glype!') the odd screech of a seagull now and then, and, faintly, distantly, the rattle of what sounded like diesel engines, pumping out invisible soot. When he opened his eyes again, and looked up Castle Street, he could see the cause: the 'black hacks' (mysteriously transposed

London taxi cabs), chuggering away without moving, or only just occasionally, waiting for enough souls – six – to fill up the interior and let the driver away. You could almost see the smoke, the soot, they produced. But it wasn't that which made him want to turn round and leave Castle Street, and give up on a visit to Harrisons, but the sudden feeling of something like dread, knowing that just beyond where he could see, as far as he could up the street, was his school, St Mary's Christian Brother's in Barrack Street. And with school came all sorts of thoughts and feelings he'd rather not deal with right now. He was free after all! The Brothers had given their dispensation! What was he doing here?

Feeling the full force of that, Christopher, instead of keeping to his plan to march forthwith to the Central Library and get all studious, succumbed to the need for a brief dander past The Bank Buildings and down the adjacent lane on the left. It was the draw of… Fresh Garbage, with its incense and hippy clothes, and, more importantly, the 'chick' who worked there and kept Christopher awake at nights thinking about. It was only as he approached the entrance, which could well be termed humble were it not for the near-life-sized stand-up sign of Jimi Hendrix done in psychedelic colours, that he thought it best not to enter. He had at least half the Ardglass mussels yet to get through, and he didn't want to be told off for eating on premises – or for lusting after the girl in charge, either. Indeed, just as he stood there, contemplating all this, the girl of his before-dreams stepped out in her bell-bottoms and long primped hair, and lit up a fag (A.K.A. 'cig', 'cancer-stick', or something even less salubrious, in moral terms, which Christopher could fantasize about later). He promptly turned round and hoped she hadn't seen his furtive presence.

He returned to Castle Place, enjoying its openness after the closed-in-ness of the lane he'd just been on, a sliver of street sandwiched between two nineteenth century behemoths. Here was a good place to just position yourself and take in a 360-degree view of all the grand old buildings, and to look off down into the unfolding of Royal Avenue (proper), with its buses and pedestrians bustling away, and… was that *Jaws 2* showing at the Avenue? ('Must ask the Da about seeing that', he mused.) Prone to a self-consciousness that wasn't always unhealthy, he wondered what anyone would make of him as he navigated the city centre like this, either with eyes closed and an intense look on his face or pinioned to one spot and looking all round him like a wide-eyed tourist. He was enjoying himself, he knew that. Spying a break in the traffic, he crossed over the road and proceeded to scoot down what he thought was High Street (maybe because he could see the Albert Clock at the end of it), but was in fact still just Castle Place, past the British Home Stores and its unenticing window display of an extended family of clothed dummies in various poses. The only item that caught his eye was the one that probably wasn't on sale: the glorious orange Space Hopper, being motionlessly sat upon by a dummy kid wearing a silly yellow cap. What fun they'd had bouncing on them, Christopher reflected, and wondered if a sixteen-year-old could ever do that again. His mind resisted the impulse to say 'No'.

The same mind also reflected, faintly, on what he had meant when he had used the plural there –'they' –'what fun *they* had had…'. Ivan Stacks the first Protestant he'd ever met? What a joke that was, he had to admit. Sure, my best friend is a Prod. I grew up with him and his family next door to us… *another faraway world, but not of dinosaurs and spaceships…* Dinosaurs and spaceships were easier, Christopher heard himself state. The thought had the finality of a realization, one he didn't fancy dwelling on, and, anyway, another internal voice was calling out: 'Cornmarket, here I come!'

After stuffing the now empty mussels tray into an over-filled lamppost-attached yellow litterbox on the street, Christopher veered off Castle Place and entered a side-street on the right. He chose to walk on the right side of the side-street, also, falling for the allurement of Thompson's Bakery. He didn't linger very much though, just allowed his eyes to feed tantalizingly on the arrays of sugar-topped Paris buns, flowery baps and rolls, and the pasties. Cornish pasties were his favourite, dressed in brown sauce and liberally sprinkled with salt. That, he realized, would be the lure of Victor's once again, calling out to him in his innocence. The adjacent Enlander's, with its display of fine rings and necklaces luxuriating on their white velvet open cases, dragged his mind far enough away from his stomach to put Victor's to bed. He walked on, somehow then gravitating to the left side of the street, drawn by the chance to peruse the extensive shoe stacks outside Saxone and Trueform. That's where the biggest 'buzz' seemed to be happening -even if 'buzz', as in 'Belfast is Buzzing', wouldn't become a buzz word until quite a few years later. Like many Belfastians (if he qualified as one, his house just technically beyond the boundaries), he didn't realize the street with the bakery, the jewellers and the shoe shops was what constituted Cornmarket proper, and the rotunda at its end was actually Arthur Square. It didn't make any difference to his sense of achievement upon reaching the -circular- square, which he thought was called 'Cornmarket', as his mind fleetingly conjured the sight of dray horses from yesteryear pulling massive, wheeled barrows chock full of cornstalks, prancing around in endless circles, men calling out unintelligible things and bargaining for the best price they could get. He had never taken the trouble to think past why Belfast would be marketing corn anyway, a crop which, if he did think about it, summoned the vasty fields of America or somewhere decidedly warmer than here, that was for sure. From time to time, a breeze would take it upon itself to harry the pedestrians and remind them there was nothing exotic about *their* climate.

The option to sit awhile at the centre of the rotund 'square' was mulled over, but the circular seating seemed to be occupied, and anyway, Christopher told himself, 'I shouldn't get too waylaid. I am going to the Central, but now that I'm here, a quick peek into Caroline Records can hardly hurt.' There was also the projected image of him sitting there reading the *News Letter*, and the strangeness of how it would strike others, a badge-proclaiming Christian Brothers fellow happily engrossed in the periodical mouthpiece for the Protestant community. So, with an alacrity which surprised him, he suppressed his desire to find out what had happened to the Sceli-something and the Mega-somethingelse and opted instead to indulge the materialist in him. He did so after wandering slightly centre-ward, toward the general vicinity of numerous magazine and newspaper stacks, speed-reading the titles as he did so, wondering 'Should I take a look at that *Radio Times*?' And then, spying McManus's in the background: 'Why are there so many bloody shoe shops in Belfast?' (*Maybe*, a voice within proffered, *so people like you can clod all over the place willy-nilly.*)

Christopher made a – busy, buzzy – beeline past whatever else might tempt his gaze and resumed his trajectory down Ann Street, with its own assortment of attractions. He took in the sights of the various shops on either side, walking right down the middle, noting 'Woolies' [Woolworths Department Store] on the left, and the Capstan Bar just next to it, with its curiously attractive little red awning over the entrance on one side; and then, on the other, the giant and slightly disturbing black & white 'SHOES McMANUS SHOES McMANUS SHOES', giving way to Littlewoods [Department Store], whose front and name felt happily understated in comparison. He walked on, now veering to the left, dodging and weaving past others. Being a pedestrian precinct, the Cornmarket area was a great attraction for shoppers and general wanderers, if your collision antenna was working properly, that is. Christopher ambled on, past Eason's, resisting the urge to browse the magazines or check out the latest bestseller lists, past Joy's Entry, and then, after a brief 'shufties' at the desiderata of sexy camera gear in Amateur's Nook, past Pottinger's Entry, with its standing wood-board sign advertising bottles of Guinness for a measly 25p at the Morning Star – he had that and much more in his pocket! As ever, proximity to a city bar would give him the same distant sense of longing he had felt eyeing the Capstan: the wonder of what it would be like to enter a bar and order a pint of the black stuff. For how much longer was that to be denied to him? Another thought: Why did Pottinger's Entry, with its thick black stone and its incredibly low archway, look like the Entry to Hell, and yet still remain so alluring for that?

He crossed over, passing between shoppers and sundry ambulators, and right past a small crowd of very young kids who were pantomiming a fight, prancing around each other with exaggeratedly big steps and issuing the occasional mock-roar as they did so, as though they were monsters. Maybe they'd just seen the latest Godzilla? Christopher wondered. He also wondered if he'd heard that there was a new one out, fond memories of *Godzilla vs Meca-Godzilla* seeping back. Why weren't they in school? thought Christopher, more to the point. Was it International Class Cancellation Day, or what? Anyway, he was almost there, and he didn't care. He was at Caroline Music, just beside Bogart's clothes shop. He loved this place as it always had unusual items, never just the mainstream fare. He would come here to enjoy seeing what they had in the way of jazz, which in recent years had become an obsession. Last year, he'd visited New York with his parents and watched in amazement as jazz musicians played on the sidewalk, sax, stand-up double bass, and even drums. He'd then run round to the nearest record store and asked his Da to get him the cassette of *Charles Mingus, the Atlantic Years*, which request his Da had gladly complied with. The album had since become one of his favourites. He had been shocked and saddened at the very beginning of this year to see that the very same Charles Mingus had died. He remembered watching an impromptu tribute on BBC2 with great sadness for the fallen great. They'd showed a video of him playing 'Goodbye, Pork-Pie Hat'.

He had received Miles Davis's *Bitches Brew* for his fifteenth birthday, an album he had also asked his father to get him, many times, and then sat in something like horror as he endured the cacophony which emanated from the 40-watt Waltham speakers in his bedroom. What madness! His brothers had taken pity on him and bought him his next choice, *Diamantina Cocktail* by the Australian pop band The Little River Band instead, allowing him to consign *Bitches Brew* to the top of the wardrobe, where all the headache-inducing vinyls went, Chick Corea's *The Brain* among them.

Since then, however, a kind of musical maturity had blossomed, allowing him to re-visit Miles and branch out in any direction. The trip to the US had helped. Christopher was now heavily into John McLaughlin, and his adventures with the Mahavishnu Orchestra, and Shakti; the progressive rockers YES; Weather Report, and their bassist Jaco Pastorius, and other luminaries of the jazz-fusion, jazz-rock progressive rock world. He knew it, but didn't know it, that this music, with its intense and colourful modes, created pathways out of the 'ugly reality' of life in a place in which violent death, thuggish behaviour, state-endorsed murder, sectarian strife and general fear, were part of the picture of daily life, usually in the background, but occasionally, if you knew someone who had suffered, in the painful foreground, too. Where he lived was fairly quiet, thankfully, but how insulated could anyone be living here? Music was a way out of this, or a way *through* this, or… music was just *another* world, an infinitely more enriching one.

They were playing Gil-Scott Heron and Brian Jackson's 'The Bottle', when he entered. He guessed that was the title from the number of times the singer would scream it out -and then confirmed this by noting the handwritten display on the counter. It was just up his street, even if the drum/percussion solo went on a bit. No, it was good; it created a groove within the confines of the shop, near-trance-inducing, too. Good background for the business at hand, searching through the titles, these large square artworks of delight -like Lindisfarne's ink-etched purply *Fog on the Tyne*; a seemingly untitled Earth, Wind & Fire album, with the *de rigeur* Egyptian iconography; Heart's indelibly erotic (to Christopher) *Dreamboat Annie* cover; Van Morrison's *Saint Dominic's Preview*, with Van sitting on those steps, playing that old acoustic, his far-off visionary look spoiled only by the unappealing tcat in his trousers. Then there was Jaco's monotone head-and-shoulders portrait, which Christopher had bought in New York the year before, his eyes intense, looking like he owned the keys to far off mysteries… And then, Christopher found an album he suddenly felt he should have. The moment coincided happily with the moment when the percussion solo exploded back into the band returning to take up the theme of that most powerful song, Mr Scott-Heron soon getting back the chance to shout once again, 'The Bottle!' The album Christopher was eyeing was called *Splendid*, a guitar collaboration by Larry Coryell and Philip Catherine. The artwork showed the two of them looking out at Christopher, their images done by some matrix of printed words, computer code, blunt red stencil of the title and their names at the top left. Larry, in his suit, big glasses and even bigger hair, looked like an eager office-worker, but somehow that added to the spark, and nicely complemented Philip's Belgian cravat-wearing Bohemian look. The titles of the tracks attracted, too. What was 'One Plus Two Blues'? Might listening to it help with the 'O'-levels? What were 'Snowshadows'? Number 8 was 'A Quiet Day in Spring', and that, Christopher noted, was what it was right now, a quiet day in spring, in Belfast city. He had to get it. He suffered a brief moment of panic, however, over finances -£2.95 was not to be sniffed at, after all. This would leave him with only 5p to get home... But, he rattled his kecks and found, to his eternal delight, that he had bus tokens aplenty. And of course, the library was free. So, he then strode up to the counter and bought it from a long-haired bloke wearing a Led Zeppelin T-shirt. Christopher exited a Belfast shop for the second time that day with something like ecstasy coursing through his sixteen-year-old veins -he felt... Splendid!

All of ten minutes later, having passed through the out-security barrier/ Ring of Steel at the end of Royal Avenue, Christopher then skipped up the grey-black marble steps of the radiantly-red red-sandstone Belfast Central Library, and only just in time checked himself to avoid getting slapped in the face by the massive and ineluctable revolving doors. He stood back, girded himself, placed his plastic Caroline Music bag into the same hand that held his school bag, and waited for the space to open up and welcome him into the dark interior of that most venerable building. With the energy of youth and expectation of great things, he soon found himself bounding up the huge, elegant, rounded staircase, past the large bookcase after the first flight, filled with books -whose only purpose, it seemed, was simply to impose their gravity upon those who had the privilege to walk past them. He soon gained the second floor and, with fitting reverence, pushed open the stately doors that gave access to the place where he could steal an hour or so, coming to terms with his ignorance.

· · ·

Time travel is a sci-fi-nub if ever there was one. It might be H.G. Wells's *Time Machine* contraption one might imagine you'd need to scoot through the millennia at the drop of a hat, or an engineered wormhole in space. A precisely timed slingshot round the sun might also do the trick, but for one unsuspecting creature in the history of existence, all it would take would be a little bit of fudge. Not the kind you might pop in your mouth, or 'gub', but the kind which is a mix of a lie and a hope, resting precariously on a wing and a prayer. Somewhere in the fug of an inebriated chat in the Dobbins Hotel lounge and the puzzlement of a hungover morning, coupled with a touch of ribbing on one side and a touch of 'chancing yer arm' (what novices with more enthusiasm than knowledge often do) on the other, it was possible for the innocent Scelidosaurus to be rudely transported away from his familiar surroundings in the Early Jurassic Period and carried forth a few million years in time to the Middle Jurassic Period. All it would take was a pen, someone to push it, and an indulgent uncle with the authority to publicly disseminate such to an unwary public to accomplish that wonder of wonders. This punter and that would read of the new (old) reality and accept it as carved in stone, belief aided by hope, and, for one solitary seeker of new worlds, further aided by the mysterious forces of sleep, which possessed him as he lounged in his comfy seat on the second floor reading room of the Belfast Central Library. He had soon pushed aside the deathly boring *Guide to Mathematics Stage 4* and had instead taken out the long-forgotten quires of the *News Letter*, eyes awash with wonder, unprepared for the waves of sleepiness that wonder, requiring as much energy as wonder invariably did, brought to the door of his consciousness. And so it was done, Christopher transported to a place of slumber and dreams, and the poor ancient beast transported to a harsh and alien environment, where beasts much larger than itself strode perilously close by, shaking the land with their hooves...

On the horizon a veritable nest of volcanoes could be seen, spewing their fumes and torrents of red-hot lava into the sky from their well-formed blackened cones. In the air all around raged the screams of beasts seen and unseen: sequoia-high trees would seem to accompany some of these sounds by a sudden swaying or even a cracking of branches. Giant pterodactyls passed overhead, swooping low on occasion to terrify vulnerable-looking potential meals on legs, or to actually capture them in their extremely teethy gubs to the intense horror, of course, of each shrieking victim. Huge two-legged animals with heads as big as the creature viewing all this trotted by gnashing their banana-like teeth and clacking their jaws with sickening regularity. The poor Scelidosaurus looked around and wondered what was going on. He didn't know Ivan Stacks, or even the genus *Homo Sapiens* to which Mr Stacks belonged, as it had not yet evolved, but one felt sure that *if he did know Ivan Stacks*, and if he discovered it was he who had put him there in the midst of this maelstrom of chaos and terror, he would have a few words to say to him, so he would!

It didn't take long for one of the huge two-legged beasts to take notice of the bewildered Scelidosaurus. Normally, in his quiet corner of existence, the Scelidosaurus would hardly have raised an eyebrow in the presence of such a fellow, confident that the rows of scutes and plates on his body would deter even the hungriest of predators from taking an interest. And covered he was, in hard, knobby plating, even sporting horns on his head that doubled as signals to the fairer sex that he was a beast worth rubbing noses with. Somehow, however, he was unable to coax his usual calm at the approach of beasts with something to say. Of the thing on two legs coming his way now he had no name for, in the pictorial lexicon of his experience. It was simply different. At least, he consoled himself briefly, it doesn't have two heads.

It was a Megalosaurus, but of course the Megalosaurus didn't know that. Does a tiger know he's a tiger? Well, yes and no. He knows he's a something, but he doesn't subscribe to human language or nomenclature, so he wouldn't know what you were talking about even if you addressed him politely or repeated the word over and over. The Megalosaurus, however, had, and has, escaped the scrutiny of even some of the most important palaeontologists in history, and remains somewhat like the elephant which is discovered by a band of blind wise men, who each tell different tales about what shape it is, based on the fact that each is touching a different part of its anatomy. So, that its head might resemble a well-known politician in Northern Ireland wouldn't necessarily take the biscuit as being the most outlandish thing anyone could say about the beast: it could even be partially true. That head now turned toward Scelidosaurus (who also didn't know his own name). With the intelligence of a small dog, it's possible that 'ole Mega', if we may thereby abbreviate the onomastic mouthful that he tends to be, might have done a dinosaur version of a double take, as the creature he beheld did not tally with anything in his memory banks of known walking fodder. Actually, on that thorny question of 'fodder', this one, with all those hard bits sticking out, looked a mite thorny itself, or horny. Or was that 'horned'? Whichever it was, it was unlikely old Mega would have simply rushed over and gone for a bite. Even his imperious descendant, the Tyrannosaurus Rex, wouldn't have been so incautious as to expect everything to go his way, even with little 'uns like this. Ah, the joys of the pack! Why try and kill something by yourself when you can make it a community effort? Ganging up on fare would always be about comradeship and teamwork, and not about the cowardice that lurked within even the meanest meany, when push came to shove. And, of course, they didn't do hard drugs in the Jurassic Period. And no dinosaur sniffed glue, either.

Here, Mega didn't quite have the option of enlisting any fellows of a similar kidney, however, having drifted far from his own territory, and yet he was eager not to let a sprat like this spoil his day, or to put a dent in his masculinity… And, come to think of it, gender did play a part, for if he wasn't mistaken… that smallish unknown horned (horny?) creature looked actually rather feminine… Those soft curves, the elegant tilt of its cute head, and the pert and almost alluring uplift of the creature's rear-end. To an audience of humans more accustomed to eking out their lives on the northern hills, plains and valleys of the island of Hibernia millions of years hence, the face of that Scelidosaurus might even look *familiarly* feminine. Did it possess some features in common with the face of the one and only Bernadette Devlin, or was it just a case of you only see what you always see – especially if it's on TV? And while in 1979, even in dreamtime 1979, Bernadette, the face of working-class socialist Republicanism, had dropped off the radar a little in comparison to her heydays in the late sixties and early seventies, she still possessed massive star appeal, and had much left yet to say, or, as her critics might put it, much yet to shout about. What a surprise, or a coincidence, then, that her apparent admirer, or was it her would-be assassin, the Mega, coming from a world she knew nothing about, a world in which portraits of Queen Elizabeth II and framed tracts from the Bible, like *Thou Shalt Not Steal*, adorned walls in scrupulously clean front parlours, looked like none other than her perfect nemesis, the Right Reverend Ian! Ian Kyle Paisley himself! Those teeth! That mouth! That look of God-fearing hatred!

Just then, not terribly far away, on a dusty track unused by others, passed a ten-ton armoured Triceratops. He moved forward with no heed to what was around him, happily monolithic and unwavering. If you squinted, you could just make out what looked like a metal grill round his flamboyantly hooded head, and/or the nub of an exhaust from his glorious behind, from which issued, moment by moment, a malodorous puff of noxious fumes. Dotted here and there, other smaller beasts of similar shape and industry patrolled the nooks and the crannies of this Jurassic scene, kicking up dust and exhaling a collective whine, as though their lungs were mechanical bellows, huffing and puffing but with no houses to blow down, unless they were lucky. Flak-jacketed raptors scurried in packs, rounding up herbivores, with the occasional slash of their foot-length-long claws, and much gnashing of teeth. Victims were not all destined to die, but those who were destined to live wondered if there was life before death... The Scelidosaurus felt a oneness with them, and this helped as the Mega made its first move.

'Do you dance, Bernadette?' roared the giant beast. 'Who's asking?' replied the Scelidosaurus. 'I'm askin'', replied the towering monster. Somehow, despite the throaty gutturals, a Liverpool accent could be discerned for both.

Then, from an entirely different quarter came a shout of 'Cut! Cut! Cut!' and into the prehistoric scene strode a tall leather-faced black-sunglasses-wearing man in casuals, holding a megaphone and a camera-lens and looking not unlike Sam Peckinpah. The Sceli and the Mega looked round in unison, like two kids who know they're doing things all wrong. The man appeared to huddle with the two, as much as one can when there's such a disparity between heights. Whatever was said was nothing anyone else could hear, which was, incidentally, a variation on whatever you say, say nothing. But actions speak louder than words and no-one could deny that whatever had happened, the two beasts were now, miraculously, clad in dinosaur-sized black balaclavas. Sam retreated out of shot, brought the megaphone up to his leathery lips, thrust his lens-holding right hand skyward and bellowed: 'Roll 'em'!'

It wasn't Sunday night viewing. The Mega lorded it over what he thought was his quarry, blocking the sun at one point, his great jaws a-snapping, Master of all, if not yet master of his balaclava, the cloth of which tended to inhibit the gnashing. The Sceli knew now what it meant to fight for your life, and your way of life, and hit back, whipping her tail round with force, sometimes on target, pummelling the Mega's meaty legs. Yet, the physics of size were against her, and it wouldn't be long before the Mega's teeth caught its prize, tearing a chunk from her neck, dripping with blood. Instead of succumbing, however, the Sceli grew in rage (although the balaclava obscured the niceties of facial expression) and in fury *and* in incaution, doing what only the desperate will do when up against the wall, and projected her own head toward the danger area, pushing against her best herbivorean instincts to snap out with her ferocious beak as good as she'd get at the monster's fleshy underbelly and legs. Blood from them both splattered the ground and coloured the air, as then their vocal chords came back into play. This from the Mega, this time in a North Antrim accent: 'Die, Fenian, Papist whore, die!' This from the Sceli, in tones of acerbic Tyrone: 'I'll die when I'm ready and not at the hands of a Unionist fucker like you!' Never in the history of the ancient world, in the land that time forgot, had two beasts been so diametrically opposed in hatred (or maybe something deeper) that they'd pushed through the limitations of animalistic utterance to voice their thoughts with such eloquence.

Unbeknownst to them both, their struggles and toil born of deep mutual contempt, distrust and, it had to be said, a shocking lack of acquaintance, had brought them into a kind of frenzied dance, and not the kind which had initially appeared to be on offer. This dance carried them away from the dusty *tabula rasa* ground they'd begun on to a place which looked ever so different, where the man-made replaced the natural, buildings replaced trees, the far-away volcanoes became lost to view, as angular stone and right-angled brick shot up all round them and became a street, or an avenue (if one without trees), not unlike the one at the heart of the North Eastern metropolis of the island of Ireland, Royal Avenue shining and new and resplendent in the late afternoon light – or was it Donegall Place?

It was now B-movie stuff, as the two, unaware and uncaring, their balaclavas now shredded and long fallen away, roiled in their anger and rage and frothing frustration, smashing windows in shops selling men's and women's fashion items, bridal accessories, vinyl records, cassettes, diamond rings, and size thirteen shoes, spilling blood everywhere... *Smash! Bang! Wallop!* Up the street they careered, past the Avenue Cinema, which was showing *Jaws 2*, with its tagline 'Just when you thought it was safe to go back in the water...', the partial irony of which was lost on the grappling behemoths, if not on the few bystanders, guffawing loudly, who had braved danger to witness (pre-) history being made. The Megalosaur's own jaws dived for the Scelidosaurus' already blood-spouting neck once again, giving impetus to said Scelidosaurus to scoot with unseemly alacrity up into Donegall Place proper, with what felt like the last of its energy, if not the last of its pride. It was a race to the finish now, but the smaller had a card up her sleeve. Neither gave much heed to the mess they were making, the fine window displays shattered here and there, lampposts pushed over, one red & white Citybus knocked over, the passengers inside shouting out for help... The army and police were in high dudgeon, dismayed at being left to look so helpless, officers with automatic rifles screaming out to their subordinates to 'Get movin'!' and 'Secure this area!' Running this way and that, the Mega closing in with giant Coltrane steps, the Scelidosaurus was facing imminent collision with the Ring of Steel. Somehow, however, it managed to tweak the momentum forcing its mass forward, making it hurtle ever more left-wise and into the jewel of the street, the windows of Robinson & Cleaver's, and its display of fine perfumes, *Mystère de Rochas*, by Rochas, and the newest, top-of-the-line Estée Lauder, *Cinnabar*, anachronistically packaged as a 'New 1980s Kind of Fragrance', as though to speed this decade to its conclusion. The Mega had of course been following the Sceli, who'd given up the ghost of surviving this battle, focused more on some dim intimation of a long, generational war, for all her peaceful upbringing. And with it, the promise of martyrdom had now taken root in her breast, allowing her to see individual death as just a milestone to freedom and victory...

The two had landed, with earth-shattering force, against the ground floor corner of the grand Robinson & Cleaver building, at the head of Donegall Place, a stone's throw (pardon the idiom) from City Hall, in the centre of Belfast, Northern Ireland, twentieth century, Friday, April twenty seventh, nineteen seventy-nine, having time-travelled millions and millions and millions of years into the future, their fury having sustained them throughout. Masonry flew up and out, and the air was lacerated by flying glass and perfume bottle tops. There was a sound of cracking somewhere, deep and disconcerting, as the building appeared to be shaken to its foundations...

The dinosaurs seemed to have become aware of the gravity of the situation and had ceased in their labours of hate, the Scelidosaurus' head now serendipitously nestled in the fleshy throat area of the Megalosaurus, as though they were lovers, the eyes of each looking out at the assembled strange-looking dinosaurs with circular legs and smoke pumping out of their behinds... As one looked to the other, from the ancient dinosaurs to the modern mechanical ones, and then the modern mechanical dinosaurs to the two ancient ones, it was, for some hardy bystanders, becoming increasingly difficult to say which was which...

One of those bystanders stepped forward. He was a slightly rotund man in a powder-blue-coloured suit and cream shirt and tie, with slightly protuberant eyes and bloated cheeks, and he swayed slightly, as though not quite in control -well, who could be in a situation like this? The hair on his head could be described as 'dirty-fair' and not as kempt as it could be. 'Do not go gentle, sweet creatures, into that good night,' he let out of him, punctuating that with a half-suppressed burp. 'Old age should burn and rave at close of day, and all that stuff you learn at school,' he appealed to the pachyderm pair before him, '...but don't you think you're taking things a little far? Rage, rage, against the dying of the light, certainly, but look what too much will bring...' The rest of his words were occluded by the sudden intrusion of a series of cracking sounds, like you'd hear if a sequoia were keeling over under some cataclysmic pressure, cracking and warping and breaking and... for those who could bear to watch, the upper stories of the giant building began shattering and falling, and then, with a last enormous whoosh, down came the oxidised turrets, tumbling, tumbling and falling and hitting the deck and exploding, turning road and all to rubble and, co-incidentally, preserving the dinos in silicate for their journey here, or just up the road, as it would be, with the action of tectonic plates coming into play and shifting the ground round a bit here and there, in the Garden of Eden, millions and millions and millions of Fridays and countless plates of chips into the future....

Whatever the racket them turrets made, it was enough to wake Christopher up, and he did. With an unalluring snort.

Chapter Five: Tidying up, pt.1, Saturday, April 28

Professor Tweedy's shoulders were slightly hunched as he sat at his desk in his office at Queen's University, his head down and lower lip pushing up against his stiff upper lip. He looked very much a man pondering the imponderable. In fact, he was simply pondering the best choice of words, and the best tone, with which to address the two students who had caused the recent upset. He wasn't very good at telling people off, or even just talking to them, and students presented a particular challenge, being generally so immature, impatient and inordinately inarticulate. He liked students best when they were quiet, taking notes at his lectures, or raising the occasional hand to ask a pertinent question. He wasn't pally-wally with them, and never addressed any by anything other than their family name.

If he was honest with himself, he was also a little upset by having been seconded onto this project, having been happily engaged in his own studies and pursuits in archaeological, not palaeontological, digs. Why hadn't the geologists been asked? Instead of pursuing the record of ancient human settlements in Belfast and environs he had now been spending most of the year basically holding the chisels for the insufferable Heinkle. No wonder they called him Herr Heinkle! 'Don't! Don't! Don't!' was hardly the most diplomatic way for the visiting Professor to address his well-meaning and extremely welcoming local Professor, exhorting Tweedy not to even touch the rocky outcrop they'd come across early in the dig. It was so infuriating being talked to like that, and yet, he had gladly complied with Professor Jope's 'request' that he offer 'our German friend' every assistance, as it would 'reflect well on our global standing'. Tweedy was vexed by the behind-backs phrase that was used about him from time to time, as 'Jope's Hope'. *'Jope's Joke', more like...* And, Lord, oh Lord, yes, both disciplines did involve digging into the earth, but the Permian surfaces they were working with had to be about the most uninspiring and, quite frankly, uninteresting substances known to man -unless you happened to be lucky and came across the tiniest speck of ancient calcified organic matter, the wingtip of an Early Triassic mosquito, perhaps. *Oh, joy, oh, celebration! Let's open the Champagne!* This was probably what Heinkle would do, but Tweedy, no. Tweedy would just have to pretend to be in raptures over the enormity of it all, smiling for the camera, engaging Heinkle in rapt conversation over the 'significance' of this, when, in reality, he didn't care one iota for a mosquito's wing, even a Triassic one. He would have been the first to swat the creature it belonged to with the flat of his palm. *Die, little thing of no worth, and don't show your face round here for the next hundred million years!*

Yes, and no. Yes, he did entertain such frivolous channelling of his inner frustrations, but no, he also knew the thrill of any exploration of what lay below our feet, however far back in time, and was – relatively – happy to be part of this enterprise, partly, at least. Uncompromisingly obstinate characters appeared to populate academia anyway, whether they had German accents or not. Jope was nice, of course, but he, like Tweedy, had to answer to higher forces within the university, the ones who called the shots and from time to time interfered with the happy course of their work. 'The University envisions this enterprise as a bridge to international cooperation for a department sometimes too closely focused on Northern Irish rock and soil.' This was particularly galling as a policy tweak considering they had lassoed Professor Jope, who was already as international as archaeologists got, and made sure he kept his nose in Northern Irish soil and rock during term time. It was hard to keep up with the powers that be, and not wishing to second guess anyone, Tweedy had felt it better just to accept – accept all he was given, be it on a silver platter or in a dirty paper bag, metaphorically speaking.

Oh, the joys he derived from uncovering the tangible past! What ineluctable pleasure Tweedy had derived from even just reading about that giant beaker rescued from the depths of the mud and clay in Cluntyganny Townland last year! (The pamphlet was still on his desk.) That was work and a half! He well recalled his meeting with the authors Brennan, Briggs and the curiously named ApSimon – those funny Welsh names were always a wonder, too! Had that one-and-a-half-foot tall pot been part of a burial chamber or had it been a utensil used daily for a family in Neolithic times? That had led to some wonderful discussions... Even today, in the *Telegraph* he'd read about what the people at Historic Monuments were doing down in Armagh. It could only happen here of course: how to find a four and a half thousand-year-old pot? Just blow up the local Woolworths store or have the local terrorist organization do it for you, and then start digging! He'd done plenty of digging himself, of course, at Shantallow, in Londonderry, and closer to home, up at the Malone Ridge, where pre-historic settlements in this area had begun. With what painstaking care had they worked, day in, day out, chipping away at the past, tenderly wiping away dirt here and there, pulling away the chaff of the relatively modern, to get at the kernel of ancient habitation and culture and life! How many months had he spent, endangering his family happiness in the process, working upon those three-dimensional jigsaws to restore the various vessels and utensils, sherd by loving sherd? All for the goal of being able to re-construct the most precious artefacts of the past, for ultimate display either within an academic institution or, glory of glories, at the Ulster Museum... Yes, it could be very satisfying to delve into the dirt and pull out jewels which would lead to a great understanding of our past, ourselves, and this great Province – but where was the greatness in exploring the deep, dark past Heinkle dwelt on so much? Who cared about trilobites?

And now, in the midst of all this, the world – potentially – was focused on what they were doing up in Eden, that so inappropriately named hellhole past Carrick! No, they hadn't struck gold and discovered two dinosaurs locked in mortal battle. They had discovered evidence to suggest two dinosaurs had, coincidentally, died in this particular area, but with an enormity of time in between, and absolutely no connection to each other beyond spatial coincidence. Quite possibly they had even died very far apart, of course, and the rocks had simply 'floated' toward each other in the Pangean flux: Heinkle was working on that theory. The 'discovery', as such, had occurred last year, courtesy, apparently, of someone's else's hard work, and this had led to the arrival of The Magnificent Heinkle, as Tweedy now mischievously tagged him. Tweedy hadn't really bothered to clarify the origins of the enterprise and gladly took Heinkle's word as gospel, even when wrapped in the flubby inconsistencies of a far-from-perfect command of the English language. Furthermore, the nature of the work, digging into clay in all weathers in a territory devoid of any trace of human settlement told Tweedy all he needed to know. Yes, it had initially been immensely satisfying to be part of that team, the team that had discovered this chance 'meeting' of ancient fauna, but knowing Heinkle, Tweedy knew his part would be downplayed to the smallest of footnotes in history. He, Professor Tweedy, unknown archaeologist in a corner of the world better known for violent conflict than anything uplifting, would be forever known as the second man on the moon…

And… the second man on the moon now had to tidy things up, his Eminence upstairs happily ensconced in his work, or still just reeling from his own professional embarrassment. Like the old crustacean he was, Heinkle could easily retire back inside his shell and let the underlings take care of things. Tweedy brought his thoughts back to the matter at hand, broke out of his slumped posture and released his face from its rigour. He had to look as professional and as unruffled as possible, the Professor at his desk, able to accept his visitors with nary a whisker out of place on his professorial moustache. The Tweed jacket played its part, too, and he couldn't care less about whoever wanted to call him 'The Tweed', 'Tweedy Professor Tweedy', or 'Tweedy Bird', as he had heard. He liked these clothes. They imparted a certain dignity, necessary in the big bad world of academia and among the poorly clad students, in their bell-bottoms and cheesecloths, looking like lost hippies.

He surveyed what was on the desk immediately before him and found it largely uncluttered and expressive of an uncluttered mind. The 'paperweight' Heinkle had given him, however, stood out like a sore thumb. It looked like a fossilized elephant's toe. He hadn't even understood exactly why the German professor had given it to him on their first meeting: was it a souvenir of the old country? Heinkle had done his best to explain it, but that had been at the official Welcome Reception and, well, with drink taken on both sides and Heinkle's English not always as mellifluent as it might have been, Tweedy hadn't bothered to pursue the matter. At least it was good for holding paperclips, and, less fortunately, dust. Otherwise, he told himself, for today's purposes, only a pen and a QUB Bookshop memo pad would suffice, oh, *and* the framed family shot of Abigail and he and Tommy and Jenny, at Scrabo Tower two summers ago. *What a day that had been!* He repressed the moment that floated to his mind when Abigail had implored him to stop examining the soil at the base of the structure – which he had been doing for the previous twenty minutes – and instead play with the kids: 'Don't! Don't! Don't!' *(Did she really say it three times?)* He didn't want to believe that he was always being berated for following his instincts, or that the world was a mite too harsh for a man who only ever wanted to pursue the foundations of civilisation, to be left alone with his scraper and brush, to uncover who we were, who we had been...

His office door opened and a young female head, enveloped in an over-abundance of dark frizzled hair, popped out from behind it and spoke: 'Is it OK if we come in now?' Against his better judgement, Tweedy found himself giving way to his annoyance: 'Couldn't you knock first?' 'Oh, I did, sir,' said the girl, suddenly looking worried, 'many times, but there was no answer...' 'Oh, come in then, come in...' instructed a slightly flustered Tweedy, who realized he'd been so caught up in his thoughts he simply hadn't heard. He wasn't sure he wanted to apologize, but as the door opened further and the female student and then her male companion were revealed, standing there looking defenceless and apologetic, he did endure a moment of conflict, wondering how he might reconcile his impulse to give at least the most casual of apologies and still maintain a façade of sternness and stolidity. Had the meeting been for some other reason, he would likely have thrown out: 'Dear me, how silly of me, come in, come in, sorry to have kept you waiting. Us professors sometimes live in the clouds! You need to knock pretty hard sometimes, ha ha!' (Something told Tweedy he would never have said that, but then something else whispered into his hair-filled ear, *what a nicer professor you would be if you just opened up a little... smiled a little, became more openly friendly with your students, played with your kids a little, too...*) Repressing this feeling and whatever his inner voice was telling him, Tweedy now found himself barking out commands a little too loudly, as he suggested they (a) 'come in, come in', (b) 'take a seat' (c) 'oh yes, bring that other seat over from there' (berating himself for not having arranged the seating himself), and (d) 'just sit, just sit down'. Tracey and Manny felt they were getting the treatment they had expected, as, at the same time, Professor Tweedy felt he was giving them the treatment he had wished to avoid. Realizing this from the looks on their faces and feeling upset at having spoken too loudly, he did what he hadn't expected himself: Professor Tweedy smiled.

It was an awkward smile, one forced up into his facial muscles by a flurry of feelings, including a new one, a sudden awareness that Miss Tracey Whatever-her-name-was was a bit of a corker. Her hair was a marvellous network of dark filaments, her eyes shining like jewels in a face that belonged in a magazine… Tweedy had also taken in the hair and face of her companion, Manny Something-or-other, and, despite having met him so many times before on the dig, viewed him now, and the brown skin on his face and his hands, as though for the first time, like he was a being from another world. (A voice inside Tweedy barked: 'Don't! Don't! Don't!' eager to suppress anything which detracted from the enlightenment he held so dear. 'We are all God's children.') Tracey and Manny smiled back, if also a little forcedly. It was going to be one of those meetings, alas, thought Tracey, a total cringe event.

'Now,' pronounced Tweedy, having soon dispensed with his 'smile', 'thank you for coming to see me. You've already expressed your regrets over the recent incident, so I'm not looking for an apology or to grill you… I'd just like to have the chance for us to talk a little about things and see what we can achieve going forward.' It was a classic little speech, perfectly reflective of his educational principles of fairness and decency, albeit allowing a bit of space to explore further, or to, if not grill, then lightly toast the two for their indiscretion. 'Well,' spoke up Manny, as though beating Tracey to the mark, 'we'd still like to apologize anyway, sir,' at which point Tracey found her chance and echoed that with, 'Yes, very much. We had no idea our little joke would become this big… *story!*' Tracey had employed a dramatic pause before her final word, which, when spoken, kind of exploded from her – Tweedy noticed: faintly metallic-ochre painted – lips. And that word had an edge to it, as though to emphasize the chasm between what they had done and what the journalist they had spoken to had created. Manny threw in some further similar-sounding comments, with the idea of a 'joke', Tweedy soon began to note, being promoted very much by both. He could see this was their defence, a defence they were building right in front of him as he sat there in his august chair in his august Tweeds in his august office. He wasn't having it.

'Joke?' he threw back. 'Joke? Is that what it was?' This silenced Tracey and Manny, as did the subsequent lecture unloaded upon them for thinking in terms of how humorous this all was, how amusing, how delightfully funny it was to do something that could bring ridicule down on this serious enterprise to uncover the past and learn the secrets of the natural world of ancient prehistoric times. In order to deliver this Tweedy found himself using more energy than he had thought he would and wondered why he hadn't poured himself a cup of tea or water beforehand. He ended his monologue with an appended question he regretted asking the moment it jumped off his now somewhat dry tongue: 'What was the precise nature of this joke, may I ask?'

There was a moment of silence, but only a moment, until Tracey, with the metallic-ochre lipstick and the filament network of dark hair, and, Tweedy now noticed, semi-circular low-cut pale pink blouse which, no matter how much he tried to stop it, led the eye to take in – fleetingly – the topographical prominences of her breast area, spoke. 'April Fool,' was all she could say. 'April Fool?' echoed Tweedy, his eyes now squarely focused on hers and enjoying the fact that he could do so without appearing too intensely focused on her jewel-like, star-shining-in-daylight eyes: confusion gave him the right. 'Yes,' said the lips, opening and closing before him like waves at the seashore…. 'April Fool.' Manny spoke up, feeling the need to add a little detail, and maybe break the deadlock in communication, or whatever it was, unfolding before him. He said something, which Tweedy didn't catch, and then appeared to reach into his shoulder bag, eventually fishing out what was clearly a newspaper, and, it soon transpired, that newspaper. 'You see,' Manny was saying, head down as he scanned the article – *that* article – and found the part that he was looking for. 'You see,' repeated Manny, stabbing his finger into the page with what he hoped wasn't too eager a gesture, 'April 7th he wrote, this…blo.. [struggling not to pre-fix his name with a swearword] Ivan Sticks fellow, April 7th. You see?' 'No, I don't see,' replied a visibly unimpressed Professor Tweedy who not only didn't like being corrected, if that was what this was, did not appreciate having to obediently look where some annoying and disruptive student was asking him to look. Never mind that he was obviously from a different world from the one Tweedy inhabited.

'I think Manuel is just trying to point out something we both noticed…' spoke the fair Tracey. Tweedy heard her words and softened his response to the Manny or Manuel fellow. He didn't speak, but gave the tiniest suggestion of being about to, allowing Tracey to then reach over, take the rag from her companion and with her fairer and much more pleasurable-on-the-eye hands, and point, delicately, to the place in the article where it read: 'Discovery of the dinosaur fight was recorded as April 7th, a date which will likely go down in history…' 'I'm all ears,' said Tweedy. 'Well', explained Tracey, 'obviously Mr Stocks didn't realize we were pulling his leg, and….' Tweedy's eyes narrowed; he wondered if this made him look more attractive to the young beauty before him. 'And?' he inquired, now enjoying the moment for what it was, even if what it was was different for all involved. 'Well, we wrote April 1st! Not April 7th!' As Tracey said this her eyebrows rose and her face flushed with radiance and cheeriness. It was a vision of joy, Tweedy found himself thinking, being so close to such bursting feminine youth. He could almost reach out with both hands, grip her by the shoulders and pull that Helen of Troy face up close to his own, to make contact with the metallic-ochre lips, the metallic-ochre lips…

Somewhere inside the dark chambers of Tweedy's mind, a light switched on in a lonely room, and he felt the swish of an uxorial hand pass through the air and slap him roundly on the right cheek. 'Oh, I see…' he said mechanically, processing, synaptic gears whirring… This called for action. 'My paper and pen!' Tweedy exclaimed, over-gesturing and fluffing about like a man in a half-panic, sweeping the useless paperweight off the desk in the process; he didn't bat an eyelid when it thumped heavily onto the floor, spilling whatever paperclips it had once proudly held. This, and the fact that his pen and notebook were already right there in front of him was clearly deemed comedic enough for both Tracey and Manny to feel it acceptable to smile broadly, point pointedly and even utter a few words of excitement to accompany the actions of their professor. 'Ah, yes, here we are!' said a now bubbly Tweedy, bringing the pen and the memo round so that Tracey could use them, adding 'Darling girl, just write the date that you wrote for poor Mr Sticks here.' (No-one made anything of his term of endearment and Tweedy was too engrossed in the fun of it all to even care.) Tracey took the pen – *a fountain pen, Parker, gold trimmings, nice* – and wrote 'April 1', turning the memo paper round for the professor, who took a long look at it. 'My dear,' he pronounced in his finest professorial tone, 'with that overly long upper serif and a miniscule foot at the bottom of the stalk, your "one" looks eminently more like a "seven". I'm afraid our Mr Sticks mustn't have realized his leg was being pulled! How funny, how terribly funny that is!' And at this Professor Tweedy let out that rare thing for him, a laugh in the presence of students. It was a laugh that was infectious enough to spread to Tracey and Manny, and in no time at all, the three of them were laughing and laughing at the hilarious revelation of it all.

'How is it,' asked a still cheery Tweedy, 'that you happen to write like that? Not standard British calligraphy that, I venture.' The 'I venture' added a millisecond of pause to Tracey's response, either as she wondered if she'd ever heard anyone use that phrase outside of old black and white films like Mister Chips or what it meant precisely, but then she was on it: 'Oh, I've a wee bit of the Continental in me, don't you know?' As she uttered the three-word tag, her delivery shifted from a reasonably flat working-class Belfast accent to a noticeably posher, more Malone-Road-like, register. It got Tweedy's attention and he laughed again at the delightfulness of it all, or the delightfulness of her all. 'Pray tell,' he managed to throw her way, enjoying his own acme-ancient-Professor delivery, glad that he had touched up his pencil moustache a little the evening previous (which gave him a touch of the Errol Flynn, he always half-imagined). 'Oh aye,' blurted out Tracey, availing of the old Norn Iron linguistic stand-by, even if it did burst the potential balloon that 'Continental' had added to her profile: 'I was schooled in Paris, no less, yonks ago, mind. The Da had work there.' 'Paris!' Tweedy's enrapturement rose. He worked to suppress, however, whatever physiognomic messages he may have been giving, ever more aware of -in the most negative sense- of the presence of Manny / Manuel, *who hailed from God knows where*. 'Is that a fact, is that a fact? What line of work, may I ask, was your father engaged in?' Tracey winced, but only slightly, then brightened, like a person who knows if they just do something quickly, something they don't like, then they can move on: 'Err... well... Socialist... Agitator.... I think that's what he said anyway... Part of the movement... and all that...' Tweedy's mouth momentarily popped open, with no discernible purpose. For want of something to do, it moved, and sound came out: 'Oh, I see...

socialist agi… agitator,' he stuttered, wondering what he could say next, as little internal voices scolded him for his indulgence in lusting over one of such lowly background: 'You see,' they seemed to say, ganging up on him, 'what do you expect from a student who causes such a ruckus? Her and her brown friend! Shouldn't you be telling her off, not letting her get away with almost ruining the project. The project… the project… the project….' Tweedy had become lost to these voices and to the chant of 'the project, the project' coursing through his otherwise vacant mind, and didn't snap out if it until voices outside his own head broke through the din: 'Professor! Professor! Are you OK?'

To their vocal joy, Professor Tweedy did snap out of it, and, encouraged by the cheerful and friendly faces and voices before him, now did his damnedest to put on an even bigger smile than before. Something, also, had spoken to him, a softer, more personal voice of his own, maybe nurtured since childhood, one which chimed in with the feeling of the students here before him and… with that other Tweedy who was also rebellious and, deep down, buried under layers of politeness and academic courtesy, not quite so committed to the project after all. It said: 'Oh to be an *academic* agitator!' It said it only once, very swiftly, and then retired back into the depths of Tweedy's personal consciousness. But it added a certain shine to the smile he now projected out towards both of his wards. They – yes, even the boy – had added a sense of unexpected happiness to his day. 'They', yes, but 'she' most of all.

After that it was impossible for Tweedy to return to any kind of sternness or professorial stolidity. He found himself inquiring about what they would do now, and cautioning them against any hasty action, that what they had done had obviously been blown up out of all proportion and perspective and that it was hardly a hanging offence. He didn't feel like inquiring about reports he'd heard from others that these two had sometimes shown less than devotion to the project, knowing that young people sometimes need to explore different avenues in order to see which one they would eventually head down in life, and if digging in the dirt and labelling jars hadn't quite suited them, well, life was long and open. He knew that some students' commitment to archaeology was not quite what his had been way back when, and that some had chosen this not quite knowing if they would ever use the skills they learnt here in their future careers. It was, after all, success enough, he often thought, if a university student came through the experience simply having learnt how to look at the world, and how to think. That, he concluded, was something worth encouraging, and gave him encouragement when he had witnessed student after student end up working in general science education, or in completely unrelated areas, like banking and TV or whatever. Tweedy was an educator first and a committed teacher of archaeology second, at least as far as the students went.

He had one ulterior motive for being soft on Tracey and Manny: their actions, while disruptive to Tweedy and all, had ended up delivering the kind of treatment he had sometimes wished he could deliver to Herr Heinkle. *Professor Heinkle, rather.* Yes, this had been a difficult time for one and all, but it had been priceless to see the look on the old German's face. That look of horror would sustain him as he tidied things up here and got on with the project that had taken him away from his cherished pursuits, not into the animal past, but the human one. There was also, he had to admit, and then did his best to suppress the thinking of it even as he did so, the fact that he had been able to spend even a short time in the presence of so delightful a young lady. After they had gone, Tweedy sat back in his -still august?- chair and closed his eyes. Not only was he happy with the way he had handled things, he was simply recalling the proximity he had enjoyed to one so sweet, one so cheery, one so radiantly beautiful, one so young...

Outside, Tracey and Manny walked about a minute until they were safely outside the building, before Manny exclaimed: 'What a dirty old geezer! You see the way he sized you up! You're lucky I was there! He mightta jumped you!' Tracey smiled, then caught herself on, and found herself slapping away at Manny's head and shoulders, uttering vigorous, if mild, swear-word-laced denials at even the suggestion of such. But she was laughing, too, caught between knowing what he said was true and blushing at how she felt about it.

Chapter Six: Tidying up, pt.2, Tuesday, May 1

As Professor Ronald Tweedy looked down from the street-facing window of his No.17 University Square office, the sight of students parading or protesting within the grounds of the university across the street displaced whatever residue of disappointment about the last few days he'd been feeling up till then. There was a note of discord to be discerned down there certainly, with one small group seeming to taunt and jeer another who were holding up hand-made banners plastered with the initials UUP [Ulster Unionist Party] and various slogans. *That would be Bradford's supporters*, Tweedy mused. A good man, if a little overzealous. Tweedy winced as he observed one student seemingly thrust out a hand to grab one side of an apparently offending banner. 'Tut, tut,' he tut-tutted, thinking, *oh not here, please.* Thankfully some other – adult – figure entered the fray, so to speak, and appeared to calm things down a bit. *The sooner this election is over the better... Why do we have to live like this?*

Retreating from the window, the memory of his own failings in the last few days resurfaced briefly, among the most pressing of which was his failure to have watched the UTV broadcast last night, of Professor Heinkle refuting the ridiculous dino-battling story. Tweedy shook his head in the minimal way people do when no-one is looking and it's just a theatrical gesture designed for oneself. He concentrated, as much as he could, only on the fact that his kids had erased the piece that very morning on the VHS. Inadvertently, mind, but for some pop music transmission. *Technology and kids, what a recipe for disaster*, he told himself, when another part of him was saying: *take the blame yourself. You should have watched it live... (And not have shouted at Jenny!)* Heinkle would be displeased, but he guessed he would be able to request a copy, special delivery, from the boys at Ulster Television –'for our archives, if you don't mind'. *Oh, he'd wing it with Heinkle and say he had watched it all in its technicolour glory.* The main thing was that this would draw a line under the 'crisis', and they could get on with the project post-haste, making way for a return for Tweedy to things archaeological, not geological or… palaeontological. (Was that even the correct term? he asked himself.)

Post-haste, now-or-never, ASAP, *tout suite!* Or was that 'tout de suite'? And as Tweedy wracked the memory of his middling French, the very mention of that language opened up a crack into a room he thought he could keep safely closed. No! No! and again, No! *Hadn't he spent the weekend seeking to satisfy his lust for that trampy student via the convenient medium of his wife?* 'No!' he spat at the third person incarnation of that other person masquerading under his nomenclature. No, no, no! (Echo of…. *Don't, don't don't!*) This was no way to think, he reprimanded himself automatically and swiftly went back to the window to see if the disruptive students – *political agitators?* – could fill the void of his early morning vacuity. Never mind Robert Bradford! Margaret Thatcher! *Yes, Margaret Thatcher would do just as well.* Her stern face and faintly bronze coiffure came to Tweedy's eyes like a salve against the weakness of emotional and sensual breakdown. Yes, yes, yes, it worked a kind of magic on his brain, which, actually, was still dealing with the residue of wine and Scotch he'd over-imbibed the night before. OK, so he'd compensated for his wife's refusal by having a few too many tipples, but life was never easy for anyone, and we always had work to steel us, man us up… *Get on with it, man*, Margaret's face was saying sternly to him, be bold, be true, and we will prevail. 'Oh, why can't we vote directly for her?' Tweedy whined, whisperingly, to the bookshelves and the desk. He winced again, knowing he'd be giving his vote to Bradford in the end, but mindful that, within days, victory would be theirs, and that the Iron Lady would prevail. Order, order.

There were more pressing things at hand than dealing with all this. He'd report to Heinkle within a few minutes about his meeting with the rapscallions who'd sought to torpedo things and then do his best to praise the UTV broadcast without letting on that he hadn't actually seen it. (It wouldn't be too difficult as he rarely got a word in edgewise.) These things needed preparing, and so, feeling good about having identified what was what and what he needed to prioritize, Tweedy walked calmly round his desk, as he would do on any normal day, and took his seat, observing with pleasure a desk uncluttered, polished, shining and clean. It was a mirror for his mind.

It was only 9.41, he noted, spying the wood-framed wall-clock he'd been gifted by the students of '76. Two thoughts occupied the same space at once: 'What a class they had been!' and 'I've plenty of time. Heinkle doesn't usually stir until noon on a Tuesday.' He dealt with the first first, memories seeping back to the class excursions they'd enjoyed together. The most strenuous had been at the Malone Ridge, where they'd spent an entire early summer's day picking at straws in the ground, Tweedy sometimes barking commands as to what was of worth and what was not. And yet they, as a group, had made progress! They had persevered and he had instilled in them the need for patience and care, to be wary yet open, and gladly willing to spend hours doing what seemed closer to child's play in a sandpit than anything remotely delicate or academically important. They'd all listened to him, and never a word of disobedience did he hear. Not, of course, that he, Tweedy, instilled blind obedience in his students – no, he didn't want to think he was like Heinkle in any way – but that they had respectfully listened to the words of one who knew what he was about. And he did. He was an expert of the earth below our feet.

It wasn't the deep earth that Heinkle loved so… deeply. It was the earth which was almost within touching distance, the earth… or the water… Yes, the water which flowed through this city, for example. How many people knew that the river that gave this city its name still ran, and not simply through it in the way it always had, but *under* it, right beneath the feet of the shoppers in High Street? It wasn't well known, but the Farset (from which was derived the 'fast' of Belfast) had been culverted and hidden just below the surface of the city, and yet ran there still, vigorous and strong, disgorging into the Lagan at high speed. Whoosh! He had seen it himself, the pedestrians oblivious as they passed by above in the Belfast of now. Shopping for shoes and treats for the kids at Woolies now occupied the hearts and minds of the citizens of Béal Feirste, to give it its proper Gaelic nomenclature, whether you liked it or not –'béal' meaning 'mouth' and 'Feirste' the name everyone had betrayed for the last two centuries by hiding it away out of sight. Out of sight, out of mind… Out of smell! It had reeked a bit.

Then there was all that wood no-one would ever see. Not quite [Robert Lloyd] Praeger's 'City on stilts' but a fair few buildings on larch timber stilts, not the least of which was the supposed jewel in the crown, the City Hall itself. Sinking! Imagine it sinking! Into the soft alluvial, all alluvial sleech! Of course, as they discovered not thirty years after its grand unveiling in 1906 – that monstrosity which had been the death of the infinitely more appealing and sophisticated White Linen Hall! – it wasn't quite the vertical piling which had been the trouble, but the horizontal cross-beams, imposed upon the builders by lesser minds who were never happy unless they were poking their noses into things beyond their ken. (Add to this, the same sloppy, shabby workmanship which would also give us the Titanic!) Tweedy flinched, as though these engineering missteps had happened on his watch, could be laid at his door, or just possibly because he'd said the unthinkable about the supposedly unsinkable. *(It was the rivets, the rivets… poor quality rivets, not the good men shooting them in.)*

'The Venetians had it right!' Tweedy found himself vocalizing, for the second time that morning, himself the only audience. He was glad to get back onto territory he felt safer on. 'The shift to concrete was an ugly reminder that at the end of the day,' Tweedy confided in himself, 'Belfast would never have confidence in its own engineers, those who had sought to build without the interference of committees asking for this adjustment and that, until, of course, the damn building would sink.' *Sink without a trace would be the best!*

To wit, this year, 1979, was supposed to be the year Tweedy would reach out, at the university's expense of course, on a research trip to Venice, to study first-hand the techniques which had resulted in one of the true wonders of the world, an actual city territory on stilts, by the use of vertical piling... of larch timber, just as in Belfast! *If the Italians had The Tower of Pisa, by God we had the Albert Clock!* The lean, so endearing to so many, and so embarrassing to those who knew what it meant. Again, to keep things Belfastian, the Albert Clock's leaning was due to the incorrect application of the engineering and architectural genius which had given the world Venice, the blame for the tilt pinnable on the lapel of the poor-witted committee who balked at the original plan, aghast at the price tag for a monument to a man still warm in his grave. 'Follow the Venetians to the letter!' had said the voice at the back of the room, drowned out by the drone of the witless curs in charge of the purse strings. Oh, no, don't listen to the engineers and the craftsmen, except when it pleases – *please may we have more trills on the outside?*

Tweedy felt only contempt for municipal committees, historically and now, envisioning a city ravaged by their feckless judgements, likely to pull down every edifice which didn't make quite as much money as possible, or for reasons beyond the grasp of even the most reasonable man. How many listed buildings had been torn down? The Old Ulster Club in Castle Place, built by none other than Charles Lanyon, who designed this wonderful palace of academia, looked certain to fall prey to the greed and philistinism of the Divisional Planning Office, damn them. Even Betjeman's plea for the preservation of Lanyon's old Deaf & Blind Institute had fallen on, pardon the pun, deaf ears. It was the old tactic of letting the premises fall into disuse and then sweeping in to demolish and replace. *And why not be creative and re-purpose what we have?* mused Tweedy. That old power station on East Bridge Street, with its towering chimneys, was an eyesore, but it had character! Once it was down, beautiful red brick by brick, as it happened, *that was it*. Its sixty-year contribution to the city's skyline was gone forever! Couldn't they have turned it into a museum? There was something in old [C.E.B.] Brett's quip about 'the lunatics of Belfast' pulling down the old lunatic asylum on the Falls which resonated still. Belfast was a palimpsest for fools. Concrete was the Play-Doh of a bunch of unqualified men who saw the city as their play-pit, and wood as suitable only for trimmings. 'No, it won't decay, if you do it right. No air, no oxygen enters the mud and the compacted space of the pilings. Hear me out, I know whereof I speak,' said William Joseph Barre to the committee in regard to the construction of the Albert Clock and its foundations. They did hear him out, and then reneged on their apparent promise to follow whatever he said. Oh, ye of little faith, mused Tweedy, feeling the regret which must have attended the poor architect... who never lived to see what would become of his beloved project. At least he didn't have to witness that unsightly tilt.

There was only one thing Professor Ronald Tweedy of Queen's University hated more than municipal committees and that was... dinosaurs. Dinosaurs and Tweedy shared little in common, perhaps only Professor Janek Heinkle, of the Palaeontology Department of Heidelberg University... and, Tweedy reflected with sudden added distaste, the damn committee at this university that had thrown him into Heinkle's unendearing embrace. Tweedy closed his eyes. In the blackness of sought-after nothingness, however, it didn't take long for a massive creature to materialize, as though from a dark wood, poking out its pince-nez glasses-wearing snout, and grunting, grunting… 'Don't, don't don't!'

Tweedy did two things very rapidly; he opened his eyes as quickly and as wide as possible and at the same time brought the palms of his two hands into immediate contact with his cheeks. Entirely autonomic, it had the effect of erasing the nightmare image before his consciousness, waking him up in no short order. But it also forced out a sudden and unexpectedly loud blurt of sound from his mouth, something like 'Buuaarrkkk!'

Buuaarrkkk? For the space of about two seconds, Tweedy could swear the sound had come from elsewhere, in space and maybe even in time… It had a vaguely prehistoric register to it, suggestive of animal brutality… By the third or fourth second, he'd calmed down enough to know it was just him making a gulder – Belfast-English for something between a shout, a grunt, and a burp. He'd definitely had a drop too much last night, not to mention all those canapés…

Then, with the kind of timing that only usually happens in films, there was a knock on the door, one that was all too audible in the compacted silence after his own unexpected dinosaurian grunt. Tweedy's eyes widened even further. And then just a smidgeon more as he noticed, horror of horrors, the white panelled door shudder ever so little, the ineluctable precursor to an unwanted opening. For a millisecond or three, Tweedy felt a shimmer of déjà vu, half delighted in expectation and half cowed by a sense of impending doom. In another millisecond, Tweedy retracted his palms from his cheeks, then reemployed one of them to towel his face and the other to pat down his coiffure, as the last best hope of a man staring embarrassment in the face. But… it was just Sheila, one of the office ladies from downstairs, and, joy of joys, she was smiling innocently as she seemed more occupied with handling the sticky door and suggesting that last month's lick of paint had left it 'all gummed up'. 'Oh, sorry to disturb, Professor, but I did knock a few times and, well, sure, the post always has to get through, eh?'

The middle-aged and somewhat dowdy Sheila (a tiny voice inside Tweedy asked: 'dowdy in contrast to whom?'), head partly down and still muttering about the painters, padded in and over to Tweedy and perfunctorily handed him the post, a few flat envelopes and one bulkier one, which he guessed was a book he had ordered recently. 'You're very kind, Sheila,' Tweedy said, almost getting up as he did so. 'No, no, no need to get up on my account. I'll be out of your way, I know you must be very busy.' 'You're a dear,' Tweedy responded, feeling relief and a renewed sense of his own importance, to be sat on his august chair and brought the post by an underling. Just as she reached the door on her way out, however, Sheila turned, and for the first time lifted her face to catch the eye of Professor Tweedy: 'I thought he was wonderful,' she said. She tipped her head backwards ever so slightly, making it clear to her interlocutor, whose eyes had narrowed ever so slightly at her utterance, whom she was referring to. Tweedy, just when he had thought himself relieved of her annoying presence, able to return to his free-floating ruminations on the vicissitudes of local history, now felt pressure once again, this time to utter something in response which he knew would be an outright lie. She was referencing the TV broadcast last night -which he hadn't seen! But life, like Belfast in July, is littered with obstacles and so when he said 'I thought so, too' he didn't feel one iota of scruples about lying through his freshly brushed front teeth. Emboldened, indeed, his subsequent 'Wonderful! Wonderful!' bellowed from his lips with hearty delight.

Sheila looked at him. Tweedy looked at Sheila. Had he, Tweedy suddenly wondered, done enough to satisfy the figure before him, a figure which, the longer she continued to look at him, transformed from a dowdy middle-aged office underling into something closer to a.... dominatrix, her eyes holding his, boring into them, torturing him as he felt himself begin to squirm on his so-called august chair. Tweedy couldn't fathom her, and he couldn't speak, until, like a cartoon sun passing out from behind cartoon clouds, Sheila smiled and spaketh: 'Sure, you'll all be glad when this is forgotten about. Round here that shouldn't take too much doing!' With a wry laugh, Sheila, accepting the paltry thing on Tweedy's lips as a returned smile, and all that she was apparently going to get from the man, who remained silent, disappeared behind the panelled white door and out of Tweedy's world.

At times like this, and occasions like this were rare, august Professor Tweedy allowed himself to indulge in the expression of choice taboo phrases. 'Thank Fuck!' seemed the most appropriate here, and so Tweedy let the remark escape his august lips, at a volume, however, which satisfied both his paranoia about chance eavesdropping and his need to really say how he felt. He loved his white panelled door, and the paint which had 'gummed it up' all round, sealing it as firmly as one of those jars ole Heinkle seemed to love so much. Tweedy added, just above a whisper: 'I needn't have worried. I could sing God Save the Queen in here and no-one would hear me!' He now smiled, broadly and contentedly. Enough of those ruminations on the horrid past, he thought. This is May: my birthday month! I should be thinking positively, ever onward, ever forward!

Little pre-august Ronald Tweedy had already found his inclination turning to things of the past while a student at Inst (or The Royal Belfast Academical Institution, to give it its full title), eager to follow up whatever he had heard about this or that event in Belfast's past, and to go exploring at the weekends down lanes and in and out of cemeteries dotted around the city. But it was the discovery that on his day of birth, May 21st, if forty-two years before he'd actually seen the light of day himself, that Queen Victoria's grandson, Prince Albert Victor, had visited Belfast and been given a gala reception by the city that had made young Tweedy really fall in love with the past. As an impressionable schoolboy, he had felt some mystical connection to that day, that time, that world beyond the one outside the school library windows. The grown-up Tweedy sat back in his chair and sighed. Oh, to have seen it! To have been able to join the festivities that day in 1889, even as a bystander, waving to his Majesty as he rode by in his carriage from the 'Free Library', or what was now called the Central Library, down Royal Avenue, up Donegall Place, Donegall Square, May Street, then down Cromac Street, soon to arrive at the site of the new bridge, which would be named after their illustrious visitor.

Thousands had gathered, cheering and waving and clapping hands. What a sight it must have been! Tweedy allowed his eyes to close once more, giving himself to the reverie of long ago, as though to meld with it… the Bishop of Down, Connor and Dromore, rubbing shoulders with Grand Master R.R. Kane of the Grand Orange Lodge of Belfast, not a speck of tension between them, all brothers of the one city, and that city one of the leading lights of the Kingdom. Sure, back then the Orange Lodge had close relations with the Catholic hierarchy and Irish speakers aplenty in its ranks; it was no coincidence that the Dr Richard Routledge Kane, Grand Master of the Orange Lodge of Belfast, borrowed from the older language when he declared to the Right Royal visitor: 'A hundred thousand welcomes!' (from the Gaelic Céad Míle Fáilte). Would the Robert Bradford I'm to vote for soon do that? mused Tweedy. Could Belfast ever hope to regain that level of togetherness it once had? It was too unrealistic a question for Tweedy to properly entertain, after a decade of bombs, bullets and violent chaos on the streets he had grown up on, so he kept his eyes closed just a little bit longer, his mind's eye roving over the crowds and the carriages and the decorations and the bunting, and …. the Venetian ship masts covered with crimson cloth and carrying a host of maritime flags… Had there been a delegation from that fair city? Or was it just a token of Belfast's love for the jewel of the Veneto, an elegant gesture of appreciation by the engineering or architectural guilds of the city? Tweedy daydreamed away… until the package and letters in his hands, back in 1979 Belfast, fell from his grip and spilled onto the floor. 'Dear, dear,' he mumbled, sitting forward and doing his best to suddenly bend down and regain what he'd let slip.

'Dear, dear', he repeated as he got out of his chair, swept them up and deposited the bits and pieces on his uncluttered desk, cluttering it now. His 'Dear, dear' this time was for Belfast as it was now, war-torn and creaking under the weight of a municipal drive towards modernity which threatened to destroy the city even more comprehensively than the bombs of the terrorists. Whether he believed that or not, he now took comfort in the execution of his duty in surveying what was before him physically, the various envelopes and packages, or package, singular. 'I really must go and see ole Heinkle,' said Tweedy, as though addressing the post and hoping for its understanding that he wouldn't be opening anything quite yet. But then one piece caught his eye. It was perhaps the simplest, plainest envelope, stamped from Antrim, but because it was addressed to 'Members of the Carrickfergus Dig', and not to Boss Heinkle, Tweedy felt it would be perfectly acceptable to peruse its contents. It would give him something to employ as a conversation-buffer if Heinkle happened to want to press him on any points from the broadcast he hadn't seen. He took his seat.

Professor Tweedy slipped his gilt letter-opener (gift of the class of '74') in under the backflap of the envelope and carefully and delicately extracted the crisp pages of the small letter within. He laid them out on the desk surface, clearing away the other items with his right hand, and began to read.

Dear Members of the Carrickfergus Dig,

My name is Roger Byrne and I am a teacher at Antrim High School. Last year I contacted the Archaeological Department at Queen's in connection with a find of fossilized bones I had made on the Antrim Coast in 1978. I wrote explaining about my find and after a period of about a month received a response from a Professor Thompson suggesting we meet for discussion and a sharing of information. We arranged a date and time and met at the site I had been visiting for the past few years. I showed him the specimens I had found and he asked me if he could borrow them for the purposes of analysis. I acceded to this and awaited any word as to the results. I was a little anxious because I felt this find had the potential to be quite significant: Thompson was excited by my suggestion that these fossils were dinosaurian in origin.'

This was not entirely news to Tweedy, but it still felt like he'd been left out of the loop. He'd simply been told that the fossils had been found by an amateur, with very little else being mentioned. He had never heard of Roger Byrne, or he'd forgotten... No, he was sure no-one had mentioned these things to him in detail. And Thompson wasn't even on the team! Why had he not been told this? He was looking at the words on the page, but felt the sudden need to look away, to get his bearings. Was it the hangover or was it just shock?

After a moment, somehow, his focus returned and he could read on:

'I have heard nothing since my last meeting with Professor Thompson, making it about one year of silence. Imagine my surprise...'

Tweedy could see the rest of the sentence, but the strain of processing it was too much for him. Simply looking away was not enough. He had to get up – and he did –, tear off his constricting, useless tie – and he did –, walk around the desk – and he did –, and jump up and down and scream and shout at the top of his lungs – which, only at the last moment, he did not. He did manage a wee leap and a fierce flap of his right and left arm, but he was careful not to let even the tiniest of sounds escape from his agape mouth, gummy door or no gummy door. He stood there for all of five horrible, quaking seconds and, like a shot, went back to his chair and eyeballed the innocuous-looking piece of paper on the woody surface of his august oak-panelled desk, reading on:

'…when I saw in the paper that my find had been mentioned, and yet without any attribution to me, AND that the find had been characterized in such a way, as evidence of a battle between dinosaurs! I confess that I found the story to be concocted and, frankly, silly and I really do think I deserve an answer as to what is going on. It didn't even get the location right!

I am sorry to be so blunt about this, but I do feel this is a situation not of my making and I would really appreciate if any member of the dig, perhaps Professor Jeinkle – I saw his name in the article- could reach out to me, and do so in short order.

Sincerely,

Roger Byrne,
Antrim HS

Ps I wrote to Professor Thompson towards the end of last year and again in February of this but received no reply, and I don't know Prof. Jeinkle, so I just addressed this to the Team. My postal and telephone details below.'

Tweedy sat and re-read the missal from beginning to end a further three times, each time hoping for some chance element which would unlock the mystery of it all and defuse the nightmare that this seemed to entail. 'So much for hoping to draw a line under the recent crisis!' his mind screamed. 'So much for resolution, some light at the end of the tunnel! A new one had just opened up, threatening to swallow us all whole… What on earth was going on and how on earth could this have ever happened?' He was beginning to feel as though his worst fears were confirmed by this letter. How low down in the chain of command was Tweedy not to have been told all of this? These and other questions flooded Tweedy's mind as he began to lift his head back, and then further back still, until he was staring up at the featureless white ceiling. White signified purity and innocence, a world of joy and light. But white was also the colour of death.

Chapter Seven: Time is a Harsh Mistress, pt.1, Friday, April 27

Christopher had a busy evening of 'ekkers' [homework, or exercises] and TV, with a single hearing of the Larry Coryell/Philip Catherine record sandwiched somewhere in between. He and his two brothers agreed *Splendid* was the best thing since sliced bread, even toasted sliced bread with Caerphilly cheese on top. Christopher had enjoyed *The Streets of San Francisco*, as he usually did of a Friday evening, and had a peep at what big-eyebrowed Alastair Burnett had to say on the *News at Ten*, after its ungodly serious-sounding Westminster chimes. He'd also given up on the 'awful' Friday Film *Cat Ballou*, except for the fact that Jane Fonda had been drop-dead beautiful. About eleven thirty, Christopher took a wee stroll outside to get a breath of fresh air – to get his head showered.

He went out the back door, of course, and then sauntered up into the drive, stalling halfway up so that when he looked up at the sky the streetlamps wouldn't spoil his view of the stars. Or the satellites, if he was lucky enough to see one. This was the quasi-protected dark space of the area between the gables of his house and McDonald's next door. It wasn't particularly cold, and while there was some cloud, there were patches you could see through to the black of the night sky. There were twinklings there, to be sure. Christopher had his hands in his pockets and it felt nice to just be there, away from the TV screen and its noisome noise. The family had been quiet for once and there'd been no shouting about anything. He was a member of a cast list of exceptionally strong characters who were often pulling in different directions. Christopher was never really sure of his part in all this drama, making the far away and the other ever more attractive to his being. And you couldn't get much further away than the stars in the night sky.

He could succumb to the orderly, and vaguely scientific, part of his brain which said: *go back inside and fetch the paper to check what satellites are passing over, and grab Da's Tasco binoculars*. But he knew how it would end, with him sifting through the fine print, in the dark – oh and don't forget to bring a watch – and then straining his neck, and his eyes, as he peered upwards at massively distant points of light, coaxing them to move. Sure, which way was even north or west? Christopher had to admit he was pretty hopeless at things astronomical, but it didn't stop him being an avid viewer of *The Sky at Night* on BBC 2, falling on every golden word that came out of the mouth of the one and only Patrick Moore, doyen of TV astronomy. Better to just look up and enjoy the moment. Even if it was a bit lonely. This time, he was thinking not of his Ma, Da and brothers, but the fellow of his own age living just there, behind that giant dark gable, Michael. His best friend. Or had been… He'd thought about him today, too. In the city centre, seeing those Space Hopper things in the window of BHS, and remembering the fun they'd always enjoyed together. Like now… yes, only just a few short years ago, he and Michael would get together under the clearest night sky, up at their shared gates or between the gables, and look up and wonder at it all. Or share a laugh at it all, the vastness of the universe, or… that day's stupid happening at respective schools. It had always been fun, to stargaze together, jump up and down when one of them had spotted a satellite in its trajectory. 'Look at that! How can a star just move like that?' 'Because it's not a star, ya berk! It's bloody Skylab!'

Wasn't that causing a bit of a stir now? Christopher then thought, opening the door to a whole slew of overly-excited internal observations: 'Come down sometime soon, that article said. Maybe even hit something! Eighty tons and more! Maybe even over a big city! It was hard to believe but 1979 could be the end of the world… for some poor buggers anyway… Imagine it lands here!' Christopher then mused on that. He wondered if anyone would notice, with all the regular bombs going off. Instead of 'Bomb-Damage Sale', it would be 'Skylab Damage Sale', he quipped. And more: 'End of the world it could be. Not like the ones you see them advertising round the town of a Saturday afternoon, the walking signboards. No, we're talking massive damage from space. Destruction on a scale heretofore unseen… **Belfast City Hall Reduced to Rubble. Royal Avenue in Ruins**. What a headline or two that would be in the papers… certainly very alliterative anyway…' Christopher loved his internal monologues; talking with himself was often more fun than talking with others. His father had asked him how he had happened to come into possession of the *News Letter*. Christopher had told him. 'You've met a genuine man of the press, then,' he said encouragingly, even if Christopher suspected he wasn't too admiring of that particular rag. They usually got *The Irish News*, or the *Tele* of an evening. But later, Christopher did notice him taking his time to peruse the other stories, ending up most satisfyingly checking through the classifieds. 'You never know, they might have a wee piano in there…'

End of the world… had he dreamt about dinosaurs today in the library? He had, but it was all a haze, even soon after waking up. 'Did I grunt or make some silly noise?' he quizzed himself. 'The look on the old fella to my right seemed to confirm that. Funny seeing that piece in the paper tonight, beside the TV guide, entitled: "The Beasts on the Lagan Bank"…' Which had opened: 'They come in all sizes and colours and the ones to watch out for are those great bouncing beasts that thunder towards you…' Christopher had put it down as soon as he'd seen it was about dogs, not dinos. He had flinched at the idea of the mysterious being deflated, the dramatic image conjured by the words on the page suddenly wrested away from the exotic.

Christopher had seen the phrase 'The End of the World' stencilled on semi-dilapidated walls on the Shore Road, and York Street, followed inevitably with 'is Nigh', along with other choice Biblical graffitied messages: 'Ye Must Be Born Again', 'Give Thyself to the Lord', and 'Sinner, Beware!' And 'The end of the world' had been the first thing out of his lips that early morning a few years ago hearing the first of two nearby bomb explosions. *The bombs, the bombs….* Yet, it had had less to do with an avenging God and more to do with the kind of cataclysms Christopher had seen in science fiction films… He'd been rudely woken with a sudden huge noise and all he could think of was giant meteors and evil alien motherships blasting the neighbourhood. His well-thumbed book on the 1906 Tunguska Event had given him plenty to think about. Had it been a force-field beam smashing into the planet at 50,000 miles an hour? **Kaboom!** 'End of the world!'

He had made straight for the window, throwing back the thick curtain, then the inner lace, glimpsing debris flying, breaking up, and falling, falling… 'Get away from the window!' screamed his eldest brother Paul. 'What the hell are you doing, Chris?' threw in Jim, the middle brother, 'There might be another blast!' Christopher, having seen enough, and convinced by the logic, threw back the curtain and hurried back to bed, excited, terrified and expectant of either worse or better things to come: he wasn't quite sure how he felt about having aliens attack.

He knew it wasn't aliens, of course. After five seconds anyone who woke up in Northern Ireland hearing a sound like that would know it was a bomb. But aliens had more allure. Like dinosaurs. Their violence was at least exotic. The brothers talked where they were, Paul in the lower bunk, Jim in the upper, Christopher in a parallel bed on the other side of what was a very small room (making it even smaller). And within a few short minutes, it did happen: the second bomb. And this had a different effect, having been anticipated, the red carpet rolled out to welcome its coming. You could hear bits of building or masonry or wood hit other things too in the general after-blast. Paul and Jim took it in with a few 'Jesus'-es and 'Holy Fucks,' while Chris remained stoically silent. The rest was all scurrying here and there, the three brothers piling out of respective beds, consulting clocks, throwing back the curtains for light to illuminate where their jeans or long-sleeved shirts had been discarded the night before. At the end of all this, all three thundered down the stairs where, to their surprise, and chagrin, Ma and Da had already gathered, looking shocked not just because of the explosions but because their three sons were wearing outdoor clothes. 'You're not going out!' Mother screamed. But no-one was moving, all just in a state of high expectation and excitement, and genuine worry, peeking out the Venetian blinds in the living-room, if only to see what others were doing, even if it wasn't yet six in the morning. The Gormans were opening their front door, Bobby putting his head out, looking worried. He couldn't stop his kids however, who forced past him and got into the drive. Soon, this picture was being played out in other people's houses, everyone just standing in their driveways or up at their gates, waiting, waiting, talking, talking, listening, listening…. Until they heard the signal which seemed to alter the course of things. If the emergency services with their sirens were coming, then, sure, now would be alright to unlatch the gates of the various households and pour into the streets. And once this happened, it became a force not to be resisted, wherein, if everyone was going out to see what happened, whatever Christopher's Ma and Da said no longer had much force. The three brothers piled out the front door, past their front garden, into the drive, and up to the iron gate, unlatching it and joining the great exodus of everyone to see if what had happened had really happened.

It had been an attack on Doyle's Sweetshop, as it was generally called, but properly Doyle's Newsagent's, with the adjacent Nellie's Bakery an unfortunate casualty of the target blasts. Doyle's was a regular haunt for eleven-year-olds like Christopher, and his friend Michael, who was wearing a white vest, pyjama bottoms and slippers when Chris saw him (and laughed). Every kid, having hurried there in flocks from different streets, had a look of absolute shock on their face contemplating, as they now were, the complete abject ruination of the sweetshop -and the adjacent bakery- that had been their near-daily destination, both blasted open to daylight, a light but awful smoke enveloping them, and a strong smell of cordite everywhere. (The Mace mini-supermarket next to Nellie's was untouched.) But there was compensation. All over the road in front of the shops were remnants of what had been inside, dented cans of juice, packets and even -some shattered- jars of boiled sweets, bags of crisps all shrunken and burnt, packs of biro pens, and books and magazines spilled everywhere, and, to the illicit delight of just about everyone, bars of glorious, if more than slightly smoke-damaged, chocolate and other confectionery delights. It didn't take long for a few to bend down and pick them up, one by one, ecstatic to get their hands on something so desired and now for free...

And if this behaviour wasn't bad enough, thought Christopher, who secretly felt like chiding Michael for grabbing a virtually untouched *Mars Bar*, now kids started to see what else they might do. And so, before the arrival of anyone you might call an adult, before those sirens got any louder, one by one, and then as a mass movement, all the kids of the neighbourhood, it seemed, threw off whatever inhibitions they might have entertained upon arrival, even those who had looked behind them and seen the blown-in windows of the houses opposite, and made like a horde past the partly twisted railings, down the three steps, and into the heart of the sweetshop proper, raiding as a group, shouting out their glee and common mad excitement as they stuffed *Mars Bars, Crunchies* and *Bounty bars*, and all manner of bars and packs emblazoned with names known to all – and loved to death after school – into every available pocket, pouch, rolled-up shirttail, sweaty palm, or even just directly, minus the annoying wrapper, down the hatch.

As the sixteen-year-old Christopher thought about this, remembered this, re-experienced this, here in the dark space between the house gables late this Friday evening, the names of all these desiderata came into his mind, like a rollcall of juvenile exotica, each title given all the weight of words in a poem he might study at school, or read back to himself at nighttime, before dreamtime... *Cadbury's Milk Tray, Twix, Nut Crisp, Curly Wurly, Marathon, Tiffin, KitKat, Buttons, Treets*... savouring each word lovingly... *Fry's Chocolate Cream, Picnic, Cadbury's Fruit 'n Nut, Milky Bar*... They might be sacred words, he thought, the language of some obscure religion... *Aztec, Aero, Peppermint Aero, Bar Six, Rolo, Golden Crisp, Maltesers*... intoned with gravity and mystery... *Dairy Milk, Toffee Cup, Cadbury's Brazil Nut, Flake*... fragments of a code to paradise, some promise of beyond... *Turkish Delight, After Eight, Munchies, Smarties, Toffee Crisp, Caramac* and *Butter Snap*. And that was just the chocolates.

Christopher had just stood there, watching, wide-eyed at the scene, wondering how he felt himself, and would he start, and step toward the melee? But no, he knew the Doyles, was best friends with Paddy, their son, was always given special attention by Mrs Doyle when he entered the shop. He couldn't steal from them. Not that scruples mattered now, as unbeknownst to the frenzied kids, grabbing all and sundry, the adults had arrived - and how. They were wearing black berets, flak-jackets and carried automatic rifles, and were barking out commands that no-one listened to... until 'air-support', in the shape of a dark green army helicopter, came in and did the honours by making a sudden vertical drop down from the sky to about thirty feet above the ruined shops. The fierce down-thrusting wind from the whirring blades combined with the intense, near-deafening noise it made, had the desired effect, and every last child, pockets/hands/shirttails brimming with illicit sweetmeats, got the message and turned and ran in terror, like rats, in unbecoming haste, left and right and straight ahead, down Collinward Avenue, round into Elmfield Road, or up Elmfield Park, dodging every soldier their terrified eyes could see. Christopher hadn't moved, though, like just a few other kids who'd lingered, watching only. He hadn't looted Doyle's, but he had enjoyed the thrill of seeing that mechanical beast swoop down so dramatically, and, even more so, the madness of seeing everyone else behave badly. Michael, he noted, wasn't there. Michael had a side to him, he remembered thinking. The soldiers barked out more commands, and other authority figures rushed round checking houses and calling out for help from time to time, the sound of walkie-talkie voices, blips and beeps pervasive. The Valkyrie-like helicopter rose and resumed its hover far above, with its constant thrumming, back where it would often be in Troubles-torn Northern Ireland, like some weird flitting tadpole of the sky.

The incident hardly made the newspaper. No deaths. No injuries, beyond the shock of those in the immediate vicinity, those whose windows had been blown in, the splintering glass miraculously being caught by lace curtains, protecting sleeping babies from wounds and worse. Chaos, screaming, madness, terror, shock, but nothing worth the attention of the radio or TV. It was, after all, during the Ulster Workers' Council strike, when basic services, amenities and facilities all over Northern Ireland were under constant threat and attack from forces who controlled everything you could think of. Christopher recalled the evening he had walked down the O'Neill Road, then looked over Elmfield estate and watched in fear as all the lights of the estate, in one fell swoop, had blinked off. Just another power cut, but this one actually witnessed *as it happened*, not seen on telly – the place where he lived reduced to awful blackness at the snap of someone's fingers. It had frightened him. It was part of the process by which Christopher's perception of what was in the papers, what was on the news, what his Ma and Da talked about, what Father McClafferty sometimes talked about in his Sunday homily, became real. The attack on Doyle's cemented this, hugely. It was really the first time the 'Troubles' had entered the protected space of the Elmfield estate, situated just beyond Bellevue, just across the boundaries of Belfast proper. 1974. A Friday in late May, near the end of the strike, when the 'forces that be' really wanted to put the foot down, as the Da had spelled it out to his youngest son, 'blowing everything up that opened against their orders.' Doyle's had done that and so had been targeted. Mrs Doyle and husband Peter had not allowed the attack to deter them, though. That very Sunday, just two days post-attack, saw them setting up trestle tables outside what had been their shop, on which they laid out all the Sunday papers, magazines and crisps and sweeties, with a cardboard box as cash register. The residents loved them for it and, despite the smell of cordite, which hung around for months, the whole estate was determined not to let the bombers have wrought any lasting damage, at least to their spirit.

Christopher had other problems, though. In May 1974, he was happily enjoying St Bernard's Primary School, just round the corner, and indeed, within a stone's throw of Doyle's shop. He had done the '11-plus', the test which determined the course, and quality, of a child's subsequent lifelong education. He'd passed, as had Paddy Doyle, but Michael hadn't – 'on purpose' he said, part of his plan to enter Glengormley High. It was the beginning of the end of something, Christopher and Paddy and Michael guessed, but sure, the line was: 'we'll all still pal around anyway'. But, somehow, things did not turn out like that. Paddy's family was moving anyway, and Christopher would start at St Mary's, Barrack Street, going each day on the bus into town, a new routine to get a hold of, from that September coming. Then, somehow, Chris's friendship with Michael started to fall apart. What used to be little points of contention between them ballooned into something worse, until, finally, that summer, not long before starting at different schools, they had had a fight, a real one, with fists flying and punches landing. Michael was the stronger. Christopher could never forgive Michael's Da for not doing anything, as he saw him purposefully turn away and walk into the house while Michael belted the prostrate Christopher repeatedly in the face at the bottom of McDonald's garden, saying 'Take that, ya wee fucker!' Chris had lost the fight, and he'd lost his friend, too. And, if he had thought about it just a little more, he had lost a whole way of life... his childhood.

Whether he was aware of things in precisely those terms at that time is unsure, but Christopher knew that *something had altered,* something awfully big -bigger even than that explosion in the neighbourhood, or explosions, the two of them, ten minutes apart, set off by timed detonators, attached to what would otherwise be perfectly innocent gas canisters. The innocent and the guilty roped together, wreaking havoc...

Grammar school in September plunged the knife in further, cutting out a hole where before there was just the merest hint of weakness in the fabric... The innocent in him was confronted with an alien environment of boys who didn't always smile, and weren't always nice, and boys only... not a girl in sight. Killen, from Antrim town, couldn't be described as a mere 'boy' that was for sure. He'd more adult in him than Christopher could ever have imagined someone the same age as him. And something else, too, a darkness, an edge, a violence just waiting to be provoked. Any disobedience would bring it out, for sure. 'You'll not do my homework for me and you'll get your face scarred, fucker.' So, Christopher did; he did Killen's homework for him, week in, week out, until he was caught, and underwent a shame before the class, picked out by the master for his dishonesty. 'We don't tolerate dishonesty here, Maguire. You're going to find that out. Dismissed.' Great pain and shame and tears and fear along with it, expecting retribution anytime, any day of the week. Within three months of entering, Christopher had grown emotionally old beyond his years. He'd just turned twelve, but no longer was he the carefree, smiling child he'd been just one year before. School had soon become a kind of hell.

Time could not be taken back. Time was harsh and unforgiving. Time like the time he'd seen referred to in today's *News Letter*, that 'sixty-six million years' was nothing to the time he felt now gone from him.

And yet, he persevered. Human nature, inurement to life's vicissitudes, whatever. There was too much going on right now to keep him thinking of the past, even if part of it was still living right next door to him.

Ah, Mickey, couldn't we be friends from now on? Sure, we could try. Occasionally, in the intervening years, they bumped into each other, not so difficult if their houses were only separated by a four-foot fence. They'd exchange a few words, greetings and the like, the odd question, observation, then go on their respective ways. Christopher noticed, more than before, how Michael's words were not as delicate as his, or what he talked about never seemed to go beyond the stuff of every day. One time, Christopher threw in a reference to what he'd been studying, about Shakespeare, but Michael laughed it off, almost as though he thought Christopher had been patronising him. He wasn't, but then Chris wondered if he had been, after all. Had he thrown that Michael's way to embarrass him, or to show off his new learning, something they'd never ever shared?

Mickey, of course, had taught Chris quite a bit. How to swear, and why, and when, even if Chris's idea of 'when' didn't quite strike Michael initially as normal. For years, Chris had maintained a swear-word-free discourse with his friend, schooled by his parents to be proper and polite. Michael didn't mind. He didn't 'give a fuck'. They could still talk rubbish with each other and get on fine. Then, however, one Sunday, of all days in the week, they had walked up Carnmoney Hill, one of the two hills on either side of them, and talked about recent life. Chris had been going through some family stuff, and Michael had asked him what, finding out his friend shouldn't be keeping things in. 'Just let things out, Chris,' Michael had advised, talking about emotions. Christopher had thought about it as they ambled about in the country lanes, here and there, not too far from home, but away from the estate, and under a not-too imposing summer sun. Coming across a sheep poking its nose through the barb-wire fence keeping it inside its field, Christopher suddenly decided to let loose, directing everything he said at said sheep: 'You… fucker!' Michael laughed. Chris was not laughing. He was deadly serious. He went on, staring at the animal, eye to eye: 'You… stupid fucking … cunt!' This had Michael in stitches. He exclaimed, 'Oh, Chris, ya man ye!' 'Aye,' continued Chris, squaring up to the poor creature now, pointing his finger, too, unleashing, 'fuck ye, you piece of shit with legs. You're just a fucking cunt like all the rest of them! Look at ye, you wee bastard stupid sonofabitchfucker!' Michael clapped his hands and stamped his feet amidst his tears of laughter at his friend now coming of age before his eyes, and before the eyes of someone's poor unattended and quite innocent wee sheep. 'Sure…' said Michael, half unable to get out what he wanted to say, 'what the bloomin' hell did thon wee creature ever do to you?' It was a rhetorical question, beautifully registered in contrast to his friend's expletive-laden rant. From now on, it was perfectly ok for both to lace their interchanges with choice swear-words, and, Chris made it clear to Michael, blasphemous ones, too. Fuck God, too.

They'd never had a problem belonging to different religions, Christopher, Catholic, Michael, Protestant. They'd met first at the age of six, when Chris's family had moved from Liverpool and taken up residence in Elmfield Crescent, next door to the McDonald's. It hadn't taken long for the two boys to meet and become friends. Religion wasn't high on the agenda of six-year-olds. So, after a year or two it didn't require much thought when Michael asked Chris to join him in that year's Orange Parade, his Da being in the Orange Lodge. Chris's Da had done a double take, however, and they'd had to bring it to the Ma for a discussion, but Christopher just couldn't understand what problem there might be, knowing very little of Irish history, William of Orange, the Battle of the Boyne, or Protestant triumphalism. The Ma and Da, realizing that to explain their awkwardness about allowing their Catholic child to enter a Protestant Orange march on the Twelfth of July would do more harm than good, gave their blessing. It was only then that Chris explained he wasn't just taking part, but that he and Michael would be 'leading the parade', 'twirling sticks and all.' For years, Christopher wondered why his parents had looked so aghast, if even only for a moment, making him also wonder if there wasn't something bad in doing this at all. The day turned out to be a lot of fun, however, with him and Michael twirling sticks, and dropping them, and throwing them up ridiculously high, and laughing at the marchers in their black suits and sashes and their funny bowler hats. The following year, somehow, Christopher had gained enough awareness to think twice about joining, but had joined anyway. Thereafter, though, even if he didn't quite understand why, he would never join Michael in the parade again.

Michael taught Christopher about fishing, introduced him to the group Queen, *and* to Elvis Presley, showed him how to play darts, and shed important light on universal human anatomy: that women didn't have penises was cataclysmic news to innocent little Christopher... Now, however, Christopher was gaining information Michael didn't have, Shakespeare, the Gaelic language, what the French ate for breakfast. And, beyond what constituted education in the classroom, he was learning difference, too. Learning not about difference, but to *feel difference*. He was becoming academically inclined and bookish, and Michael was not. Christopher was growing ever more aware of fundamental political injustice in the state they were a part of, while Michael 'couldn't give a fuck'. And, miserably, cruelly, stupidly, almost evilly, at the end of the day, Chris was learning to be Catholic and learning that his friend Michael was a Protestant, the son of an Orangeman, who would later become an RUC Reservist, and that they were destined to inhabit - miserably – separate realms, and to have separate experiences and outlooks.

Nothing happened you could call explicit. It was just a bit of this, a bit of that, accumulated points of difference, and difference in what they now did, post-idyllic childhood... difference as a way of life, a way of looking...

And yet... something in them wouldn't die, something like a friendship that could never peter out... just wait it out, it said, the difference, *all the crap things that we call experience, or education, when what it is is just a kind of fog, seeking to occlude or muddy up what matters... wait it out, man, we're friends forever...*

As Christopher stood there, in the dark space between the two houses, no longer mindful of twinkling stars or stupid bloody satellites, he noticed he was crying, and soon, uncontrollably so.

Chapter Eight: Time is a Harsh Mistress, pt.2, Saturday, April 28

With the 'O's fast approaching, a trip to the library would be in order, thought Christopher, and so, after stuffing his face with the requisite Saturday morning Ulster Fry, washed down with two beakers of hot milky tea, he left the family home with a bag of books and walked down the street. (A bit of time away from the 'fam' wouldn't hurt either, he added in his mind.) Kids were out in the Crescent, messing around, playing tag, and a few were even doing what he'd seen kids doing yesterday, one acting like Godzilla and the other on his hands and feet, attempting to ram his friend. This set off a train of thought which brought him back to Ivan Stacks and that story. As he ambled, right-wise, in the vague direction of the Glengormley Library, which would only be reached after completing an extremely circuitous route, taking nearly half an hour, he thought about that story. It was, after all the dust had settled, really amazing to think that someone had discovered the first Irish dinosaurs; it would be big news soon enough. It was highly ironic, too, that they'd been found preserved in the midst of beating the hell out of each other. What are the chances of that? he wondered, as he passed by the shops (the ones which had been blown to kingdom come, now good as new, if with different owners). He could go through the (St Bernard's) church grounds and take the messy, and technically illicit, route over the stream and up the embankment, bringing him up near into the middle of Glengormley, but the ground was likely a bit wet at the moment, so he headed off down Church Road, taking the back way. (The front way was up to the Antrim Road, with its noisy traffic, through the heart of the village, past shops he'd only want to enter and buy stuff he couldn't afford. Of course, just opposite the library sat the huge, and hugely attractive, 'Crazy

Prices' supermarket, crammed full of goodies, but he wouldn't be drawn from his goal: of stuffing knowledge in his head, just as he had stuffed those rashers of bacon, potato farls, fried eggs, baked beans and pair of sausages, all coated with a visible layer of table-salt, into his slavering gub.)

'Two libraries in two days; I must be getting bookish indeed!' Christopher congratulated himself, whatever maudlin feelings about the dear old past he had nursed last night now well and truly vanquished. Or was that vanished? Thankfully, it being Saturday before 10 am, he could grab a desk to himself and get out his books. It wasn't the biggest library in the world; you could walk from one end to the other in about fifteen seconds, but it felt nice to be in that quiet atmosphere, conducive to learning the world's knowledge. He had to concentrate on science, maths, and geography, only the last of which he had any interest in, loving the diagrams and graphics elucidating precipitation, mountain-formation and such. He also took a moment to just relax after his jaunt to get here, stretching out his legs and even doing a two-arm stretch that probably looked like a conspicuous yawn. There were only a handful of kids and maybe two or three 'old codgers', as he might ungraciously call them, perusing the stacks or sat reading the morning newspapers. The receptionist was very quiet and slow-moving, and she seemed to want to instill this sense into all who entered, making sure to present the studious features of her sharp face and the glacial pools of her eyes to everyone who passed by her perch. It was a small library, in the middle of nowhere, but, Christopher mused, to her it was the centre of learning and self-improvement – *so no picking your nose and laughing with yer mates!*

With what struck Christopher as uncanny fortune the first page he opened of his soberly titled *GCE Science Book 2* was about dinosaur fossils. It was even eerie, he felt. And… he wondered, how hadn't he realized he studied this stuff before?

He had only been focused on what he'd read in the newspaper and what he'd heard at school about the big find at Carrick, and... he wracked his brain... he hadn't realized that those kids, yesterday and this morning, were acting out that precise same dinosaur story! Nothing to do with Godzilla, but the real thing. And here, in Glengormley Library, the official middle of nowhere, *the real thing* was on the page right in front of him, staring him in the eye: *dinosaur fossils!* A kind of fuzzy graphic depiction of them anyway. 'Knowledge!' he felt like exclaiming out loud. 'It's there for the taking!' Thereafter, he engaged happily, and studiously, with the text.

Under the picture there was a caption. It read: 'This dinosaur fossil was found in a piece of rock.' He liked that sentence. It was simple, clear, unintimidating. The next was a question: 'Why is the dinosaur described as a fossil?' He knew the answer to that: 'Because it had become very old, in fact, become a stone.' 'Write down the types of rock in which dinosaur fossils can be found' was the next task. This section was about getting the student to do a mock version of the test, writing in answers, to be later checked against the proper answers at the back of the book. *OK,* he thought, *the answer to this question is... well, of course, really old rock...* He thought of basalt. He knew basalt from what they'd learnt about the Giant's Causeway. Northern Ireland, he'd discovered, had a lot of basalt. Basalt came from volcanoes. It wasn't basalt until the lava came out and cooled down. But, he wondered again, was 'basalt' one of the kinds of rocks you'd find dinosaur fossils in? Or was it sedimentary? He mused on this, allowing the phrase 'Sedimentary, my dear Watson' to bring a smile to his lips, and then moved onto the next question: 'Why are fossils so important to scientists?' That was easy: 'because they contain images, or imprints of dinosaurs, and other things, like trilobites and fish'. He wrote that in, and then looked at the whole three-question exercise. He had filled in all, but... he noticed with some chagrin, there had been ten blank lines for each answer and yet he had only used about one line for each. Was he supposed to write more? And if he was, what was he supposed to write? He thought he could probably add more to the first one, waffle a bit on the second, but for the third, he could really go to town. So, he did. Here's what he then wrote: 'Scientits [sic] can use these fossils to reconstruct the dinosaurs they came from. Yes, they can pick out all the little bits and pieces, using a brush and tweezers, or tongs, and stick them together, with glue and steel pins, and make them look like they used to look. And, they can then reconstruct their whole world and make it come to life. They add some green bushes behind them and paint in a few volcanoes on the wall behind and then put the dinasuars [sic] in the middle and it looks really like it looked millions of years ago, in the Age of the Dinosaurs.'

Strangely, he felt a mixture of satisfaction and sleepiness at the conclusion of his efforts. Before going onto the next section, he took a quick peek at the 'proper answers' at the back of the book. He read through each very carefully, then looked back at his own work. The discrepancy in terms of level of knowledge and even the level of English was immediately dispiriting to him. His typos hit him like little slaps in the face, and the obvious childishness of his approach sickened him like a kick in the stomach. He became flushed in the face realizing the mountain he had yet to climb in order to be able to pass the exams. He recalled what he had been trying to not think about ever since February: he had failed both Science and Mathematics in the 'Mocks'. He was facing disaster, an end of the world with greater potential ramifications than the local shop getting bombed or Skylab divebombing Belfast. And yet, despite this, or maybe because of it, Christopher felt his eyes becoming heavy. He thought it would be the nicest thing in the world to just lean forward and rest his similarly heavy head on the inviting fine-grained wood surface of the desk, with whatever books were there to act as cushions... Why, he wondered, did he always become sleepy in libraries?

At this point, what should happen but he heard his name being called out. Was it the steely-faced bitch behind the counter, Christopher wondered desperately -and uncharitably? No, after a two-second wait, his wobbly head set to scan the area around him, who should poke out of the metaphorical bushes but an old friend from primary school. 'Sean McIvor, as I live and breathe!' 'Christopher! Me old chum! Long time no see. What's up wi' ya, mucker?' This exchange, Christopher soon noted, had attracted the attention of the receptionist, who was now throwing eye-daggers in their general direction. Sean noted the concern in Chris's eyes and looked round, but he then smiled and turned back to Christopher: 'Wouldn't worry about the ole bat!' he said, but sufficiently quietly for her not to catch it. He soon sat down beside Christopher and they started talking, if as mutedly as they could manage given their mutual sense of fun at having made acquaintance after all these years. It didn't take long for Sean to see what Chris had been looking at. 'Science? Aye, I can't stand it, but our teacher's dead-on and he gives us all As.' Christopher: 'Where was it you went to? St Malachy's?' At this, Sean delivered a mock slap to the side of Christopher's head, saying 'Where's your imagination? Wouldn't set foot in the place. Nah, St Peter's...' Christopher knitted his brows (as they used to describe it when knitting was more popular). Sean: 'Up the Whiterock! You know where that is, don't ye?' 'The Whiterock?' Christopher echoed, drawing upon his miserable lack of knowledge of Belfast and West Belfast, to proffer, unconvincingly, 'Oh, aye' (the mainstay response of those at sea), adding, to cover his tracks, 'I'm at Barrack Street.' Sean grabbed it and ran with it: 'None of yer CBS Sparta regime for us! The Brothers! God help ye! But we still have our fair share of retreats we have to go to, mind.' 'Aye, it's like Colditz, Barrack Street, can't stand it', countered Christopher -or was it acquiesced?. Yes, Christopher couldn't stand Barrack Street, but he wasn't sure how he felt about a fellow from -the unknown- St Peter's getting the boot in to his school. Timidity had the better of him, however, as it always did in almost every interchange with others, and he let it stand that they both thought Barrack Street was 'crap'.

It wasn't long before they were sharing the fact that Science was 'bollocks', *and* the fact that one of them had failed the 'mock', but only one. To change the subject quickly, Christopher thought it best to ask Sean about the dinosaur story. 'Oh, that, aye, sure it's doing the rounds, that one... I'll be the Mega and you can be the... whatthehellwasit? *Skellig Michael* or something like,' cracking up as he did so, to the obvious displeasure of the receptionist, who now seemed about to leave her perch and maybe even swoop down upon them. 'Scelidosaurus, actually!' piped up Christopher. 'Oh, you sound like a regular scientist now!' This added fuel to Sean's fire of a laughing fit and it was only a matter of seconds before they would get the third degree. Rather, the librarian lady did unlatch herself from behind the counter, but simply made her way to the general area of where the two friends were talking, making it difficult for them to make the same level of noise. They waited for all of two minutes for her to hover away and then Christopher resumed the topic, explaining that he'd bumped into the same journalist who'd written it just yesterday in the city centre. 'Get away! Was he wearing a Robin Day dickie bird?' asked a newly chortling Sean, gesturing a bow-tie as he did so. 'Well,' replied Christopher, a little disheartened his news hadn't made a bigger impact, 'he certainly looked the part...' But now Sean was laughing too hard, having become inconsolably consumed by the giggles, and this time the receptionist lady came over and addressed them directly:

'I beg your pardon, but this is a library, not a café. Other people are trying to read… books!' This sobered Sean up a little, but also gave him the idea to ask Chris to go for a coffee somewhere. But Chris declined. He knew he was going to hell if he didn't study now and give himself some chance to erase his negative thoughts. *What would be the point of making all this effort to come here if I now just left and had a bit of fun?* 'Sorry, Sean, I'm up shit creek and ….' '… a dino ate yer paddle!' finished Sean, again unable to control himself, waving at his friend from St Bernard's, as he now found he couldn't even control what came out of his mouth so it was best to just keep it shut, retreating back, entrance-wise, still waving, smiling, desperately trying to suppress the giggles, until he was gone.

Christopher spent the next two hours straight solidly reading the science textbook, the mathematics textbook and the geography textbook, reading and taking notes and setting himself mini-goals to see if he could remember stuff and if his writing might improve. He also wrote, and re-wrote. Writing, he told himself, was not just putting words on the page, but doing so with an idea, an approach and a seriousness injected into the exercise that surprised, and even delighted him. He could do it, he was beginning to think. He would pass these 'O'-levels if it was the last thing he ever did.

His body also had claims on what to do with his free time. His bowels were murmuring to him, but it would be ages before he took heed. Somehow the mission before him blocked out everything else. Until…somehow, eventually, the message got through. He got up and went to the toilet. It was locked, so he returned to his books and waited. After a reasonable amount of time, or what he thought was a reasonable amount of time for some other human entity to do what they had to in there, he pushed his chair back and went and tried the door again. And again, it was locked. He had positioned himself in such a way as to ensure that he could see if anyone had entered that hallowed space, and so he wondered if whoever it was was (a) luxuriating (b) in trouble (c) had fallen asleep, or (d) had died. His bowels now madly clamouring for his attention, Christopher decided action was his only recourse, and so, he approached the receptionist librarian lady, if rather timidly. She noted him coming and inclined her head slightly at the hearing of some utterance from his mouth. At this stage, Christopher was only able, like some very little child, to articulate the word 'toilet'. The lady turned away briefly and Christopher wasn't sure what that meant, but she turned back, and, before he could say/blurt out 'I'm about to burst', handed him what he noticed with inordinate relief was a key, attached to a long transparent block of plastic engraved with the golden words 'Property of Glengormley Library'. He understood this was the library's system; in fact, he now even remembered having been told that the last time he had visited. He accepted the key and plastic block with as courteous a smile as he could muster and went on his way toward enormous relief.

His sojourn at the table after this episode was then coming under serious attack from another part of his body: the stomach. It was getting on for one o'clock and he hadn't had a bite since around nine, even if that had been a bite and a half. The words on the page before him were at times beginning to go in and out of focus. It helped that he would close one eye and then the other, inspired by a section in one of textbooks about the stereo vision of fish. Doing this repeatedly almost gave him a headache. *And so*, he concluded, *with all these parts of my body rebelling against my better instincts, it's high time I got off my arse and got something to eat, or at least had some air*. Within two minutes, Christopher had stuffed all his books and stationery back into his bag, abandoned his desk, left the library, with a heartfelt nod of gratitude to the librarian receptionist lady -not reciprocated – and had walked over, zombie-like in the general direction of Crazy Prices supermarket, to see what he could get to assuage his cravings. Which, after entering its vast interior and scanning every edible product known to man, turned out to be a (well-salted) pastie from the bakery counter for 10p and a carton of Rathkenny Milk at 14p, just pipping the one from Dale Farm at 16p, in observance of good economic practice, as, he often surmised, had been inherited from his Da, who would walk an extra mile to save 5p. Crazy Prices had lived up to its name, thought Christopher, as he munched into the pastie, standing up outside the giant shop, and awkwardly then opened the milk carton, almost dropping it in the process. Not dropping it added to his feeling of glee. It all went down a treat, and he was soon sated.

Once completed, Christopher disposed of the unwanted paper wrapping and carton and slapped his hands together to banish the crumbs: the action looked indivisible from a man celebrating the completion of some hard task. He would go home now, feeling like he had indeed completed some hard task, and then he asked himself what that might have been. Before he could get very far with an answer, he realized he might as well take a quick re-visit to the library and actually borrow something. There was something about not having done so which nagged at him, as the way to really complete operations. Fifteen minutes later, he was on his way, his bag just that little bit heavier now that he had borrowed, with great excitement, *The Lost World* by Arthur Conan Doyle, and *The Moon is a Harsh Mistress* by Robert A Heinlein, the first a paperback and the second a hardback, both well thumbed through. The first he perceived as his real treasure, his eyes widening at the discovery of a book by the Sherlock Holmes master but centring on his now-favourite topic, dinosaurs. (And he had seen the film.) The second book had intrigued him simply by its title and its cover image of strange mechanical happenings on the grey surface of that disc he loved to watch in the night sky. Again, these were doorways to another dimension and while he had the 'O'-level exams to combat, he was sure he could still find some time to nestle up with a book, now that he had gotten over his long-running problem of not enjoying the experience of reading.

What *had* he learnt in his morning at Glengormley Library? Again, he deferred answering that directly and instead recalled his chance meeting with Sean. It had been fun, and fun to regain a tiny bit of life as it been lived just a handful of years before. And life at St Bernard's Primary had been fun, fun incomparable with the hell -sometimes- of life at Barrack Street. There were aspects to his new school life he enjoyed, of course, but he really had felt like he'd been cast out of the garden of Eden and left to wander amidst the flotsam and jetsam of uncivilised humanity, be it in the form of his fellows, not all of them though, or some of the (non-smiling) teachers, the Brothers, or maybe just the top man, McCrohan. As Christopher walked to the end of Carnmoney Road and made a left onto the Antrim Road, taking the straight way back past the traffic and the shops, just for something to look at, he winced as he recalled Head Brother McCrohan's evil technique of pinching a student's cheek, pulling out the skin so that he could get a good, viciously rapid slap at it, and always in front of everyone. It wasn't just physical pain he wanted to inflict, it was humiliation he wanted his victim to suffer – and suffer they did. That was his reality now. That and fellows like Killen, or like Harry McNulty and Kevin Brady. The former was a nutter and the latter a boxer. It had been sweet to beat Brady that one time last year, but it had also been a terrible, vicious and violent ordeal. Then there were the 'O'-levels fast approaching. Why, oh why did life have to change so swiftly and so terribly?

With almost Biblical timing, it started raining. It was not a heavy rain, but more of a drizzle, a simple indication that the world was, alas, not this amazing thing, but some rather sad imitation of life, half-baked, weary, and now getting a bit soggy.

This line of thinking, if it could rightly be called 'thinking', brought him back to his feelings of the night before, an irrepressible sadness at the loss of time, the loss of a world he had known and cherished… Something about *this* then intrigued him.

It wasn't long before he had it… *The Lost World.* He had it in his bag of books. And it had nothing to do with dinosaurs. It wasn't a book title, but a sad fact of his own experience: he had lost a world. Then, as he allowed the little train of his thought to continue to chug on, the other book came to mind. He ruminated on it as he had done with the first, from the angle of the title, until he had come to the conclusion that it wasn't the 'Moon' that was a 'Harsh Mistress' – it was… 'Time', mulled over and re-done as… *Time is a Harsh Mistress.* (A real bitch from hell, in fact!) He even spoke/embellished the phrase out loud to himself, to the sad drizzle, and to the traffic of a humdrum brown Ford, an unwashed white Leyland van and a wee man on a bicycle getting soaked: 'Time is a Harsh Fucking Bitch from Hell!'

As Christopher continued to walk down the Antrim Road, happily, finally being able to take advantage of the shortcut through the church grounds, and past his old school St Bernard's, he decided to go back in his mind and re-ask the question he had posed just outside the library: *what had he learnt today?* (He didn't mind at all that his clothes were becoming soggy in the developing rain.)

He recalled his first stab at answering the question about fossils, or all three in fact. He might wince again to see how poorly he had done, but thereafter, he had seen what was at the back of the textbook, had read that, had thought about it and had then taken out his notebook and made notes. From these notes he had then asked himself questions about how to link this part and that, and whether this sentence or that were more acceptable. He had written and re-looked, and then re-written. He had rapidly drawn bold pencil lines through words or phrases which now struck him as childish. He had sat back, looked up at the ceiling, and around at the shelves and allowed his mind to work as he did so, mulling things over and weighing things up. And then he had gone back to a freshly turned-over blank page of his notebook and had attempted to write down his ideas, or his answers to each specific question in the textbook. He had concentrated on that, mightily, for – he wasn't sure how long, as his sense of time had abandoned him – and… eventually… he had succeeded in writing something he had to admit was coherent and flowing and logical and… nice. 'Don't use that word!' his brother Jim would always tell him. But, in the absence of Jim, he felt he could throw it in, no problem. It felt right. It was nice what he had written; it flowed. Like a river. Like music, even. Music flowed. Water flowed. Rain… *fell*.

Yes, he had forgotten time. His sense of time passing had become secondary to him when he'd been writing. The reason he had felt a keen need to go to the toilet had been because he had ignored his body and ignored time when writing, his mind furiously engaged in dreaming up the best way of describing what a fossil was or why they were important to scientists (and not *scientits*). When he had started at one section, it had been about quarter past eleven. When he next checked his silvery Sekonda alarm watch, after his flurry of active thinking and writing, the time had jumped more than half an hour, getting close to noon. At that moment, exterior time had suddenly become relevant again, and the exterior world, in the shape of his bowels, had managed to upgrade its faint tap on the shoulder to a huge slap about the head: *Get thee to a lavatory! Now!*

There was something else in all this, too. Initially, Christopher couldn't quite catch what it was but it had to do with the satisfaction he had felt when viewing the sentences he had eventually created. Through trial and error and a massive cross-examining of what was good and what was absolute childish rubbish, he had managed to formulate a working and full-proof description. There was no simpler way to say it: in Glengormley Library, on the outskirts of Belfast, County Antrim, in the official middle of nowhere, Christopher Maguire had captured a fossil. He had used words – not a brush, tongs or tweezers – to dig it out of the filthy muck of inarticulacy. And it now shone radiantly, deep within the folds of his Eason's pale blue Exercise Book.

What other marvels might this lead to? wondered a smiling, slightly soggy Christopher Maguire, as he opened the backdoor of his house and wiped the soles of his shoes on the mat.

Chapter Nine: Janek Heinkle reflects,
Tuesday, May 1

It was a beautiful day over Munich, as Professor Janek Heinkle, of the Palaeontology Department of Heidelberg University, coasted slowly and gracefully down from the clouds. Left and right arm extended, palms flat to catch the air, torso and legs straight as a fuselage, he glided slowly and gracefully over the old town, his eyes bright with excitement and the special joy that comes into the heart upon returning to one's hometown. Heidelberg may have been where he had worked for the last twenty years or so, but Munich would always be his home. (Correction: München! Heinkle abhorred Anglicisation.) And now, here, miraculously, or not so miraculously, considering his past life as a Luftwaffe pilot, Heinkle was flying – yes, flying – over the centre of his cultural and emotional universe. Coasting downwards in slow motion, brushing past the magnificent -but sharp!- green-oxidized steeple of Peterskirche to a point right over the main area of the Marienplatz with all its bustling multitudes, he marvelled at the intricate detail he could pick out on the façade of the Neues Rathaus. 'Hallo!' he called out with vibrant enthusiasm to the pedestrians far below. 'Hallo!' he called again, throwing out: 'Es ist wunderbar dich zu sehen, meine Landsleute!'

That, or it was a crap day in Belfast and Professor Janek Heinkle, of the Palaeontology Department of Heidelberg University, was slumbering on his Queen's University office desk, left cheek flat on the grained wood, and left and right arms abjectly extended out on either side, having rudely dislodged a number of items in the process a half hour previous, when he had flopped into an irresistible slumber. Saliva trickled out of his mouth, along with the occasional febrile saliva-bubble, caused by the even more febrile working of his mouth pathetically attempting to form the words 'Hallo' and his greeting of joy at seeing his fellow countrymen. Only the coldness of what he at first thought was the air but then, as consciousness began to awaken in him, realized was the coldness of the wooden surface of the desk, perturbed him. However it happened, the multifarious spiky protuberances of the Neues Rathaus, or New Town Hall, which was the picture-postcard jewel of München's Marienplatz, began to shimmer and dissolve, and the feeling of flying was suddenly, and sickeningly, replaced by a brief feeling of falling - like so much deadweight. And he woke up.

It was with some effort and a feeling of considerable vexation that Professor Heinkle managed to lift himself off the surface of the desk and do his very best to recover his professorial poise. A crumpled handkerchief, extracted from the back pocket of his trousers, came in very handy to wipe his dripping nose and mouth. He mumbled words from his native tongue as he did so, sounding remarkably unhappy, or as unhappy as anyone might be if extracted from the safely unseen back pocket of paradise and dumped into the conspicuously visible front shirt pocket of hell. That, he conceded, might be too melodramatic a way to describe his present predicament, but he was past caring about anything like a sophisticated response to recent problems. He had been embarrassed by the newspaper story and that was that. He had looked a fool, and that was that. He had attempted to restore balance with the TV broadcast that went out last night, didn't feel at all like he had, but that was that. 'That was that' had become his new slogan/philosophy in life, a crude distillation of French Existentialism and something out of the mouth of Immanuel Kant when talking about the importance of empiricism. Talking of which, the actual only words of comfort Herr Kant was offering Heinkle these days was this annoyingly apt phrase, not comforting in the least: 'Wer sich zum Wurm macht, soll nicht klagen, wenn er getreten wird!'

Or, 'One who makes himself a worm cannot complain afterwards if people step on him!' He had, and they were! That was that!

Had he? Had he been responsible for all this? One critique of pure reason suggested 'no', but another, derived from his military training from another epoch, another universe, suggested 'yes'. You, as the commander of any team, it lectured him, are responsible for the slightest error made by even the lowliest member. It was never enough to command and to train, but to ensure and to insist, and if that didn't work, cut! CUT it out and cauterize the wound (just as he had once done in the forests of the Ardennes, on the run from the Allied forces, nursing a bullet in the thigh). At the first squeak of insubordination, or rather, the first indication of laxity among the ranks, it had been Heinkle's duty to act, and to act without mercy. Oh, he told himself, how I have become soft over the years! He absorbed this realization with the measure of vague but salving equanimity he had learned to impose upon himself, just as his nation had learned, over the long, long years since he was a young man, rearing for action...

No, he told himself, I will not fall into that emotional trap. I, we, deserve to have equanimity stuffed down our throats for what I, we, did. I know this to be true. He winced even so.

He winced once again as memories of last night's broadcast fiasco came back to him. As he mused: 'Why did I have to mention Winston Churchill – *your* Winston Churchill, no less- and place him together in battle with Alexander the Great?! What a silly thing to have said!' He consoled himself with the realization that this overly simple comparison reflected his years as a teacher of the young, or at least the most recent generation, who needed all the guidance they could get, even if it meant reducing complexity, sometimes absurdly so, on a routine basis. Einstein had never done that, Heinkle told himself, adding, 'Yes, but his poor students often wondered what he was saying and scribbling on the blackboard...' Try as he might, though, Heinkle's embarrassment was immoveable. This turned his thoughts momentarily darker, as he then wondered what he would do if he ever met this Ivan Stocks [sic] face to face... No! He then pictured a firing squad and the final moments as poor Ivan squirmed as he stood tied to a vertical post, with no hood to hide his eyes from the horror about to be unleashed against him. *No!* Heinkle baulked at the idea of such, cursing himself for even the merest hint of the emotion it brought up through his veins. Anger, militarism, fighting, stupidity, he had seen what it did to him, to his nation... He could see what it was doing to *this* nation, too. If it could be properly called so. A nation, that is.

A nation once again... a nation once again. Somehow that poignant phrase from the famous traditional Irish Republican song came into his mind. As did a flood of memories... Heinkle had been here before. To Ireland. He had flown here. Not as a passenger, but as a pilot. From France. On a bombing mission over England that had gone awry... 'Heinkle in the Heinkel', his fellows always laughed at that one. In the Heinkel He111H-5, to be exact, mid-range bomber, hoping to have added a little spice to people's daily life in London, had they not been intercepted, gone off course and ended up flying westwards over the Irish Sea... It had been chaotic inside the fuselage, the fuel tanks hit and the needle on the dashboard going completely in the wrong direction. They could never hope to make it back to Juvincourt [Airfield, in Picardy]. Then from below, literally from the waves, or more literally from some ship among the waves, came death. It came in the form of gunfire, bullets smashing through the glass of the plane's nose and into the body of Unteroffizier Rister. His agonising dying screams caused panic and extreme dismay among a crew already feeling their time was fast approaching. Incredibly, fate was to be kinder to the rest, and the spying of an emergency landing strip on a beach made the remaining members put away emotion and focus on the business of survival. An hour later, having jettisoned their deadly payload in the sea, and Heinkle having pulled off the landing of a lifetime, Heinzl, Voigt, Hengst, Galler and himself, Janek Heinkle (of München), holding the body of poor, dead Gerd Rister, and exhausted from their efforts, watched as their beloved Heinkel (not Heinkle!) went up in flames -by their own hand. Never let the enemy capture your plane, that was the edict drilled into each and every Luftwaffe crew. There was no embarrassment among the men when tears began to course down cheeks and sobs went up, for their dead colleague, for their failure, and for the destruction of their 'Zuhause am Himmel', or 'Home in the Sky'.

They were very far from home now. Disclosure of precisely where here was, however, managed to lift the spirits, with Hengst the navigator declaring: 'Gentlemen, we have flown past our target of London and somehow managed to land in the very arsehole of Ireland!' To show that he wasn't merely being facetious, he whipped out the charts he had recovered and pointed, with gusto, at the map: 'Here!' And 'here' was just as he had said, precisely at the south-eastern nub of Ireland, where the teddybear (as he later learnt to call it) sits, or as Voight shouted out: 'This is where the shit comes out! Ya!' This nugget of knowledge played its part in raising the spirits of all and it wasn't long before they were singing 'Bomben auf Engelland' [Bombs on England] at the top of their voices. They not only didn't care if they were discovered, they hoped they were.

Wir fühlen in Horsten und Höhen
Des Adlers verwegenes Glück!
Wir steigen zum Tor
Der Sonne empor,

Wir lassen die Erde zurück.
Kamerad! Kamerad!
Alle Mädels müssen warten!
Kamerad! Kamerad!
Der Befehl ist da, wir starten!
Kamerad! Kamerad!
Die Losung ist bekannt:
Ran an den Feind!
Ran an den Feind!
Bomben auf Engelland!
(Etcetera!)

A stray donkey might have taken the credit for the capture of these enemy combatants but for the intercession of some members of the local militia, astounded at the sight of them: all were dripping with a combination of blood, sweat and tears. They also all looked radiantly happy, pausing only briefly in their rendition of 'Bomben auf Engelland'. The rest is history, as they say, thought Heinkle as he mused on the images of that incredible day (within the safety of his private Queen's University study), and that incredible time thereafter, living as internees in what turned out to be a remarkably friendly country. Oh, Ireland, he sighed, feeling, for the first time that day, a positive emotion toward the place he had now taken up residence in. But, he checked himself, was this Ireland, here? Not the Ireland he knew, certainly. 'Why are all northern regions cursed by bad weather and societal chaos?' he asked himself. How he abhorred the arrival of hordes of Northern Germans for the football or the Oktoberfest! How uncivil they were! How uncivil the Northern Irish, too! With their bombs and bullets and ugly graffiti scrawled everywhere! And yet, as he thought this, another voice told him to remember the reasons, the politics, the fact that Ireland had been subjected to British imperialism for almost a millennium…

The stories Nora, whom he'd met and fallen in love with back in '42, told him of the brutality the Irish had lived under, under the boot of the British. It was all coming back to him, all the love he had felt in this country, and the oneness with their struggle. They were continuing it now. Rubble and ruin was inevitable if you wanted to build a new world, or reclaim one that had been stolen from you...

Heinkle hadn't told anyone of his wartime adventure. He kept it all to himself in the years after, building up a career in science, in geology, and then in palaeontology. Who needed to know his affairs and his past? Did NASA invite the press to interview Von Braun? So, when Heinkle had flown to Ireland this time, to Aldergrove, as per his university's contract that he work for the main university in the North of Ireland, he made simple tourism the excuse for his visit down south one weekend soon after arrival. He brought with him a copper tankard for beer he'd been given by the remaining brother of Gerd and paid a solo visit to the German War Cemetery at Glencree near the Wicklow mountains. He brought also a six-pack of some lager he'd picked up in Dublin, and, after a bus journey that was only slightly less hazardous than a trip in the Heinkel He111H-5, he located the plaque adorned with Gerd Rister's name, and drank can after can as a tribute to his fallen fellow. The beer was warm, a sad imitation of what they served back home, but by can number three he was reduced to tears, tears that didn't stop until he had finished them all. He'd used the tankard for each, and, with as much solemnity as he could muster, he left it there as a memento of familial love for Unteroffiz. Gerd Rister, 03-10-1918✝03-03-1941. Just seven days before his birthday... Boys aged only twenty-two and younger were dying in the city Heinkle was living in right now, for a cause understood only partially and bathed in a light so bright it blinded...

Heinkle's education, in death, in war, in political grievances beyond his own shores, and, most unexpectedly, in science, had begun in Ireland. After an initial period of unendingly tedious incarceration, in the 'Curragh Camp', they'd all been given a degree of freedom unthinkable had they been prisoners of war in England, just across the water. It was freedom, freedom to roam, to roam outside the confines of the camp, into the nearby town, to mingle among the natives, to even go to dances, and bars! All under the trust system, to which all the fellows gladly acceded. He had met Nora, they had dated, they had loved, she teaching him English, and… giving him the precious names of the local fauna and flora, the 'saw-sedge', the 'black bog-rush', the 'purple moor grass', the 'fan thistle', 'butterwort', 'fragrant orchid', 'fly orchid', 'marsh orchid'! Admittedly, she had borrowed a book from the local library the week before and practiced the pronunciation of each a few times, asking her 'Da' on occasion what was what and how did you say it. Janek lapped it all up, and then asked to be taken to the library himself, where, to her annoyance, he would spend hour upon hour, devouring the books that they had. Soon, it was things closer to the earth that fed his developing hunger for knowledge; this was both metaphorical, in his gropings with Nora in the dark of the barn, and literal, with his sudden enrapturement with rocks. 'Tell me their names!' he would implore Nora, but Nora didn't know, nor did Nora's Da. Janek was not to be outdone. With a small hammer, lent somewhat reluctantly by Nora's Da, and a notebook and pencils, Janek Heinkle set out into the wilds of Kildare to document all he could see. By the end of the first day, he had filled the entire notebook, and the drawings he'd made were accompanied by descriptions devoid of the proper terms but rich in the language of the layman, using colours and texture and shape and simple measurements to record. It was the start of an obsession.

Incredibly, again, in a country where he had only known

incredible experiences, he soon found himself chosen to join the very select ranks of those eligible for formal training, in Dublin. It was wondrous news for Janek Heinkle, but sad news for Nora. He had begun teaching her German; she had begun loving him; they had begun to look like a couple; she had begun to think of a future, far beyond the backwater she lived in... Now, at his desk in his study at Queen's University, Belfast, Northern Ireland, 1979, Janek Heinkle could find another reason to feel melancholic, in love with a past that lingered as Nora's natural-made 'crushed-orchid', perfume had lingered, on the bus northwards to Dublin, and over the decades since, persisting through marriage and the getting of children and his rise to eminence as a world-authority in his field. What had he done, back in 1942? Taken the step that his mind had ordered, suppressing his heart? For, even if it was only now, thirty-seven years later, he thought that perhaps he had, in fact, loved Nora Murphy just as much as she had loved him.

There was a knock on the door.

Chapter Ten: Heinkle vs Tweedy, same day

Ten minutes previous to said knock, Professor Tweedy had stridden into the corridor outside his room and bounded up the steps that would bring him to the third floor, where Heinkle's office was. At the top of the steps he had then stopped, feeling a sudden, intense bout of nerves. What was he doing? he asked himself. Rather, it wasn't so much what he was doing as what he was thinking, and then again, not so much what he was 'thinking', as what was going through his head could hardly be classified as coherent thought, but rather, *what was his attitude?* Yes, it was his 'attitude' that was giving him pause, intense and almost painful pause, as he fathomed the depths of how he would frame his words to his 'superior'. Was he going to accuse Heinkle of lying? Would he be so forthright? Yet, what else could account for this information gap, the failure to share with his colleague vital aspects of their mission? How could Heinkle have left Tweedy so in the dark? And… was he stealing the work of that poor Byrne fellow. What a disgrace to the university! This could be a scandal far eclipsing the fiasco of the Duelling Dinos!

And yet, could he say all that to Doktor Heinkle? World-authority figure, gracing the cloisters of Northern Irish academia… Contemplation of this reduced Tweedy even further, to the point where he now, at the top of the stairs, uttered the pathetic whimpering of a man who has been dealt an impossible hand, the utterances accompanied by an attempt to muffle what was coming out with his – Scottish Tweed-enclosed – left arm, his body folding in on itself, as he leant forward and, knees bending, sank slowly, slowly down, falling into something like a paroxysm… IF Sheila had come up at this time, she would have rushed to him like a nurse. Tweedy looked like a man undergoing extreme physical – stomach-centred – distress after all. Moments later, however, he had recovered sufficiently to force himself to return to his office, to think things over, or just to recover his poise and his breath.

'Intelligence' he said to himself *sotto voce*, 'intelligence…' What was the intelligent thing to do, he now queried himself. What indeed? It took a few moments or so, but gradually it dawned on him that he really should extricate himself from his emotions. To be deadpan and disinterested was always the best way, when no other option seemed viable. *Play the innocent*, he told himself, the boy who has no idea who broke his toys, *and, fellows, sure I have plenty of others!* Yes, yes, yes. This would be Tweedy's opportunity to take the No-no-nos and the Don't-don't-don'ts of his life, crush them into a ball and toss it/them back where they/it came from. Toss, or fling… No, 'toss' implies a carefree approach, 'fling' carries too much intention with it, too much 'attitude'. While he wondered what had made him employ children's terms into his way of figuring things out, and guessing it derived from too close contact with his kids, it was working. He was beginning to calm himself down and find the right strategy for dealing with this potential calamity. Tweedy had heard Japanese people often went into paroxysms at the prospect of even minor disagreements at the office with fellows, had even developed complex linguistic strategies to mitigate the stress of conflict, a useful formality of regular address… but here, in the enlightened West, we were no better at dealing with inter-personal conflict. English let us down, he believed, the old pally-wally system of employing informal address from the first moment of meeting. It was all a sham, after all. At the first sign of disagreement, even – *especially!* – among academics, the knives were out, even if the knives took the form of only the merest of skewed smiles.

Tweedy decided it was wise to review how this had all started. He cast his mind back like a Sunday fisherman casting his rod, his head nodding back ever so slightly. The cheer of Christmas and New Year had hardly subsided when he'd gotten that call from Professor Jope, asking him to come in sometime for a chat about 'an exciting new project'. That turned about to be the suggestion that Tweedy be seconded onto the about-to-be-launched team headed by Professor Janek Heinkle, of the Palaeontology Department of Heidelberg University. It had sounded so wonderful, even just the man's title and affiliation had a resonance that echoed through the cloisters. Tweedy's enthusiasm, however, took a knock, or two, early on upon learning what his part of the bargain actually entailed: acting very much in a secondary position and having to spend endless days up beyond Carrickfergus, often in bucketing conditions. The name Eden, everyone soon agreed, had been entirely ironic. The more Tweedy now examined, not the soil and muck they had to work through and pore over, but his interaction with the German professor, the more he realized how secondary, or even tertiary, his role had been. Tweedy, he could now see, had been little more than a glorified student-worker, reduced to doing the donkeywork and whose comments, perhaps because he was not a palaeontologist *per se*, were invariably given short shrift. How had he allowed this to happen? Had he been asked to give up his dignity in the cause of affording Queen's some sheen of glorious internationalism? Tweedy acceded he had; he had been played for a fool, left in the dark and hung out to dry. That was a run of idioms that jangled and even brought a smile to his face, if only because humour could be the only way to deal with the ridiculousness of this situation. He now had the evidence, in his pocket, to explode this sham, and to extricate himself from what he would probably look back on in years to come as 'just one of those things'. He even started to hum a jazzy tune he somehow remembered that had those five words in the catchline. Tweedy was smiling again. 'It was just…. one of those things!' he sang to the white walls, and to the ceiling which, not long before, had made him think of death. The line, *I laugh in the face of death*, suddenly ran through Tweedy's mind, like a cartoon train in a cartoonishly dayglo landscape.

'To hell with it,' pronounced a now philosophical Ronald Tweedy, seeing there was no option but to confront Heinkle in as non-confrontational way as possible. *Allow him to tie himself in knots, that's what I want to see. Ha ha ha!* Tweedy moderated his glee, according to the same principle which told him to put away his stress and worries, and then exited his room once again.

Heinkle, upon hearing the knock, felt suddenly bitterly robbed, interrupted, that he wouldn't be able to dwell further upon time past, here in the comfort of his office, his mind's eye only now beginning to see Nora's freckled Irish face, with a backdrop of gorse and the cry of the curlew... That, and he had also wanted to put closure onto his question of what he had done, and why, all those years ago... He always kept his office door locked as he abhorred the prospect of some unexpected and unwanted person walking in, be it that Sheila woman or a student, and now took advantage of the few moments it would take to get up from his desk and make his way to the door...

Thinking back, he knew his sudden obsession with geology hadn't been just some noble quest for knowledge, a sudden desire to know everything. It had also been a strategy -yes, he could employ that most military of words here-, a strategy to block out the reality before his eyes. Not that of the beauty of Nora Murphy, and what she had offered to him (only happiness), but the reality that he had belonged to a war-machine that, as he had heard report upon report through the enormous radio in the Murphy's house, and through the newspapers, was responsible for atrocities in Poland and France... The persecution of Jews, and the wholesale execution of families in the Warsaw Ghetto... He, Janek Heinkle of München, lover of adventure and... now in love... he had been an implement of that torture and cruelty, that destruction on a vast scale… Oh, that the bombs they had intended for London had only been delivered to the fish in the Irish Sea was a blessing! Failure was a blessing… Only by altering his focus would he ever be able to deal with the reality of his life and the world he had been an active player in… This world was evil, or this world had evil in it… while humans devoted their energies to killing and tyranny… Thereafter Heinkle had found himself definitively less interested in his own species, happily entranced with the past, a past as far back as it was possible to go…

'Yes, yes, I'm coming,' said Heinkle in as perfunctory a tone as he could manage it. *What could be of such great import to disturb him? What could be of such great import to vie with what he'd just dwelt on?* He turned the latch and opened the door. 'Ah, Tweedy!' said Heinkle, in as upbeat a manner as he could muster. 'Come in, come in.' Tweedy, according to his own strategy, had so fixed the features of his face as to look like a moustachioed doll, one with a vapidly cheerful demeanour. Heinkle motioned for him to sit down and returned to his own seat behind the desk, noting as he did so that Tweedy had not yet uttered a word. Mischievously, Heinkle wondered if his colleague had transformed into the Sphinx. Unsure that his guest would break that impression any time soon, he felt obliged to give voice to another perfunctory utterance: 'So…' followed fairly soon with, 'How are you…' hesitating slightly before continuing, '…getting along?' Heinkle decided he couldn't really care less.

'Oh, fine, fine…' said Tweedy, in a perfect illustration of the clipped style of speaking. His teeth had opened and closed like a portcullis. His doll-like smile remained.

'Very… good,' said Heinkle, hoping that the pause between his words would give his interlocutor the opening he needed to explain his presence. Moments passed, however, and nothing was forthcoming from that moustachioed mask before him. Tea, thought Heinkle, tea is what is used in such situations this side of the Rhine, not 'Kaffee und Kuchen!' (*Oh for a Dampfnudel!* thought a suddenly homesick Heinkle.) 'Tea?' asked Heinkle. Feeling the need to clarify that, he added: 'Would [pronounced 'Vud'] you like a cup of tea?' Heinkle was beginning to feel like a man who has received a telephone call from a friend who then refuses to say why he'd called. It was with no little relief, then, when his guest appeared to react, first with a near shriek of 'Tea?', as though it were some exotic material, and then a less excited: 'Tea? Yes. Thank you.' Heinkle had thought he'd been going through a lot lately, but perhaps his colleague had been under even more stress... He was glad to be able to stand up and walk over to the small counter and sink and make preparations for that most magical of potations, magical in that it could extricate Heinkle from this present hell.

'How was I?' asked Heinkle, searching for items here and there at the counter. Hearing nothing, he clarified: 'On the TV last night.' Tweedy's ears suddenly turned reddish. 'Very good!' he piped up, his mind in a panic, knowing that to say so was a complete lie, as he hadn't viewed the broadcast at all. Heinkle: 'I don't think so. Oh, I think it was a damn waste [pronounced 'vayste'] of time and effort... I just want this whole thing to...' His next word was difficult for Tweedy to catch, but he felt enormous relief that he hadn't been quizzed on the contents. 'Eh?' asked Heinkle. Tweedy, not sure of the question he was being asked just threw out what he could and hoped for the best: 'No. Great. Wonderful. *Wunderbar!*' His attempt at German struck an incongruously upbeat note, causing Heinkle a moment's pause for thought, one, however, which he decided not to follow up on.

In a cunningly strategic move, Tweedy decided he had better cover his tracks, and fast, and so started talking nineteen to the dozen on a different topic. With not a little confusion, Heinkle found himself saying: 'Whoa!', followed by: 'Please forgive this old German und speak a little slower, har!' He was glad at least that a communication of sorts had begun. He was never really sure what to say to Tweedy... 'Of course, terribly, terribly...' squawked a rather flappy Tweedy, half getting out of his seat as though to give added weight to his apologetic words and tone. 'I was saying I saw those students... the Williamson girl and the... Jal fellow...' 'Gut, gut!' sounded Heinkle, glad to hear what he had unconsciously been dwelling on recently, the prospect of some kind of chastisement for the offenders, the authors of their present troubles. He allowed Tweedy to speak on, as he attended to the various aspects of tea-making, filling the kettle, plugging it in, washing out two cups and opening the Giant's Causeway-printed canister he was using for teabags. What a wonderful trip that had been, if wet, he reflected as his colleague continued.

'Well, I told them straight, Professor Heinkle. I made it clear to them the trouble they had brought down on our heads, and made it clear they would have no place in our team from now on,' pronounced a bold and righteous Tweedy, almost banging the desktop with the fist he had unconsciously made as he was speaking. It was the first time Heinkle had felt sorry for the students, remembering his own youth, and the world-altering folly he had been engaged upon... 'Vell,' said Heinkle in response, now delivering the two cups of steaming tea to the desktop, 'I just hope they vill learn from dis incident...' He hesitated between going back to the counter to retrieve some biscuits, and, feeling the need to throw in his own comment, he flopped for the latter: 'I'm sure there was some reason for their... indiscretion?' Tweedy did his best to unravel the ins and outs of the mis-communication between them and the reporter from the *News Letter* and, seeing the triviality of what it now looked like, allowed himself to go where Heinkle, and his sensitive-looking eyes, seemed to be going, and relented in his tone and then in his approach. 'Well, of course,' Tweedy said, 'young people will be young people… they didn't kill anyone after all.' This appended phrase had a seemingly direct visible effect on Heinkle, who then suddenly looked extremely pensive and, after a moment, uttered 'No… No…. No….' like the tolling of some bell signalling the approach of doom.

It was, Tweedy found himself realizing, a moment he had been looking forward to just a few short minutes ago, the opportunity to take the No-no-nos of his life and toss them back where they came from, but, somehow, it didn't feel like victory. Heinkle was obviously more upset than he could fathom, or had been through things he couldn't begin to imagine… And yet, even in the midst of this old man's existential angst, if that's what it was, Tweedy knew he couldn't put off what he knew he must broach. With a sudden turn of his head and an audible sigh, Tweedy signalled the approach of a different kind of doom. Heinkle missed the theatrics of the moment, however, his thoughts a million miles away, and about four decades in the past… He didn't notice either when Tweedy reached into his inner jacket pocket and pulled out an envelope, which, accompanied by Tweedy's far-off drone of meaningless words, was then held out, over the surface of the desk, piercing the twin twirls of rising tea-steam from the cups. Only then did Heinkle break free of the past and take cognizance of the white, flat thing being held out to him. He took it, autonomically, noticed the delicate steam, and, ignoring the thing now in his hands, declared solemnly: 'Prost!'

They raised their china cups at the same time and even tipped them toward each other in a gesture seemingly incongruous for two men in the midst of a professional crisis: nothing to celebrate yet. There would be even less once Heinkle opened that envelope, thought Tweedy, a surprisingly devilish anticipation rising in him. 'I received an envelope like this twenty years ago,' said Heinkle just then, sounding suddenly serious. Tweedy stopped himself from commenting that he had probably received quite a few envelopes over the years; he had the guffaw all ready, too. Yet, something about the way Heinkle had said what he'd said militated against exterior comment. Tweedy needed to just sit tight and give his eminent interlocutor a bit of space. As it turned out, however, Heinkle didn't need very much. He opened his mouth and said: 'It was to tell me that Nora had died the year before... She had never married.'

Tweedy had no idea what he was talking about, but he suddenly felt the need to retrieve the envelope; he had no desire to heap misery upon a soul already in pain and misery. And yet, Heinkle, with the same autonomic movement he had employed to take the envelope, and hardly even glancing toward it as he did, put his fingers inside the flap and began to extract the letter inside. He knew he had spoken of his past life, his past love, but the words had been spoken as though in a trance... he had no desire to explain them, as his audience had not really been Tweedy, but himself, or his bared soul, his raw heart, in this most unlikely of settings, finally ready to listen to the emotion he had always ignored. Nora, Nora, his mind called to him, and to her... Janek, Janek, she called to him... *My love, my life!*

Heinkle snapped out of his reverie. He had pulled out the letter and pulled back from Tweedy, who, he did not know why, was attempting to snatch the letter out of his hands. 'It's OK,' Tweedy was saying, 'it's OK, I will take care of it, Professor! Please!' 'Vat are you doing?' snapped Heinkle. 'Let me see what has got you all ... flust....' He couldn't quite recall the full word 'flustered', but repeated 'flust' a further three times, enjoying the fact that it sounded quite Teutonic. Tweedy was flapping and Heinkle was snapping, but then, once the latter made oracular contact with the object of all this commotion, everything just stopped dead. Tweedy could see Heinkle's eyes flit from left to right, and left to right, like a typewriter on speed. Was he going to explode? thought Tweedy. And then: why am I not enjoying this moment more? Emotional confusion had clouded his view of the man in front of him and he was willing to forgive him anything, and even… crawl back into his own shell of enforced obedience… he was a lowly figure after all, a minion of the great Heinkle, sat here in his literal shadow, with the sun streaming in from the window behind him.

Then, as he continued to observe Heinkle's reading of the letter, unable to discern what sort of effect it was having on him, Tweedy regained his claim on contempt. Why should he be ready to forgive this man for his sins? Heinkle had kept pieces of the jigsaw from him, after all. He had no right to do that! Tweedy was not his minion, or his underling, his hireling, his proto-student. Tweedy had every bit as much right to know what was going on in this operation as the next man, and certainly as much right as Heinkle. And, as he sat there, Tweedy's view of the man before him returned to what it had been earlier, the view that concluded that Heinkle had wantonly ignored his so-called 'colleague'. And, watching what Heinkle did next did little to detract from that view. 'Thank you, Tweedy. I'll take care of this,' spoke the German, an utterance which did nothing if not enflame the seemingly patient man before him, who, however, was patient no more. 'Take care of it?' shouted Tweedy. 'Take care of it?' he shouted again. 'What the hell!' Heinkle's eyebrows visibly lifted behind the pince-nez. 'I beg your pardon?' he countered.

'Beg your pardon?' echoed Tweedy. 'What do you mean "I'll take care of it?" I certainly hope you do, but don't you think you owe me an explanation?' Heinkle fixed Tweedy with a look that demanded more from his interlocutor. He didn't have to wait long. 'And what about this poor Byrne fellow? Don't you think he has a right to be upset?' 'Of course he does!' shot back

Heinkle, 'but I'm taking care of it! Don't worry! I made clear mention of Byrne on the TV last night...' From the look of surprise on Tweedy's face, Heinkle felt it necessary to inquire: 'You did say you saw the programme, no? I mentioned Byrne twice I recall...' Tweedy's face was now doing what his ears had done a few minutes previously, and the blush was palpable enough for Heinkle to comment: 'Your face betrays you, sir.' This was too much, Tweedy felt, and pounced: 'You... You...' but he couldn't say the next word, knowing that that alone was clearly accusatory. Heinkle was now reluctant to say anything.

Tweedy composed himself and then composed this: 'You have kept me in the dark, sir. I am supposed to be your colleague and yet I have been kept in the dark about the very origins of this project... I find it... galling!' Heinkle didn't actually know what 'galling' meant, or had forgotten, but he knew he should respond. Before doing so, though, he got up from his seat and walked back to the glass cabinet behind him. He extracted a small key from his pocket and unlatched one of the cabinet glass-panels. Within a moment, he had returned to his seat and had placed a box about the size of a small batch loaf on top of the wood surface. As Tweedy looked on, his brow creased with the pressure that comes when curiosity is piqued, Heinkle started to open the box. He then stopped. He looked at Tweedy.

'I apologize, Professor. My... English is not good... My... approach was not good... I... live in my own world and... I don't always think about those around me... I should have explained things better... I am heartily sorry...' Tweedy could hardly believe what he was hearing. He had expected the big guns, but here he was being offered an olive branch, a token, even, of submission. He had won, but there was no joy in winning without an equitable display of magnanimity. But Heinkle hadn't quite finished. 'I thought I had explained enough on our first meeting, but we had both had...' Heinkle smiled expansively, '…a few welcome drinks…Guinness is Good, no?' This raised a small smile on Tweedy's face, as the atmosphere between the two men warmed ever so slightly. 'Thompson… he had become sick, so I had heard… they needed an expert, they called for me… I… thought you'd been informed of all the circumstances of the find… I can explain about the location, if you'd like… I gave you one of the two pieces for safe-keeping…' Tweedy felt a jolt. 'But, dear Professor Tweedy, please excuse an old man who didn't think. We have been given a great gift. A wonderful – vunderbar, as you might say it! – gift of two fossils. The first ever instance of dinosaurs in Ireland! We, you and I, Tweedy, we are the… guardians, the… protectors of an ancient secret, of ancient beings who walked this earth when the earth was young… *we have been chosen!*'

Tweedy was beginning to feel sick. He was hearing all that Heinkle was saying, but after 'I gave you one of the two pieces for safe-keeping' it felt like his stomach had suddenly hollowed out. A deep pit at the centre of his being had opened up and he was standing on the precipice, about to fall in. Heinkle continued: 'Do you know that a fossil is an extremely rare object? Do you know that among a *billion* living organisms on the face of this earth only one is… destined to survive as a fossil? Yes, everything else will decay. Everything else will disappear… This means that any fossil we find is a scientific *treasure*, a… glory, a gift from some… very mean giant, who only ever throws out a bone from his daily feasting once a millennium…'

As Heinkle spoke, finding an eloquence that astonished Tweedy, Tweedy thought of the 'paperweight' he'd slammed onto the floor of his office last Friday, overly excited by the metallic-ochre lips of the fair Tracey, where it had remained since then, down among the piles of the carpet and surrounded by paperclips… Had he chipped it? Was it damaged? *Would this be the end of his career?*

Heinkle produced a pair of light-blue thin rubber gloves and carefully pulled these over his fingers and hands. He then opened the box. 'This,' he said, removing the stone-like item from the soft-matter interior of the box, 'is the fossil of part of the tibia of a Middle Jurassic Megalosaur. You have the fossil fragment of a femur of an Early Jurassic Scelidosaur. We are spending all our time and efforts now just to see if there might be any trace fragments of either of these fine fellows in the dirt and muck of our very own Garden of Eden. These beautiful things were found in Islandmagee, a few miles north, but they were *ex situ*. Based on data accumulated by Thompson, there was ['vos'] reason to think the Eden site might disclose more items…'

Tweedy looked at the fossil before him, its smooth largely black surface possessing lines, contours and striations whose nature and origin flummoxed him completely. He was like a child viewing a picture by Kandinsky: possibly enchanted but definitely devoid of the vocabulary to even begin to describe it. The more he stared into its mystery the more he saw the gift he'd been given, cast aside like a useless toy, an abject fate for so precious a thing.

'I think I need to go now,' said a chastened Tweedy. 'I am very sorry for everything, Professor Heinkle. I will dedicate my every waking moment to the success of this mission.'

Heinkle was a little taken aback that Tweedy was leaving so soon, but he was also glad that their *tête-à-tête* had suddenly become resolved. He knew not why, but it mattered little. Heinkle called after him, just as Tweedy had, somehow, managed to make his body move according to the necessity of getting the hell out of there: 'Tweedy, bring the femur here, if you don't mind. I can teach you all about the features of both! I'll make a palaeontologist of you yet!' It was all Tweedy could do with the remainder of his strength to respond with a call of 'OK!' which, somehow, came out incredibly, and embarrassingly, high-pitched.

. . .

Tweedy, perhaps because he was undergoing a mental strain so acute it limited his vision and perception of the immediate world around him, didn't notice that the fair Tracey, and the not-so-fair Manny, had been standing to the left of Heinkle's doorway, having finally summoned up the courage to think about apologizing to Professor Heinkle in person. They seemed glad not to have been noticed by Tweedy, as now both were smiling broadly, and even... somewhat mischievously.

Chapter Eleven: Violence, pt.1

Professor Janek Heinkle knew quite a bit about violence, and what he didn't know he could infer pretty easily from the batteries of steak-knife-like teeth in the jaws of a T. Rex. Yes, they might be like Saturday night diners at the Grand Hilton Restaurant, giant napkins somehow held in place from the neck down as they sat down to a nice plate of recently deceased Triceratops, but it wouldn't be stretching the imagination terribly either to suggest they were quite capable of raiding the Hilton kitchen, snapping their way through some of that night's juicy still-live candidates, or even the cooks. Conversely, you could be forgiven for insisting that the Triceratops's conspicuous bony neck frill was evolved body armour designed to prevent a nasty predator's *Jaws-II* 'Just When You Thought It Was Safe to Hang Out in the Kitchen' attack. Yet, it might just be something 'TrickyTops', as once dubbed by the child of a friend of Heinkle's, had evolved to make its own jaws bite a mite harder, part of the mechanism of the mouth. It might even be just a frill, something TrickyTops had picked up from some fancy dinosaur boutique to catch the eye of some ten-ton babe passing by. It all depended on how carefully you looked and checked the evidence. And even then, at least for the moment (at this historical stage of palaeontology), it would all be open to debate and interpretation. Yes, and no. Heinkle simply could not envisage T. Rex as never succumbing to its bloodlusts, even when up against a foe of comparable deadliness. Dinosaurs, he knew (or guessed), sometimes threw caution to the wind and allowed themselves to be lured by their most feral instincts. In this regard, they had quite a bit in common with humans. They didn't always come in when it was more or less safe, and they didn't always need a pack of like-minded fellows to prosecute a quick kill.

The Megalosaur and the Scelidosaur at each other's throats! It would be only funny were it not for the publicity fiasco that came with it. *Ah…. That was that!* his mind shouted. Heinkle's pain returned at the memory of where he was, metaphysically. He knew that was *not* that if he still continued to feel as bad as he did. Closing his eyes tightly and burying his head in his leathery hands, he did his best to expunge or occlude his miserableness. When the telephone then rang, in the dark of that enclosed space, it veritably exploded. This was the violence of the unexpected. How Heinkle managed to break free of his statuary, pick up the receiver and find himself passing words in as normal a voice and tone as ever was beyond him. Furthermore, whatever dark feeling he had been in the grip of was miraculously now beginning to dissipate… Heinkle was learning that Tweedy would not be coming back to Heinkle's office. This, it seemed, was the import of the call. Something about having to take care of his… 'what?' 'What did you say, sorry?' Heinkle hadn't quite caught the last word, but he'd heard enough to get the general message. He didn't really care why Tweedy was no longer coming back to his office, just as long as he wasn't coming back to his office. Peace and space to think, or not to think, was a wonderful alternative. (Unbeknownst to the German professor, his colleague downstairs was busy cradling the Scelidosaur's fossilized femur like it was a newborn baby, thankfully perfect in every way, unchipped and undamaged by its rough handling of a few days ago. Professor Ronald Tweedy was whispering to it, touching it tenderly, even delivering soft kisses to its smooth exterior/posterior…)

Heinkle tried thinking nothing, getting up to look out the window and observe the comings and goings of passers-by down on University Square, but something was nagging at him and he quickly sat down again, his eyes re-encountering the fossil, the fossil of the Megalosaur's tibia. Of course, it was too early to announce to the world that this was definitively from a Megalosaur as such, or even that it was a fragment of tibia, but Heinkle had a way of intuiting fossilized bones. It came from his years of work in the Trossingen and Solnhofen quarries, even sometimes in the company of the great Friedrich von Huene, when he worked as his apprentice, uncovering pterosaur fossils. Von Huene had a knack for 'seeing' that Heinkle liked to think had been passed onto him. With his encyclopaedic acquaintance with dinosaurian taxa, the master could see the whole from the tiniest fragment, although he also had a knack for not allowing his intuitions run away with his scientific need for actual evidential confirmation. Heinkle wondered if he were running away with his hunches, his vision of the whole from the smallest, broken part. But that was part of the fun of it all, the creative joy that this kind of work brought into his heart. Instinctively, Heinkle passed his right hand down to his right leg and touched the area just below the knee. Here, this is where it came from, Heinkle told himself, feeling the electricity of connection with a beast that had walked the earth a hundred and sixty million years ago.

How had it looked? This, of course, had taxed the experts down the ages, with wildly differing anatomy being foisted on the poor, mis-named creature. It was a 'Mega'-losaurus because it was BIG. Nothing particularly scientific there! Well, he reflected, who could imagine the astonishment of the early discoverers, when things like this had been dug out of the earth? Megalosaurus was one of the first to be found, after all, and it didn't take a brain-surgeon to see how it got its name. Interestingly, Heinkle then mused, Scelidosaurus was one of the first actual dinosaurs on the planet. Interesting how these two did have something in common after all -both had a claim on 'first dinosaur'. They were a funny pair, though, Heinkle had to admit. A kind of Laurel and Hardy of small and big, or was it…

the Walrus and the Carpenter? One had fangs, the other a saw, but the only violence they did was to scoff all the oysters that had happily joined them for their sojourn on the beach. At this, Heinkle reached behind him to the lower bookshelf where he kept not his tomes on palaeontology, but the bits and pieces he would pick up from time to time on his days-off in town. He soon picked out *The Complete Nonsense of Edward Lear* and found what he was looking for. Unexpectedly, these stanzas in particular grabbed his attention:

> The Walrus and the Carpenter
> Were walking close at hand;
> They wept like anything to see
> Such quantities of sand:
> 'If this were only cleared away,'
> They said, 'it would be grand!

> If seven maids with seven mops
> Swept it for half a year,
> Do you suppose,' the Walrus said,
> 'That they could get it clear?'
> 'I doubt it,' said the Carpenter,
> And shed a bitter tear.

Upon reading that, Heinkle found himself almost shedding a bitter tear himself: the Walrus and the Carpenter were not the Megalosaur and the Scelidosaur after all, but himself and Tweedy, doing the work of all those seven maids with seven mops up at the Eden site, sifting through all that muck and sand and soil! It didn't take him much, linguistically, to recall that other nonsense pair: *Tweedle*dum and *Tweedle*dee! The sudden realization of this called for another burying of face in leathery hands, combined with something like a muffled scream, and even a few actual tears. Heinkle was feeling the pain again, the pain of having fallen into a vortex of stupidity and professional shame. A good wee mope was well in order, as you might hear it said in the German's adopted city.

'Oh, in München zu sein!' [Oh, to be in Munich!] exclaimed an exasperated Heinkle. He was feeling homesick, too.

Within a few minutes of well-earned self-indulgence, however, Heinkle recalled another essential aspect of British/Irish culture and made himself another cup of tea. It did the trick, and he could go back to his mental deliberations. He would write a letter to Roger Byrne, explaining and apologizing for the mix-up and the lack of communication. This would be a step toward a rehabilitation of purpose, and a re-focusing of energies on what mattered, not on what could not be helped. Maybe they could even invite Byrne to take an active part. (Oh, to replace his hapless colleague!)

The tea was hot, though, and the fossil still upon the desk, so back his thoughts went to the creature it had come from, the mighty Megalosaur. Sip by sip, he fell back into contemplation of the animal's graceful form, stalking the savannahs in search of something to fill its demanding stomach. It wouldn't have been so graceful as it swooped upon some unsuspecting individual, however. If Belfast wanted to see real duelling dinos, then Heinkle realized, they might look no further than the famous preserved fight between the Velociraptor and the Protoceratops, described by John Ostrom. That was the only evidence ever found of an actual prehistoric battle. They might note the close-up detail of the Velociraptor's lethal pedal claw embedded in the midsection of his rival and its foreclaws grasping the no-doubt blood-gushing head of its poor unfortunate prey. What had happened next was unfortunate for both, of course, but fortunate for mankind, for had they not been then drowned in sudden hot Vesuvian sand who would have known, or cared less about their deadly battle? Not one in a billion, that. One in a million billion.

It was easy to view violent death at a distance. The fact that it involved strange beings made it even easier. Heinkle then relented, remembering the silly newspaper article. Perhaps he didn't need to take so grim a view. No doubt the article had entertained its readers and took their mind off all contemporary woes. He was living in a city where violent death was part and parcel of everyday life. Instead of the velociraptor's claws you had human hands gripping onto another human's torso, inflicting death wounds, spilling blood… No, in fact, it was usually done at least at the distance of a gun-barrel, or even quite remotely, the victims unsuspecting that innocent brown saloon car, parked outside some random shop… not knowing it had been fitted up with a half-ton of explosives and a mercury tilt-switch. 'Oh, in München zu sein!' Heinkle sighed. To be back home where all such violence – and even worse – was safely buried in the past.

'Duelling Facking Dinos OK!' said Heinkle, just before dropping his tired head back down to where it seemed to have always wanted to be, resting upon the *tabula rasa* wooden surface of his office desk.

Chapter Twelve: Violence, pt.2

Christopher Maguire's own brush with violence hadn't been quite as blood-curdling and nasty as that faced by the unfortunate Protoceratops, but, sure, everything is relative. It had started with one quick smack in the face from Kevin Brady just moments before Brother Walsh was expected to enter and start the last class of the day at Barrack Street. Being an amateur boxer, Brady knew how to deliver a punch. Christopher had been standing up for PJ, who was often the butt of Brady's bullying, and now he was lying down on the cold wooden floor for precisely the same reason. With help from PJ and another boy, Paddy Lappin, Christopher managed to get up and return to his seat just in time, none of them wishing to incur the wrath of the Brother for not being seated and quiet. Christopher nursed his bruised mouth and nose as inconspicuously as he could manage and suppressed the urge to cry.

Once home, and after spilling the beans, his brothers not only urged Christopher to go back the next day and 'beat the living shit out of that fucker', they made it a point of honour upon the family name: 'You *don't* do this and your name is *mud.*' Life throws things at you, and now life had thrown this at young Christopher. He went to bed that night knowing what the following day would bring, or what the evening would bring if he didn't get even. And so, it came to pass that on Wednesday, May 17, 1978, Christopher Maguire shouted out to one Kevin Brady at 12.11 pm in the courtyard of Barrack Street Christian Brothers Grammar School, Belfast City, as said Kevin Brady was proceeding toward the school gates (it might be presumed to avail of a snack from Ann's corner shop next door, which, among other desirable items, sold 'singles' of Player No.6 cigarettes – and a non-safety match – for anyone who had 2p).

Christopher shouted out that Brady was 'a bloody eejit' and left it at that. It was enough. Kevin Brady had no fear of Christopher bloody Maguire, and was best mates with Harry McNulty, who would go into Bruce Lee killer-mode if anyone looked at him the wrong way. Brady turned immediately and faced the one who'd dared to call him 'eejit'. 'You talking to me?' he said quietly as a response, his hands visibly balling into fists. No-one knew he'd culled this from Martin Scorsese's X-rated *Taxi Driver* that Brady and McNulty had seen the year before at the Curzon, smoking cigarettes and throwing chewed-up chewing gum around. No-one except Brady, who was getting into Travis Bickle Mohican hair mode. Kevin Brady wasn't tall, or even heavy-set. He was just bullish in demeanour and had fists like bricks.

It wasn't a pretty sight. Christopher had no idea how bad it'd get, but ploughed on against his better sense, punch after vicious counter-punch and kick after savage counter-kick. The urging of his clan was in his blood and wouldn't let him go, even after getting mercilessly punched about the head. Get in close and whack away, as any Velociraptor worth his salt would advise. Thankfully, neither of them had claws, or rude horns sticking out of their heads either.

It wasn't long before the first intervention happened, from a couple walking past the gates. They looked in and shouted out: 'Stop! Stop this fighting now!' But neither of them were teachers, Brothers, or anyone connected with the school, so they could both 'go shite' as far as Christopher and Kevin were concerned. They were having too much 'fun' for that.

Unlike in the days of dinosaurs, the biting of the arms, or any other part of the anatomy, was outlawed, and looked upon as 'girly', a shame beholden to the one who tried it. Yet Christopher had done so, locked within his adversaries' grip, unsure how else to break away, Brady's arm against his face. He couldn't give a fig, he might have said, what anyone might think about his action, least of all his rival, who shouted 'Girl, don't bite!'

It wasn't Christopher's only dip into dishonest play. Brady had him on the ground and was walloping his face; Christopher knew he'd had his chips, but the urge had not quite died within him and he wouldn't say the word that Brady urged him to shout out. It was like a blessing, then, for Christopher, when an elderly gent -presumably another passer-by- broke in, having actually entered the schoolyard, and did his best to tell the both of them to stop. Brady felt the tug of authority dictate to him that now was time to say 'OK'. Yes, alas (for Kevin Brady), poor Kevin Brady listened. He hadn't reckoned on the principle of unfair play and looked immeasurably shocked when Christopher Maguire revived beneath him, took Brady's proffered hand and then delivered a kick so ruthless to his rival's shin it would bring tears to the eyes of an elephant. Brady fell in sudden biting pain and Christopher fell on him, smacking him with all his might and pushing off the 'oldie' who must have felt they'd just gone mad and what's this world coming to, and such like. Christopher now stood tall over the body of the fallen boxer Brady, basking in the delight of final victory. The old gent went away.

Accompanying the old gent was one more vestige of the innocence Christopher Maguire had been clinging on to since leaving St Bernard's Primary School. It soon detached from the 'oldie' and went off for a walk into the city by itself, never to be seen again, head down and tut-tutting all the way.

Chapter Thirteen: The End of the World
as We Know It, pt.1, month of May

Sixty-six million years ago, something happened to the dinosaurs, and very suddenly. They all died. All the big ones, anyway. It might have been something they'd eaten the night before, but likely not. In 1979, no-one really knew. Had it been some volcanoes getting out of hand round Siberia or India, or a massive Supernova, light-years away? Had the world's plankton all gone Bartleby and said: 'I would prefer not to... be eaten', or had the Sun thrown a tizzy fit and hurled a few million ionized flares Earth's way? Or... had it been a giant space rock happily roiling through eons of spacetime until its relax-time was rudely interrupted by an annoyingly large obstacle? (Us.) Professor Janek Heinkle didn't know either, but he kind of guessed – yes, even eminent scientists guess – it was the latter. He was right to think so, of course, but he wouldn't know that until the following year, with the discovery, thanks to *père et fils* Alvarez, of a layer of iridium stretched over the entire planet, iridium being the calling card of brainless extra-terrestrial matter. Heinkle had read Max Walker De Laubenfels, after all. De Laubenfels was not a palaeontologist but a spongiologist. As a token of respect, Heinkle had instigated wrapping his fossils in natural sponge not long after reading De Laubenfels's paper (and thereafter swotting up on his vast research into these marine wunderkinds). In one 1956 paper, De Laubenfels, Professor of Zoology at Oregon State College, had proposed that the mass extinction that ended the Cretaceous Period might have been triggered by an impact with an asteroid. Four years later he would be dead himself, and the world would have to wait for another twenty to learn the truth.

The six-mile-wide asteroid slammed into the Gulf of Mexico, before it was the 'Gulf of Mexico', travelling at more than fifteen miles per second. It was not messing about. It flew in at about a thirty-degree angle and became superheated with the friction of pummelling through the atmosphere to many times the heat of the surface of the Sun. When it hit the water next to the Yucatán Peninsula, the explosive force was more than a billion times that released in the atomic bombs dropped on Hiroshima and Nagasaki. It was not messing about. It obliterated everything for thousands of miles in all directions. It created tidal waves and threw up an enormous mass of material from the ground, which then circled the globe, cutting off the sunshine and turning the Earth into a cold, dark place for decades. The dinos who died immediately (incinerated, vaporized) were the lucky ones; the rest of the behemoths either choked to death slowly, starved to death slowly, froze to death slowly, or just gave up the ghost and lay down on the ash and cinders and said 'Goodnight, Vienna.'

And then there were no more dinosaurs. Not the ones we think of as dinosaurs, anyway. No more big T. Rexes, no more cute veg-munching Stegosauruses, no more giant but graceful Brachiosauruses, no more not-quite-sure-what-they-look-like Megalosaurs, and no more armoured-car-resembling Tricera-topses, either. Of course the Scelidossers had long gone, eons before, and in a much less dramatic manner. Fair play to them. They knew how to exit a scene. In 1979, though, no-one knew for sure how any of them had exited the scene. All that was sure was that life on Earth immediately after the Age of the Dinosaurs must have been pretty damn boring.

Well, now something similar was about to happen, sixty-six million years on. It wasn't an asteroid, like the 1937 'Hermes' that had inspired a zoologist with a penchant for sponges to think about the end of one world, or the United States space-station Skylab -even though the latter was just about to re-enter the atmosphere with the potential for city-wide destruction and the former was officially 'lost' in space and therefore potentially headed back our way sometime/anytime soon. No, what was about to hit wasn't even in space, and it wasn't flying anywhere, except around England in a bus, with a consistency somewhere between a rock and a sponge. 1979's Earth-smashing flying blunt instrument was actually just one human being. And that human being was a woman. And because most people only saw that human being from the waist up, indeed above the breast-area, it was really just a woman's face, filling out the screen. An enormous woman's face with an enormous head of hair, redolent of the contrail flames on an asteroid plummeting through the atmosphere. This face and hair was hurtling toward the unsuspecting and the innocent at an unstoppable speed into the living-rooms of the desperate and the helpless, and the living-rooms of those too indifferent to vote, resigned to a system that they knew was stacked against them. It was the face of Margaret Thatcher.

When it hit, that face – and that quintessential *shock* of hair – and the realization that the Conservatives had won and wrested back the power of government from Jim Callaghan's Labour, no-one died as a direct result. There was no massive explosion, no tidal waves racing around the globe at the speed of an airplane, or even the speed of a bus. No-one was vaporized. Nor were giant behemothic animals suddenly wiped out as a consequence, either immediately or in agonies that lasted months or longer. Giant, but not-so-giant, behemothic, but not-so-behemothic, animals existed now only on the plains of Africa and India or in the oceans, and none of them had even heard of Margaret Thatcher. But… in the little city of Belfast, in the North of Ireland, or as some would exclusively term it, Northern Ireland, and casually as 'Norn Iron', *something special did suddenly disappear.* For, from the early morning of Friday May 4th, 1979, year of our Lord, no-one in that city, or its environs, could be bothered hearing anymore about thon silly bloody yarn about the stupid fighting Irish dinosaurs. That particular story had suddenly lost its feet and was fading quicker than the remnant sparks in a fag butt dropped on the Ormeau Road on a rainy winter's day. Goodbye Duelling Dinos!

This was of course great news for Professor Heinkle. The election was just the ticket to draw away all the unwanted attention on him and the 'mission'. Indeed, he knew it wasn't likely to last much longer anyway. They'd been digging away at the same place for months now and largely to no avail. Homesickness and a tiredness borne of too great a human interaction (often the way with those whose only joy is digging up the relics of the past) had taken a certain toll upon the 65-year-old man. Proper scientific analysis of the fossils would take months, years even. If he oversaw the start of that, he could then pronounce his duties over soon enough, and get himself back to his beloved country, back to Heidelberg… no, he'd want to spend his time in München. *Oh, in München zu sein!* And, he appended… *'Weit weg von Tweedy!'* [Far from you know who.]

The Editor at the *News Letter* was pretty happy, too. Thatcher's win would erase all trace of the fiasco that had been his nephew's first foray into the field of investigative journalism. Coverage of *Election '79* had had a balming effect for days now on the poor man's soul. The *Iron* Lady's eventual victory he described in an Editorial as a *'godsend'* which would *'change the political climate'*. The Editor had no way of picking up on the eerie resonance those phrases might have with the – as yet unknown – *iron*-sulfide-rich asteroid *sent from the heavens* sixty-six million years ago which would radically *change the climate of planet Earth!* He wouldn't have cared less anyway. News was news and news was money.

Even kids forgot about the dinosaurs, and about that German Prof they'd seen on telly on Monday night, although you wouldn't have thought so earlier in the week. 'What an eejit!' was a common exclamation on the morning after the broadcast, a televisual event which had done nothing whatsoever to quieten down the wags and the jokers around town. Indeed, on Tuesday morning, there were those not only still mimicking battles of the prehistoric behemoths, but those acting out the histrionics they'd witnessed on the screen just the evening previous, with the added spice that the bloke was a 'stupid Kraut' to boot, and a 'specky' one at that. In primary schools and the like, kids at lunchtime would try their best to capture what they'd seen, delighted to get the chance to do a German accent, with the likes of: 'It vud be like yer Vinston Churchill, ya?, punching Alexander ze Great on ze fuckin' neb and… the two 'o them beatin' the shite outta each other on ze feckin' ground!' Kids would collapse at this and then another one would try. There was mileage in the old yarn yet. And yet (to use another 'yet') just three days later, mention of a dinosaur or a 'Kraut' or a 'Jerrie' wasn't worth tuppence anymore. Each area of Belfast had a brand-new horde of stories about who'd won what and what had happened at the polling stations and 'What did you do with the free time?' -as the polling stations were often borrowed schools. In other words, daily life acquired a new football to kick about, and even if it wasn't quite as exotic as prehistoric dinosaurs or foreign blokes with funny accents, *it was what it was!* The new topic, to be twisted in and out of shape and dragged around the houses and beyond by all and sundry, *wuz here*, as inescapable as the latest expletive-loaded graffiti. Sure, politics was bread and butter in ole 'Norn Iron' and everyone wanted a bite of that.

Christopher also learned to live without the dinos, taken up with all the latest chat about what Thatcher's victory might mean for the Troubles, and what might come from the 'RA now – they'd already dispatched her friend Airey Neave just over a month before. The Iron – suphide-rich – Lady had already been

159

talking up the return of the death penalty. It was retribution she wanted, everyone knew. This was now the chat at Barrack Street, when, that is, they weren't being drilled into the ground by their teachers in matters academic. Christopher was 'sweating bricks' about his chances of passing mathematics. He wasn't looking forward to the *viva voce* in Irish, either, not having nailed the prefixes – the 'an', 'dea', 'dearg', the 'so' and the 'ro' and the damn aspiration they'd wreak on the subsequent word. Considering all the study he had to do, he thought anything not related 'could go shite'. The news of the world and, sadly, the news of the one which had existed so far in the past, where fantastic beasts had roamed gleefully about, never having to study anything, could go shite, too.

What he'd learnt that day in Glengormley Library stayed with him, about the need to concentrate and focus and compose with all brain cells switched on. He was making progress in leaps and bounds and bounds and leaps. The experience also helped beyond the study stuff, though, as he discovered, on those rare occasions when a gap in time might open… Pen trials, he called them; little jottings in his notebook, where there was space…

For years, he'd been handy with a different kind of pen and a different kind of notepad, executing illustrations of the weird and wonderful that seemed to wander in and out of his mind from time to time. In class-time, doing such in his study notebook would attract a regular shouted rebuke from McCaughey, the bearded leather-jacketed Maths teacher: 'Stop doodling, Maguire!' He had, eventually, but kept at it within the confines of his home, using multi-coloured felt-tip pens on fancy Basildon Bond letter-writing paper drawing out exotic scenes of starships, aliens, or abstract shapes and juxtapositions. Or he'd reinvent the five-pound note, reproducing the frame and Lizzy's portrait, but then excavating the interior until it looked like a complex of mysterious caves, with waterfalls and jagged rocks and bats flitting here and there about. He also did a series of black-ink fine-pen cartoons for no-one's entertainment but himself, as when he created the family of the portly 'Grots', who stood around looking portly, void of thought, and yet vaguely menacing, eyes glazed in front of their ink-drawn telly. But somehow this was not enough, or not quite the only thing he felt inclined to state. Words, then, filled a gap.

The pen trials with words could take aim at anything that happened or anything that conspicuously did not. It started as a diary, which merged into a journal, just as words merged fluidly into little doodles on either side. Margins were an invitation, all the blank space staring out at him. The doodles often made more sense than any words or phrases he threw down. It wasn't easy to capture much with a palette of twenty-six immoveable symbols. Reading helped. Initially, Christopher had never been a keen one for the books. The wall he had to crawl over just to get the kernel of the tale had always proved too high for him, until a few short years previous, when he'd found the joy of 'film tie-ins', books created as a textual replica of whatever new film was out. Films he couldn't see because they were rated 'X' or even 'AA'. *The French Connection II. Taxi Driver. Shaft.* His brother Jim had asked the Da if he'd allow Christopher to read a book with swearwords in it, and the Da had assented. So, Christopher, at the tender age of thirteen, could see the likes of Popeye Doyle or Harry Callahan blow people away with Magnum 347s, shout 'Fuck', and 'Cunt', and witness wanton bloodshed on the page. It was great.

Then there was Lorca. Gabriel Garcia Lorca. Christopher's understanding of Spanish was limited, enough for the 'O'-Levels for sure, but hardly native, so when his eyes pored over the opening pages of his brother's copy of *Romancero Gitano*, the unknowns outweighed the knowns. That, however, only added to the thrill. What precisely did it mean that the moon ('luna') had come to the forge ('fragua') with her 'polisón de nardos'? The latter phrase Christopher just couldn't get: he was like the boy in the next line simply watching: 'El niño la mira mira./ El nino la está mirando.' He was watching the words dance line by line, in grace, in mystery. What did 'Verde que te quiero verde' mean? 'Green I love you green' just didn't hit it; made no sense, was ugly. English could be ugly. The phrase could only be in 'Castellano': that double 'l' that made the word a word beyond the words he knew. And *words beyond* the words he knew sounded suspiciously like *worlds beyond* the worlds he knew... Attracting him...

Between the gunplay and the mystery, books were doing something to his head. Jotting down his random thoughts in words became his way to add dimension to diurnal life.

Of course, there were professionals for this kind of thing. The writing, that is. A whole raft of poets for starters, as announced – just in case you didn't know – in the Blackstaff Press's just-hot-off-the-press *Poets from the North of Ireland.* Mr Heaney wasn't the only one holding a pen and digging into the metaphorical earth... Mr Hewitt had been doing it long before him, and Mr MacNeice (défunt) along with him. And Longley, Mahon, Montague, Simmons and Fiacc *et cetera*, were fairly jostling for attention in the crowded streets of people's minds. The rising stars of Messrs Carson and Muldoon had yet to twinkle in the eye of the adolescent Christopher, but once the 'O's were over, you could never tell where he'd wander next.

Some writers, though, were truly professional in the sense of earning money from the Word. There were those at the top of their game, interviewing politicians, old and new, the new names everyone had to talk to now, and the ones who'd just held on by their dirty fingernails in the last election. Some writerly types were not so lucky, though. One wee man had been demoted from the heady heights of top-flight journalism and was now occupying a lonely, isolated seat in the backrooms, in charge of that most miserable of jobs, the one which dealt with Birth, Death & Marriage Notices.

This was typical:

'Good morning, Notices.'

'Morning. I'd like to place a Notice for a recently deceased family member.'

'Certainly. May I take your name first, Madam?'

'Of course. I'm Muriel Doakes… you want my address?'

'Well, we can have it in a moment. Would you like to read me the Notice first? Or if you give me the details I can suggest a wording for you.'

'It's OK, I've written it out. It reads like this: "Doakes, Joseph. Much-loved husband of Muriel, died May 12, 1979, in her loving arms. [sound of quiet sobs] Always remembered by his sons Anthony and Peter and his loving wife Muriel. Funeral on… [sobs, choking up…]

Etcetera…

This was not typical:

'Good morning, Notices.'

'Morning to ye, Mucker. I wanna place a wee Notice, like.'

'Certainly, Sir. Birth, Deaths or Marriages? May I take your name first?'

'Oh aye. Nay problem. It's Dinny.'

[pausing] 'Dinny? Dinny What?'

'Dinny… Armstrong.'

'OK, thank you. Dinny…. Armstrong… And, would you like to give me your Notice… Or if you just give me the details, I can suggest the best wording for you…?'

'That's alright, Mucker… here: the bloke who died is Ivanovich Stoki.'

[another pause] 'Ivanovits… Stoki? Could you spell that please?'

'Sorry. It's Russian. Nat sure o' the spelling, like.'

'You don't have the spelling?'

[sound of something like sobbing] 'No… I only knew him a bit.'

[pause] 'OK… Well, how about…. well….. [another pause] …Address?'

'Oh aye… [similar sound, with pause] … just off the Woodvale.'

'I beg your pardon, Sir. You mean the Woodvale Road?'

'Oh aye. Mucker.'

[considerable pause] 'Address, with numbers?'

'[sounds of something like sobbing, but probably not] … Enfield Drive…[more unintelligible sounds]… number fourteen…'

'Fourteen Enfield Drive, Woodvale?' [considerable pause] That's my address! Are you having me on? *Who is this?*'

[sound of what might have been sobbing now transformed into full-blown laughter, all-too familiar to the man behind the desk at Notices, who then exclaimed]

'Ya ballacks ye! That Davy Wilson? You're a bloody glype!'

'That's no way to talk to a customer!'

'See the stew I'm in now because of you, ya gaunch!'

Before Ivan Stacks had slammed the phone down, Davy (also known as 'Abe') threw himself at the mercy of the court:

'Only having ye on! C'mon, you have to see the funny side of it! …*And…*'

'Yes, ya ballacks?'

'…I got some new hot news about the dino story…'

'You what? The dino story? Are you kidding me? That's ancient history!'

'I like that! Ha!' At this even Ivan could allow his tormentor friend a bit of slack. 'Ancient? It's actually *prehistoric*, don't ya know?' [exploding in chortles]

'OK, OK, get on with it…' [allowing himself the tiniest bit of a sympathetic giggle]

'Well, it's got the makings of a scandal, I can tell ye that, Ivan, but better than spilling the beans here… never like these fucking things anyway… telephones? Who fucking invented them, some cunt I can tell ye! Anyway, how about we meet for a wee jar?'

And there it was. Despite the knock-out punch from Asteroid Thatcher, despite the devastation that had seemingly wiped out all trace of that tale of Northern Irish dinos beating the bejeepers out of each other, *something had survived*. Davy/Abe had survived, and with his story, he hoped this might just be the way to have their friendship survive, too. Ivan was always good for a tap, after all.

It worked. Ivan Stacks, cursing him still, found himself slowly but surely inveigled once again into the world of possible intrigue and, you never know, a doorway back into the spotlight. Talking of which -being in the spotlight, that is-, as soon as he had replaced the receiver, Ivan couldn't help noticing that everyone around him in the office seemed to be looking at him. And they were just sitting there, as though temporarily frozen. Shock, and not a little disdain, was written into every face. Not knowing what else to do, Ivan smiled, sheepishly, and then, despite his best efforts, 'went up a redner', as it is rendered in the less than sophisticated patois of some parts of Belfast and its environs.

(Any resemblance he might have had to a giant speeding asteroid about to slam into Mother Earth was purely coincidental.)

Chapter Fourteen: The End of the World as We Know It, pt.2, Thursday, May 17

Much to the chagrin of Abe, the 'wee jar' would be much 'wee-er' than Abe would have liked, Ivan insisting they meet first just for a liquid lunch, to 'strike when the iron's hot and all that'. He'd be lucky to get two pints over the one he'd have to buy just for appearances, but Ivan was a man possessed and couldn't wait to get the 'griff'. So just two days post-telecommunication they sat down for a tipple or two at The Morning Star, just up Pottinger's Entry, off Ann Street in the centre of Belfast. It was an old haunt of Ivan's and he couldn't help making that clear, with 'Look at the sheen on that wood, now, would ye?' and 'Best ham sandwiches in Belfast!' Abe, who was not familiar with this establishment was all ears, and then all lips and tongue when tackling his frothing pint of radiant Tuborg Gold. 'I like this,' he said, smiling from ear to ear. 'I like this.'

Ivan said 'I like this', too, just before he tucked into his pint of Guinness. He *savoured* the foam and the *torrent of dark liquid* that ran beneath it, over his tastebuds and down his *cavernous* throat. That, at least, was how he might have worded the experience. Ivan had recently gotten into the habit of noticing words and how things in the world were described; it was either an occupational hazard for a hard newspaperman like himself, or a measure of how much he yearned to be back at a proper desk typing away about stories that were happening. He wouldn't admit it to Abe, certainly not yet anyway, but the Notices job was doing him in, sucking out the marrow from his writerly bones, and dancing on whatever brain cells he might have left. So, however it happened, he recently found himself falling into the habit of *writing in his mind*, as he looked around him. The Morning Star had plenty for him to write about. Yet, Abe was going on about his job at Gilpin's [the furniture store], complaining about his boss and all the snotty customers who would come in just to 'give me feckin' grief'. He had to break in. 'Aye, Davy, got it, but you know...' at which Abe/Davy momentarily stopped, expecting, perhaps, a clarification question or something to confirm that Abe was in the right and the boss was 'a right cunt'. 'Aye, I hear what you're saying, but would you look at this place? It's a wee palace!' Davy/Abe, not quite sure if they'd return to his tale of woe felt the need to indulge, sympathetically looking round him and smiling to a tee. 'A bit of alright that, aye, the way the bar curves... bit like your Ma's arse!' Ivan replied in his greatest mock-solemn voice: 'No jokes about the Mother!' which Abe heartily echoed, and the two of them clinked glasses and supped. Around them – as one wee man who yearned for greater things might put it, if he could put it at all – the beautiful ship-like dark polished wood bar shone, the nineteenth-century wooden chairs graced with green leather seats shone, the bronze and silver taps from which a range of draft beers would come frothing out shone, and the mirrors advertising Guinness, Tuborg and McConnell's 'Old Irish Whisky, Belfast' *shone*. Even the wee rings of beer on their tabletop *shone*, a bit anyway, in the late morning Morning Star light.

Then Ivan caught himself on. 'So, ya ballacks, what's this bloody scandal you're selling me? And remember, once bitten twice shy, I didn't come up the Lagan in a bubble, and if you're pulling my leg, I'll have yer guts for effing garters!' At this display of linguistic invention, Abe raised his glass and so did Ivan and they clinked and drank again. 'Well,' said Abe, once he'd savoured his sup, and assuming a face more designed for business than pleasure, 'it's like this...' And at this, he did a mock double take and announced that his pint was almost finished and that he 'probably' needed a refill 'to get through the telling', and, 'Lord God, that fish 'n chips over there looks like the job!' Ivan took the hint and was up getting another round and a bit of 'grub'.

When all was said and done, bar-wise anyway, and Abe had trumpeted the joys of fried potato soaked in Sarson's vinegar, liberally speckled with local sea-salt (no less), Ivan, through a mouthful of bread-soaked stew himself, said: 'Shoot!' (even if it sounded more like 'Hoot!') So, Abe did: he shot -or maybe even hooted. 'Aye, well, I've been hearing again from my sources.' 'The gal who knows the bloke, or the bloke who knows the gal who works with yer other man?' fired off crackshot Ivan, quick as you like. Abe found that confusing, until he realized he was getting 'the piss taken out of him'. 'Yes, yes, I know… but this is from the horse's mouth, wait'il I tell ya.' Ivan was smiling, having decided he would happily give his friend enough rope to hang himself.

'Well, apparently there's this bloke who found the fossils in the first place and he's pretty ticked off that no-one's giving him the credit!' Ivan's eyes narrowed, metaphorically anyway, sign enough for Abe to extrapolate without interruption. 'The very same wee girl who blabbed about the fossils in the first place, she and her mate…' 'Oh aye, the nig-nog, met him…' said a not very enlightened Ivan, 'aye…?' 'Aye, well, they overheard this barney the two professors were having up at Queen's, and one was stark raving mad about the other not letting on about that.' Abe let that hang there, like a moment stuffed with drama and not a little confusion.

Ivan could see potential in all this. His eyes had widened, as they had before, but this sounded like the real thing, and it had happened only days ago, not millions of years in the distant past. That was encouraging. He asked for clarification; Abe gave it: 'The bloke who found the dinos is getting pissed upon! And I think it's…' 'Yes?' asked Ivan, starting to ignore The Morning Star in all its glory. 'Yes?' he asked exasperatedly. 'Yes?' Abe: 'A wee bag o' Tayto'd go down rightly right now. Here. Let me see if I can get us two bags…' Abe, taking excessively long to rifle through his various pockets, had Ivan where he wanted him, noticing that Ivan's impatience had gotten the better of him and was propelling him up to the barman to get the 'damn crisps'. Abe pounced, so to speak, shouting up to his now vertical friend: 'And a wee McConnell's, Ive, if ye don't mind!' Ivan needed Abe's deft nod toward the mirror ad to make it clear he meant the local whiskey and then barked out the order double-quick. 'Make it two, while yer at it, Pat,' said Ivan/Ive to his portly barman acquaintance. He was, as he entertainingly fashioned it himself as he stood at the bar waiting for his order, 'in thrall to the thrill of the thrunt'. (© Ivan Stacks, wordsmith, '79.)

'You were saying?' he asked half-coyly upon his return to their table, satisfied he had his man, and that, yes, now he would get the griff, all that he needed to get back to the glitzy world of investigative journalism, digging better and deeper than any bloody German dino-hunter ever could.

Less than an hour later, both reluctantly protesting the late hour that it was, nigh on quarter to one at that, Ivan and Abe supped their last and ambled out into Pottinger's Entry, and down to High Street. They would part at Castle Place, so they had decided, as Ivan would have to return to the *News Letter* in Donegall Street, and Abe to his own destination, 'a bloody paint warehouse in Brunswick Street'. The chat had turned from things dinosaurian to things feminine, and to their better halves, Abe lamenting his for her endless nagging and 'Ive', as he was sometimes abbreviated, lamenting his for her endless *inexistence*. 'Dinny worry, Ive. The right bint'll come along soon enough.' 'Dinny indeed! Dinny effin' Armstrong!' exclaimed Ivan in a moment of total recall – of a telephone conversation best left forgotten. 'Aye, Dinny Armstrong, that's me!' threw out Abe, along with his right arm, in a fitting power gesture. As they paced up High Street, past Dolcis, the shoe store, H. Samuel, Smiths the Chemists, then Wallis, the British Home Stores, and... another Dolcis, Ivan then quizzed Abe on the Russian angle, asking where he'd thought that up.

'Ah, well, ye see, there's this wee man I know... and...' said Abe teasingly, to Ivan's complementary 'Oh aye?' 'Aye, well he's got a Belfast accent you could hammer nails with, but me and him were talking, and he turns round to me and tells me he's actually fecking Russian!' 'Get away!' said a suitably impressed Ivan. 'Aye,' continued Abe, 'well, his Grandda was, like, and well, once he tells me that here's me looking at his gob [gesturing that as he spoke], and whaddya know?' Ivan wondered what it could be: 'Made in Russia stencilled on his lip?' Abe laughed: '*As good as* – big fecking Josef Stalin moustache over it, don't you know! Funny how I hadn't noticed it before! Bushy feckin' eyebrows to boot!' 'Funny that alright!' said his laughing friend, who, somewhere at the back of his mind was wondering what a silly conversation this was... and how he'd always have silly conversations with Abe. *Funny that!*

Now they'd gotten to the junction, it was time to say 'Ta ta', but Ivan's curiosity was getting the better of him; with all his 'sources' and his stories he could never know just what pies Abe had his finger in at any one time. And the Russian angle had a certain allure to it – was it his journalistic instincts telling him so? A Russian in Belfast – another exotic avenue to pursue? So, when Abe let it out that he might bump into this fella at the place he was going to now, for some Gilpins' business thing, Ivan glanced at his watch and asked if he could tag along. Abe looked surprised: 'Well, I'm not sure...' They were standing outside Van Allan's fashion store, the traffic going between Royal Avenue and Donegall Square light, just a pair of single-decker Citybuses moving northward. The cold in the air, not much noticed until now, was suddenly enhanced by the beginning of the lightest of drizzles. Ivan couldn't catch why Abe wasn't sure and his face

said so. Abe: 'Well, you see, I think he's doing the double, like.'
'It's OK, Abe, I'm not in the DHSS!' 'Right enough,' said a
placated Abe, 'and don't tell him you're a reporter either!' Ivan
laughed but thought he'd heard enough to convince him not to
go now...

Just as he was about to say so, however, Abe suddenly
assumed his best shifty-looking-character mode, looking around
about as though to check no-one was listening: 'Actually,' he said,
'we're working on a wee project...' 'Abraham Lincoln,' exclaimed
Ivan in exclamatory fashion, 'you're always working on some
fecking project!' At this, the two of them chortled heartily, until
Abe precipitously resumed his shifty-character routine and said
in his best secret agent tones: ''Nuff said. Nudge, nudge, wink,
wink and all that.' It should have been 'enuff' to convince Ivan
to say 'Ta, ta, see ya next time', but curiosity's a funny thing and
before you could say 'Grigor Ivanovich' (the Russian bloke's
'secret' Russian name) or 'Gregory Ivans' (the name he went by)
the two friends were off striding down Donegall Place together,
in the general direction of the paint warehouse on Brunswick
Street. 'Just up th'road', as Abe put it so delicately. 'Go on then,'
said Ivan, 'sure, never met a world leader before.'

The drizzle continued to fall, but they hardly noticed it and
cared even less. They didn't carry umbrellas, and if you looked
at any of the shoppers and pedestrians in Donegall Place, up the
length of which they were now walking, City Hall-ward, nor did
anyone else. It was a societal thing. Everyone had an umbrella,
but no-one used them very often. The two friends did up their
collars, and that was plenty.

After passing through the security barrier checkpoint, the
two ambled over to where the buses assembled and then walked
down the right-side of the City Hall. Turning right, after crossing
over the busy street, into Howard Street, Abe was still thinking
of his stomach: 'If you want *the real Russian experience*, mind, we

could always drop into the Skandia and tuck into the best Pavlova in Belfast…' 'Oh aye, well if you're talking that, I'll raise ye a wee place called The Crown just beyond Brunswick Street, and they do the finest pint of Irish in Belfast, I can tell ye that!' Abe mock chortled at that one, with a wee raise of the eyebrow, duly noted by Ivan. Was it the mention of 'Irish'? he wondered.

The drizzle had dried up by the time they entered Brunswick Street. Now that he was soberer, Ivan was thinking that maybe he had come here against his better judgement. He knew he could take an extended lunchbreak today, but this was 'ripping the hole out of it', as he might have phrased it. What was he thinking by wanting to meet this Russian bloke? Was it important? Hardly! But, sure, he was here, and he could snook off soon enough anyway. His mad thoughts about nudging Abe into a wee illicit daytime crawl or just having a quick one in The Crown by himself, were dissipating fast. Sure, they both had to work! And yet, his journalistic instincts were resisting the sobriety of rational thought, as they had in regard to the dino story. That and… to be perfectly honest… Ivan Stacks had no desire to fly back to his desk and take phone calls from grief-wracked souls! ('Grief-wracked!' -I like that, said Ivan to himself.)

A blue van drove past them and half-parked down the street just as they were walking toward what Abe had said was their destination, the unprepossessing (in name and in appearance) Brolac Paint Warehouse on the right side of the street. Both Abe and Ivan thought it strange that the van had stopped so abruptly, but they were too much in the grasp of a momentum propelling them toward their destination to think too much about it. When the occupants of the van got out and put something down on the street and then got back into their van, Abe turned to Ivan and said: 'Those fellas were a bit young, don't ya think?' 'I do, aye,' replied Ivan, just as said van then suddenly sped off down the street. They looked at that, and then at the pile of what looked like paint-tins on the pavement, still walking ever closer to the warehouse front itself. Then Ivan stopped. And, as he stopped, he put a hand out to stop Abe walking, too, shouting: 'Stop! Stop, Davy, stop!' It was a voice seared with panic: Ivan, ever the vigilant, felt something wasn't right. They froze, watched as the door of Brolac Paints opened and out walked a man. He was smiling ear to ear, and between ear to ear was the biggest moustache Ivan had ever seen. His eyebrows were bushy, too. God, he was Josef Stalin's younger brother if he was anyone. He was also looking straight at the now motionless Abe (and companion) and had just opened his mouth to shout a cheerful: 'Ah, Davvy!' ('Davvy?' thought Ivan) when, abruptly, madly, fiercely, violently, suddenly, a rude bang madly flashed and all three men fell down.

And paint-tins were flying through the air.

Chapter Fifteen: The End of the World as We Know It, pt.3, May 17-18

Blackness, shock, confusion. Alarm bells, sirens, screaming. Smell of smoke and chemicals. Pain. There were no verbs in Ivan's thoughts for the first few moments after the blast. Not much comprehension either. Until some impulse pulsed and the need to find out what the fuck had hit them kicked in (Ivan's instinctual phrasing). The opening of his eyes did not go well, as acrid smoke was everywhere and gravitated rightly to his delicate sight organs like moths to a flame. The ears were working, though, and beyond the big sounds, like the obnoxious mad ringing of the alarm bells and the ghoul-like wail of steadily strengthening sirens, he could make out the less imposing sound of moans in his immediate vicinity. Abe, it had to be, and what was Abe moaning exactly? Ivan concentrated, trying to make out in which direction he should reach his hand out in the chaos that was now, hearing: 'Fuckin' cunts… fuckin' Fenian cunts!' That was plenty for him to throw his arm out left-wise, shouting, if weakly: 'Davy… Davy…' Ivan's hand caught Davy in the face and this made Davy moan again, with this time: 'Fuckin' cunt… trying to break my fuckin' nose?' But Ivan knew he hadn't hit with much force really, and hearing Abe say anything reassured him he was alright. Then, with 'Fuck this smoke!', Ivan opened up the peepers full and tholed the pain of all those dirty fumes, fighting back against his better reason that he'd see just what was bloody what. He could just make out Abe lying right beside him, his torso moving slowly, arms not in play at all, moaning still, eyes closed, and something on his face that looked like dark satin, vaguely glistening, his moustache and beard moist. This produced another shock within Ivan's already shocked mind and his head went back the three inches it had raised itself off the tarmac and he closed his eyes and let the black flow over him, and into him and under him if it bloody wanted to... He couldn't give two fucks.

And then he could, because he'd started coughing. This became convulsive soon and electrified his own torso into a paroxysmal fit. It was bad, but even worse was noticing that Abe was not coughing, not even slightly. And then the sirens, which had been like a kind of BGM you try to ignore, began to roar and roar and roar...

Shouts and screams. And whistles. Thudding on the ground. Faces, hands, sounds of metal sliding over metal, voices, strident, some directed his way, most not, and then a sensation of being held, lifted, something horrible and rubber slapped upon his face. Voices. Screams. Echoes of these sounds in close proximity, the mad alarm bells ringing all the while. Within minutes, when minutes felt like an eternity, somehow now the two of them, Ivan knew this much, were side-by-side, but this time not upon the tarmac on Brunswick Street, but deep within the sterile plastic metal glass interior of an ambulance, and medics were working, working, working, not so much on him, but on his fellow right beside him. Banging on his chest and... the last thing Ivan saw before his consciousness gave out was the insertion of a tube down Davy Wilson's throat...

Inside the RVH, which he knew was the RVH because a kindly nurse, looking more like something out of a Catholic convent, had spoken the first words to Ivan since being unloaded from the wailing vehicle: 'You're in the Royal Victoria Hospital now, dear, and we'll take care of you.' He read her name tag, making out 'MAGUIRE' before slipping back to black. Slipping back then to wakefulness, how many moments/minutes later he had no idea, Ivan Stacks was feeling horrid, much abused and angry, enough to want to complain, or at least say something to fight back against the madness he was going through, speeding down a corridor flat upon his back, wondering whose idea it was to place the windows up above, the clashing sunlight pouring down like acid rain into his febrile, teared-up eyes. What sort of torture were they subjecting him to? And who were all these nuns? And who or what was doing all that screaming? And where was Abe? Where the Russian? The last query forced itself into such manic importance that Ivan found himself now vocalizing just that: 'Where's the Russian? Where's the Russian bloke?' Staff Nurse Maguire returned at this and told him, in the same kind tone she'd used before: 'Dear, are you alright? What Russian do you mean? There was no Russian at the scene.' Ivan, contemplating what she had just said, blurted out: 'That rhymes!' And then: 'The Russian... big moustache... looks like Stalin's bro...' And then the effort he'd expended on this interchange took its toll and knocked him out again.

Injections. A light pen to his eye. The cutting off of clothes. Fear. Disquiet. And yet, something like relief to be in safe hands, among the nuns, in their white finery, the smell of Dettol permeating all. 'Where's Abe?' he asked as slowly once again the wakefulness receded... 'And what about the Stalin bloke?' This set off a series of images within his dimming mind, leading him to end with: '...the Revolution, comrades, s'just begun... line 'em all up against the wall, and.... shoot them feckin' Taigs...' Out.

. . .

Ivan would be ok. He'd been out a solid four or five hours, and, he was told, would be up and about 'in no time'. They weren't so informative about his friend Abe, and no-one wanted to indulge him much about the Russian anymore. He'd been visited by Staff Nurse Maguire again, and by the red-tunicked white-aproned Sister O'Hanlon – the inescapably 'Taig' names amplifying the sense that he was indeed in a convent –, who'd lectured him on the importance of taking all the pills he'd been given and having 'a positive mind-set and that'll get you through'. Ivan wondered what he'd need that for if all it was was getting back on his feet, but no-one seemed about to clarify that. Nor would they say much on the state of his friend, except to say he was being taken care of. 'He's in Mr Rutherford's hands and you couldn't get better, safer hands anywhere.' Ivan didn't know Mr Rutherford, but, he reflected, with a fancy name like that he couldn't be half bad. But why did Abe need someone like that? That's what he wanted to know. And as he lay there, Ivan felt a chill, a chill that had started the first time he'd noticed Abe unmoving and uncoughing right beside him on the street. He didn't want to dwell on it. 'A positive mind-set' that's what he'd been told to adopt.

'Nurse,' asked Ivan an hour or so later, catching Nurse Maguire as she passed through on her tour through the ward he'd been put in, '… a wee quick question… is he a doctor?' 'Who?' she responded. 'This "Rutherford" bloke…' 'Of course! He's the best we have.' 'So,' asked Ivan, 'why is he called just Mister, then?' Staff Nurse Maguire smiled an unexpectedly wide and warm smile at that, and replied, 'Oh, "Mister" is reserved only for the highest surgeons. Not 'Doctor'. Now Ivan had her: 'Then he's in a pretty bad way, right? My friend, that is.' Nurse Maguire smiled again, politely refuting that implication and made her way past him, onto the next patient, feeling all the stress of the day coalesce behind her facial mask of goodwill and cheeriness.

Ivan had other chats. The police came in the evening, after the first ritual of communal dinner: Ivan was in a ward with about twenty others. He hadn't touched the custard, and only eaten anything because a nurse called 'Carson' had nagged him. At that time, Ivan had felt he had material there for a joke to share with Abe about nagging women; certainly he'd share his feeling that with a good Prod name like 'Carson' she could hardly be a nun, but thinking about Abe then put him in a funk, and not the kind Earth, Wind & Fire were good at. It was two RUC officers who had come to see him, and they closed the round-the-bed curtains behind them so they could have privacy. If they wanted to ask questions, Ivan did so even more. They had to bat a few before it was their innings. To cut a long Q & A short, they couldn't tell him anything about his friend, just about what had happened earlier that day. 'Aye, the wee bastards got clean away and dumped the van round Divis. Just outta their nappies, but the 'RA'll have them doing bomb runs for them and then throw them a few sweeties. Feckin' sick, pardon the French.' To elaborate, Officer McAllister, with the very thick glasses, continued: 'I heard you're a *News Letter* reporter yourself, so you'll know the history. The one the IRA let off outside your offices back in '72, killing and maiming innocent people going about their daily life, was the reason we got the Ring of Steel in the first place. Now, wee shites like today's boyos, or much worse, their Das and Uncles, attack easy targets *outside* the security barriers and… pooof!' He gestured an explosion with the fingers of his right hand. They were beefy fingers, Ivan noted. 'Sorry you and your friend were caught up in it. They're the… scum of the earth.' Ivan had been sixteen when the Donegall Street bombing had happened. His Da, who worked in the *News Letter*, had been there that day, and when he'd come home later that evening, he was exhausted and looked like he'd seen hell. He said the word 'carnage', and Ivan had never heard that word before.

Now that it was Ivan's turn to open his beak [pronounced 'bae-ek' in true Belfast fashion], he told them about the Russian. 'Big bloke he was… came out the door before the bomb went off… big moustache… shouted out "Davvy!" to my friend Davy, then a big flash and we were all on our backs. 'Aye,' said Officer

Hamilton, according to his nameplate, 'we heard about that… but… aye… we're still looking into that one. Thank you very much, Mr Stacks.' The two officers seemed to want to cut the interview short right there and then, but Ivan wasn't having it. 'There was a bloke there, I tell you.' 'Oh,' countered Officer McAllister, 'I'm sure you believe it, but the shock and trauma of something like this can do things to a person…' Hamilton added: 'There was no sign of another casualty in the place you mention, and no-one identifying as Russian there has come forward at this time.' 'I'm not mad, you know!' shouted Ivan suddenly. 'I saw him with my own two eyes, and Abe was the one who told me about him. That's why I was going there in the first place! Because he's called Ivan, too, and he has this big moustache…' Hamilton: 'You went there because he's called Ivan, too? And he's a wee moustache… OK, Sir, we'll check that.' 'Big one!' half-shouted Ivan, 'big bloody moustache! Looked like Josef feckin' Stalin, I tell ye!' 'Aye, aye,' said McAllister then, 'we're looking into that and we'll get back to you when we hear anything…' They were noticeably retreating now and opening up the curtains. Ivan didn't know what to say. He even started to wonder if he'd dreamed the whole thing up, or that the drink had played a part. Instead of returning their farewell greeting he just laid his head back on the pillow and stared into the middle distance. The effort of the whole experience soon knocked him out.

. . .

Ivan dreamt he was in Hell. It was a pretty nice hell, mind. It was a kind of cave, dark and a bit ominous and lit only by primitive burning oil rags wrapped around the ends of wooden sticks protruding from the walls. There was a smell of sulphur. There were demons there. But the demons were ambling through a corridor, and they were all friendly and even courteous, in the way people can be in country areas, doffing their hats, as they passed him, nodding their heads (and some of their heads were quite hideous, but in a pitiful sort of way), the occasional 'Good afternoon' thrown out. Ivan – dream Ivan – wasn't sure precisely where he was headed but he did know or feel he had to get there pretty damn quick. He knew there were hordes of people (or demons) waiting for him to arrive, maybe for him to entertain them, or even teach them. He didn't know what or why. He carried a heavy bag in his right hand and found himself walking faster and faster down through the mysterious shadow-filled cavernous and winding natural corridor, past all the not-so scary horned and scaly figures who seemed to dwell there. By the time he got to his destination he was late. They were all looking at him, little demon children sitting at little demon desks tapping the wooden desktops with little demon fingernails. A feeling of dread began to descend upon him – not the dread of being among demons, but the dread of not knowing what the hell he was supposed to do. This was the 'hell' in 'what the hell', in Hell. He knew there was only one thing to do: open the bag and start the lesson. Yet, when he reached in and grabbed at the contents of said bag, he pulled out not papers or books or files or even pens and paper, but a gun. It was a ray-gun, too, a laser gun, all chrome, with tiny blinking multi-coloured lights along the side, and as he looked up, over the heads of the children he could see what it was for. The Imperial Commander of the Soviet Union of Disaffected States, Josef Stalin, in full battledress and medals, a giant handlebar moustache and a shock of hair that would make the Bride of Frankenstein jealous, was standing there ten-foot-tall, his eyes burning like anthracite. This figure then opened his mouth/gob/beak (bae-ek!) and out came the most terrible sound Ivan had ever heard, delivered in a deep register that shook the walls and the desks: 'DAVVY!' Dream Ivan knew what he had to do: he raised the ray-gun laser thingy and aimed it right at the tyrant's enormous head, then pulled the trigger with all his might and concentration... KAPOW! Out shot a blast of blue light and all the demon kids screamed. The Imperial Commander of the Soviet Union of Disaffected States, Josef Stalin, gesticulating wildly, desperately, and uttering curses in visible Cyrillic script which flew from his spitting gob, was glowing and shimmering and shining and.... yes.... evaporating!

And then he was gone.

. . .

When Ivan woke in the wee hours of the morning in the dark ward, he felt like he was in Hell again. A hospital ward at night can be a scary place, with either very little noise at all, or with the noise of just one patient somewhere whimpering in a pain that never stops. Shadows drape all. You want to go to the toilet but you don't know if you can get out of the bed. And if you do, how to navigate through the shadows and the silences and then incur the ire of the night staff? The eidetic residue of Ivan's dream was also a factor: demons might be about, and even if they were friendly, he didn't feel like bumping into one of them. As it turned out, one bumped into him, as his panicked brain initially surmised. One moment Ivan had had his eyes closed, the next, he was staring at a face at the end of his bed -or towering over it, more like. The face was 'as black as the ace of spades' (standard Belfast simile of the time), and the whites of its eyes were locked onto him. Ivan started whimpering, drawing the bedsheet up to his face, to hopefully cover his own eyes, and banish the vision from his reality. But no, the face spoke: 'You can't sleep, Mr Stacks?' Mr Stacks shook his head, as though his life depended on it, one false move and all that... 'You're already on sedatives, so I'm afraid I can't help you there,' said the black face, which then smiled. This had some effect in calming Ivan, who managed: 'Who are you?' 'Doctor Dyran [pronounced 'Dye-ran']. Just happened to be passing by.'

They were more or less whispering, and Ivan was now coming to grips with his first ever meeting with a person of colour. (No, he reminded himself, second, but that fellow was just over-tanned, not... dark ebony!) He was also noticing that his interlocutor was very tall, very slender, and very dapper, too, an expensive-looking grey suit and waistcoat visible under the white doctor's over-coat. Doctor Dyran indicated he would now move on, but Ivan was now more interested than afraid, and so he asked: 'Where are you from?'

'Nigeria.'

'Oh.'

'How are you feeling, Mr Stacks?'

'Do you know about my friend David Wilson? He was with me during the bombing. We came here in the same ambulance.'

'I know. I was there.'

At this Ivan became extremely excited and sat up. Dr Dyran added: 'Well, you came in two different ambulances, actually.' This Ivan asked him to repeat, and even when he did, he refused to believe it. 'Not at all. I distinctly remember lying side by side with Davy. What are you talking about?' 'Well, I'm sorry, Mr Stacks, but the mind plays funny tricks on people who've gone through a trauma like that...' The doctor seemed to want to leave now, reluctant to carry on a conversation which might wake others and, more importantly, to indulge a patient still coping with things after such an event. To close the matter, he said: 'I was in the ambulance with Mr Wilson. You were in a different ambulance, with medics...' Dr Dyran realized his news might disturb Ivan even more, so he smiled again and said: 'Listen, you'll be alright, and I'm sure your friend will be alright, too. Just try and get some sleep now...' 'But... Doctor...' 'Goodnight, my friend,' said a smiling Dr Dyran, his white teeth flashing in the dark, if not literally. As he paced away toward the corridor, Ivan called out weakly: 'What about the bloody Russian?'

The episode had taken it out of him, so it wasn't long before Ivan slipped back into a welcoming unconsciousness.

. . .

After morning ablutions, breakfast, and the pill-round, Ivan was to have yet another visitor. This time a woman, with two very young kids in tow, a boy (about four) and a toddler girl. They were giving their mother, who looked about twenty going on forty, a hard time, wanting this and that, and, most of all, wanting to leave. Ivan had never seen her before in his life, until he realized he had. She was Sandy, Abe's wife! He hadn't seen her for at least four years. He smiled, half out of courtesy that she would come and see him and half out of relief that he'd remembered her. He attributed her own lack of a smile to the battle she was having to fight with her young'uns. But then there was something more to it, he noticed. Sandy asked him how he was anyway and they both expressed surprise at not having met for so long. (Well, Ivan knew, he and Abe would only meet to jar, sure.) 'So, Sandy, can you let me into the big secret: how's your hubby doing? They don't tell me anything in here.' At this point, the little girl was making it clear that she just had to go to the toilet, and so the mother couldn't answer Ivan just yet until she had come back. Ivan then had to endure five minutes in the company of wee Stevie, asking him about the plastic truck he had and, eventually, running out of things to say, asking him if he liked dinosaurs. 'Nah. They're crap.' Ivan didn't usually pray, but now he was praying for Sandy to return. Relief ran through him when she did, but he was still not entirely comforted because she didn't look particularly happy. He dreaded to find out why.

'What was him and you doing there?' she asked Ivan straight.

Ivan thought it best to keep it simple: 'He had to go there for some business thing, Gilpins and that paint warehouse…' He was then about to explain about his own reason for accompanying him when Sandy threw him a look. She seemed to want to communicate with him but couldn't do so easily, with the kids scampering around and she having to check they weren't disturbing others. That, or she couldn't bring herself to say what she had come to tell him. Therefore, she just raised an inconspicuous index finger to her right temple and all but murmured 'damage…' It was enough to provoke her tears. Ivan looked at her in complete shock. He tried to ask simply by his facial expression if it was really true, and then, whispering: 'Will he recover?' 'They don't know' was all Sandy could say and then she had both hands on her face and was doing her damnedest to suppress her sobbing in front of the children. She soon stood up, as though determined to change her attitude, flashed a not very convincing smile Ivan's way, reached out and squeezed his hand, and before Ivan could say 'Do you know about the Russian?' she, and wee Stevie and his even wee-er sister, were out the door. Ivan was in shock. He closed his eyes. On the world.

• • •

Later that day Ivan got to see Abe, who was half-comatose, his head bandaged up. He spent a few minutes trying to speak to him and even tell him that things would be alright, but when Abe hadn't seemed to even register his presence and the nurse in charge was dropping hints, he left, squeezing Abe's hand before he did so.

• • •

Ivan had plenty of time to lie in bed or sit up watching the communal telly. He preferred it when it was off, though. An hour wouldn't go by without some reference to action somewhere, be it a news flash, or a notice for keyholders to return to their premises to deal with the aftermath of some bombing.

. . .

His parents came in and made a fuss, regaling him with bottles of Lucozade and Cadbury's Fruit 'n Nut. They assailed him with questions about why he'd been there and urged him to be more careful in future. To which Ivan could only answer by asking, miffily, where exactly was safe? 'Can't live under a rock!'

. . .

Fellow workers from the *News Letter* paid visits irregularly. By end of day, Ivan had scored three large bottles of Lucozade, four big (or 'big, big' according to the adverts) bottles of C & C (Cantrell & Cochrane) Sarsaparilla, 'Brown Lemonade', Red Lemonade, and innumerable bags of Tayto and Perri crisps. Even a few packets of fags, too.

. . .

The Uncle/Editor showed his face, too. Unlike the others, he wasn't smiling, but he rarely did. He was tut-tutting, engaged with the bigger questions of what all this meant, and eager to disclose his memories of the bombing outside their offices seven years before. By the end of their encounter, Ivan was tut-tutting a lot, too.

• • •

The upshot of all this activity was to prevent Ivan from engaging with what any of this meant, or even thinking at all. He felt like asking for some sort of muscle relaxant to help his face get back to normal, after all the mostly cheery interactions. Imagine being famous, he reflected, and having to do this kind thing all the time.

• • •

But think he did, eventually. It was late, about 11pm, and virtually everyone was obediently asleep. In the dark, it wasn't so much thinking, as seeing, seeing all the faces from the day, and the one, eyes heavily lidded, he didn't want to see among them. Poor Abe. Poor Sandy and her kids. He rolled over on his pillow, as any kind of change of position might help to dislodge the feeling of misery.

Logic and reasoning helped, too. Yes. He had had to think and re-think things. What he'd been told by that black doctor had shaken him and his belief that he thought he knew what was what. That had soon crumbled. It didn't take much for him to shift, ever so slightly, in the direction that all the hints were telling him, too: that his insistence on the Russian bloke being real might go the same way. Abe had said that guy was a Belfast bloke, after all. More than that, he had intuited that the very reason they weren't letting him out was that he was still showing signs of delusional thinking, as a consequence of the shock and the trauma. In a dazzling moment of brain-surgeon brilliance, then, Ivan realized he would give them what they wanted: he would accept that he hadn't seen any bloody Russian and give every indication that he was cured and no longer suffering from delusions.

He smiled. He was James Bond. He was Batman. He was Columbo. He would use cunning to get out of a tricky situation and then he'd get to work with his detective skills once back out on the streets. Gumshoe Stacks would 'make inquiries', re-visit 'the scene of the crime', 'interview the witnesses' and, from the apparent void, fish out a story his uncle would just have to print! Josef Stalin in Belfast!

Suddenly Abe was looking down on him. 'What are ya doing now, ya sausage? What about them dinosaurs? Did ye forget them, boyo?'

Ivan sat bolt up straight in his bed, shocked at the sudden vision. He was on the verge of calling out for the nurse, to insist they go and check on his friend. He stopped himself just in time. At the very start of his plan, he'd be damned as delusional -again!

What was he bloody doing? Ivan wanted to know this more than anything. He was crying. That's what he was doing. He only noticed this when he raised his left hand to explore the sudden itchiness on his face. Tears. Tears for Abe. He lay back in the bed, and put his head under the pillow, where he allowed more of the tears to come out, in 'torrents' and 'streams' (his 'words', as he re-adopted his recent tendency to thesaurus-ize his reality).

It ended like this: after enough sobbing and heart-break at the misery he'd encountered, Ivan Stacks decided to relinquish his insistence on the need to follow up on the mysterious Russian, and, as though suddenly connected, all interest in dinosaurs, too. It was all rubbish, he'd decided. It was clear there was only one story worth expending any energy on, and that was... the Troubles. He would take up the mantle of the serious reporter and get to grip with the everyday, not the fantasy, get to grip with the unfortunately real, if deadly, violence stalking the streets and wreaking havoc on society. He'd tell the stories of victims of an evil that had no morals, and no justification, and no mercy. The Russian bloke? He now couldn't care less. Dinosaurs? The scandal Abe had enticed him with? It would be another 'chase in the dark after shadows' (Ivan Stacks ©). Dinosaurs were now not merely a thing of pre-history. They were a thing of the past – *his past.*

Chapter Sixteen: Awkward Encounters, pt.1, Saturday, May 19

At around 1pm on Saturday, Ivan Stacks, not quite sure if he was a little bit broken or a little bit resolute, or a maybe just a little bit of both, exited the Royal Victoria Hospital and crossed the road to hail a taxi back to Woodvale. All the traffic on the hospital side was going up the Falls, and he didn't think he'd want to be spending much time up there anytime soon. He'd thanked all the nurses, Staff Nurse Maguire most of all (secretly thinking all along that she was 'bit of stuff for a middle-aged woman'), and also Sister O'Hanlon, whom he had just before this engaged in conversation on the weighty topic of all this madness. 'Sister, what do you think when you see a bomber brought in with injuries? Do you...', but she hadn't allowed him to elaborate, the features of Ivan's face and the position of his hands making it clear he would be all into dealing out some sort of nasty bedside punishment. Prefaced with a brief moment of eye-contact that would fell a bad-mannered goat, she answered, in her beautiful Belfast 'brogue': 'We treat every patient the same. I've seen it all, perpetrators and victims, and once they enter this building... they're *only* patients.' Ivan wisely asked no more. 'Hope you can get back to some normality, young Ivan,' she piped cheerily. 'Good day to you.'

Ivan surveyed the road, firstly up the Falls, seeing it soon curve round, closing off further visual inquiry, and then down, which similarly didn't disclose much beyond the traffic and a few trees, except for the huge brick building across the street, which he guessed was a church. He crossed over to it, still trying to keep his eye out for any passing taxis which were not 'black hacks' (which would only take him down the Falls, just as 'black hacks' only went up and down the Shankill). The church at his back was radiating an oppressive aura, as though it had just too many bricks and not enough windows, or… that it was too much of a cloyingly Catholic symbol to be this close to. The wee *fleur-de-lis* spikes on the iron fence, punctuated with overly-ornate circular crosses that might have served some purpose during the Inquisition (which he'd learned about in great detail at school), were hardly inviting either. He walked on, crossing another little turning in, past McPeake's Wallpaper and Glass Merchant, and then on until he was standing outside an establishment called The Saloon Bar. Before he could become too intrigued about what he might find inside – portraits of the Pope and the Virgin Mary behind the bar, perhaps – his attention was taken by the discovery of a fonaCAB Vauxhall taxi motoring leisurely down the Falls on his side. Up went his arm, Ivan more eager than he had ever been to get back to his home and out of alien territory.

More indications of precisely how alien this territory was came in the form of occasional green, white and orange flags (the 'trickelor'), stuck here and there, out of second floor windows or tied to lampposts. He knew they were illegal but that the police wouldn't lightly decide upon any removal operation around here. As the taxi turned up the Springfield Road, Ivan also made note of the other items tied to lampposts, SDLP [Social Democratic and Labour Party] election banners not taken down yet, but, with Gerry Fitt's mug plastered all over them, many either ripped or splashed with green paint, or graffitied with rude words. Even Ivan knew Fitt wasn't universally loved in West Belfast, despite his big win recently. Ivan had been relieved when, upon telling his address, the taxi driver had just grunted neutrally. You never know, one part of his brain would tell him: 'Might be some hard Nationalist in disguise ready to spirit me off to a backroom somewhere where I'd get done in.' Then: 'Nah, you can always rely on the taximen of Belfast, West, East, North, and definitely South ('hoity-toity territory'). Decent chaps the lot of them.'

After being in hospital for a few days, Ivan's eyes ate up the surroundings, the shops and terraced housing on either side. His stomach-eyes picked out SPRINGFRY and he thought of eating a deliciously unhealthy chip after all that mush he'd had in the ward. And then, just two shops on, he feasted on MAGUIRE'S PUBLIC HOUSE, where he envisioned himself having a very slow pint of Guinness, to settle him down and... But two thoughts interrupted this reverie: bittersweet memories of being in the Morning Star with Abe, and some keen worry that if he did enter this pub, he'd soon be identified as a Prod and taken out the back for a beating, or worse.

A few shops and a few tricolours on, the scenery changed to just residential housing either side and Ivan wondered where all the brick came from. There were fine terraced houses on both sides, and the aesthetics of the beautiful brown brick and the elegant two-storied bay window projections either side of the front doors did their bit to soften his thoughts and his feelings. 'This could be anywhere in Belfast,' Ivan decided. 'Anywhere half nice.' He also started to reflect a little on what he'd just been thinking as they passed Maguire's pub. Maybe it was because he usually stayed in his own part of the city or around the city centre; some illogical fear had seemed to creep into his soul and just tell him things. Or was it that the whole recent experience had done something to him? He recalled his chat with the Sister and wondered if he'd come across as embittered. He had every right to, of course, by the playbook of most people's experience in this city and around, but Ivan's family had never been ardent, just shocked when this or that happened. The father hadn't encouraged any talk of demonizing the other side; he took the moral high ground every time, and in the course of this decade there was plenty of opportunity for that, the bombing outside the *News Letter* 'taking the biscuit'. The father had pulled strings to get Ivan into temporary residence in Woodvale, against Ivan's first choice of digs in the lower Shankill. 'Environment is education', was the father's favourite phrase, adding, 'you'll not stay in lodgings strewn with bunting and the kerbs painted red, white and blue.' Ivan was glad of his upbringing; he knew a good reporter had to be dispassionate, not take sides. He had to nurture understanding in division, not hate. Even so, he wished the fuckers who had left his friend a vegetable would get run over by a bus, and very fucking slowly.

Soon after passing the giant Mackie's factory on the left ('more brick!' noted Ivan to himself), the taxi made a sharp right off the big road. This jolted Ivan out of whatever train of thought he'd been riding and into some kind of awareness that not only was the landscape changing, but he was also leaving 'alien' territory and gaining entry to all points East. The biggest indication of this was not only the expansive space opening up either side, but the sudden appearance of ugly, graffitied, paint-splashed impenetrable-looking blocks straddling the road, which was itself punctuated with speed-bumps in the tarmacadam, to discourage drive-by shootings. This was one of the sites of the 'peaceline', he soon realized, going through the usual lip-curling sense of outraged irony at the use of word 'peace' in the title. Once through, Ivan sat back as he hadn't quite done so until this time, at least metaphorically, and allowed some as yet unprobed sense of territorial safety to flood through his being. He was going home!

Too soon to think so. 'Just a wee min, there, Mucker. Gotta drop off some eggs and things for ma sister,' spoke the up-until-now taciturn taximan, angling the car right until they were driving down a side street. On either side were houses that had seen better days, many with windows covered with corrugated iron or plastic. On the street were signs of either vandalism or riots, with the occasional burning pile here and there. Ivan wasn't feeling good about the sudden detour, but the taximan seemed genuine and friendly and after parking, he rushed out carrying what he had in the passenger seat and was back within a minute or two. 'Sorry, mate, I'll get us back on track now,' he explained as he started up the car again and made a big turn. Back on the street, he soon sailed back into the left lane.

'Know what they call this street, Mucker?' shouted out the driver. Ivan said he didn't. 'Nathin'!' replied the driver, head turning as he threw that out. 'I don't get ye,' said a confused Ivan. 'Well, it's officially "Merkland Street", but since almost everyone's escaped, the city took the name away. Just my wee sister and her family and two other families and that's about it.' Ivan was still confused, but from what he could make out and from what he could see, this area was more like a battlefield than a place to live in. 'Fackin' shacking!' confided the taximan, in his best Belfast twang. He then capped that with: 'Man's fucking inhumanity to man…' Ivan decided not to pursue this, seeing and hearing enough from his guide. The 'peaceline' they'd just gone through… From the late sixties and early seventies, families had been intimidated on both sides, until Belfast had gotten what it wanted, everyone of one religion inhabiting their own wee world, with no overlaps. Prods here, Taigs there. Or if there were overlaps or too close a proximity, they always had the barriers, the walls, the 'peaceline'. Anyone messing about got shot, kicked senseless, knee-capped or murdered. The gates opened during the day and closed at night, the division writ large for everyone to see. Ivan closed his eyes and waited for the journey to end. *Man's inhumanity to man…*

He didn't keep them closed very long. Funnily enough, when he did have a peep, the first thing he saw was election posters for the DUP [Democratic Unionist Party] attached to lampposts, and the more than occasional Union Jack here and there, too. He also made note of the kerbstones done in red, white and blue, just beyond the junction leading into the Shankill. Ivan couldn't help thinking what a crazy world he was living in, where in the space of one short car journey of about ten minutes he could travel *from one universe to another.* It was like parallel worlds, too. The poster paper was probably just the same, and they both painted their kerbs; they just used different words and different colours. Enjoying his moment of philosophical insight, Ivan extrapolated in his mind: 'they could probably even order the materials from the same shop, the owner of which would be rubbing his hands at the business to be had.' *Roll up, roll up, ye fightn' Norn Ironers, all the ink and all the paint ye need! And, sorry, we don't have guns, but that's alright: your words and symbols are much more dangerous!*

'That's a nice-looking church!' exclaimed the taximan. They were passing by St Matthew's Parish Church on the Woodvale Road. 'It's not Catholic, is it? It's got a wee Round Tower thing going on there, like.' 'Anglican,' answered a cheery Ivan, cheery now that he'd almost gotten back to base and that he'd hit upon a funny set of never-before-thought-about insights into life in the Province. 'I see,' said the taximan, even if it sounded like he didn't. 'Well, would you believe it,' continued Ivan, eager to instruct, 'if you could see it from a bird's eye position and you looked down, you could see it's in the shape of a shamrock!' 'Gettaway!' responded the driver, head flicking back to show his smile of happy disbelief, which he added to with: 'A shamrock up the Shankill! Never thought I'd hear that!' Ivan chortled in response, glad he'd spread a little enlightenment. 'Oh, yes, but of course, this is Woodvale, strictly speaking, you know...' 'Oh aye,' said the driver, and Ivan could hear he wanted to ask more, but suddenly the driver had become intent on what he was supposed to be doing. 'Enfield Drive, you said?' 'Aye, just turn right here down this wee street,' advised Ivan. 'Never been up here before, mate,' confided the driver. 'Fuckin' nice church, that.' Ivan winced momentarily, but fell back on the old mainstay, in order to fill the hole created by his interlocutor's unfortunate linguistic juxtaposition: 'Oh aye.'

Two minutes later, in slowish traffic, past the place his Da had made much of telling him a famous artist had once lived in, then turning up one little street and down another, they finally arrived at Ivan's destination. Ivan gave him a tip of a pound note on top of his fare and the taximan was 'made up', as they say, beaming thanks, and saying in farewell: 'See ya round, Mucker.' Ivan was genuinely glad to have made his acquaintance, but also genuinely glad he was now driving off, with Ivan thinking the likelihood that they would see each other around was about a million to one.

He turned to his front door and shook his head with gratitude to see it. It was gratitude to his father who had wangled this wee place, if only for this year. While there were a few gable end murals dotted around here, extolling the virtues of the UDA and King Billy, they weren't visible from where he was now. And no painted kerbs, either. (That artist fella, he quipped, mustn't have been very busy.) It was a pretty wee house, and the brickwork radiated warmth and love. He was home. As he walked over the threshold, it felt a little strange that he wasn't carrying anything -he was the mysterious traveller who'd gone on a long journey and had now just returned with nothing in his hands but his keys. Well, he had something invisible with him he hadn't had before. Experience. He shook his head and uttered something like, 'Ah, well, now…'

He was thinking of visiting the kitchen first, to set the kettle for a nice cup of tea when, to his great surprise, he heard the doorbell ring. Immediately he thought of the taximan. 'Had I left something in his cab?' 'Was he lost and needed my help to get out?' He smiled at this as he reached for the door latch. He could make the shape of someone behind the frosted glass. Still smiling, he opened the door. As the sunlight was against him, he had to peer a little to make out who it was. Or what it was. For what he saw first was not so much the whole face as just the bit below the nose, and the bit below the nose was dark, and stringy, and bushy. It was a huge moustache. He looked further up the man's face and noted the similarly bushy eyebrows. He then noticed, as his eyes had grown accustomed to the light, the eyes of the man standing before him. They were cold, and unmoving. And if he still needed any prompting about who the man with the cold, unmoving eyes was, the man's mouth opened and out came these words: 'Good afternoon, Comrade! Dovry fuckin' Din! Josef Stalin at your service…' in a Belfast accent you could cut bread with. 'Got something for ye.' And at this, the man with huge bushy moustache and huge bushy eyebrows smiled evilly and pulled out something metallic and smooth and shiny from his jacket. It was a gun. And… Ivan noted, whimsically, ludicrously even, as one might when feeling a complete and utterly paralyzing panic, *it was not a fucking ray gun!*

Chapter Seventeen: Awkward Encounters, pt.2, same day

At that precise moment, Professor Ronald Tweedy was just about to launch into a mini-lecture to a mini-audience of three: his wife, Abigail (39), his daughter, Jenny (12), and his son, Tommy (8). It was on the subject of the Crown Bar in Belfast, where, as a pre-celebration of his forty-eighth birthday, he had dragged them. They had managed to snag a snug. ('To teach our children a little culture and history, darling. Not because I'm "an alcoholic."') Tweedy had an as yet untouched pint of Guinness stout before him, Abigail, a Babycham (bottle, and now filled champers glass), Jenny, a poured Britvic Orange Juice, and Tommy a half-pint glass of Cantrell & Cochrane Red lemonade. Before said lecture, however, Tweedy indicated that a toast was in order: 'A bit early, but who celebrates their birthday on a Monday?' He was lost for words then, weighing the wisdom of adding: 'To me!' Thankfully, Abigail stepped in: 'To Professor Tweedy, your very clever father, children! Happy Birthday, Daddy!' They all grabbed their respective drinks and touched glasses, all except Tommy, who had to be shown that that was what to do. Once they had all clinked and had their first sup of respective drinks, Tweedy couldn't be held back. 'The Crown Bar of Belfast! As old as the hills... in a manner of speaking...' He realized he had to qualify that particular linguistic flourish as it brought him uncomfortably back to digging in the dirt -something he didn't want to think about today. 'Or... at least as far as... 1839.' He spoke the date with great force, as though it possessed some special mystery or power. *Eighteen thirty-nine*. Capitalizing on the moment, he then quizzed his family: 'What happened in 1839, then? Would anyone like to answer that?' As quick as a jackrabbit, Tommy spoke up: 'Was that when you were born, Daddy?'

Buoyed by the Guinness and the attention, Tweedy subsumed the hilarity which this remark (delivered in all innocence) caused among his wife and daughter, and responded with a smile: 'Well, Tommy, how's your mathematics? That would make me a right old age now, wouldn't it? 1839 was a hundred and forty years ago, after all. No, I'll give you all one more chance...' It was Abigail's turn, and herself buoyed up by the first delicious sip of her sparkling bubbly-like drink fired off: 'Man on the moon?' and laughed heartily. 'Mummy, you're terrible,' spoke a similarly laughing long blonde pony-tailed Jenny. 'Oh dear,' said a visibly – slightly – crestfallen Tweedy, 'history, people. Know your history.' When they had calmed down, Tweedy continued, in all excitement: 'The opening of the first railway line between Belfast and Lisburn, no less!' This piece of intelligence was not received with any reciprocal enthusiasm, Jenny doing her best now to nudge her mother and ask about something completely different. 'To here!' exclaimed Tweedy now, 'To Great Victoria Street!' This added information was met with more stony looks.

Realizing the energy in this story was all on his side, he immediately followed things up with a quick run-down of what he had been hoping his captive audience would find of enormous fascination. 'The Ulster Railway had opened a new chapter in Belfast's life, and in came even more people and trade. They needed a little spot for light refreshments, and so was born The Railway Bar. And, a few years, I beg your pardon, a few *decades* later, it got the best treatment of any public house in the city. Spruced up like a palace. Right here! Think of all the hustle and bustle!' 'From Lisburn?' asked a sceptical Abigail, only interested if she could pick at his story a little: 'Hardly the centre of the universe, Lisburn!' Yet, the significance of all this was not to be so easily dismissed. 'Hustle and bustle aplenty! And no luxury spared!' shot back Tweedy. 'And it's still here!' Hereafter,

Tweedy launched into a mini-treatise on the 'spruced up like a palace' part of the story from the 1880s, highlighting the work of 'fine Italian craftsmen' whose main purpose, he expounded, was to work on Catholic churches, not pubs! 'Oh, the Italians! The Italians!' he exclaimed. 'Lovers of art and makers of the finest cities in Christendom!' At this, Tweedy gave a conspicuous look around him, his nose, by default of the fact that it stuck out, pointing out the Victorian gaslight lamp above them, the black tufted leather for the comfort of their weary backs, the metal strip for striking MATCHES, the richly ornate stained-glass panels, the general weathered woodiness of the snug's interior, ending with a final proboscidial flourish at the rampant woody lions in their lofty frozen poses, guarding all within. 'This place is a time machine!'

To be fair to Tweedy, the noise of punters laughing and pinting and calling out orders and slapping backs and scraping stools across the intricately pattern-tiled floor was certainly classifiable as hustle and bustle -one that had Abigail wondering about the wisdom of having brought their kids to this den of iniquity (as her strict Presbyterian father might call it). Reading this in her eyes, Tweedy, after a long and languorous slurp of his stout, pounced: 'Darlin', next door used to be a Temperance Hotel, would you believe it! Your father would be impressed!' He guffawed. 'The passengers were not all fond of a tipple, you know!' He then proceeded to explain in even greater detail about not only The Crown but about Robinson's, two doors down, which was originally called The Dublin and Armagh Hotel, punctuating his talk with the names of all the major players, be it owner Michael Flanigan or architects E and J Byrne et cetera et cetera. As often happened when giving a lecture at Queen's, Tweedy so angled his head in an upward direction and spoke without break to some point above the heads of his listeners as to appear as both a metaphorical *and* literal 'Fountain of

Knowledge' (with the occasional ejection of micro-spittle). And as also happened in said lectures, his listeners here soon tired of what he was going on about and started speaking, if in hushed tones, to one another. Jenny really wanted to get out and visit the shops, as did her mother, and Tommy was hard at work playing with two little toy figurines he had picked out of his pocket. When Tweedy finished, he brought his head back down to earth and looked around – he was not happy with what he saw: Abigail and Jenny in a quiet but animated discussion of which shop to visit first, Anderson & McAuley's or 'Marks 'n Sparks', while Tommy was in a different world entirely – playing with… plastic dinosaurs! A T. Rex and a Stegosaurus!

Tweedy reached for his glass and downed the last. He had promised Abigail they would only be here for one quick drink, but somehow he felt like another, and quick. Indifference was bad enough but being reminded of his enthrallment was unforgivable. He hated dinosaurs now. They entered his dreams at night and his reality by day. They pranced all over his other dreams, too, like that of escaping the all-too-familiar here and visiting Venice – to inspect that city's wonderful piling, no less! Dinosaurs, despite having become indubitably extinct in the Dark Ages *before the Dark Ages*, had somehow returned. The lumbering louts had broken their chains and threatened to break Tweedy's, too. Well, not his chains, but his dreams! (His mind was mixing metaphors…) That, or he was summoning excuses to tell himself he needed to get just one more alcoholic beverage, because if he couldn't have perfect happiness, he could at least taste a little oblivion (having now decided that a Bushmills would have to accompany any pint he had next).

Cheeriness would carry his plan through to fruition: 'Young man, are you enjoying your aerated water?' Tommy stopped playing and looked quizzical. 'That's right, young Tommy. You're drinking "Aerated Water"!' Tommy said: 'It's Red Lemonade,

Daddy.' His father smiled, in a gently, and of course ironically, patronizing way. 'Yes, Tommy, that's what they call it now, but back in the day it was called either "Aerated Water" or "Carbonated Water". Did you know that, now, me lad?' Abigail was watching this interchange with some delight, delight in seeing her husband engage with the children directly. She kept watching, pulling away slightly from Jenny who was listing all the items she wanted to see in the department stores. 'Well, listen to this. Belfast was once the world centre for such drinks! The largest producer of fizzy drinks anywhere!' He said this with as infectious a cheeriness as he could manage, knowing he was on his way toward victory. Tommy was looking cheery now, too, even uttering the odd chortle now and again. 'Well, let me tell you, boyo,' said his father getting well into his stride, 'that Red Lemonade may be all very well, but you haven't lived until you've tried the genuine homegrown, baked-in-history thing itself, Belfast-born Ginger Ale!' Tommy chortled again and seemed won over entirely.

Abigail could see what was coming and thought it best to intervene: 'But, Ronny, wee Jenny here's itching to get shopping and you did say we'd be here for only one…' She was never quite assertive with her husband, but there were times when she said what she felt she needed to say. 'Jenny,' said Tweedy / Ronny / Daddy, addressing the more strategically important of the two females, 'we'll be out of here like Jackrabbit, but you'll never forgive yourself for not trying this Belfast Ginger Ale. Something to tell your friends…' It was clear Abigail was about to speak and make the decision for them to leave, but Tweedy was too close to his goal to have his urge denied at the final hurdle. 'Dear, I'm sure you're enjoying that tipple, too. And did you know, you might never get to drink it again!' This seemed to floor Abigail, who shrieked, slightly, wondering what actually was coming next. Her suddenly widened eyes asked 'Why?', as then did her mouth.

'Because… dear, the French have their knives out for that little drink…' Now Abigail noticeably frowned, even more mystified by her husband, wondering how a single pint of Guinness might wreak such an effect. Tweedy: 'They sued Babycham!' This produced a laugh from Abigail's throat which was also a release of tension. 'Sued Babycham? Whatever for?' Tweedy: 'The "cham" in Babycham, that's what's for! If it *ain't* produced in the Champagne area of France, it *ain't* Champagne!' said Tweedy, buoyed by his sudden licence to speak casual, like, if only for the duration of that sentence. 'There are no people quite like the French to hold on for dear life to their culture! Just look at Paris! Its beautiful architecture!' This prompted Tweedy to add, with a tinge of rancour in his voice: 'Look at Belfast!'

He had opened a different topic entirely here, but he realized this was neither the time nor the place for recriminations about Belfast City Council's criminal destruction of their city, not least the beautiful Terminus building designed by John Godwin in 1846 just across from the street. *Oh! That the last remnant of its magnificent stone glory was pulled down no less than three years ago! And that horrendous Europa Hotel they put up in its place!* But… *that* was another story. Here, he had the chance to linger awhile in a Victorian structure that had survived the brutal test of time, one rescued only last year by no less an august committee than The National Trust. He rejoined The Babycham Express with gusto: 'They failed, Abigail. The French failed but they'll no doubt try again! Hold on to your Babycham, dear! Hold on tight!' This exhortation produced such a moment of hilarity among all of them that Tweedy could virtually taste the Bushmills he knew would soon be his to sup. Up he got and he went out beyond the stifling confines of the snug.

Tweedy was like a man released from prison. All he surveyed was glorious, and the smell of freedom was so tangible he allowed himself a conspicuous sudden, but deep, intake of breath. The impulse to close his eyes as he did so was offset by the desire not to miss even a millisecond of the beauty of this wonderful bar. It was a wonder which dwelt in the figures all around him, the happy tipplers, young and old, swapping stories and jokes, vivacity and pep written into the contours of each and every face. But for their clothes they might have been the very same as those who trudged in here to The Railway Bar a hundred and forty years ago – their Welcome to Belfast! The air was permeated with little twirls of smoke here and there, and all was bathed in the sweet glow of sunlight filtered through stained glass and refracted off the luminescent, but orderly, tiles of the floor and the dark, but glossily dark, swirling arabesques of the ceiling. You could get drunk just by taking all this in. And then, just over there, steps away, was the bar, with its pink marble counter, its recessed arches, holding, alternately, cask-ends in triplicate, intricately piped and tapped, and shelves of glistening gravity-feed bottles of spirits and whiskey, beckoning lavishly, voluptuously, uproariously, to Ronald J Tweedy.

He took the three steps that he needed to take and was gladdened there was space between those sat on high stools at the counter. Soon he was leaning on what early critics had called a butcher's slab, not that he cared, and looking at the brass beer taps, announcing **Guinness, Harp, Bass, Tennents**, and **Kronenbourg**. He'd made a quick decision on what to have; with a Guinness taking minutes, he ordered a half of Bass, to 'tide him over' as he waited, with a wee Black Bush on the side. And, as he called out the ones for the fam, his eye spied a handwritten sign for 'Fresh Strangford Lough Oysters' just to his left. He'd have some of that, he decided right there and then. It was his birthday after all!

Five minutes later, Tweedy walked back to the snug, a tray full of liquid goodies before him, brimming with delight. 'I'll be right back,' he announced, Abigail looking askance. He didn't wait, and in his rush, he left the snug door open.

This was a mistake. Not because Abigail and the two kids could clearly see him return to the bar and somewhat slowly knock back whatever drink he'd obviously left there, but for the much greater shock which followed.

Having downed the half Bass and turned round to return to the snug, he was suddenly assailed by a woman more than half his age. Assailed, no less.

They talked, he animatedly, she even more so, until... she then pounced.

As Abigail, Jenny and Tommy watched from the dubious comfort of the snug, Jenny, a bottle of *Ross's Belfast Ginger Ale* snug in her hand, felt strongly compelled to ask: 'Mummy, why is that woman kissing Daddy?'

. . .

Meanwhile, two miles away, back at Rancho Deluxe in Enfield Drive, up the Woodvale Road, Ivan Stacks was contemplating eternity. He was being slowly forced to step backwards into his hallway by an enormously tall man whose most prominent feature was what experts in the field would call a 'walrus' moustache, much beloved of the former leader and dictator of The Soviet Union, just celebrating his first quarter century underground. His eyebrows weren't exactly un-bushy either, with plenty combable real estate up top, too. As the light was behind this imposing figure, Ivan was even more compelled to think the figure more than mere mortal, his panicked brain flailing at the resonances with figures from his ancient knowledge of The Holy Bible, demons from the underworld, or the Big Bad Boy himself, Satan. Memories of the sermon he'd witnessed himself only three years before at the Free Presbyterian Church of Ulster in Ballymena by none other than the Right Reverend Ian Paisley suddenly began to flood into his mind. It was never so much Satan or the demons on which Paisley dwelt, but on the sinners destined to fall within their clutches, were they not to repent and see the fatal error of their ways. Ivan was now like one of the 'three men,' bellowed out with passion, 'this very day, all living in Ballymena, going to hell'. As he had listened to the Reverend's thundering voice that rainy day in February, he remembered his own thanks to God that he was only there for *that* day, thanks to his Uncle Samuel, and would return safe and sound to the comfort of his Belfast home.

Safe, no longer, alas. He had become 'Mr Obstinate', as Paisley had termed a certain kind of reprobate. He knew it! Somehow, he was now remembering the words he had heard that day with the crystal clarity of Revelation! The Reverend Ian had been quoting from The Book of Samuel (no doubt making his uncle a happy man in the process) and had hit upon the theme of 'Stubbornness is as iniquity and idolatry', delivered in his inimitably robust Ballymena accent. (It was also heavily modulated and – yes – nuanced to bear the drama of whatever he happened to be delivering forth about.) The lesson that day was a simple one: 'Do not be *playing* with your soul! Do not be *gambling* with the time that is not yours! Do not be treating Eternal things as *trivialities!*' Ivan might have breathed a sigh of relief that he never did the horses, or even the Pools, but *play* he certainly did, and *trivialities* was his speciality! Drinking, smoking, running after women (but so far only at church fêtes), and chasing… chasing… it was on the tip of his tongue… 'chasing after shadows … in the dark!' That was it! *Like the bloody dinosaur story!* And that's what he'd been doing in his life, as Uncle Sammy was forever lecturing him on, pointing out his fallen ways, and what he wouldn't give to knock some Christian sense into him. And… fallen Ivan had, into *Presumption!* Presumption that he could carry on his unChristian self-indulgence and wait around until he just felt like coming at last to Jesus Christ Our Lord and God. 'Oh, hearken ye, ye of little faith,' the Uncle would say, exasperated after hearing about Ivan visiting the dens again, in 'yer big fancy city'. 'I wouldn't spit on Belfast!' he would add, shocking Ivan, in his student days at Queen's. Ivan used to wonder how his fellows managed to get through each and every Friday and Saturday night at the Student Union bar, 'The Speakeasy', without incurring the wrath of the Almighty. He never did that, mind, only a few quiet sips at The Botanic now and again. Until… until he had started meeting up again with his school friend, Davy Wilson.

Ivan kept backing up, his eyes wide and dry with shock and horror as he saw the metal of the gun in its entirety glint dully in the interior light. They were still within the hallway, but the figure had reached his hand round without taking his eyes off Ivan and closed the front door to. He towered within the small space, and Ivan knew his time upon this earth was at hand. He could see the man raise the gun slowly up and point it in his direction. His last thoughts would be the Reverend Ian's, pronounced with all finality and just for him… had he only listened, had he only listened:

> 'You stubborn, obstinate, hard-willed, hard-hearted sinner, brought up in the evangelical tradition, brought up in the evangelical Protestant tradition, God says you are just as filthy and iniquitous in your sin as a pagan idolator who bows down to wood and stone. Stubbornness is as iniquity and idolatry!'

Spliced upon this voice within his teeming, self-destructing mind, another voice boomed, too, in a decidedly East Belfast, true docker tone. 'Where d'ya want it? Right between the eyes? Through the heart? In yer fucking gut?'

Ivan saw the circle of the barrel, heard a bang, and fell.

. . .

'It was just a birthday kiss, for heaven's sake, Abigail!' exclaimed Abigail's suspiciously radiant husband upon re-entry to the snug, a pint of plain in his hand. The flushed look in his face belied his innocence, with the result that Abigail was very much less than placated. Jenny, too, was looking querulous at Daddy, and with the truly innocent eyes of youth was noticing what was different: 'You've lipstick on you, Daddy, look!' But Tweedy couldn't look, of course, and yet that didn't stop him from doing his damnedest with his left hand, flicking out of nowhere at the offending mark with no idea of precisely where to wipe. This attempt at inconspicuousness just made him look even more ridiculous than Abigail thought was possible. 'She's a damned student, wouldn't you know? And not a very good one, either!' he confided before sitting himself down. 'You looked pretty happy to see her, anyway,' said his wife in a tone that hadn't been heard since the last time they'd rowed about some other perceived indiscretion on her husband's part, a tone of marked distrust. 'Oh, for God's sake, Abby,' pleaded Tweedy, 'I said it was my birthday. What was I supposed to do? Back off and shout "Untouchable!"' Abigail didn't like where this might go and so she let it drop, and this inclination was aided immeasurably by the visitation of one of the barmen, delivering the food Tweedy had ordered and paid for. 'Look at what we have before us! Fresh Strangford Lough Oysters! And brown bread!' Whether it was this or just the sight of the bivalves glistening in the orange stained-glass-strained sunlight, a slice of lemon reclining by their side, everyone's attention gravitated table-ward and the joy of what they saw was plenty to displace whatever had gone before.

. . .

The bang that Ivan had heard was the English word 'bang', spoken loudly, and precipitously, by the man with the walrus moustache. In combination with the sight of the gun barrel and the general bad vibes he was receiving from the situation -the likelihood that he was about to be shot to death-, Ivan Stacks did what any self-respecting ordinary person just going about their business might do, and fainted. While this had the effect of ending the craziness of that particular moment, it wasn't quite enough to end the unexpected nightmare that coming home had become. Josef Stalin was still there.

Ivan had only been out for a minute or so, but not in the dimension he had felt himself to be in. Dreams have a way of stretching out time. Ivan had been flying over a place that, if it wasn't Belfast, it was certainly the dead spit of Belfast (notwithstanding Uncle Sammy's nasty comments). Somehow his memory had decided that today -March nineteen, in the year of Our Lord nineteen seventy-nine- was Total Recall Day, because not only had Paisley's long-ago-heard sermon come back in full strength, but in his dream-ear, he was hearing the voice of local comedian Jimmy Young, reciting one of his poems, word for word. It was about a wee man in a similar predicament, who'd lost consciousness, or had quite simply died. He'd then gone, for all the sins Paisley had warned about, to Hell, but a Hell uncannily like the city of his birth. 'Surely to God, they were joking,' said the man in the dream, 'surely Belfast... wasn't Hell!'

> But there, before me, God love it,
> The big City Hall stood in state.
> With a tricolour flying above it
> And two Civic Guards at the gate.

That was only the start of the torment
I soon was to learn all the facts.
The Pope was living in Stormont
And Paisley was cleaning the jacks.

There was definitely something about the Head of the Orange Order coming next, but now the body, not the mind, was sending Ivan messages… Slap, slap, slap…Slap, slap, thud, slap. It took a while, but it worked, the messages, that is. Ivan's eyes popped open. Before him was the man with the conspicuous facial hair and, he winced to realize, a bad case of halitosis. 'Wake up! Wake up!' it said. 'I can't shoot ye if you're lying on the ground now, can I?' Ivan hoped this was a joke.

Ivan was where he had been, in the hallway, but now on the floor, the first step of the stairs right behind his bonce, and Josef, as he felt safe naming him, was bending over him, precariously so, and delivering slaps to his cheeks every few seconds. Now that he was coming around he thought it best to say so, issuing a 'Gruugh, gruugh' and a 'whaaa….whaaaa'. Despite the linguistic simplicity of these utterances, they did the trick of communicating that he was awake and no longer in need of being slapped into consciousness. It made the Josef Stalin figure resume an erect standing posture and even mutter a few words of what Ivan thought sounded like encouragement. Whether he felt encouraged or not, Ivan was certainly glad he was no longer getting a noseful of rotten ashes and buttermilk. 'Get up, ya shite ye,' said the towering figure, but in a tone which also seemed to suggest: 'The emergency's over. Calm down.' The man shifted his big booted feet and ancient black denim-clad legs, away from Ivan and stepped back a bit, back in the direction of the front door. Ivan showed some movement in the direction of doing as requested, but he was still as weak as a kitten. He wiped the side of his mouth with his sleeve -sensing a touch of saliva present, or was it blood? – Ivan felt the need to say something. Noticing that the gun was no longer in the man's hand helped. 'Excuse me... but I've done nothing to you. Please don't hurt me.'

'Aye, so ye say,' said the man, his tone now a tad harsh. 'But you've been asking the world and his wife after me, and that, fella, is something I can't have. No, no, no.' With something like horror, Ivan, still horizontal and feeling very vulnerable, noticed the man now move his hand toward the inner part of his jacket – a rough-looking dark carapace of a jacket, like something you might see on a shipyard worker from fifty years ago. 'No!' shouted Ivan, his panic level suddenly shooting up. 'I'll not say anything about you, I swear, mister!' The tone of desperation in his voice seemed to help assuage the man, who now muttered to himself unintelligibly, as though conflicted himself. 'Davy told me you were Russian! I wanted to meet you! My name's Ivan, too!' Ivan spat these intelligences out in rapid succession, in a tone of exasperation not lost on the other. Ivan's words had a strange effect: the man smiled. It was not a smile to adorn a poster or a book on How to Achieve Happiness, but it was as radiant and beautiful as a flower in bloom to Ivan. Had the (Russian) ice been broken, at last?

'Aye, Dyaedushka... that's Grandda to you... a sailorman, jumped ship, liked it here...said it was warmer than Vladifuckingvostok... Ha!' He chortled at that, giving Ivan hope. Ivan wanted to make a riposte in kind but thought it best not to, yet. (What could he say? 'I saw *From Russia with Love*? *Doctor Zhivago*? You look the spit of Omar Shariff?') A little refrain was coursing through his head: 'Whatever you say, say nathin'... But now Ivan had it: *he's chortling, so you should at least smile*. And so smile Ivan did, if not very convincingly. The giant man noticed Ivan smiling and accordingly stopped chortling -his eyes seemed to become angry, if not quite like two bits of anthracite, then something pretty close. 'Get up on yer feet!' he bellowed. Ivan wasn't even sure if he could, but the voice was so startling and terrifying, he knew he had to try. 'Get up, get up on your feet!' With this, the man approached Ivan violently and started to pull at his lapels or whatever bit of clothing he could grab and made it abundantly clear to Ivan that getting up was what would happen. This action also made it clear to Ivan that he was in grave danger once again, that a man who could behave like this wouldn't be averse to inflicting pain and suffering to a much greater degree, so as Ivan scrambled/was half-pulled to his feet, he couldn't help crying out in desperation and fear: 'Don't hurt me, mister, don't, please, don't!' This enraged Josef even more, who approached the now standing Ivan one more time to deliver a slap to his face, accompanied by a shout of 'Shut up!' Ivan shut up, and did his best to control himself, to stand with only the tiniest of quiverings in his erect body, and virtually no sound coming out of his mouth. He could read the man's actions like an open book -he didn't want to shoot a pathetic sobbing excuse for a man lying on the ground. He wanted to do it man to man, face to face.

Or... The man spoke: 'See, I don't like the fucking spotlight. In my area of expertise, the less heat I get the better. Don't need people nosing around, you get me, pal? Especially when they're fucking reporters!' Ivan: 'Of course! Of course! I won't say a word. I promise!' The man: 'You said plenty in the RVH anyway...' He said this with a curl of his lip that had Ivan worried again and wondering how he could have heard. He had to try and explain: 'I was...' 'What?' cut in Belfast Josef Stalin. Ivan: 'Confused! I was confused!' Stalin: 'Oh, aye?' Ivan: 'Oh, aye... I thought you'd been killed or injured... I thought the bomb had got you, too! But everyone thought I was crazy talking about a Russian bloke...' At this, the man hung his head, ever so slightly and was silent. Ivan thought it best not to speak, and not to utter the sentence dancing around naively on the tip of his tongue – 'I was worried about you!' When the silence dragged on for a few seconds longer, the pressure to throw this whimsy out became stronger and stronger. Thankfully, and just in time, head still down, the man threw out his own utterance: 'Poor fucking Davvy.' Ivan noted the familiar mispronunciation. '"Visselchak" I called him. "Komik"… he always cracked me up. Davvy, stupid fucken cunt.' 'Is that Russian?' asked Ivan, ignoring the Anglo-Saxon. 'Aye. Davvy thought it was cracker… Wanted me to teach him…' 'Aye, well,' offered Ivan, 'me and him have been friends for ages, now. The docs say he might recover, but…' and he let his explanation trail off, sensing the other didn't seem to be listening. It was better not to say too much, Ivan decided, better just to cling to this as a moment of shared sorrow.

The man suddenly started speaking again, venomously: 'Them wee fuckers setting off that bomb… Was probably meant for me… I'll get their goat… wee Republican cunts. I'll fuck their families up and all…' Ivan didn't want to hear this -it might make him even more worthy of silencing. 'Please don't involve me, mister. I won't say anything about ye, I swear to God in heaven.' The man: 'I'll catch up with them, and …' At this he looked up, and his hand started to reach into the inner space of his jacket again. He was now smiling, but in a manner that wasn't radiant at all. Ivan wasn't sure what it meant. The man's hand stopped. His smile stopped, too. Only his mouth moved: 'And if you come round asking about me, or if I hear a feckin' word of any reporter coming round asking for the Russian, I'll cut yer ballacks off and then shoot ye in the fucking head. You understand, pal?' Ivan: 'YES! I got it. I will never say anything to anyone ever in the world, in my whole life, anywhere, anytime to anyone. I swear to you, mister, please, please…' The man looked back at Ivan with a deadpan expression on his face and said in his flattest, gravelliest, ugliest voice: 'Thought so, pal. Sure, you're one of us after all. Just making sure o' that.'

Ivan felt disgust. Eye contact between the two was held for interminable seconds. Ivan wondered should he indicate assent – when he rather felt like saying: 'Go fuck yourself!' It was a difficult ten seconds.

Thankfully, the Mexican standoff came to the welcome anti-climax of the figure making to turn round to then fiddle with the latch, until he had found out how to turn it to open the door. Still with his back to Ivan, the daylight forming a kind of corona around him, he then grunted, audibly: 'Fucking nice day the day.'

He didn't close the door. Ivan did that. Even if it took him all of two minutes to free himself from the statue-like pose he had assumed. He closed the door to, and then walked slowly back up his hallway. He then slipped quietly into his front parlour and slumped onto the faux leather light brown settee, with all the mindlessness of a sack of Comber potatoes. Not that Comber potatoes said: 'Fuck!', as Ivan did, letting the word out after about a minute of staring into the middle distance. And then another one, as he had liked the sound of the first.

Questions came into his mind, like flies he wanted to wave away. How had that monster heard what he'd been saying in the hospital? It really was a case of whatever you say, say nathin'… With a shudder, Ivan remembered how the police who visited him had been so unwilling to follow up on the Russian… *Might they have…?* No, he couldn't accept that. *No way! And how could Abe have been mixed up with that bloke?* Or 'Davvy', as he'd been rechristened. *And who was he? Big in the UVF? A lone wolf? How many people had he…?* Here, Ivan demurred. Somehow, he didn't want to finish the thought. The shock of the whole thing began to grip, staunching thought. Images of violence flashed before him. The barrel of the gun not two feet from his face. That malevolent smile. The moment of the bomb going off on the Belfast street made an unwelcome reappearance. Abe, lying on his back, shouting 'Fenian bastards!' *Why would he say that? Was it like he knew something...? That bloke had said 'the bomb was meant for me'. Had Abe been in cahoots with Josef Stalin? Was Abe in the UVF or the UDA?* Ivan shook his head. He couldn't accept that idea either. He knew him to be as uninterested in hard-line politics as himself. Abe liked drinking, drinking, talking about shagging (pre-marriage, anyway) and making jokes about anything that came into his head. Ivan couldn't imagine he'd been living this other life. It was better not thinking, he then decided. Living in Northern Ireland was bad for the soul. *Bad for the soul!* Better to get the hell out, go and live in Blighty, maybe. Aye, that might do it. *Get my head showered...*

Thereafter he surveyed the room about him. It wasn't really his style, but he'd been told not to change it, as he wouldn't be living here permanently. If he was, he thought, the first thing to go would be those horrendous white-as-death pampas grass things un-adorning that ugliest of bulbous vases. Yet, he had to admit, from where he was looking, it made for a nice wee tableau of calm life in the face of adversity. As did the lace curtains, and the wee decorations on the mantlepiece, corralled by the two china dogs on either side. In the corner stood an empty birdcage. It reminded him of years ago when they'd kept a budgie. Maybe he could do that again. He thought about it... It would be good company... a wee companion... 'I'll have to make a wee fire,' said Ivan, only beginning to realize his nightmare was over. 'And that wee cup of tea I was just about to...'

Ivan froze. He could hear a noise at his front door again... Someone fiddling with the post slot, or flap, or whatever they called that thing where the letters came through. He could make out a distinct thud on the door, too, striking enough to have him jump out of the settee and into an erect standing posture in the middle of his parlour. *Is he back?* wondered Ivan, dread beginning to flood through him. *Let it just be the postman!* It was a dread that became confirmed as he edged his head round the door of the parlour to look down to the front door, seeing an enormous figure blocking the light of the two panes of frosted glass, as it seemed to struggle to pass something through the letter slot in the middle part of the door…

The figure now banged the door with blunt force and shouted something unintelligible, but along the lines of 'Blood!' With horror, Ivan watched as slowly but surely what seemed to be a blue envelope, creased and stained, passed awkwardly through the flap and, with an accompanying precipitous, and considerably angry, grunt of what sounded like 'Nakaneets!' – whatever that was – from outside, it fell down and onto the welcome mat of Ivan Stacks's dwelling, glowing with the mystery and the menace of a missive from Hell.

The figure left. The light once again came into the hallway. And once again Ivan fell on his arse.

· · ·

'Tracey Williamson, you're a bloody flirt!' exclaimed a smiling Manny Jal, perched on his stool at the entrance end of the counter at The Crown Bar, Belfast. He was welcoming back the said Tracey from her unexpected mini-tryst with their -former?-supervisor, Professor Tweedy. They weren't quite sure of their status yet, a point Manny was eager to ask Tracey about: 'Hoping he'll take us back?' Tracey smiled gloriously, basking in the rays of attention and the residue thrill the moment had imparted. 'You had to see the look on his face!' confided Tracey. 'He was all for it!' Then she started giggling. 'I shouldn't,' she protested, seemingly against herself, 'but his wife and kids were watching!' This confession added depth to the giggles, which now infected her partner, to the extent that one of the barmen threw the smallest of glances in their direction. It was OK to enjoy yourself, but there was a line, the glance seemed to suggest. 'I can just see the headlines,' Manny managed to get out, doing his best to calm down, at least to the point at which he could speak intelligibly. 'Queen's Professor charged with…' but he couldn't get it out, and now he was reduced to an even greater bout of giggles and unending chortles. Tracey knew they were on thin ice and held out a hand to Manny's shoulder: 'C'mon, they'll throw us out of here if we don't wise up.' It had an effect and the two of them returned to something vaguely approaching a merely cheer-filled interaction, looking not necessarily that much merrier than any other pair of punters.

What was behind their temporary loss of control was not simply their inherent natural inclination to not take things seriously, nor what they had drunk -Manny on his second pint (Kronenbourg following Bass), and Tracey, only on her first Gin 'n Tonic- but what they had done prior to entering: smoking a spliff. It had become their habit of late to push the envelope of public decency by lighting up illicit 'cigarettes' while ambulating the city streets. Tracey had been completely against it, but Manny had calmed her thus: 'You wanna see Birmingham, doll. It's common practice.' Tracey had responded: 'Maybe in your estate, mate, but not on the High Street, surely.' 'Well…' Manny had acceded, with a smile and the merest nod of the head. Yet, this is what Tracey liked about him, his natural lack of concern for Big Brother, a kind of way of being which made him stand out from other boys around her. Having brown skin, of course, helped in that department, too. He only came from Birmingham across the water, but it sometimes felt like he had swooped in from another world entirely, where rules were never taken that seriously and everything was always going to be alright. It helped that she had been brought up strict, even if her Dad had been something in the Socialist Movement. He'd been maddeningly conservative in his views on what his children should or shouldn't do. Underneath all the activism and the speeches he was supposed to have given, he was a hardcore oldie, who had basically thought his girls should take a backseat while the men went about changing the world. Because of this, university had become the education she had never dreamed of. It was so open, and the possibilities endless.

'OK, Trace, let's take it real slow, now,' advised Manny. 'Let's talk about... the future.' 'Oh, feck off. I didn't come here to talk about that. I don't wanna think about it,' replied Tracey, her smile and cheeriness taking a back seat for the moment. 'Yeah, but...' continued Manny, 'I think I'll have to make a decision soon...' 'Ah,' sighed Tracey, 'decisions, decisions, can't we just enjoy this trip?' She had a point. Manny reflected on it: marijuana had the unusual effect of either making him as carefree as possible or as intense and focused on whatever the big topic happened to be at that time. That was the thing about drugs: once you took them you were prey to behaving like a doll with some unknown being's hand up your back, manipulating you this way and that. If they made you laugh your head off, that was fine, but you might also be launched into some desperately serious pursuit of the truth, and while that might enervate you, it had the potential to bore the tits off everyone else, as he once put it. Drugs could be as treacherous as ordinary life.

Tracey and Manny seemed to agree not to talk future stuff, or anything of great import. They continued to sit idly, propped up on their high stools, enjoying the effects of the Morrocan Gold Manny had 'scored' from a wee man in the Holy Lands (in South Belfast, not the Middle East). The strangeness had not been lost on him: his family hailed from the island of Zanzibar, off the coast of Tanzania, and here he was in a city not usually noted for its exotic ties to the world. Birmingham wasn't much better, but it did at least have a huge percentage of black and brown people walking around and that was something you didn't see here very often, unless they were wearing berets, flak-jackets and carrying Army automatic rifles. He didn't know his own family's exotic past. His first memories were of life in a concrete high-rise, getting in and out of scrapes with his brothers, putting up with routine racism at school or on the street. When he asked his parents one day was he a 'Paki', his father suddenly got angry and started shouting about 'this damn country'. Manny didn't understand why and cried. It was Day One of his real education, the other one, that is, besides what they told him at school. Having to learn two at the same time was a challenge, and it was made even harder by having his father and uncles continually inform him that what he was learning at school was not to be trusted. He trusted it enough to pass what he had to pass, but when the chance to see another life came up, he thought it best to go for it. That other life was life in Belfast, studying at Queen's. Why had he screwed that up? he now wondered.

'Do you not think that pillar looks like a dragon's tail, Man?' Tracey had been enjoying the vista. Their position gave them one of the best views in the establishment, all down the length of the inner bar, where they could view not only all the brass and the wood and the marble, but the rushing around of the barmen near swept off their feet. (They did their best to not look at themselves in the mirror set into the ornate wooden arch to their right.) The pillar Tracey was referring to was the nearest ceiling-supporting pillar, beyond the taps and the wooden arch with the mirror. Like all the other ones dotted throughout the bar, it was decorated in such a way as to look like it was covered in scales, downward-pointing thick scales, all done in winedark brown, the tips of each scale edged in what might be gilt. The longer they looked at it, the creepier it became. The ceiling into which it was projecting was an organic-looking mass of flattened tendrils, circles and curving lines, done in the thickest of thick dark brown gloss paint, inviting Manny and Tracey in their state of heightened awareness to just look and follow the lines and…

imagine. 'Azi Dahaka,' pronounced a dreamy Manny, and then once more: 'Azi Dahaka…' The nearest barman threw another glance their way, but was suddenly too busy to say anything, distracted by another punter.

'Yer wot?' said a similarly dreamy Tracey, in her best adopted working-class British accent. 'Azi Dahaka,' replied Manny, his eyes tracing out the curlicues of the ceiling to such a degree he had to noticeably swivel his head, and the enormous shock of hair that came with it. 'The three-headed monster.' 'Oh,' said Tracey, as though her partner had just said 'Azi Dahaka, three to one odds at Chepstow.' It took a while for the young lady to process the import, leading to another iteration of 'Yer wot?' To which Manny answered, as an upstanding Brit, 'Darlin', you wa'ant born in the East End of London, so don't come a clappers with me.' Tracey decided this sketch was getting too silly and so asked, straight: 'Look, Manny, what are you going on about?' To which her partner/boyfriend/friend responded by explaining that he had been told stories as a child about this monster called Azi Dahaka and how it had three heads and was a 'really nasty piece of work', but that some 'bloke' had caught it and trapped it, but his parents had strategically not told him that part until he was much older, making him believe that they'd just used the story to intimidate him into going to bed or not fighting with Yar, his younger brother, or to stop picking his nose and eating the contents. 'Gross!' complained Tracey, adding: 'They should have let it loose every time you did!' They cracked up at this and didn't stop until another barman entirely threw them a more pronounced dirty look.

'Tell me again about your family's religion, Zorro,' asked Tracey, her eyes still firmly wandering round the décor. Manny obliged, but he had done so before, wondering why he she had to keep forgetting. Her nickname for him, usually used sparingly, derived from the fact that his family adhered to the Zoroastrian faith, which had been 'mega' back in ole Zanzibar. Halfway through his re-introduction to all that, she blurted out: 'You know, you're bloody Othello, that's what you are.' She had to explain that one, Manny having not studied much beyond the basics of 'England's greatest writer', as his teacher had framed it. (He'd been science-leaning, not arts.) 'Well, imagine I'm Desdemona, his "bit",' explained Tracey. 'And, I'm as white as...' She had to hit the pause button here as Professor Tweedy and his wife and two kids trundled by on their way out, Tweedy nodding and raising a politic hand in farewell greeting and Tracey, and Manny, too, excitedly shouting out: 'Bye, Professor Tweedy! Lovely to see you,' etcetera. Tweedy seemed to blush, his smile an awkward concoction of cheeriness and loss.

'Right, well,' continued Tracey, 'I'm whitey-girl and you da big dark-skinned fellow who sweeps her off her feet.' Manny smiled, asking 'And?' 'And? Well, Othello tells her all this guff about his journeys to Patagonia and meeting the... the... Anthro... pophagi!' Manny laughed at the contortions she had to go through to get that out, combined with the exoticness of what his partner/girlfriend was talking about. 'Well, Trace, don't get too excited. From what I've heard, Zanzibar's not all sand and sea, natives dancing around with shells in their hair! Our family was escaping, so the story goes, from poverty, pure and simple!' 'Oh, don't tell me that, Manny! Don't puncture my dreams. Feed them, ya eejit!' This had the two of them laughing again, perhaps at the ridiculousness of the conversation. Until Manny had to ask: 'So, they end up waltzing into the sunset, then?' which was his follow up question about the Shakespeare play he had no knowledge of. Tracey stopped laughing, paused and said: 'Not quite.' Manny gave her a look, puzzled. Tracey took a huge slug from her glass, savouring the alcohol, and the bubbles, and looked Manny square in the eye: 'He gets all jealous and.... strangles the poor bitch!' At this, she exploded in giggles, so infectious that Manny, despite his initial shock at hearing the end of the story, joined in, slapping the counter with both hands, and accidentally dislodging a random utensil, which flipped up and hit an empty glass which hadn't been cleared away yet. It fell over and caught the attention of the barman, who called out: 'Oi, whatcha'!'

Whatever the barman had intended to say thereafter was lost to eternity as a sudden commotion took over proceedings at the entrance to the bar. In had rushed three soldiers, looking dead serious.

Tracey and Manny looked round to see all this happen and to watch as the soldiers approached the bar and exclaimed in no uncertain terms: 'Everyone out! Bomb scare at the Europa! Everyone out. NOW!'

. . .

Ivan continued to look in horror at the blue envelope adorning his WELCOME mat. He didn't dare go near it, believing it as potentially dangerous as the strange and menacing person who had dropped it there, squeezing it through his letterbox -for what purpose? Was it a list of demands to be met, which, if not, would lead to his execution? More pertinently, as it now inhabited the hallowed space of the inside of his residence, having shown that a front door was no real barrier to exterior threat, was it a letter-bomb? Unlikely, as it looked as flat as a pancake and would have been activated surely when being passed so roughly through the metal flap. But you would never know. It happened a few years ago, if memory served him correctly. The IRA that was. Might lose a hand just touching it. Might be radio-operated! Or, might it be not a bomb, but some weird substance that infected whoever opened it? Or was it just some disgusting stuff inside, designed for Joe Stalin's remote evil pleasure? These and other thoughts and worries continued to pass through Ivan's mind as he hemmed and hawed about what to do.

He knew he'd have to do something. He didn't want it to remain where it was, a nasty, potentially deadly, unknown item to be always stepped over every time he had to go outside or side-stepped every time he had to deal with someone at the door, like the gasman or the postie. He had to act, now. Feeling so, Ivan went into the kitchen, noticing the kettle and wondering why God hadn't made it easier for him just to sit back in his own wee parlour and have a decent cup of tea without having to go through hell first. He'd just come back from the hospital, after all! But, Ivan knew this was no time for self-pity or self-indulgence: *he had to act*. A broom leaning in the corner spoke to him: 'Use me.' So, he did. He could see clearly what he had to do. He didn't particularly enjoy holding the broom by the wrong end, with all the dust and the flakes of whatever stuck through its bristles, but he could use it to poke the envelope… But, Ivan then wondered, what if it was a bomb? There wasn't much distance in the length of a broom… So, he replaced the broom and put his thinking cap on. Two minutes later, he had accumulated a variety of smallish items he had hit upon the idea of throwing at the envelope, with plenty of distance in case anything might happen. These were mostly kitchen utensils, knives, spoons, forks, the complicated tin-opener which looked like it had been designed by and for military engineers, and a few cans of Heinz Beans, and Campbells Soup. Before launching the operation, Ivan reflected that he was well stocked, and he really should open some of these tins sometimes and not just have them sitting around in cupboards gathering dust, and rust.

Standing halfway between the door of the pantry and the start of the stairs, he made a start by lobbing a spoon. It didn't go anywhere near the envelope. Then he threw a fork. It crashed into the door and Ivan worried that he might have dinged the wood. A knife followed, and even managed to hit the outer corner of the target, but its impact on the door again gave him pause for thought. After a brief conference with himself, it was decided that the survival of the door in pristine shape was sufficiently less important than his own survival for him to stop. But, he was starting to lose confidence in the utensils, or, more accurately, his aim. Ivan could see there was only one thing left to do: to up his game and bring out the big guns. He looked at the can of Heinz Beans, wondered what the '57' referred to, decided he didn't care as long as it got him out of this scrape, and then positioned himself to lob it at the envelope. It wasn't going to work from this distance. He should have realized this before, he told himself, but by now he had become bolder, knowing the only way to get a direct hit would be to drop the bloody thing right on top of the envelope. This, of course, was dangerous -pronouncing it 'dang-er-roose', to cheer himself- but with one little genius adjustment, Ivan realized he might just prevail. He went back to the kitchen and retrieved the broom.

One minute later he was holding desperately onto the correct end of the broom while balancing a Heinz can of beans on the other, nestled within the dirty, dusty bristles, leaning out as much as was humanly possible. With all the care and attention to detail of an army bomb disposal expert, Ivan brought the broom end to a position directly above the envelope on the WELCOME mat. He then deftly edged the broom end to one side, sweating from his brow as he did so, the effort to hold onto the handle taxing him mightily. With one slow, meticulous turn of the broom, which also involved slightly turning his whole body at the same time, as he didn't trust his wrist, the Heinz can of Beans fell. Direct hit. It fell right onto the envelope, leaving the tiniest of impressions. Nothing happened. Ivan was delighted, but not finished. It took multiple repeats of the operation, employing a variety of other cans, Heinz Oxtail Soup, Campbell's Soup (many varieties) and something he looked twice at and wondered how he'd ever bought it: Newforge Irish Stew, 15½ oz. That was the last one he dropped, and the last to confirm that whatever was inside the envelope was certainly not explosive. He was so happy to make sure of this he told himself that that was what he'd be having for lunch – if he survived the next stage.

The next stage was a tentative push around with the broom, eventually sweeping it toward him, out of the field of fallen cutlery and cans, as though he'd earned the right to play with it, like a cat with a mouse. It was a thing of little import, and he, Ivan Stacks of Enfield Manor, had prevailed. He would no longer be intimidated by such nonsense. Gingerly, having leaned the broom to one side, Ivan picked up the envelope and, happy to see the flap was only pushed in, not sealed, inserted his index finger. It was done with the greatest care. Seeing that the contents appeared to be only a normal letter, he summoned the remainder of his courage and picked at the edge of the interior letter paper, drawing it out with all the delicacy of an antique dealer handling Victoriana. He was rewarded by discovering that that indeed was what it was, two sheets of normal letter paper, inscribed with words. The words seemed to have been written quite roughly, in a sometimes-smudged black biro, but to Ivan, they gave off a very positive vibe. These two pages of rough handwriting did not look awful at all; they were normal and innocuous, a bit like himself, he suddenly thought.

What was written on them, however, could hardly be described as innocuous, but they certainly gave Ivan plenty to smile about, even if it raised his eyebrows in the process.

. . .

Outside the Crown Bar was the kind of commotion usually only seen during a major disturbance, which this was, but without any visible sign of damage, yet. White-tunicked chefs, still wearing their long white headgear, along with other hotel staff in smart uniforms, were running out from the carpark area of the Europa just across the street. Police and army personnel had already stopped all traffic and were calling out and vigorously gesturing for all pedestrians to move as quickly as possible up the street, and only in the direction away from the city centre and toward Shaftesbury Square and the so-called 'Golden Mile'. Some Crown punters had exited with pints still in hand. Sirens from the emergency vehicles filled the air, as did the expectation of something nasty about to happen. The Europa had already garnered the title of the 'most bombed hotel in Europe', and everyone knew the routine by now. Manny and Tracey were laughing, but mostly out of nervous excitement, never having been in such a situation, only having read about bombs going off in the city centre. They were just two in the gathering crowd of people now being herded away from the danger area, people asking questions, people swapping chat about experiences they'd been in before or things they had heard about this area always being under attack. People who didn't know each other would pass comments easily with others and, if nothing else, the event had created a sense of community in the midst of adversity.

Tracey had to press Manny on their unfinished conversation, though, prompted ever so slightly by the sight of the quaintly ugly GREAT VICTORIA STREET BAPTIST CHURCH on their left. 'When are you going to tell me more about this Zoro… Zoroastrian – is that right? – religion of yours?' 'In the next bar, doll?' replied Manny. He didn't have much money, but Tracey was apparently 'flush', her mother having slipped her a few quid recently. 'Oh, go on, we've got plenty to walk up to Queen's from here. Tell me a bit anyway.' Manny looked back at the chaos they were walking away from and repeated the title he'd said in the bar: 'Azi Dahaka. I told you. The three-headed beast. Maybe he's behind all this. Lord of chaos and all that.' Tracey tried her best to be satisfied, but it wasn't enough. 'Ok, more?' 'Trace, my parents didn't really bring me up religious. And anyway, if you look at it, it looks a lot like Christianity... You have Adam and Eve, we have... Mashya and Mashyana!' 'That's interesting,' said Tracey. But, somehow, still she wondered if that was enough. She thought to ask him more, contemplated doing so in the next watering hole, took his arm and nestled her head at his shoulder, but said little else beyond her short reaction. Manny understood this to mean he'd have to come up with something really Othello-like to charm his 'doll', the wonderful Tracey Williamson, with whom he felt every day more and more worried about losing, especially since he had to decide on what to do next, stay here in Belfast, against the plan, or head back to Birmingham.

They would stop now and again and look back but waiting and staring for any length of time felt a bit ghoulish, like they were hoping to see something explode. Better to walk on, at an idle pace, enjoying the rest of their uncluttered Saturday – neither of them wishing to get into how many more of these they might have left. But now Manny stopped precipitously, edging Tracey to inquire, using that phrase again: 'Yer wot?' They had crossed over a side-road and were now standing outside the unprepossessing Bradbury's Surgical Instruments. Uninspiring as that location may have been, Manny was suddenly smiling, beaming, like a man who'd suddenly seen the light – because he had. 'Bismillah!' he threw out, not necessarily to Tracey, just out, although he did follow that up with a repeat of the word, and this time for the ears of his doll: 'Bismillah!' Tracey asked: 'Is that another one of your strange Zorro words, Zorro?' 'Maybe,' replied Manny, a little mysteriously, adding: 'Ever heard of it? Or just heard *it?*' They had now both stopped and were just standing talking on the pavement of this most non-descript street, only the occasional car or truck passing by, as most traffic had been stopped. Tracey shook her head, but she had to admit there was something about it which rang a distant bell. 'I give up, Zorro. Put me out of my misery…' she half-groaned. 'Something you might have heard on *Top of the Pops*, perhaps?' teased Manny/Zorro. It only took a few seconds, but Tracey had it: 'Queen! *Bohemian Rhapsody!* Got it!' 'Aye,' said Manny: 'Bismillah!' To which Tracey chorused: 'No!' and Manny responded: 'We will not let you go! Will not let you go!' To which Tracey joined in and they went at it together, the music's spirit, *and* the residue of the illegal substance from the Holy Lands, helping things along nicely.

After they had done that to death, Tracey somehow had the presence of mind to ask: 'So, what was all that about, then?' To which Manny leaned over, confidante-like, and whispered close to Tracey's left ear: 'Freddy's a Zoroastrian, too!' This garnered a huge reaction and an admission that she had never known that. But that wasn't to be the final intelligence to be imparted. For that, Manny leant over even closer and whispered so quietly and right into her ear that it did indeed feel like a genuine confidante giving over only the most highly sensitive information.

At this, Tracey literally screamed. 'Your cousin?' she gasped.

· · ·

Meanwhile back at the ranch…

At the top of the first sheet was written: 'Please write the Russian words for these, Grigor. It'll make my day!' On the left side of the sheet were the words in English, a litany of the taboo vocabulary so dear to Abe. On the right were the Russian equivalents. 'Shit' was 'Guv'no', 'Fuck' 'Blyad', 'Cunt' 'Pizda' and 'Tits' 'Siski', or 'Bufera'. It was an education. Ivan felt a tremor of shock just looking at all these words exposed here in black and white, even if he'd never given them a second thought in the midst of drunken conversation with his friend, or with others. Did he, Ivan, swear like that in front of others? (Others = not Abe.) A quick moment of reflection told him that no, he did not, at least not very much, realization of which set him wondering just how much his acquaintance with Abe dragged him down a peg or two... No, he winced, *that's the language of my parents*, Abe 'dragging him down a peg or two', along with 'why couldn't you have made a clean break with him from university?' Well, he had told them, 'because we're friends, that's why!' A tone of exasperation had added an edge to that fairly simple explanation, and the subsequent slamming of his bedroom door had sharpened that edge, making his parents think twice about reviving the topic. Part of Ivan's distaste came from the fact that he could see that his experience at university had opened up a chasm between the school friends, but he was determined not to have that push them apart. University was, after all, 'only an old cod's game anyway', he liked to tell himself, full of la-di-la idiots and poseurs. He always remembered to watch his Ps and Qs whenever he had a drink with Arthur Campbell B.A. and William Savage effing B. A., too. Anyway, this sheet of dirty words was a true education: it exonerated Abe and clarified everything!

Yes! Abe's 'wee project' had been innocent! As innocent as Abe had always been. All he wanted to know was how to say some dirty words in Russian! Ivan could just picture Abe slipping in a few words over a pint of two, maybe a 'Look at the "Siski" on her!' or 'Fancy ordering a "Pizda"?' Ivan laughed out loud at that one; it was as though Abe was right here with him, swapping tales and funny talk, and nothing bad had ever happened at all. Inevitably, perhaps, Ivan's laughing soon descended into a bout of sobbing, not only in the realization of what had happened to his friend on that non-descript little Belfast side street, but as a kind of physical release of all the tension he'd just had to put up with from the headcase with the moustache and the gun. When he'd recovered, and recovered his posture, he sat up straight on the sofa and looked again at the sheets. It was like an epistle from Abe himself, telling his friend he was fine, not to worry.

With a smile, Ivan noted that 'Dinosaur' was 'Ginazava'; 'Ginazavas' had been the start of all this malarkey! He then wondered was that a soft 'G' as in 'Gin 'n Tonic' or a hard one, like 'Gung-ho'? It was a little window -or a sympathetic echo?- into Abe's own fascination, his eagerness to discover things -not the preserve of the uni-crowd that! Yes, Ivan grew more excited to note the non-taboo words, the 'Kak pozyivaite' for 'How are you?' and the standard response of 'Ya voraikiya, spaisiba', 'I'm fine, thank you.' It was a sign that Abe had been truly interested in the language and had possessed a desire to learn. Where would it have taken him? 'Death' was 'Smeirt'. 'Life' was 'Zhizn'. How on earth was that pronounced? Ivan wondered if he might visit the library and find out. Maybe he could buy a wee cassette or something at Smithfield. They had everything, sure. 'Man' was 'Mooshina'! 'Woman' 'Zhenshina!' 'I am Mooshina'!' exclaimed Ivan, feeling emotion swell within his breast once more. 'I am Mooshina'! Then: 'What is 'Friend'?'

He might have fallen for the tears again, but parallel with the sadness he was feeling for the brutal – temporary? – loss of his pal, Ivan was beginning to feel something else – the rise of curiosity. Curiosity about the Russian language, and the cold hard landscape it came from. Belfast had Smirnoff Vodka posters on every corner, but that wasn't Russia. All that 'Leaves me breathless' shite? That was Russia for the masses, a wee sip of the exotic without getting off your backside. What was real Russian Vodka like? Ivan wondered. What was real Russia like? Maybe I should go there, he thought. 'Sure, with a name like Ivan, I'd be welcomed right in!' shouted out Ivan at the pampas grasses in the vase. 'Comrade Ivan Fucking Stacks, no less!', delighting in the swear word, as though Abe were here... He briefly also wondered if his sudden outburst had offended the pampas grass, decided it had and took that as licence to throw his head back and laugh like he'd rarely ever done, at least in the company of only himself.

A moment of two later: 'Davay na pumsika benibud!' exclaimed Ivan once again: 'Let's get drunk sometime!' The final phrase on the second of the two sheets. Abe had thrown that in, no doubt hoping to share a table with the other Ivan in his life, to pick his brains about the land far, far away, where the wind blew hard and icicles hit your face like nails from a nail-gun.

Ivan contemplated that, Russia, like, the cold, like, the wind, like, the icicles and all... saw himself trudging through the barren wastes of the Tundra, arm in arm with the giant Josef Stalin, singing Cossack songs and sipping now and then from what Joe had stuffed away beneath his tarpaulin-like cloak, a bottle of the real stuff, fiery and ninety nine percent, the two of them swapping stories in a fluent Russkie dialect of the Steppes...

And then...

...contemplating that...

Ivan said quietly 'Nah'.

A pause, then:

'Belfast's fine by me.'

And finally, returning the sheets of paper to their envelope:

'I think I'll put that effing tea on now.'

. . .

'Err... second cousin, more like...' said Manny, hands in pockets, hoping this qualification wouldn't dampen down the excited fair damsel by his side. It didn't, but he felt he should throw in a little more detail anyhow. 'Well, from the same place my Mum and Dad came from... you know?' Tracey: 'How could

I forget? The one and only Zanzibar! Did you know him there?' 'Nah,' baulked Manny, 'I was born in Birmingham! You know that! And he's much older than me!' 'Right…' said Tracey, processing all that, but with a look that suggested to Manny she might lose interest anytime now. 'We'd see him sometimes, at festival time, or big family get-togethers… in Brum, of course.' 'What's he like?' she then asked. Manny released his hands from his pockets and allowed them to paw Tracey's long frizzled hair: her excitement was infectious. They were in serious danger of launching into a bout of lumbering here on the street, until Tracey, with her keen eyes, spotted a little side street just up ahead. 'C'mon!' she called and tugging his bomber jacket, ran with him down the street and left into the ever so slightly more discrete territory of Downshire Place, as it was proclaimed on the wall. No-one in sight, they instigated a frantic series of hugs and deep passionate kisses, Tracey holding Manny's jacket with such strength her nails threatened to tear the fabric. Manny pushed her against the brick wall and let his lips wander from her tongue and lips to her face, to her ears and back to her lips. Tracey's hands were no longer gripping his jacket, but bear-hugging her boy ever closer to her, massaging his back, with the occasional pass of her outstretched fingers through his own frizzled but stiffly abundant hair.

Sensing that this might not be the best thing to do even on the most non-descript of little side-streets, she started sending him signals that enough was enough. These were understood in short measure and Manny, ever the gent, desisted, but they still kept close, as though unwilling to break the magic of the moment of their sudden togetherness. Now, though, Manny had a new idea to entertain him, and his left hand went searching in his inner jacket pocket. Tracey looked on as Manny's dark-skinned hand soon re-emerged and holding what she had half-expected it to hold -a joint. 'Here?' she asked, tone and her suddenly widened eyes trumpeting her concern. 'It's just a small one, a few puffs, that's all,' explained an innocent-sounding Manny.

He dragged more than she did, but within a minute it was thrown down the gutter. Tracey couldn't handle too much marijuana, but a little made her merry; Manny's mellow smile told her that he was more than merry. But, for other reasons, they were more than merry together anyway. It wouldn't hurt to walk on air for a bit.

They returned to the main street, hand in hand now, feeling very hippy-ish, and it was as though the Hippy God had blessed them, for not ten paces away was Hippy-Heaven, Sassafras Wholefoods, and the cool Elvis Presley wood cut-out on the pavement advertising Music Heaven just up the stairs: *Good Vibrations!* Tracey loved this shop. Today was turning out to be one long trip.

With her boyfriend's newfound status as a bridge to the heady heights of the rock world (or not), Tracey passed on perusing the Miso cups and packets of dry barley and scooted up the dingy narrow stairs, followed by a dreamy, smiling, slighter slower-of-pace Manny. If anyone would have asked him why it was taking him so long to go up, he'd reply he was already quite high, thank you very much.

Tracey had only ever bought one record here, but it was enough, having garnered all the publicity it did as a home-grown effort of this shop and its illustrious owner, Terri Hooley. (The single had been 'Teenage Kicks' by the 'amazing' Undertones.) And there he was, locked into a typically robust conversation with some other music-mad fellow of a similar age. She had only ever passed a few words in his direction but his glance -and smile — over at her as she entered the small area of the shop, showed he remembered her. He remembered all his customers.

Manny made the last few steps up like a man twice his age, prompting Tracey to ask, laughingly: 'You alright? You better get your puff back!' Still, if it had been an unexpected effort, Manny's smile was still intact, a smile which one might imagine would take World War III to shift.

He followed her lead and, in slightly bemused fashion, started perusing the vinyl record stacks which took up the central part of the shop area (which was so small it had him looking round in a state of stoned incredulity). Tracey and Manny thus maintained this somehow soothing, somehow brain-calming activity for the space of minutes, two or ten they couldn't say for sure, the sounds of the owner's talk with the other fellow drifting in and out of their consciousness, melded with a bit of Jimi Hendrix on wailing guitar. Manny was floating.

It was only when Mr Hooley paused, no doubt for dramatic effect, and then reached down below his counter and ostentatiously took out what seemed to be a copy of his latest pressing -if Tracey squinted, she could just make out 'The Outcasts'- that the dreaminess stopped. 'This!' Terri Hooley virtually shouted, with a vigour and an energy that only the uninformed might have taken as anger. Actually, as anyone could see, it was just passion. 'This is what we can make by ourselves! THIS!' the owner reiterated strongly, holding out the large black and white square single cover. And then, with more than a touch of tonal flourish, he added: 'EMI and Polydor are dinosaurs! DINOSAURS, I tell ye!'

At this Tracey looked straight at Manny and Manny looked straight at Tracey and their minds swapped the same uncanny thought, uncannily: 'How and why was it that the owner had happened to say "dinosaurs" just now?' Had 'their' story and all that razzamatazz with the journalist and the publicity, not to mention the painful embarrassment of it all, so permeated this city as to have become part and parcel of Belfast's linguistic repertory?

Tracey wondered how she'd go about asking that. Contemplation of precisely how she might ended up causing her so much existential stress she started giggling.

This giggling started Manny off, and before you could say 'Cross Town Traffic' the two of them were cracking up. Again. Just as they had done at The Crown Bar, but this time, with no overly sober barmen looking on.

Terri Hooley looked over at them, smiled warmly at the two young people having fun, then resumed his animated conversation, jabbering away about how he felled the frumious behemoths of the music industry with his vorpal sword amidst the brillig, mimsy borogoves.

It was a beautiful day in Belfast.

Chapter Eighteen: Time Warp, Sunday, May 20

Christopher woke about nine o'clock and was gladdened to see it was wet and miserable outside. Central heating, soft carpet and the prospect of whatever he wanted for breakfast shone all the more for it. Yet, sat at the dining-room table, halfway through his bowl of Sugar Puffs, eyes scanning the *Observer* for stories of interest, his cheery feeling took a knock as he realized he would have to loaf it round to St Bernard's for Mass at eleven. 'Grumble groan,' he said to no-one in particular, echoing a catchphrase from The Goodies [TV comedy show]. The only story that caught his eye was one about poor Johnny Weissmuller, who, now at the grand old age of seventy-three, had been reported doing Tarzan calls inside the retirement home he was now confined to, causing a fair amount of bother to his fellow residents. *Well,* thought Christopher, *where's the harm in that? That would be quite amazing, surely,* before moving onto another story ('Ooooo-Ooooooooo-Oooooo-Ooooooooo' sweeping through his mind like Tarzan through the vines).

His mother entered from the living-room and said, 'Good morning, Christopher,' to which he replied likewise. Little by little they swapped other little linguistic parcels, the most striking of which was the news that his mother had taken care of the *News Letter* reporter Ivan Stacks. 'Aye, you said you met him, isn't that right?' she threw out. 'I did, aye,' replied son to mother, adding, with noted concern, and some excitement: 'He was in a bomb explosion? And you nursed him? That's incredible.' Whether it was incredible or not, to be a victim of a bombing in Northern Ireland in 1979, Christopher felt it was so because he had actually met this person, and his mother had taken care of him. 'Well, he was discharged yesterday,' she said. 'Glad to hear it,' replied son to mother, 'thank God.' His mother had been making toast and tea and was now in the process of transporting that back into the living-room, but she paused, holding said tea and toast, and added: 'Well, his friend wasn't so lucky.' Before elaborating, she carried on and deposited the tea and toast on the large rectangular stool near where she would sit and came back to fill in the rest of the news. By the end of telling all, Christopher looked up at her and said: 'Ma, you have a hard job there, I can tell ye. Thanks for telling me. Sorry to hear that. This place...' Nurse Maguire, who was now Ma Maguire, looked down at her son and wondered how she would feel if he were ever to befall the same fate as any of her patients. Then she turned, closed the door and went to have her breakfast.

This place... Yes, thought Christopher, this place is... madness. After that he took to scanning the paper with even more vigour but less delight, and then soon realized he should be scanning his textbooks instead. The 'O's, the 'O's....are coming. The 'Ooooooooooo-Ouooooooooonooo-Ooooooooooo-Ooooooooooooos!'

. . .

Mass was even more miserable than the weather. Christopher and his father had arrived late. Arriving late – to Mass or to the pictures, or wherever – was a common enough occurrence, as his Da, forever 'footering around' with last minute to-dos before leaving the house, even called himself 'Paddy Last'. They couldn't take a pew inside the church proper, as all were filled with parishioners, so they stood in the not particularly roomy entrance area, which was at least dry. Older people were sitting on the benches on either side, all listening intently to every blessed word out of the mouth of Father McClafferty, the much revered and respected local priest at St Bernard's Parish. Standing for forty-five minutes was no joke, but it would be at least punctuated by a little trip to the altar to receive Holy Communion. Today's

Homily was based on the parable of the talents 'from the Gospel according to Saint Luke', as enunciated beautifully and commandingly by the priest.

Christopher, in part attracted by the drama in that voice, listened intently to the few words he could make out, wanting all the time to ask his father what these words meant, but knowing to do so would be embarrassing. Good Catholics, even sixteen-year-old ones, were supposed to know their parables. He couldn't get it about the Biblical father giving his sons talents and one of them wasting said talents… In Christopher's mind, talent was either something you had, or you didn't. How could anyone give you talent? Another annoyance for Christopher was the phrase 'The Infallibility of the Pope' which happened to adorn a poster on the wall next to him. He also wanted to ask his father about this. What precisely did it mean? As ever, complexities and grey areas tended to proliferate – growing out of the walls or materializing from thin air – once he was within the environment of the church. The serious miens of those around, the apparent intentness of their active listening, these were becoming increasingly difficult to account for. If Christopher was ever to stray away from the Catholic faith, he would likely do so under a cloud of confusion rather than by assuming anything like an oppositional stance. If he did try questioning what he had been brought up to believe in, logic would soon founder (because his was built on very shaky ground). Was the Pope 'Infallible' because he never made mistakes? What would happen, Christopher asked himself, if the Holy Father dropped something from his hand as he was reaching over to… like the sanctified Host! *Dropped it before he could lay it on the parishioner's protruding tongue!* Would he still be called 'Infallible'? What if he had to scramble about on his holy knees, effing and blinding, as he searched for the little piece of Our Lord's 'transubstantiated' body? This very spectacle unfolded before his mind's eye, and he found himself having to suppress the titters – which his Da duly noticed and mock-frowned at.

Christopher recalled, more soberly, his own error, when, at the tender age of seven he had gone through what he had believed was just a practice version of his First Holy Communion, even taking the Host on his tongue, and into his mouth where he had happily champed on it, having missed breakfast that morning. To be told that, 'No, that was not a trial, son. That was your initiation into the sacrament' had stunned him. Yet Christopher had told his face muscles not to give away the truth of his surprise. His horror, as he swallowed the remainder of the unleavened bread, dislodging bits from his teeth with his tongue as he did so, was his realization that his first encounter with Our Lord Jesus had likely been impious. He had then compounded this by not telling anyone, his teacher, the priest, his friends, his parents, his brothers, or even the priest in the following week's Confession. This no doubt elevated (or relegated?) his initial slip into full-blown sin. He had not only erred but was guilty of wilful concealment, which was fibbing… which was lying… which was… a venial sin. There were a million ways in which to slip into sin, and you had to be constantly on your guard.

This idea, about damnation through sinning was old hat, however, and he felt recently that it was likely just a load of old rubbish. He couldn't say so for sure, but he was slowly, and largely unconsciously, divesting himself of the mantle of guilt and the cloud of unknowingness that seemed to be the sum total of all Catholic teaching. Christopher half-looked forward to the Pope's visit later that year, but half-didn't. He liked John Paul II – with the kind of publicity he got, how could you not? –, but he still wondered what had happened to his predecessor. Had John Paul I been knocked off? And if so, would the following Pope's 'Infallibility' protect him if he had known anything about that?

And what was Father McClafferty saying about 'talents' now? Christopher hadn't worked out that 'talents' meant 'coins', and so completely misunderstood the possible import of 'wasting talent' that seemed to be central to the sermon. He vowed never to waste his own talents, whatever they might be, and felt that, if anything, that lesson was worth standing in the not particularly warm entrance of St Bernard's Church for forty-five minutes (including the relatively exciting trip to the altar to accept the Host, this time without letting it anywhere near his teeth).

As Christopher and his Da left the church and walked back under the rain in their imitation-Barbour coats, bought at Primark in the recently opened Abbeycentre, Christopher remembered how beautiful the altar looked last Christmas Eve, when they had gone there for Midnight Mass. **Gloria In Excelsis Deo** was spelt out in large pristine white polystyrene letters above that altar, and he felt that sometimes religion could be beautifully mysterious, or mysteriously beautiful. It was such elements which were the perfect counterbalance to complex inquiries and doubts like dots at the end of a sentence. He decided not to try and ask his Da about any of this and instead just said: 'It's pouring, Da.' 'Aye, 'tis indeed,' replied Da.

. . .

Christopher spent the rest of Sunday at the books, with only the occasional break for meals and the odd TV show. He was on a mission, he told himself and that would only end next month, with his trial by combat with the 'O-Levels'. But, last thing at night, before the Ides of Sleep knifed him in the back, after having spent the last thirty minutes dialling blindly between the Voice of America and Radio Moscow on the little radio set he kept under his bed, he remembered Ivan Stacks.

He remembered the dinosaurs, too. He remembered that Ivan Stacks' story had been found to be false. And yet, that discovery hadn't entirely killed the story. It had at least made it known to the world that experts were digging into good Antrim earth and rock to look for fallen behemoths, giant monsters which had roamed about and fought and killed and eaten the living flesh of their wounded prey, or whatever sad semi-carcase that happened to be lying around of a Sunday afternoon. Talking of which, back then there had been no Father McClafferty, no St Bernard's Parish Church, and no St Bernard's Primary School – the one Christopher had attended happily just a few short years ago.

They didn't play with conkers, those boys – the dinos, that is. No, sure how could they even envisage such an activity? Drilling holes in oven-roasted chestnuts and then dropping a bit of string through them, to… to do battle with another kid who'd spent his free time doing the same thing, for the purpose of… seeing which was the stronger. You held yours out -if you lost the toss- on the end of the string and allowed your opponent to take his best crack at it with his. If yours survived that, you could have a poke at his, putting all your elbow into the blow. Destruction of your opponent's conker brought glory, and a chance to go another round with someone else. Christopher tried to imagine a T. Rex attempting to participate and giggled at the sight of the poor beast going up a redner as it became increasingly obvious he hadn't the elbow for such a kind of slaying. All they had were gnashing jaws, and a serious case of bad attitude. Brutes, after all.

St Bernard's Primary had been a school and a half. Christopher amazed himself to think that he could actually be nostalgic and yet be only sixteen years old. Barrack Street had maybe done that, though, obliterating the (*pace* Andy Fairweather Low) Wide-Eyed & Legless Bliss of Childhood. He was now sixteen going on sixty, or so he would look from time to time, like an old man, deprived of his hoard of money, or whatever loveless possession that had made him happy beforehand. He was slowly coming through it, mind. Slowly coming to terms with what it meant to grow up, through changes which were always rude and sometimes a bit rough. Books helped, as did mind-forays into worlds beyond the immediate. Those worlds could be summoned, passively, by music, like that 'amazingly beautiful' album he'd bought by Larry Coryell and Philip Catherine, or, actively, by his etching and by his pen trials with words. Or such worlds could be figured forth ready-made by TV shows like *Star Trek, Lost in Space*, and *The Six-Million Dollar Man*, with their promise of a science beyond science. Given that adults forced him to believe that the unleavened bread of the Host was 'actually' the 'body of Christ' *(which he would then put in his mouth and slowly dissolve with saliva! Ugh!)*, such worlds, Christopher believed, should never be disrespected or discounted as trivial. Reality, he had worked out, had many forms. *'Transubstantiation' was as real as what happened when they beamed you down from the Enterprise to planet Deneb 5.*

Had that been a sacrilegious thought? It had. His head should know, having encountered more than a few in the last few years. Would he wave at Pope John Paul II in his Popemobile or not? That was the question.

The prehistoric world of the non-religious dinosaurs, 'actually' the bodies of giant perambulating animals, was also a world beyond the one in front of his eyes, but one which had been confirmed and was being documented even now. The likes of Professor Jeinkle [sic] was one of the ones doing the documenting, Christopher had learnt that much. The poor beasts lived on now as fossils only, but these remains could be studied and re-animated, at least in the form of pictures, moving pictures and three-dimensional displays in museums all over the world. They were on show not to satisfy fantasists but to show those who knew only this world that another *had* existed previously, an amazing world of jungles and volcanoes and behemoths and pterosaurs screeching through the dusty, or maybe not so dusty, twilight.

Why, Christopher then asked himself, am I still thinking about dinosaurs? After all, he mused, at the end of the day, I find space more attractive, if you want to know. If I had a time machine I would be zooming into the far future, not the distant past. Let the dead remain dead…

Christopher was now on the very verge – or was it edge? – of sleep. His eyes were closed. His head was sunk deeply into the pillow. His body was as inert as a log, a breathing one anyway. And yet, something was tapping him, gently, softly, if metaphorically, on the shoulder… teasing him to imagine an answer to his last question… It was about reality, *his* reality…

It was a strange kind of question.

It was a strange kind of reality.

Was he, the question went, 'actually' a character in some vast, meandering, even quite silly narrative about the beasts of the prehistoric past? Beasts who had somehow come back to life and were living in his modern nineteen seventy-nine world? Was he destined to fight them? Study them? Play with them? Eat them? Or something entirely different…?

And… as his mind began its last unloosening into the deepest void of the darkest night, he also wondered if he would he somehow waste his talents…

Did he even have any?

Should he ask his Da?

Et cetera…

His mind passed into unconsciousness before he could
formulate answers to any of these most curious enquiries,
floating
     as it was
       in the spacetime
         continuum
          dreamt up by
            a bloke
              with a
                funny
                moustache
              with his tongue
              sticking out
             born a
            hundred
           years ago
         this
       very
      ye..
    ..ar

Chapter Nineteen: Time Warp,
Monday, May 21 (and beyond…)

Whether Christopher Maguire *was* a character in a book or not was the least of his worries as he woke up on Monday morning, May 21st, at 6.25 to an insane series of sound and light explosions coming from his dreaded alarm clock. It was an all-white affair, with a taut white over-arching shade on top bordered with tassels, and an oval faced hard-plastic body and dial below. Seen in a shop window, it might be found attractive, even elegant, but, when activated for the purpose it was designed for, it struck its unfortunate prey as a piece of horrorcraft. In tandem with the strident electronic alarm, a rude light flashed on and off and none of this could be de-activated without touching, and then sliding, the incredibly small, and incredibly difficult-to-find, on/off switch at the back of the hated contraption.

It was to be another day in paradise.
And then another, and another.
So, let's just hit the fast-forward button on the VHS…

Barrack Street was not so bad, Christopher had decided, if he was to leave it and graduate up to the big school, up the Glen Road. Barrack Street may have been hard, but some of the teachers had been really great, like Mr McClean, Mr O'Prey, Mr Crilly, Ms Fitzsimmons ('Fitzy') and Brothers Maher, Walsh and Murphy, not et al, instilling a love of learning, and usually with great good humour. Even Bobby, the toothless caretaker, had always been so kind. He'd also made a few good friends, and, with his victory over Kevin Brady, had gained valuable street/school cred. Maybe he had been just too wrapped up in cotton wool from the start.

The 'O'-levels (which had caused extra-'O'rdinary stress) came and went. To his great relief, Christopher ended up passing Maths and Science, and Geography and Irish, too. Whether the examining teacher in the Gaelic viva voce was just very kind or the bar that year was pretty low is lost to history, but 'ro-minic' doesn't exist. ('Never forget lenition and the floating "h"!') The results came out in July, and from then he knew he was destined – a word with strange resonances – to start up at St Mary's Christian Brothers Grammar School on the Glen Road come September, just as his brothers had before him. His grades were even pretty good, with an A in Art and Spanish and English and mostly Bs in the other five subjects, except for Maths and Science which were scrape-by Cs. He felt like a genius. It helped that he not only detested tests but was generally awful at them. So, to actually come through them relatively well put Christopher on air for weeks afterwards.

The rest of the year was a bit of a blur, of activity and incident, full of largely unprocessable new experiences.

First off, it was big news that one of the brood would fly the coop, bringing the idea into Christopher's consciousness that change would come, even to the stable and apparently impregnable fortification of the family unit. Paul had become engaged and would move out and get married the following year. The young Christopher hadn't anticipated, however, that his first meeting with his sister-in-law-to-be, Angela, would involve him throwing her dirty looks and tut-tutting as he walked around the car his eldest brother and her hubby-to-be had rudely driven off the road into a residential wall up the Malone Road. Paul had crashed his Da's cool and very sporty light brown Datsun hatchback, after all, and that had gotten Christopher's hackles up. It helped that before this incident Paul had sometimes behaved like his two younger brothers were like dirt under his feet, so he thought, and so this was his chance to show who was who. That Paul and his fiancée were ok and had not suffered any injury was the last thought on his own ludicrously puffed-up mind-set.

July had its noteworthy moments beyond the 'O'-level results, from the sublime escapism of Christopher Reeve's Superman to the ridiculous flag fiasco in Elmfield Crescent. Seeing the street dominated by Union Jacks (for the first time ever, mind) had rather shocked and depressed the Catholic residents (who made up about 30%), as it had seemed to express the kind of in-your-face triumphalism so redolent of the Twelfth. The housing estate had always been insulated from all that kind of thing on the day, not being on anyone's marching route; but this show of bullish Britishness, seemed to have thrown that 'out the windy'. Those feeling any sense of dismay, however, had had their spirits lifted a few days before the big day. It poured one night, and by the morning, you could see that all the colours of the flags had run. The red ran into the blue which ran into the white, creating a series of ugly dripping artefacts outside each home which had had hoped for better things. It wasn't long before word got out that the flags they'd all bought were Made in China, 'and weren't worth bloody tuppence!' It gave Christopher and Michael a rare chance to share a laugh. And by the end of the day, you didn't have to be Catholic to have seen the farcical side to it. So much for the glory of the Twelfth. The real glory for Christopher came at the end of the Twelfth Fortnight with the arrival of Kal-El, from the planet Krypton -which he'd had to wait for nearly a year to see, as films took forever to make it over the Atlantic Ocean. That was more like the thing. Superman to the rescue! For two hours and twenty-three minutes, within the dark of the Capitol Cinema on the Antrim Road, Northern Ireland had ceased to exist.

Earlier in July, Skylab had finally fallen earthward, but without spectacular cataclysm or massive urban destruction. The boys at Barrack Street had talked it up, though, culminating in a whip-round for all the fish families of the Indian Ocean and sheep families of Western Australia who had lost loved ones. The final kitty came to a whopping 34p, which was spent at end of day in Ann's corner shop, on 'Black Jacks', 'Butter Balls', bars of Highland Toffee and even a few 'singles', enough to satisfy everyone who'd contributed. 'We salute thee, poor fish and poor sheep!' someone intoned before they got stuck in.

In late August, Lord Louis Mountbatten, doyen of the Royal Family, was blown to pieces in an IRA bomb, planted on his little boat in Mullaghmore in Sligo, fishing for lobsters. Eighteen British soldiers were also killed on the same day, in a double attack in Warrenpoint. The 'double' aspect came from the fact that soldiers who came to the aid of those in the first bomb were then killed by a second, remotely-operated booby-trap bomb. The news came in via TV news Special Reports, first about Mountbatten, then, much later, about the soldiers. The evening paper only had reports about Mountbatten, and the more you checked the news later on, even after it was known about the soldiers, the more it seemed that Mountbatten's death was the more important. The IRA had killed a member of the Royal Family, after all. The chimes of News at Ten that night sounded more like death knells from some graveyard scene in a Hammer film, and Alistair Burnett's face and eyes appeared to burn with unprecedented dolour, and anger. Processing all this was not simple for young Christopher Maguire.

Firstly, he was Catholic and attended a Catholic school, and many of his friends were not averse to saying 'Brits out' (and worse) and some had even boasted of taking part in rock-throwing at the army. Many lived in Andersonstown, prime Republican heartland. Next, he himself lived in a mixed area, with Protestant neighbours all around who were part of his life, and his family had never been IRA supporters, always voting

SDLP. Beyond all that, he laid claim to a simple, universal sense of outrage at any violence, albeit with a slowly growing awareness of the larger picture of a state and country-level historical injustice that, if interrogated with any rigour, might develop into ideas that would allow him to see such incidents as Mountbatten's murder and the killing of the eighteen soldiers as simply (?) part of that larger picture. But he couldn't go there, as yet anyway – if ever. To do so, he felt, would be to accept that killing was something he could accept in general, if there were ideas propping it up. Lorca had been killed by ideas, with a gun to the head. Then, on top of all this, there was a sense of outrage for the other injustice, as it seemed to Christopher to be, that here was a society expressing an inordinate amount of rage and grief for one august upper-class fellow (admittedly with others dead, including children), while relegating the deaths of so many ordinary – if uniformed – beings to some lesser utterance of outrage. It was not a good day. It was part of the 'madness', and he was glad he didn't have to go through it at school the next day, among some others who might revel in it as... victory. Furthermore, complicating matters, was he so high-minded about this not to feel a little of that, too? Some tiny admiration for an organization which could take on the might of the British Army and had connections to his uncle (twice removed?) Wish Fox, who had been one of the original IRA...? David and Goliath and all that...?

Two days later, Ma drove with her three sons to Ballycastle's Oul Lammas Fair. It was a beautifully sunny, if blowy, day. To get there they had to go through three checkpoints and the soldiers or UDR [Ulster Defence Regiment] officers at all of these looked grim. After arriving at Ballycastle and parking and making their way through all the hustle and bustle of the hundreds of visitors, enticed by ice-cream, hot-dogs, 'Yellow-man' (sweet, crunchy honeycomb), and whatever the bars had on offer, all thoughts of Northern Ireland's hell were put on the backburner. It was, Ma Maguire had realized, one of the last chances to enjoy things with all three sons, as she had done for so many years, before Paul's departure. And if the Da happened to be busy that day, it was no skin off her nose; she had them all to herself. It was a great wee day.

It was also the last chance for Christopher to enjoy things before starting up at 'the big school', reached now by not merely one bus-ride, but another jaunt in a black taxi, up the Falls and through 'Andytown'. Life was going at breakneck speed now. New surroundings, new teachers, new classes, new friends, new ideas, all happening with no proper chance to process any of it. The word pen trials continued, but the picture-drawing dried up. Words were gaining ascendency in his mind, the word-sounds he needed to produce in order to mimic the correct pronunciation of French, or the beautifully colourful idioms and phrases in Spanish, taught by the ebullient, engaging and always entertaining Pat Rice. From '¡Yo sigo en mis trece!' ['I'm sticking to my guns!'] one week to '¡Para mi! ¡Para mi! ¡Pan Bimbo!', a local Spanish jingo for bread, the next. He made the language come alive. Then, under Fergie Woods, Christopher could submit essays and original short stories, which would be given accurate and detailed feedback. Christopher's stories weren't initially very good, but he learnt from the feedback. He had had similar teaching at St Bernard's Primary under their great form teacher, Mr Herron, so he knew to listen and try again. It was heart-breaking for him to learn that such kind of class would not continue for the following year, which would focus purely on English Literature – not on his own creations! This made these classes more intense and important, for here he was given the chance to create his own worlds, or tiny glimpses of such anyway.

Then in late September, Pope John Paul II came to Ireland. From the family, only Christopher accompanied his father in the car, down to the giant field, converted for the day outside Drogheda, to join the multitudes. There had been discussion at his school, with many expressing the view that the Pope was by no means to be venerated, not a bit of it. Apparently, he would only come to tell the Irish to reject all violence and obediently put up with the continued eight hundred years of subjection, *and* he had likely put the finger on his poor predecessor, who, 'after only thirty-three days on the job', had died 'mysteriously', nudge, nudge, wink, wink. But it wasn't for these reasons that Christopher, stood beside his father in the midst of the screaming faithful, decided not to wave at the Pontiff as he glided past in his Popemobile, but because he distrusted the feeling *that he should, or that he had to*. He did put his hand up, just for the benefit of his Da, and maybe the hordes around him, but he consciously didn't wave it. If Pope John Paul II had made him out in the midst of the hundreds and thousands, he might likely have thought the boy was wanting to ask him a question.

There were a few such questions he had been thinking of, of course, 'infallibility' and 'transubstantiation' among them, but it wasn't until the following year, after Mr Dermot Tohill, their teacher of English Literature, had handed him a book by James Joyce that he would really know what it was he wanted to ask the Pope: something like – *Why do you need to scare people?* If Stephen Dedalus had received a shock during his retreat, Christopher had also received one a few short years before, one fine afternoon in Barrack Street, under the tutelage of Mr Crilly, whom everyone liked, and who had beamed praise upon Christopher for teaching Kevin Brady a lesson. 'Boys,' he said to his form class in the bright classroom, everyone sitting obediently and quietly and happily at their wood and iron desks, 'imagine you go home today, and on the floor of your kitchen you see your father lying there dead. How do you feel?' No-one spoke. There was a change in the atmosphere; some of the airiness and glee of the day had gone out the window. Mr Crilly walked around a little, in his leather jacket and his dandy moustache. He had a bit of a strut about him, and his chiselled features and general cheeriness made him popular. He was from down the country in Maghera and he loved hurling. No-one knew why he was suddenly talking like this. Maybe he'd been told to by the Brothers. 'Imagine,' he continued, 'you walk into the living-room, and there, on the carpet of your living-room is lying... your mother. Dead. How do you feel?' Well, it was a question, or a pair of questions, nobody wanted to answer. The shock of contemplating this had Christopher feeling hollowed out and extremely unhappy. After a suitably long pause, in order to let the shock sink in, Mr Crilly continued: 'Imagine this, boys. Imagine how you feel and then... multiply it by a factor of ten.' The boys thought about this, especially the ones who were good at mathematics. 'This,' the teacher concluded, 'is how Hell would feel, if you were to fall into it by straying from the path and sinning without any thought for your soul.' He then explained the various ways in which this might happen, but by that time, every boy sat there had undergone a kind of trauma and would accede to anything as long as it meant that their parents would be okay.

It would take the reading of James Joyce's *A Portrait of the Artist as a Young Man* during his second year at Glen Road, to show Christopher that this kind of instruction in the ways of the church was common, if not commonly written about. For this reason, Christopher fell in love with Joyce. And that he – Joyce / Dedalus – was an artist and couldn't care less about religion – indeed, heartily detested it – made it all the better. He would be an artist, too! Employing artistic... talent!

So, yes, if the Holy Father had stopped his motorcade, noticing the solitary boy with his unwaving hand held up in the midst of the hand-waving multitudes, and had come over and asked: 'Pray, tell me, child, what question is it that you want to ask?' Christopher would say it right to his holy, pontifical, well-meaning, smiling face: *Why the fuck do you need to scare the bloody effing bejaysus outta little kids? Is the Catholic Church mad?'* (Christopher had learned to speak like this a long time ago, inspired by a wee sheep on Carnmoney Hill…)

Alcohol was designed for Catholics, Christopher thought once. It helped to assuage the pain of exasperation that was the by-product of the Catholic Church's huge operation to swindle the mind of the ordinary (Catholic) man out of his inheritance of the riches of the earth. The Earth was not to be enjoyed as a play park; the Earth was a sub-station on the celestial path to heaven, and if entering Heaven meant abiding by all the bye-laws and rules, this sub-station was more like a training ground for the soul, with very little time left for playing around. That was a recipe for getting pissed out of your head, because who on God's earth could be expected to follow all that and still be called a human being. It was all too much; as a concept, drunkenness was much easier to swallow.

And so, it came to pass, on Thursday the twenty second day of November, 1979, just a month and two days since he had become seventeen years old, that Christopher Maguire found himself in a place he had long wanted to enter and enjoy, a pub. Properly: a Public House. Historically: everything from an Alehouse to a Gin Palace to a Bar to a Spirit Grocers. Christopher had in fact been to a pub -this same pub- on two previous occasions, but both those times had been cut short by objections from the head barman, who wouldn't sell drink to the underage. Now he had edged closer to the goal of eighteen, legal drinking age, and he was flanked by two older fellows, his brother Jim and Jim's friend Peter, whose guardianship of Christopher seemed to satisfy the staff at Kelly's Cellars, in Bank Lane. If they said he was eighteen years old, then by golly he was. They had just finished their day at Queen's, and Chris had just finished his day at Glen Road. They had met by chance in Donegall Square, under a miserable rain and fierce cold. Jim and Peter were seeking sanctuary and Chris asked if he could tag along. Jim and Peter had taken Chris downtown on a few occasions and had done their best on many occasions to get him in to see films that were classified 'X', meaning off-limits for under-18s, like, just that year, *Carrie* (X), *Rolling Thunder* (X) and *The Town That Dreaded Sundown* (X). The last two were a double bill.

Once ensconced in the dry and warm woody paradise of Kelly's, Chris tried to explain a little about what had been on the agenda during his day at school, but whatever that was, it wasn't enough to displace what everyone was talking about that day, about what was going on with Gerry Fitt and the SDLP. Kelly's was a bar where you could discuss politics, from, that is, the Nationalist perspective, and as the news filtered in from the overhead TV that Fitt had quit his party, Jim and Peter and quite a few others had even more to talk about. 'Good fucking riddance!' said Jim. 'Go and fuck the Queen!' said Peter, 'we all know you want to!' They clinked pint glasses to this and, as an afterthought, clinked with their underling, too, who had to make do with a half pint of Smithwick's. (But a halfer could be potent for a novice…)

The chat continued along the lines of how unutterably awful Gerry Fitt (with his famous 'singlet', the vest he'd been wearing once when attacked by some yahoos) was and how much they hoped and prayed that John Hume would take over, with a host of other political side swipes, but it was a conversation in which Christopher felt more like an observer than a participant. But that was okay. He was just glad to be in Kelly's. He looked around and took it all in.

Before he could take in very much beyond the cave-like atmosphere with its whitewashed walls, long turned a rich off-white by generations of tobacco smoke, or feast his eyes upon the enormous and enormously comforting glowing open fireplace next to them, or the various wall-hangings of ancient advertisements and road signs indicating how many miles it was to Falcarragh [in Donegal], his gaze was diverted toward the two young lasses who had just entered and taken up seating immediately adjacent to them. One of them in particular struck him as beyond attractive, looking like a dark-haired Jane Fonda. Or was it partly because of the effect the Smithwick's was having on his adolescent mind – or some other part of his anatomy? Chris wasn't sure of anything except that he was enjoying being there, in from the cold, supping a magical potion as he surveyed the beautiful scenery.

While everyone was discussing today's political events, it came as a breath of fresh air to overhear that the two gals, after they had settled in and had gotten their drinks, were more interested in discussing literature. And literature Christopher knew: Seamus Heaney!

'The bollocks!' said Jane Fonda, the prettier, in Chris's mind, of the two. It seemed they were Queen's students, and not because of the way they used the English language. Barbarella was apparently complaining about her professor's handling of a point she had brought up today. And now -it was clear from her holier-than-thou intonation- she was mimicking her professor: '"Of course, Grace, but, you know, that narrative about the two dinosaurs turned out to be bogus... I doubt if Mr Heaney gave it a moment's notice..." Oh, aye,' she added, 'Mr Heaney only knows about feckin' Greek literature and Scandinavian mummies!' She and her friend laughed heartily at that one, her friend throwing in, with similarly cutting mimicry: 'Don't you know, Grace, Mr Heaney doesn't read newspapers like *common* people!'

Grace! Her name was Grace! And Grace was also something Christopher knew about, because after Confession and prayers of Contrition, you would be in a state of 'Grace' until the next time you sinned. Well, Christopher felt like he wouldn't mind being *in her state of Grace*. He had to drink more – the moment demanded it – and made noises in that direction to his brother, who thankfully acceded, this time ordering a pint for the pint-sized one. This made Chris very happy, but he was also very frustratingly curious about what the two girls were talking about exactly. He could see a copy of Heaney's latest, *Field Work*, in Grace's friend's hand, but not having read that book yet, could only speculate that some poem in it must have a dinosaur reference in it. What a thought!

Christopher had long been reading Heaney. His whole family had. It seemed like an essential part of any literate Catholic's upbringing in Northern Ireland. His articles in *The Listener* or on BBC Radio or wherever had articulated with great eloquence the plight of the northern Catholics, as had his poems. Christopher didn't always understand what Heaney's poems were about, beyond the 'on the farm stuff', but all his copies, since *Death of a Naturalist* were mightily dog-eared from overuse. He sometimes thought Heaney was his teacher -of poetry, of the technical side and that which spoke on moral issues. Heaney, he knew, was certainly speaking up for the wrongs and the injustices meted out to the generally Nationalist, Catholic minority of this artificial state. *But had he also been writing about dinosaurs?* The idea was so hilarious and compelling that Christopher, halfway through his second drink, which was taking effect nicely on widening the parametres of what was or wasn't acceptable behaviour, was wondering if he might poke his nose in. Whether his interest was purely literature-connected or not was another question. He bided his time, however, sipping at the liquid he still wasn't used to, hoping that Grace and her friend didn't take notice of him, or take offence at him for… leering.

Next, they seemed to be discussing a poem Chris *did* know,

'Requiem for the Croppies', and saying more things beyond Chris's knowledge of the piece. He gathered that they were saying that Heaney had somehow made it clear that he would no longer read said poem in public, because…? He couldn't quite catch why, and because he couldn't quite catch why he felt all the more inclined to tip his head even more the girls' way and just insert himself into their chat. Curiosity is an often-irresistible force. ('As is desire,' his inner voice whispered.) Jim and Peter had now graduated from local politics onto films, and specifically the latest one by Woody Allen, *Annie Hall.* They were recounting this scene and that and chortling hugely in the process. Jim at one point told Christopher that he should see it at the QFT [Queen's Film Theatre], that it was only AA, so he'd be allowed in no problem. But Chris wasn't paying much attention, his eyes and ears locked onto what their lovely neighbours had to say. He was feeling the effects of the alcohol, too, and was getting worried that the closer he got to the dregs, the sooner the brother would announce they were leaving. He had nothing to lose, surely. He had to find the courage.

To paraphrase Hamlet, Christopher had come to the 'To poke one's nose in, or not to poke one's nose in? -that is the question!' moment. As Peter and Jim replayed the lobster-in-the-kitchen scene, cracking up as they did so, throwing out half-remembered lines and then cracking up some more, their silent charge Christopher allowed his head to appear to wobble a bit and then, as though suddenly weighing ten tons, it sidled left-wise, on compliant shoulders. 'Sorry, but is that the latest Seamus Heaney?' said an out-of-body Christopher, taking the girls, and himself, by surprise. Jim and Peter paid no attention. To Chris's amazement and no little glee, the two young ladies looked at him, smiled and Grace even spoke: 'Yeah. You into Famous Seamus?' 'Oh aye,' said Christopher, drawing upon his vast repertory of fancy phrases. He was emboldened: 'Is there some reference to dinosaurs in that book? Sorry if I overheard, but I've read all his books, but don't have that one, yet.' Grace fumbled around looking for the book, found it and tossed it over to him. Chris caught it eagerly and showed something like reverence as he surveyed the paperback cover, with its brown map graphic design; he then started to peek inside. Before he could raise his head to ask where he could find the reference, Grace directed him to the middle section of the second poem, which was in three-sections. Chris soon found that, but obviously had difficulty in identifying the line in question. This problem turned into opportunity as Grace then detached herself from her friend and shuffled over on the bench she was sitting on and pointed out the offending part to Christopher. He read, haltingly: 'Dogs in a siege. Saur...ian *relapses*...? Piss (?) mires? What the...' He then looked up at Sex Queen Jane/Grace/Barbarella Fonda, with her hazel eyes, pronounced eyelashes and radiant dark gloss vermillion lips, and, instead of saying what he had thought he was going to say, said instead: 'You're beautiful, Grace.' He was so close to her, so close to beauty, so ...he was virtually shaking with delight, desire, and not a little dread. If this was a sin, he liked it.

Grace graced her young suitor with a smile, pinched the book smartly back and retook her seat beside her friend, who then said: 'Oh, my, you have an admirer!' The two girls laughed heartily at that, and Jim and Peter, having witnessed the whole thing did so, too, Jim calling out, to Christopher's absolute embarrassment: 'We just have him out for the day! We have to get him back to the funny farm by six!' At this, all, all except the butt of the joke, cracked up in chortles. Christopher's face was quite red, but in the dim light of the interior of the bar, he was at least glad no-one would notice that trivial aspect. Even so, he'd had enough of Kelly's, enough of being little brother, enough of having embarrassed himself in front of Jane Fonda, and

'Heather', as he discovered, her not-half-bad-looking friend, enough of Seamus Heaney, too, and enough of thinking about effin', bloody, stupid, friggin' dino-bloody-saurs.

He made a promise to himself there and then never to think about dinosaurs ever again, to never care what they looked like, never be interested in them, or to find out about them at the library, read about them, watch them in crap B-movies, or enjoy imagining their stupid fat bloated bodies amble through the vegetation and the volcanoes, chomping away at tufts of grass or each other, making a bloody mess, and causing general effin' mayhem. They could all go take a hike. Dinosaurs, Christopher decided, were out! Finito! Kaput! *That's it: me and dinosaurs are over and out!*

The main barman, who had just returned from some outside engagement, brought the curtain down, thankfully for young Christopher, by approaching Jim and Peter and having a quiet word to the effect that their 'charge' looked a mite young, and would he have any identification on him, Sir?

Exeunt

BOOK TWO

Chapter One: Extreme Time Warp, Tuesday, August 6, 2019

'**M**ichael McDonald, as I live and breathe!' exclaimed a now fifty-six-year-old Christopher Maguire. 'Bout 'ye, mucker,' said a similarly aged Michael in response. They were standing in a carpark. They hugged.

They had met in 2011 – for the first time in 'millions of years' – and again in 2015, but on both occasions, only for an hour or so each time. Today they could spend the afternoon together, and where better to start than in The Bellevue Arms, the local for the lucky inhabitants of the estates of Elmfield, Collinward and wherever else was handy and thirsty.

Millions of years stuffed into forty, but with enough background details shared in the interim to make their chat in The Bellevue as unhurried and as unstuffed as could be. What mattered was the quality of the Bass, and the fact that, as Christopher pointed out, the head on it was – happily – miniscule, in great contrast to the heads on pints poured back in Japan, where he had spent the last near-on thirty years. 'This,' pronounced Christopher, 'is how it should be done. Just look at that.' So they did, briefly -look, that is-, at the two full pints of burnt umber ale, each with their miniscule frothy heads, in glasses imprinted with the large red diamond icon and name, surface clouded by a patina of fine condensation, adorning the black speckled-marble table top before them. With the thumb and index finger of his right hand, Christopher showed Michael just how large the Japanese 'British pub' froth-head was. 'That's criminal,' said Michael. 'You should complain to the authorities about that.' 'God knows I've tried,' said a disconsolate Christopher. 'Well,' said a cheery Michael, 'here's to trying!' – with which comment he reached forward and grabbed his pint from its still-life existence and, Christopher taking note, did the same and they clinked. 'Welcome back, Mucky Pup!' toasted Michael, and Christopher: 'Good to see, ya, Mucky Pup Bro!' They imbibed. Heartily.

The Mucky Pup thing had come about from long ago, way back in the sands of time, not long after they had met at the miniscule age of six. Michael's mother had dubbed them so, aghast one day at the state of their clothes from a day's play down the fields or up at Cave Hill. It stuck – not the dirt, but the name – and they would trot it out endlessly back in the day, even – back in the idyll of childhood – as they ambled down the street, arm-in-arm, singing the Mucky Pup Brothers song: 'We're the Mucky Pup Brothers, and we love our mothers!' And they did, very much, and continued to, even if now their beautiful mothers were only memories. Christopher had lost his Ma ten years previous, but Michael only the year before. But he'd subsumed the grief since, and any reference to his Mum, Ina, now brought only a smile and a sharing of stories of this and that memory. Of more immediate interest was Michael's sharing of his trials and tribulations with the Social Security people, who had turned down his request for further disability payments. He felt he was owed these due to the savaging his hands had received from all the industrial-strength bleaches and disinfectants he had had to handle in his years as a cleaner at the Post Office. He showed Christopher the letter he'd penned. It was wittily combative – whatever grievance it contained was communicated with a gracious understatement. Certainly no hyperbolic anger or indignation of man against the machine and all that. It was Michael's style, then and now. He had no interest in taking things too seriously, and no interest in nurturing stress. That said, he had no interest in playing his part as an obedient cog in a wider society that exploited you for what you could contribute, and only recompensed you with the paltriest of rewards. It wasn't his style to just take it on the chin, either, because that wasn't style, but character. And Michael had plenty of that. Christopher had long been aware of Michael's essential hippy-ness, his refusal to take part, to 'play the game', to 'roll with the punches', or whatever crap cliché it was that described the game of society everyone was supposed to play. Michael, he knew, didn't buy into the religion thing either. 'I'm no Prod,' Michael had told him another recent time. 'Maybe you could call me a White Rastafarian!' This Christopher found amusing, for what it said about Christopher's own thoughts on societal classifications (for having broached the silly subject in the first place), and on Michael's propensity to light up whenever he felt the urge.

'Happily retired? And you're only fifty-six?' exclaimed Christopher. 'Sure, *I'm* worked to the bone! Eri has me working at a part-time university *as well as* the main one, and so there's me, nose to the grindstone, four days a week, slogging away!' 'Criminal!' said Michael, deliberately echoing his earlier comment about the beer there, and they both cracked up. Yes, Christopher had gone on – from his 'O'-levels, which were now a dull ancient memory, and very, very much further on from there – to become, via Trinity and Queen's, a professor at a university in Yokohama, Japan, teaching and publishing academic papers on everything from Late Middle English literature to James Joyce and *Star Trek*. And he had even indulged his creative writing 'talents', as he now thought he had, and had published a few tomes under what was essentially his own press. (Whether it was because he knew he hadn't a snowball's chance in hell of being published properly or simply because he didn't have the patience and endurance to sell himself in the big marketplace, the jury was still out.) And yes, also, Michael and Christopher had followed very different paths over the years... but that didn't seem to matter a damn, especially because it was now Christopher's round. 'Not at all, Chris,' Michael interjected, 'you're a guest here.' He then went up and ordered two more but made Chris's a Guinness by request. The impression that Michael was flush, which would always be the impression when one of two drinking partners shelled out for a second round, was enhanced by the news that he would be 'scooting off' to Lanzarote the very next day. 'Jesus,' said Christopher, enjoying the perfectly traditional thick head on this pint now (which you *would* get in Japan), 'retired, throwing the money round and off to Lanza-bloody-rote? You're doing well!' 'Oh aye!' said Michael with a smile and a nod of the head and 'sure, I've earned it!' At that moment, serendipitously, considering the subject, he received a video-call on his Samsung smart phone from a friend who had preceded him there and was already lapping up the sun and sipping cocktails.

This gave Christopher a few moments and more to reflect on things (and to sup). He would meet Eri and his two – rather grown-up – kids a few days later when they sidled into town at the start of another of their family adventures in Europe. If Michael was going to Lanzarote, Chris would be seeing the sights of Dublin, Paris, Rome and Madrid, a mad tour in anyone's estimation. The latter city in particular held great memories for him from his sojourn there with his fellows Domhnall and Liam soon after graduating, to teach English for three or four months. Madrid was a lively place indeed. But he expected it still wouldn't be as lively as Ireland, which always involved meeting family and friends and neighbours, in, quite frankly, a punishing schedule that exhausted the two boys. It exhausted him, too, even on trips by himself when he'd get into late night sessions, the craic going ninety in the Isle of Man and all that. Christopher could never forget the walk he had endured one morning *after* a night spent in the company of his old Spanish teacher, Pat Rice, who was still going strong with his lovely Ecuadorian wife Martita. (Yes, what a glorious thing it was to have re-connected and become actual close friends!) They had ploughed through two bottles of Los Vascos 'tinto' and talked up a storm of memories and observances on the world as it was now, in both English and Spanish. It was fantastic, as always, to meet up and 'charlar' about things, but that night had also involved a mad late night taxi ride to his brother Jim's, where he had imbibed and charlared even more. Having then thrown up in his hotel room later that same night, interrupting a sleep he had hoped was uneventful and sating, the next morning had been seen him stagger, like some figure drawn by Ralph Steadman in *Fear and Loathing in Las Vegas*, from his hotel to the place of meeting his extremely respectable eldest brother Paul and sister-in-law Angela – at, to cap it all, the Belfast Hilton Hotel! It was only with superhuman will power and self-control (of his bodily functions) that he'd managed to maintain a passable smile and had acted with a cheery demeanour throughout. Christopher had certainly advanced from his early days in Kelly Cellars when a pint and a half would go to his head and give him notions...

And his relationship with his eldest brother had improved immeasurably with age. It was likely because little bro Chris had gone out and made something of himself in the world rather than just be Paul's littlest brother. They could now talk about the ordinary, and the extraordinary, goings-on in the family they'd 'graduated from', and about shared interests like music, films and travel. Whatever age, outlook, and attitude gap had existed previously had been largely dissolved with the passage of years. There had never been such a gap between himself and the middle brother, Jim. They had always been on the same level, or, perhaps more accurately, on the same planet. Books, films, music – they shared talk of these on a continual basis. The world and delight of the guitar had been shared, too, Jim having mentored Chris at the very start. Indeed, the shared interests thing had its roots in Jim's constant efforts to 'educate' his younger bro, from the early seventies, whether it was through asking the Da to allow him to read books with swearwords in them or dragging him to X-rated Bruce Lee films and the like.

Both of Christopher's brothers were now suffering from medical ailments, however, limiting the chance he would have to spend time with either -Jim, still occupying the 'ancestral' family home in Elmfield, and Paul, occupying his own much more impressive homestead with the lovely Angela in the lofty realms of posh Hillsborough. He would meet them separately, and enjoy separate communications with both, a state which had more plusses to it than minuses. Families, he had to come realize, are great institutions altogether, but just how they operate is really a bit of a mystery. Once you separate the members out, knotty things, like subtle, or even not so subtle, inter-criticisms, gripes etc., would become much easier to work out, or work around. Subsequently, Christopher navigated between the two, ceding different points to one about the other, and vice versa – anything for a quiet life –, or throwing out a sudden 'What are ye watching recently?' if that didn't work. He'd report only to himself at the end of the day about the respective progress of both. This was the fun of being the youngest.

But now Michael had ended his chat with his friend and they had come to the point of closing operations here, too, so that they could embark on their pre-arranged 'wee jaunt' up to Bellevue Zoo. 'Sure, we can walk, it's only up the road,' suggested Christopher naively. And then, even more naively, 'Michael, sure, you can't be driving after two pints…?' Michael duly informed Christopher that his constitution wasn't what it once was and, with a wry smile, that in regard to using his 'pins' [vis-à-vis 'legs'] this was Ireland, mate. Christopher, fresh from the land of strict adherence to the letter of the law, smiled, shrugged his metaphorical shoulders and got obediently into the car.

It was indeed only a very short jaunt from the carpark of The Bellevue Arms to the carpark at the Zoo – five minutes, if that – with both of them remarking on what would have been there in days of yore: the circular lion house at the entrance, for one thing, and Barry's Amusements right where they had parked, for another. This whole area had once been what was called 'Belfast's Mountain Playground', with trams coming in here from the early 1900s, packed with happy workers seeking a bit of refreshment or to let their nineteenth-century kids go wild (but in a manner likely very different from the way they did nowadays). Michael and Chris had certainly gone wild at Barry's, riding The Ghost Train, which would rudely smash through its doors and enter a darkened world of illuminated skeletons and lunatic screams, then rudely smash out again into the light, everyone on board now happily traumatized. Or they'd be smashing each other on the dodgems, with the sparks flying and the smell of electricity thickening the air. Now it was just a carpark, but still with its view of Belfast Lough, and the Carnmoney Hills to the left and wee housing estates, like their own, dotted in between. 'Titanic had sailed out to sea up that stretch of water', thought Christopher, looking at the shining Lough.

Another stark reminder of the days of yore was the first landmark they came to soon after paying the entrance charge (which Christopher insisted on) – The Floral Hall, in all its horribly dilapidated glory. It had been dilapidated when they were kids, too, but still it stood there as a pathetic token of what it had once meant to so many, a dancer's paradise, a ballroom of romance and all that. The last time they'd gotten close and looked inside it had been used for the storage of silage and animal-tending implements, a long, sad, distorted echo of the ballroom it had once been. (Christopher even briefly entertained the notion of getting in a reference to it being Hiroshima Day today, the circular building resonant with the Dome, but thought better of it.) Thankfully, the sudden appearance of little furry animals to the rear of the building, which was a grassy bank, diverted their view and gave them something to smile about: Meerkats! It was one of the aspects of Belfast Zoo they had always enjoyed, the fact that now and again you'd have the occasional bit of wildlife appear beyond their enclosures, snooking about as free as anything. And they didn't run away at the sight of those larger bipedal animals who seemed to wander anywhere they could go. So Michael and Christopher ended up spending the best part of half an hour entertaining their little friends and themselves in the process, until it was time to dander off and do the tour proper.

Michael wasn't into walking that far, however, and said so, so the two friends just visited a few choice attractions, of which the first was the best, the sealions, and just beyond, the penguins. As children, living in Elmfield, only a stone's throw away, they had regularly heard the sealions' honking away, at night, and Tina the elephant occasionally trumpeting, too. They would also hear the roar of the lions and tigers, uttering whatever it was they were feeling about being cooped up in cages in this godawfully cold corner of the world. What a place to live in, Christopher had often thought, and with glee and wonder, to be able to hear the sounds of exotic animals every night, as though he were living in Africa or the jungles of South America. (The animals likely felt something similar but in diametric contrast.) So, Christopher and Michael thoroughly enjoyed watching these seals and penguins doing their watery acrobatics and their full-throated honking, up close and personal, like.

'They made a wee movie about this place,' informed Michael. 'Yeah?' responded Christopher, 'this place? The zoo? What was it called?' Michael smiled and said: 'Err… "Zoo".' Christopher: 'Just "Zoo"?' 'Aye.' 'Fuck,' said Christopher, 'that's imaginative!' 'Mebbe they think it's the only feckin' one in the world,' japed Michael. 'Hey, I've got this film I want to show to you people,' said Christopher, now mimicking a broad American accent. 'It's about this here zoo, you see...' He prompted Michael, who was already too busy laughing, to ask about it, finally getting, in Michael's best Yankie inflection: 'Well, I just gotta hear me about this... [gasping as he spoke] ...What you'all gonna call it there, feller?' To which Christopher, half-bent with laughter himself, said: 'Wait for it... Wait for it... ZOO!' By this stage, Michael could offer no riposte, beyond a stifled 'Fuck', nor could Christopher add anything more; they just stood laughing their socks off as the sealions honked and splashed away, all of them inhabiting the same space, which was, and would be, as long as memory ever lasted, timeless.

They didn't spend a lot of time thereafter, as Michael hadn't quite the energy for it, and also because he said he'd have to pack: 'Gotta hunt down that toothbrush and the bottle of Bush.' So, they made their way back, having shouted out their farewells to the elephant, the giraffes, the wee red panda, and the tigers and the lions, and their heady smells. It had been immensely satisfying for Christopher to have done this, to have travelled ten thousand miles, and an even vaster expanse of time, and re-connected with his first ever, and best-ever friend. He'd had friends who had... fallen away, for want of a better description, and friends, the same age as him, who had died, for want of a better... reality? One way or another, it had been a tragedy of losses. Friends from school, friends from his university days at Trinity... Distance had played a part in either straining relationships or testing them. And that distance had either amplified misunderstandings or intensified bonds, nurturing slow-burn sensitivities or heightened awareness of the fragility of things. In contrast, the complete lack of contact between Michael and Christopher had somehow preserved intact the friendship as it had been at its height. The friendship, the bond, had just been as though in cryogenic stasis, untouched by the vicissitudes of clumsy interaction at an unmanageable remove, patient over decades.

In such a spirit, Christopher was so glad to have had the chance to spend time with Michael today. And yet… there had been one tiny, tiny, tiny disappointment, too. On their little stroll round the pond, which lay just beyond the Floral Hall, Christopher had spied the granite outcroppings of the Cave Hill and, as though it were his first time ever to see them, suddenly yelled: 'Look at that!' Michael did, but without understanding the drama. 'Let's go there, too,' Christopher had then suggested strongly. 'Up there? You must be kidding, Chris,' Michael had answered, and then explained how long it would take to get there, and the effort involved… 'And you can't go through the Zoo nowadays…' Christopher was still in a kind of rapture just looking up at the mysterious rock profiles, like the Cliffs of Moher, with only sky, not sea as their backdrop, floating on a sea of green. It looked like a different world. Of course, seen from the Antrim Road, on which Jonathan Swift was wont to travel back in the day, it would look more like the profile of the sleeping giant Lemuel Gulliver… Christopher soon realized it wasn't good form to continue to insist. Better to leave it there as a case of 'so near and yet so far.' *But could he return?* He wondered about this possibility from that moment onward. Might he be able to carve out just a little free time in his mad schedule of meeting the world and his wife, before his actual wife and kids came to town at the end of the week? Christopher and Michael had spent innumerable times up at those peaks, or below them, looking up at the caves, wandering around the wild landscape of dark trees and scree-covered paths. And what was his compulsion now? Was it some yearning to re-discover the ancient past of their childhood? To re-live it? As they had already made good headway in that direction so far today, re-living their past connection, he then accepted he should be happy enough just to be able to see those peaks in the company of his friend here and now. He told himself to just forget about going up there, or to put it on the backburner of all the things he, and maybe even the fam, could and should do whenever next in the Auld Sod. Thereafter, Christopher and Michael started to swap stories of what they had done, long, long ago, in a galaxy… just up there… 'Remember thon weirdo that day?' started Michael, and they were away with one story and then the next.

Before getting into Michael's Toyota -'I see you enjoy Japanese culture yourself,' quipped Christopher- Michael had them walk all the way down to the end of the carpark, away from where the car was parked. It was only when they were at the furthest point that Michael took out what he had likely been wanting to take out all the time they'd been up there. And lit it.

'Michael, you're not going to smoke that and then drive back to Carrick, are you?' 'Oh aye,' said Michael, mischievously, 'need to steady myself after all that scary wildlife.' 'But seriously, Mick. You might have an accident or something,' adding, to lessen the impression that he was being too square, 'that's a nice wee car you have there, after all…' Michael: 'It helps. See, look at these mitts.' He held out both hands, with the joint held firmly between lips, and Christopher looked. The skin on both was remarkably dry, even chapped; there looked to be rashes in certain areas, especially between the fingers. Redness. It was a life scarred by working in an environment that hadn't been safeguarded by regulatory bodies. Now, Christopher looked at Michael's face and noted, as though for the first time, how weather-worn it looked, how even leathery the skin was in places. He could see what Michael was showing him, with his body, not fancy words, articulating plenty on the exploitative nature of a society that would work people to the ground if it could, and had. That, and he knew Michael had lived things up over the years… 'The weed makes it bearable,' he said. 'Just a wee bit of relief…' 'I see, Michael, I see…' Michael had a few more drags, was about to toss it when Christopher indicated he'd like to have a go. So he did.

They enjoyed a short but stoned drive back to civilisation, laughing aplenty and, fortuitously, listening to a bit of Queen on the radio. 'Bicycles! Feckin' love this,' said Chris, and they both sang the chorus. Christopher was thankful, even impressed, his friend could handle the driving in his state. 'I'd be up against that lamppost, mate,' observed Chris, who, in his defence, didn't actually have a driver's licence. 'Takes practice,' explained Mick. 'Takes practice.'

Michael dropped Christopher at Jim's house and threw him a wee bag of plums, with a 'Here ye go.' 'Ta, that's nice of ye,' said Chris. 'Have a great time in Lanzarote!' 'Aye,' said Michael, with a wee smile thrown in, '*if* I can get to Carrick in one piece!' They laughed, still feeling the effects of the weed, and the other thing. Michael drove off, with a bit of a wobble.

Chapter Two: On Cave Hill, pt.1, Thursday, August 8

Due to one of the miracles of the twenty first century, in which he was now living, Christopher didn't have to lug himself round to the local library, or down to the Central, after an annoying bus-ride, pad up the stairs in eager expectation, show his grubby library card (if he had remembered to bring it!) and then get to work, quietly fingering through the card catalogues or making awkward inquiries to the statue-like – or bird-like! – librarians for information: he could just slip out his fancy iPhone, open up his browser and tap in a few choice keywords on the screen to get the info he was looking for. All without shifting his arse. And the info he was looking for was designed to fuel the fire of his interest in the location he had now become a little bit obsessed with: the Cavehill. Or, Cave Hill, as it might also be termed. It was part of the Antrim Plateau. If he wanted to find out what that was he could just tap that in and – hey presto! – he could learn all about… the Antrim Plateau! Indeed, at the start of his search, he had discovered that there was also a Cave Hill in Barbados, but he didn't think he needed to know. *But he could!* He could even find pictures of it, and maybe even a YouTube video of what it looked like, with a considerably different looking bunch of people wandering around it, clambering over it, and living out their considerably different childhoods from the one he had known in the considerably colder climes of Greater North Belfast.

He knew it had a history, with the United Irishmen having sworn bonds, or whatever, up at its peak, at McArt's Fort, either on top of, or adjacent to, the infamous Napoleon's Nose – infamous because many people had fallen off it. (*And* because Belfast people, famous for disagreeing over certain things, also held differing views on which prominence actually constituted Napoleon's Nose!) Now he could ascertain, no less, that the establishment of the United Irishmen had happened in 1795 with a meeting by Theobald Wolfe Tone and Henry Joy McCracken up at windy McArt's Fort, and that this had led to the also infamous 1798 Rebellion – infamous because many Irish people had been massacred by the British. This was the rebellion Seamus Heaney had written about in his 'Requiem for the Croppies' poem, way back when (in both cases). Distant memories surrounding that poem and the author's embargo on reading it in public floated back momentarily, but not enough to occlude the main task at hand, which, given the free-floating channel-surfing possibilities of the Internet, was becoming more and more difficult to maintain. Indeed, Christopher wasn't sure what it was he was looking for, if not simply to just learn something, anything, about the place he hoped he could make space for in his week's schedule. Even just looking at pictures of it made him happy. That it was 'basaltic' made him happy, too, although he wondered if he should check if, as he gathered it probably was, that was the same stuff that 'granite' was. The word 'granite' had a much deeper resonance with him, he had to admit. The term 'basaltic' sounded too scientific and clinical. Granite, however, connected him to marble, speckled marble, like the tabletop in the Bellevue Arms, and to headstones, like the one they had visited three days ago, down in Carnmoney Cemetery, to see the Da's grave. Jim and he had stood there in silence, reading the words which Christopher himself had composed, celebrating the musician that their father was: 'Music so sweet can have no ending / Love so strong no boundary'. Granite stone, a two-tone black and grey, with a piano imprinted in the top right corner. If you were very still, you could still hear the strains of Martita's 'Ave Maria', and Jim's impromptu, impassioned, graveside eulogy...

He was doing it again, drifting off course, as he lay on his back in his hotel room, whiling away the moments, a sonic backdrop of Belfast seagulls shrieking away nearby, supposedly searching for info on the Cave Hill – him, not the seagulls. Now in fact he was re-living the emotion of his father's loss, the connection having come about via a series of little steps, associations, memories, non-haptic clicks. No need for the Internet: he already had a channel-surfing mind built-in. From one point to the next, his mind would swoop down like the seagulls – and pick up morsels of this and that, or find a course to somewhere it had never intended going. It was no good. Christopher would have to make time in his schedule and just go there, up to the peaks, for even a quick re-connection with… his past? Or was it something else? What precisely had he seen as he looked up that time from the pond in Bellevue Zoo? What mystery compelled him to seek the…

…before he allowed his unstructured mind-blather to wrap him in knots, he kicked off his stasis and got ready to go down and have whatever they had for brekkie in Twenty First Century Belfast.

. . .

He had done it. It had come about by chance, his brother Jim having received word he had to go off to Antrim Hospital for a quick check up. No emergency, just a care system inundated with patients and prone to sending out precipitous confirmations for consultations that had been asked for months previously. The kind and ever-helpful Margaret, a few doors down the street, would take him, leaving Christopher with the whole morning until late afternoon free. (A lot of Chris's schedule involved spending time with his brother, their elder brother, meeting up with neighbours, friends, former teachers, extended family members – a Gertrude here, a Paula there, a Monica over there, et cetera! And even a few trips to libraries.) And so, he was off.

It didn't take long to get there, but it would have taken considerably less had he still been residing in the old house in Elmfield. Christopher had employed Google Maps to pre-walk himself up most of the way, via a little side path to the right of the Zoo entrance which was so off the beaten path as to make him wonder how Google had even thought of having someone track it. But against the virtual journey, the real one involved putting up with real mud and real branches slapping him in the face, and the occasional whiff of real dogcrap, contact with which was to be avoided at all costs. (Had Professor Challenger or Allan Quartermain ever had to worry about such?) He also had to climb over a bolted fence, ignoring the sign that said due to a recent landslide the track had been closed. Christopher had only one pair of shoes (runners, actually) on this trip and he didn't want to mess them up, or at least irreparably. His wardrobe was also rather limited. He hadn't availed of the joys of a visit to the still-going-strong Abbeycentre to deck himself out in the latest Primark cut-price fare, thoughts of which made him recall the bad news about the Bank Buildings in the city centre, of which Primark was the main business, and people's worries about whether it would survive the terrible fire it had suffered the year before. Poor oul Belfast wasn't very lucky with its architectural heritage… (He was drifting again, and creating overly-long monological sentences in the process. 'Plough on', he told himself, 'plough on!') And so, decked out in jeans, his dark blue windbreaker, Pebble Beach sports cap (gifted by a student long ago), trusty red Millet rucksack containing his water bottle, and wearing his hardy New Balance sneakers, off he damn well ploughed.

After the flat and slightly muddy path, encountering upward-leading steps, steps which looked as old as his childhood and beyond, steps which some long-ago souls had gone to the trouble to hammer into the ground, Christopher felt he was truly beginning his magical mystery tour. The vegetation on both sides was now beginning to become thick, with ferns and fronds and nettles and exposed roots on display -he could be right back on a wooded mountainside in Japan, there was that little difference in the sense of being amidst nature. He had hiked plenty, with Eri, the kids and Eri's redoubtable father, who was eighty years plus and still going strong. He enjoyed viewing the green all around and the canopy overhead for a brief moment before walking on, up another set of steps and deeper into the forest.

On and on he walked, alone, and feeling alone after all those hikes ten thousand miles away. Alone also because here was no chorus of summer cicadas serenading the nature lovers with their sonic ululations, and no chance of a monkey, a deer, or a bear coming out, either. And, if you believed the mythology, no snakes either, thanks to Saint Patrick. Christopher had seen all of these near where he lived in Japan, all except for bears, although he knew they resided in fairly big numbers in the forests not far from his home in Kanagawa. Also, there were wild boar snooting around and about when the notion took them, digging up the ground and generally making havoc for the mountain-dwellers, especially the ones with garden plots. Hill-walkers would always have to close any gates they passed through, with a hanging metal latch, to stop whatever creature happened to be in the mood for wandering about and getting out. At times, in Japan, the quiet of the hills would be punctuated with the repeated sound of rifle shots, fired to scare the monkeys off and prevent them from drifting down to the residential areas at the foot of the hills, where they might steal food, or terrorize little kids (or just play with them?). Western civilisation was more advanced here, Christopher said, his tongue more than slightly in his cheek, not wishing to dwell on its industrialization of nature and animals, its exploitation of just about everything, and, for the inhabitants of this particular corner of that 'civilisation', the thirty-year long 'Troubles', and its rollcall of the violently killed. No scary wildlife round here. Just shopping centres, building sites and tabernacles to Jesus. No flies on us.

So, with that thought in mind, it was all the more remarkable when he at last did come upon an example of indigenous fauna. Beside the occasional *skriek* of birds flying overhead, where he couldn't really look, for all the overhanging branches and brambles, the only living thing Christopher could make note of was the odd fat fly or, more rarely, bumblebee. So, when he did eventually see some movement in the undergrowth up ahead, he guessed he was just seeing things instead, seeing spots after all the strenuous efforts put into getting here. As he stepped closer, however, toward that little apparently moving thing, he realized it was no illusion at all – it must be, he told himself, a little perambulating bird. It had a longish beak and brownish dappled feathers, about twenty centimetres high. And yet it didn't seem particularly fazed by the approach of a human. Christopher was thinking 'curlew', even if he wasn't quite sure what a curlew really looked like. In his mind, curlews were a little like kiwis, and were inextricably linked to the poetry of WB Yeats. Something about hearing a curlew cry and linking that to loneliness or heartbreak – something romantically Irish, for sure. (For a professor who'd written on Irish poetry, this was a humbling moment of fuzz.) The closer he got to it, however, the further into the vegetation and leaves and the darker, muddier side of the path it ambled. Christopher might stand there and try to coax it out, but he didn't feel like he had a lot of time, and it was best to plough on, as his mind told him to, and not investigate. So, without having a proper look at the thing, on Christopher walked, eager to be out of this dark, somewhat muddy, claustrophobia-inducing place.

Then he heard a sound. It came from right behind him, and he turned round very quickly, eyes down, trying to pinpoint the source. After a moment, he could see what it was: the little bird he'd seen a moment ago had now speared a worm, and that was now wriggling on its beak. The bird occasionally opened said beak. Christopher could see a line of tiny, serrated teeth within the deadly confines of that beak, teeth which now sliced into the worm, cutting it in two. The bisected worm now fell, but the bird quickly speared one half again, and again, into the mud. Christopher had had enough. His association of poetic romance with the curlew had taken a decided knock. Time to leave. So, he did, his steps emboldened by a sudden need to concentrate on whatever his mission was. If it was just ploughing ahead, with no set goal, then so be it. He could see that the Irish countryside had its examples of raw nature still going strong.

After a further excursion along the simple path, punctuated by at one time having to climb over a fallen tree trunk, and thereby slightly muck up his – only – jeans, it felt like real progress to come upon another series of steps going up through the murk – these ones not wooden but stone, roughly cast but perfectly adequate to a mid-forest ramble. His thoughts drifted to the Antrim Road perimeter wall, with its recessed section announcing 'BELLEVUE' in large, elegant font, and the formerly beautiful steps stretching up behind that, so well-known to all Belfastians. They were like a stairway to a wonder-world for all the tired and fun-seeking city dwellers, hoping perhaps for a dance at the Floral Hall, or to take tea and scones at the Hazelwood Café, with its views of Belfast Lough. That it had become so neglected, so overgrown with weeds and grass, was a complete disgrace. A victory of time over space. Belfast needed to take care of itself... He was drifting again. Stay focused, he told himself, stay focused and you'll be through these bloody weeds soon enough.

And he was. Within the space of only five minutes, Christopher had ascended through the forest murk completely and had come out into clear space, with unobstructed views of the sky, and – once he turned round – the Carnmoney Hills, Belfast Lough and the Ards Peninsula down far below, in all their summer glory. Before him, also, as though by the design of some unseen landscape artist, the path unfolded before him with dainty little purple blooms adorning the tops of the foot-length plants – weeds? – all around. After a swig of water, and a wipe of the forehead with his handkerchief, Christopher quickened his pace and walked on, feeling free and unencumbered in spirit. It was going to be a great adventure!

It wasn't long before he could see the outline of one of the basaltic prominences that defined Cave Hill. It was just a glimpse, but it was there, and he was walking toward it, in a path that went past it, and the danger it bespoke. He could see the febrile fencing that was the only barrier between grass and a sheer drop. Christopher had loved playing on the Cave Hill with Michael and others in childhood, but he had also grown to fear the peaks. Mention of 'Napoleon's Nose', with its hundred feet drop, had given him the shivers, coming as it did from his mother recounting the various accidents and incidents which had happened over the years, people slipping off the edge and perishing below. It was a mother being over-protective perhaps, one inclined, as many living during the Troubles, to fret and worry over the safety of their child out in the streets where all manner of trouble could occur. The dangers of Napoleon's Nose, or any of the peaks, though, were rudely simple and impactful, and close. It was in the tone of her voice, relating how some child or that young teacher, he recalled, had stepped back just a step too far – or was it the wind which had tipped them over, and they'd been swept off, gone, lost forever. When Christopher played with his friends, they could all be quite lively and daring and not to take active part might be seen as acting the sissy or whatever. It was always a thing at the back of his mind when he was a child, with a close-call near-drop down a quarry nearby acting as deadly a reminder of the nearness of death as one could ever imagine. Mindful of all this, it was with some trepidation that he proceeded, cheered by the fact that other hill walkers were out on the same path, and none seemed overly worried, just laughing and chatting, or checking their mobiles in the bright sunshine and bracing breeze. Among the walkers, Christopher noted that most were families, or young people. One was a man of about the same age as himself, or, in fact, maybe a little older, and certainly a little rounder, with thinning fair hair, wearing a light-coloured mac.

It was now about ten thirty, plenty of time to roam. Christopher was enjoying himself. He wanted to peddle back and go down to where you could see these peaks from below, but it wouldn't hurt to just see where this path led. He kind of remembered. It would go to the top of the final prominence and then he could get the best view of the city and that would satisfy one of his main goals. As he walked on, however, he noticed that the solitary man was bending down and looking at something on the right side of the path. Not only was he looking, Christopher now noted, but he seemed to be taking notes, too. Christopher wondered if he was a fellow scribbler of lyrics and had just been inspired or was he the kind of hill walker who studied the flora and fauna. As he approached, he could see it was fauna, not flora that was attracting his attention. In fact, it was, if he wasn't mistaken, a bird, and one not dissimilar to the one he'd seen earlier in the depths of the forest. 'I saw one like that back there a bit,' offered Christopher freely to the intent man. The intent man acknowledged this with an 'Aye?' but didn't break his gaze from the curlew-type bird which Christopher could now see rather clearly, hopping about and stabbing at the ground. 'Wonder what that is,' then asked Christopher, but, again, this failed to spark much in the way of conversation. He decided to dander on.

As Christopher did, it was with a mix of excitement, thrill and trepidation. It felt like walking toward a sleeping giant, with the rock jutting out over the grass not far from where he was. He worried about the people he could see who were walking about on it, hoping they were responsible and not going to act the eejit. They looked so tiny, and… there was a wind blowing up here which it would be advisable not to ignore. He walked on, head down, cap re-adjusted to make it sit tighter. The path was bringing him very close to the edge of the cliff. But that was the way here, he reflected. It was the same in Clare, with the Cliffs of Moher. No fence. No officials to warn people of the dangers. There, Christopher had seen one teenage girl walk right over to the very edge and then sit down, lotus position and take in the view of the Atlantic. He himself had gone over gingerly, crawling, that is, to the point where his head was then over the edge, with the rest of his horizontal form consciously trying to imprint itself on the grass, fearful of any slipping… Maybe he'd been living in Japan too long, or, simply, he was always a bit of a scaredy cat.

He scanned the signboard which had been erected to tell visitors about McArt's Fort, as that's what the summit had always been known as, the place of an ancient Gaelic fort, long since gone, the place where Theobald Wolfe Tone had met Henry Joy McCracken to instigate the United Irishmen. The ancient chieftains before them would certainly have had the spot to see what was going on down below. From there all Belfast could be seen, along with the lough and the hills and whatever. What the somewhat weathered signboard focused on, however, was not ancient clans and forts, but birds. Birds! And the local flora, too. It was the birds which interested Christopher and had him then immediately recalling the scene a few minutes ago with the strange man looking at the strange bird at the side of the path. Here, however, there was no image of such a bird. No curlew-like creature at all. Hawks, a robin redbreast, hooked beak flying miracles, but no proto-curlew! And yet, he had seen two in the last twenty minutes. This realization prompted him to turn round and look back to see if he could see that man again. He would surely be coming this way and must be close. And yet, now, as he looked back in the direction he had come from, he could see no sign whatsoever of the man, or indeed anyone. Curiouser and curiouser, mused Christopher. Who comes all this way and turns back without making it to take in the view?

He shrugged it off and ambled on, doing up his windbreaker as he did so, and tightening his cap, both actions in response to the wind. Down he went, through the iron turnstile, then up the somewhat widely spaced steps and onto the top. The people who'd been there had ambled on, right-wise, to the long gliding slopes of green. So, he could enjoy the view by himself, and how stupendous it was! He had been blessed with great weather and clear air that revealed all, in panoramic glory.

The Lough was the most salient feature, with a broken canopy of giant white fluffy clouds suspended above. To his left, the Carnmoney Hills and the shoreline, stretching all the way to Carrickfergus and Kilroot -he could just pick out the tall stack of the power station there. To his right, as the Lough came in and became the Lagan River, he could pick out Harland & Wolff's shipyard, where the Titanic had been built and launched, and where his father had even worked for a few years -although, as he liked to add, 'not on the Titanic, of course!' He thought he could just pick out the yellow behemoths of the Samson and Goliath cranes but wasn't sure. He wished he had brought binoculars, like his Da's Tasco binocs, which he used to look at the night sky with, back in the day. Indeed, as he surveyed Belfast, it was the lack of resolution in his eyes, given the distance, that made it all into one big sprawl of buildings, even the city centre not discernible in any meaningful way. It was just civilisation, a northern Irish one, and yet the view put him in mind of something similar he was accustomed to seeing in Japan.

He had pre-checked, via the iPhone, and discovered that the hill he would often climb near his house in Kanagawa was, curiously, at precisely the same elevation of where he was now, at 370 metres above sea level. And it, too, provided a spectacular view of civilisation, Japan-style, or Honshu-style, and beyond. What you couldn't see here, looking down on Belfast from McArt's Fort, were enormous skyscrapers dotted along the horizon, the skyscrapers of Tokyo, Shinjuku, and Yokohama. Among those giants, if it was a good day, you could also see Tokyo Sky Tree, which at over a half kilometre in height, was the tallest tower in the world. Nor could you see the white Shinkansen 'bullet train', slicing through the landscape like an elongated pencil...

Beyond the man-made, you could spot islands towards the right-side of the panoramic view, like Izu-Oshima, which was volcanic. On clear days you could just pick out the wisps of smoke coming out of its caldera... Aye, thought Christopher, and back in the day, you might just pick out wisps of smoke coming out of some areas of Belfast, too, with the sound of sirens, if the wind wasn't blowing... That it was peaceful now was a blessing, he felt, and in that final sense of sobriety and acceptance of the past being the past, Christopher took in his last look. The military surveillance helicopters of back then were nowhere to be seen now; they'd been replaced by hawks and sparrows and blackbirds, maybe doing their own reconnaissance on the weird individuals below. Sure, wasn't the blackbird a symbol of the city? he quizzed himself. Co-opted by the poets into the city's emblem... Blackbirds and crows weren't seen so positively back in old Japan, mused Christopher. But neither were butterflies! He turned back the way he had come, buoyed by the view, if also a little light-headed, like a man who's imbibed too much and sees everything in double.

He retraced his steps back and then paused at the spot where he had remembered seeing that man study the bird. He looked down into the grass and gorse, his eyes scanning here and there, close and far, but achieving no joy, he thought of moving on. Then he saw it. It was not something that was moving, but it certainly wasn't grass, or the colour of grass. It was red, the red of blood, and the more he checked, what it was could best be described as a splatter of blood, with even... he felt horror as he noticed it... something like bloodied entrails – but no body to identify it. What had happened? He suddenly felt like shouting that out. He was disappointed that there was no-one there to ask or share the horrid discovery with. He took out his iPhone but thought better of taking a picture of it. Somehow it seemed too grotesque an image to have stored on the device he would have in his pocket. In fact, he wanted to run away from it. He didn't know what it meant. He couldn't help thinking that the strange man had done violence to the poor bird, that he'd struck it and killed it, and even pulled it apart! It was too horrible to contemplate! Christopher felt a chill, and ran, very fast, back the way he'd come. Back to civilisation? he wondered, he hoped.

Chapter Three: On Cave Hill, pt.2

After a while, Christopher stopped running. It was a bit silly, after all. What was he thinking? Could there really be a madman walking about butchering birds? Well, Christopher thought, as he now ambled toward the turn-off, or turn-down, right-wise, toward the area where you could view the cliffs he had just been on, there was that crazy guy they'd seen long, long ago… Yes, this was in reference to the story he and Michael had been talking about just a day or two before – 'thon weirdo!' Thon weirdo had been this extremely strange human which Christopher, Michael and their opposite-dwelling neighbours Brian, Sandra and Elaine Gorman, and Paddy Doyle from up the street, had witnessed one summery, otherwise beautiful day at the hill. They'd spotted this middle-aged man, dressed in a mac, perambulating the paths of Cave Hill and, when the notion took him, seemingly snapping at flies in the air, or something like that. His jaws would open and then slam shut with something like the sound a clapperboard made. It was the strangest sight, and the party of friends and neighbourhood kids screamed every time they spied him approach anywhere near where they were. They would run shrieking with terror *and* run shrieking with terror even if they didn't see him but expected to see him pop out of the woods, usually when one of the boys had said to the girls that they'd seen him 'Just over there!' Everyone was asking: 'What was he doing?' / 'Who the hell is he?' and… 'Is he even human?' Panic infused them all, and, somehow, lent a certain something to the day, the events of which they would then spend the next few months re-telling to all and sundry. But that was over forty years ago, at the time of impressionable youth, when the smallest thing could be blown out of all proportion. (Although, even now, in his memory of that time, the man had been extremely scary to see…)

This weirdo with the thinning fair hair was not dissimilar, and he was wearing a mac. Who was he? He hadn't responded to his attempts at conversation. What was he doing? Why had he left and turned round before visiting the summit? Or, had Christopher misinterpreted the whole thing? These were questions he wasn't sure he could answer now, in the same way he couldn't quite be sure why he was threading his way downhill, apace, now to the area where he could see the cliffs. Of course, to be perfectly honest, he could not have explained logically or coherently why he had come to this place at all, except to say that he had been hoping to re-connect with what he had grown up with, Cave Hill, in all its glory, weird or otherwise. He thought that once he had seen the caves that would be the end of the story, Game Over, and he could go back to Jim's house for a quiet cup of tea. Yes, he told himself: 'Just see the caves and get the hell out!'

He wanted to run down the path leading away from the upper reaches, but there were people coming up, a party of young men and women, and there was a small stile to pass through with cattle-gate iron bars underfoot it would be advisable not to ignore; so, he walked at an even pace, down, down, amidst the green slopes and little grassy mounds either side, towards the base of the first cliffs. And these cliffs, seen up close, were quite a sight. Walking around until he could see them properly, Christopher looked up at the imposing form they presented, 'they' being two discernibly different prominences, if paired together. He had no idea what they were called, if they were called anything, but he gathered these, or the right-side one at least, was what he had grown up seeing on a daily basis from the backyard of his house. Rain or shine, clear or cloudy, Christopher had been able to look up and see the basaltic wonder of this place, the hill's impassive face turned outwards, as though staring at some far-off world of its own stony imagination.

Before his prose-thoughts turned any purpler, he decided to press on, and, with a quick survey, again, of the sight of the Lough (and sweet civilisation on either side of it), on he went, passing under another discernible rockface, through the virtual tunnel of a few small trees and then onto the sight he had been anticipating from the beginning: the area of the caves.

Before he knew it, he had arrived. He had walked on the little narrow path, so narrow you had to step onto the grass to let someone pass, and had come to a vantage point like no other. He stopped where he was, knowing this to be the centre of his impromptu pilgrimage. He had largely put out of his mind the experience with the strange fellow, but whatever chill that had given him, a greater one, in some sense, coursed through his body now. It was the chill of confronting the ancient world, the prehistoric world, where humanity had no place, 'civilisation' being a concept that could simply never grow here. He was being purple again, and not entirely accurate, as he had heard that the caves were likely the product of human effort and that they had been visited, or even inhabited by many -from kids like himself (but only the first one, which smelt of dogpiss), and by people from the distinctly human past: smugglers, revolutionaries, day-trippers, criminals... And yet, these people had left no visible imprint of themselves. The rock was still implacable and neutral and unforgiving. Death from those eager to scale the heights to the upper caves would have been swift and brutal, with laurels for the lucky few who had managed it. It wasn't people Christopher could see when he looked at this rough semi-circle of cliffs, however, but animals. And not just animals as we knew them in the world about, but animals as had existed millions of years ago, the dinosaurs. Perhaps they had roamed here, too... Until they were dealt the swiftest and most brutal death of all, one day becoming victims of a rock even greater than Cave Hill, something half the size of Mount Everest, which had

288

plummeted down through the atmosphere at the speed of twenty-five kilometres per second – that's what it had said in the book he'd read not long ago – then smashing into the earth with the force of twenty thousand Hiroshimas…

He was becoming purple again. And he didn't like the fact that books tended to use what happened at Hiroshima as some kind of standard candle of explosive force. It was like the outdated way of describing locomotion, employing the term 'horsepower', reducing the animal to how much it could pull and ignoring the animal. Surely Hiroshima, and horses, had more meaning than that… He had to leave. He had learnt something, or taught himself something, or just felt something. That was enough. Thankfully, he'd hadn't had to share this moment with some random family and their entourage of screaming kids. He was alone, he guessed. He looked around to check. No-one. Christopher decided to have a quick pace up to the first cave area and see what he could see without trying to clamber into it. It was a far cry from when they'd been nippers, when a rope had hung from number two. Or was it number three? Having looked into the cave as far as he could from below its lip, down he then went, directly down from the caves, following another narrow little gravelly path that would bring him somewhere to the vicinity of where he had to go.

To be honest, he had no idea how he was going to come down off the hill. He didn't wish to return by the way he had come, so he just kept going down, by-passing a little hummock and coming into sight of a forest. It was then that he saw a man, a very old-looking man, with whitish hair, which looked like it had been blown about somewhat by the day's breeze. For some reason this man attracted his interest; he wasn't quite sure why. Maybe today is the day of interesting wee men, he told himself and stopped for a moment, watching the old gent amble down to the visible end of the path and then disappear, right-wise, into the forest. What had struck Christopher as a little strange, he only realized after he had gone was the fact that the man seemed to be a little over-dressed, this being August, and quite sunny with it. He hadn't adopted the common nylon or polyester, for windbreakers, of other hill walkers, nor the oilcloth-like exterior wear of the Barbour crowd. No, Christopher guessed, if anything, that old man was wearing a kind of cloth greatcoat, something more likely to be seen in the city of a winter's day. 'He must be sweating bricks!' he quipped to himself, glad to employ the kind of phrase that would only cause confusion among his students back in Japan. (Teaching English in Japan was deadly for your home dialect.)

Before proceeding, in order to, effectively, follow the old man, Christopher's attention was directed left-wise suddenly, to some movement in the undergrowth. He strained to see what it was, but soon gave up. The grass wasn't high or overgrown; most of the grass thereabouts was short and metaphorically sweet. Yet, he could still sense something happening nearby where he was. It seemed to be coming from a little clump of bushes. What it was involved not only small movements of the spiky bushes, but sound, the sound of tiny animals in conflict. Had the proto-curlew struck again? he wondered. A tinier variety? Or was it the one snake that had escaped St Patrick's gaze and had established a familial line stretching far into the future? (A secular future!) It sounded like something had been attacked anyway, and the thought of that made him just want to not dwell anymore, dwell upon the ugliness of nature up close, so he walked on, down the path toward the forest.

Christopher had only been a short distance behind the old man, so it was with some surprise and confusion, when he did enter the forest, that he could see no trace of him. Of course, he had lingered a few moments due to the commotion in the bush, but hardly long enough to allow the old man to get so far, unless he were very flight of foot, as they say. Christopher could see, quite far in the distance, a bunch of very young kids walking off, but no old man in the space between them and Christopher. He was beginning to think this day was turning out to be much weirder than that he'd experienced all those years ago, with not one, but two weirdos on the go. So, in a state of some confusion and the thrill that comes from confusion when there's a touch of mystery about it, Christopher entered the forest and began to amble down the path. He felt the atmosphere to be very different from where he had been just a few moments ago, in the 'Jurassic Park' area. Here things were peaceful and delightful -like being in a church but without thon fellow hanging from the cross, dripping blood. Forests like this were warm, comforting, magical even. He'd been in countless forests in Japan, and had never tired of the beauty they possessed, even ones he had walked through on a regular basis. The forest was always a little different, perhaps due to the light filtering through, or the change in the flora with the seasons, or with the occasional fall of this tree or that. This forest also possessed its own charm and magic, and so Christopher wallowed in that atmosphere. He had certainly come to a different world, a world beyond the one down below where people lived out their lives in boxes and went to other boxes to make things to put in those boxes and such. Funny to think, he reflected, how he had flown to Japan all those years ago, a country on the other side of the world, in order to follow his desire to see another world, and not just one in his imagination. And now here he was, not two miles from his original family home on the outskirts of Belfast, deep in another far-away place, a place not adjusted to humanity, a place where the feral was at large, and the strange was normal. He heard a noise behind him. It interrupted his thoughts, and his propensity for creating endlessly long sentences…

He looked backwards. He saw a figure, a figure which had

just entered onto the forest path. There was light behind that figure, but something was telling him that it was… the strange man, the one who mutilated birds! He could tell from the roundish shape of his body and the fact that he was holding what looked like a notebook. That man had now entered the forest and was walking his way! Christopher, already possessed by a feeling he couldn't quite describe, as though of being in the midst of a reality he had no power to escape, began to panic. It was irrational, he knew, but he felt he had to escape. (It was also good fun!)

The man's pace was faster than Christopher's – he would gain soon. What should he do? Christopher didn't think running was the right thing to do. That would lead him into the realm of when he had dreams and he could only run as though through treacle. More rationally, he didn't want to give the man an indication that he was afraid. So, instead of running, Christopher simply quickened the pace of his walking steps. He lengthened his steps also, hoping that none of this would be interpreted as strange behaviour on his part. Occasionally he would look back, and after a minute or so, he was relieved to note that now the path in front had curved, making him invisible to the approaching man. What should he do? Keep running? Or… he suddenly looked right and thought of Plan B. He could run up the forest bank and take refuge up there, in the murk of the trees. No-one would think to look up there, and even if they did, he could easily hide behind one of the trunks. It could only be a strategy of the desperate, but he was willing to take it.

And so Christopher did. Getting his already slightly mucked up New Balance runners even more mucked up was not a problem. He was just glad to be able to make his way past this tree and that, and eventually arrive at a spot even the Old Testament God mightn't notice, or Jesus, whose name he was fond of uttering at times like this – *and now*, repeatedly, under his breath. (His long-practiced linguistic religiosity had seen him briefly nicknamed 'Yahweh' in his first years at Barrack Street.)

And he could look down, and see, to his joy, after a minute, that the strange man with the notebook, was now passing by, walking on, with whatever madness had possessed him, whatever mission he was on, be it violence …or worse? Christopher didn't want to think about it. (The child in him rejected the idea that he was just projecting his fears. This fun was part of why he had come here! You couldn't do this is in a housing estate, or anywhere, usually, at the age of fifty-six.)

Christopher was holding onto a tree trunk, standing on the mucky embankment of the side of the path, at a 45-degree angle. Passers-by below would only notice him if they looked up and interpreted what they could see, as Christopher was doing his best to keep himself obscured by the trees and the foliage. It was a strange place to be, but a safe one. At his feet, ferns and fronds provided some dull green contrast to the uniform brown of the soil. He wondered if anyone had ever been here before. Was he the first? Could he explore further? Not being a botanist or biologist, however, he wondered what good he could do -just get his hands and clothes even more mucked up! He decided to wait a few minutes longer. He even slipped out his iPhone and looked at it, knowing he couldn't do much without Wi-Fi, in this neck of the woods…

And yet, on the Settings screen, which he checked idly as he bided his time, he couldn't quite understand why, under the heading 'Other Networks', there was a choice of a domain to join. 'Around here?' he asked himself. It was a little curious, but not terribly so to a person who had no real idea how networks for such devices operated, twenty-first century tech in the hands of a twentieth century luddite and all that. That the screen was giving him the chance to 'link' with another network, however, struck Christopher as certainly interesting. Was a local bear netsurfing, perhaps? Imagine a bear swiping the screen with his claws, he thought whimsically.

His iPhone screen gleamed bright into his eyes, and all the brighter for the relatively dark place he was in, so Christopher thought his eyes must be playing tricks on him. He had noticed a light beyond the light of his screen. Must be spots I'm seeing, he said to himself. To this end, he put away his smartphone and closed his eyes a little, then looked round, in order to re-acclimatize his peepers to the low ambient light. Then he looked down again, at the area where he thought he'd seen light a few moments before. And, there it was again. There was a tiny sliver of weak but discernible light emanating from the ground, through the muck and the fallen leaves, through the very soil at his feet. Had someone dropped their twenty-first century device here, disqualifying him as the Neil Armstrong of the Cave Hill Forest? Or was it weirder than that? Why would there be light coming from beneath his feet, here in the middle of precisely nowhere?

Things were certainly becoming weirder and weirder.

Chapter Four: Weird Scenes, pt.1

Christopher bent over to peer all the better at what seemed to be that sliver of weak light coming through the ground near where he stood. It was a 'sliver' because whatever light there was constituted a veritable line of light, with some lengths covered by the odd leaf or patch of dirt or fallen twig. This flotsam punctuated the line, but also enhanced the idea that it was a line at all, and not just a few random points of dull light in the forest floor. You could discern a shape, a line stretching off to where Christopher couldn't see. And then, on the other end, now that he looked, he could see that another line ran off perpendicularly, away from him. It was looking increasingly like this had special meaning, and that meaning was gradually becoming clear to the viewer stood over it: these lines of light indicated that these were the boundaries of a portal, a portal down into the forest floor!

Christopher gasped, quietly anyway. What had he discovered? Light could only mean one thing: something artificial lay below his feet. Was he dreaming? He thought it advisable to look away for a moment, again, and do something entirely different, and so he accessed the small red rucksack on his back, unzipped the larger of the two interior spaces and pulled out his plastic bottle. He unscrewed the top and knocked back a large, fulfilling draft of not particularly cold water, but enough to make him feel like he could clear his head and become sensible. To add to this, he then did a few stretches with his arms, and a roll of the head. He replaced the bottle, zipped up and then told himself, without making a sound: 'Get with it, boyo!' He looked down. Nothing had changed! He could still discern the outline of what he was increasingly beginning to convince himself was a door, or a portal, down into the forest floor. He had come to the moment of truth, the realization that he had found adventure, whether he'd wanted it or not. He would… explore!

Christopher, stepping with extreme caution and all the stealth he could muster, made moves to establish the true boundaries of the portal. By doing so, he quickly came to the decision to proceed to the next stage: to reach down and feel for whatever way he could find to lift up the door, which, he gathered, had been deliberately covered to meld into the surroundings, being covered with soil and the fallen bric-a-brac of the forest. He soon had it. Standing at what he could ascertain was the shortest on the three sides he had identified, he now inserted his fingers under the gently illuminated line. He found it surprisingly easy to achieve the success he wanted, lifting the wooden frame or whatever it was up, and up, and up. This did not reveal very much -a darkness below, but with the hint of a glow, or illumination, somehow more evident than before. He waited until his eyes became accustomed to that space, and then, to his further surprise, and delight, noted the very artificial shape of what, with a little extra checking, turned out to be a rope ladder of sorts. His mind was set on proceeding, no matter what may come. Down the rabbit hole I go! he said to himself.

Christopher of course had to turn his body round in order to be able to descend, and this is what he did next, not caring that by doing so, he would be entering a potential lion's den in the most vulnerable way, with his back to danger. There was nothing for it, he told himself, as long as he could do so without making any wrong moves, moves that might give him away. Stealth was the order of the day. Stealth, only that, he told himself, or, somehow bizarrely reminded of Joyce… 'silence, cunning, stealth.' (As for 'exile', he was a dab hand at that, sure now…)

He had to, somewhat awkwardly, keep one hand on the wooden door, holding it up, and the other on the rope ladder, and yet make no sound. But he was doing it, and doing it well.

The ladder was sturdy and didn't move much, as it was seemingly tied to the surface it scaled. Yet, he began to feel something like dread as he came to the end of the short ladder and had to close the door -the overside of which was a clever camouflage of forest undergrowth and the underside just bare wood planks- over his head. He put his feet onto the ground, which was firm, but the feeling of being enveloped by black, and of being locked into a space he hadn't been invited into was almost too much.

He didn't move, until he then did, slowly, gradually, turning, to be confronted with what he guessed was a curtain, one rigged up, he imagined, to dull the interior light, which he could now discern all the more, as the seconds passed and his irises dilated. He had a terrible thought then. What if this was the den of some paramilitary group? The Continuance UVF or Continuance IRA? Oh, Jesus! If so, he was fucked, he realized. He'd be shot with a silencer and his body would be dumped somewhere. It was a thought that might have felled him right there and then. But it was weighed against the other thought that *times had changed*. No-one did that kind of thing anymore! The moment he had witnessed one late night on Aran Island with his friends Dara and Lorcan, decades ago, where the 'RA had obviously been handing over cash for weapons, at that crossroads not far from where their tent was pitched, belonged to *ancient history*. Sure, look at the changes! Martin McGuinness had since become bosom pals with Ian Paisley, and even met the Queen! Life was different now. They didn't dub Gerry Adams or Danny Morrison on TV anymore: they were celebrities, men of culture, accepted! Belfast was booming! Economically, mind, not with explosive devices. *Paramilitary murder ain't good for business, you know!*

In this spirit of hope, Christopher threw off his dread and did what he knew he had to, now. He reached forward, and laid his hand on the curtain, feeling its rough texture, edging toward the right-side... No... He should first have a peek. Yes, that was the best plan. And so, he leaned his whole body right-wise, and his head closer, ever closer to the edge of the curtain, until, with tension building up inside him something shocking, he drew back the tiniest tincture of curtain and peeked out, into the light.

An eye stared back!

The meeting of their two eyes caused an immediate reaction. Christopher drew back sharply with sudden shock, falling back against the rope ladder and the wall it was adorning. But he stayed upright. He guessed the owner of the other peeking eye had done something similar, but with greater consequence. Christopher was sure that his ocular counterpart had fallen backwards, and hard; how else to account for the sudden issuance of what he was pretty sure was the word 'Shit!' 'It must be the old man!' Christopher imagined, reading the wheezy timbre of the voice. 'Is he OK? Is he hurt?' he wondered. He had no compunction in reaching forth his hand again and swiping back the curtain, with the impulse to help strong within him. And, he had guessed right: it *was* the old man with the silvery hair (and big coat), and yes, he was on his back and cursing, his left hand reaching behind to massage the back of his head. Christopher stepped forward and bent over to do whatever he could to show that he wanted to help. He also took note of the strange surroundings: *they were in a cave!* This was a cave, an underground cave! And it was lit with what looked like large bulbous canvas-looking lamps, stationed here and there on thin metal pedestals. These illuminated the walls around them, showing them to be curvy and warped but solid-looking, as though made of rock, not soil, and thus confirming the cave theory. Behind, beyond the man on the ground, the cave stretched back far, very far, to a point that was dark, into an area he couldn't see…

'What are you doing here? Please get out, young man!' said the old man on the ground, attempting to project authority into his voice, if not very convincingly. Maybe it had something to do with that fact that he was still on his back and rubbing the back of his head, wriggling about in his giant overcoat. It was a quite reedy voice, appropriate for someone clearly very old. Christopher reached out his hand and offered: 'Please, take my hand. I can help you up. I'm very sorry to have disturbed you.' These words mollified the fallen man to some degree, who then reached out his own free hand and allowed himself to be helped into a standing position.

Now that he was standing and they were so close, Christopher could take a better look at his interlocutor. His hair was silvery and a little unkempt and there was an accompanying -excuse for- whitish moustache doing something to add contrast to the pale and slightly mottled surface of his visage. Indeed, his skin looked taut and stretched... over the underlying bone structure... Whatever slightly or more than slightly negative impression this made was off-set by the obvious quality of the herringbone design greatcoat, which afforded the man a dignity he might not otherwise have been able to lay claim to. He had a decidedly Irish face, with a twist of irascibility etched into the eyes which reminded Christopher of the old Christian Brothers. He wasn't particularly tall, but when he spoke, you would have thought he thought he was: 'Very well, now please clear out, this is off-limits to the public.'

Christopher was willing to accept that. He was an intruder. He would gladly go and said so: 'Of course...' But he also felt the tug of curiosity. Awkwardly, he tried to voice what he wanted to say: 'Well, of course, of course, but...' But he was turning round and as he was turning round inwardly cursed himself for his inability to give voice to that tugging curiosity. It would seem that the old man would just keep standing there, holding open the curtain thing, as he put his hands on the rope ladder and then put his foot on the first rung. Thinking that, it felt like a pretty ignominious end to his supposedly great adventure. To come so far, to get so close to some mystery, for surely this was some giant mystery -a cave in the forest floor? Surely no-one knew there had been a cave here before. Surely he would have to inform someone. Christopher stopped, his back still turned to the man, as he worked out the situation. He recalled that there had been no sign whatsoever placed outside indicating that this cave existed, nor that there was some operation in progress within it. That meant only one thing: this was some *secret* operation beyond the knowledge of the authorities! There could be no way to have such a situation otherwise. This emboldened Christopher to unlatch his hand and his foot from the ladder and to turn round. 'I beg your pardon, sir,' he then said in his best James Bond tone of voice, 'but I think I'd like to ask a few questions...Fir...'

But before he could continue with his beautifully modulated utterances, it was clear that something was happening behind the old man with the silvery hair and the Regent Street greatcoat. It was a scraping sound, or a dull scraping sound, like something being dragged, irregularly, something soft and non-metallic, perhaps making staggered contact with the ground. On top of this was layered another sound, a soft sibilance, like a breathy voice, a sigh or a vocalized expression of fatigue... Yet it was dark... dark beyond the old man's silvery hair... Christopher felt a chill. Was some wild animal pacing slowly behind him, its evil eyes intent upon the two of them, waiting, waiting, ready to pounce when it had sized them both up. Christopher took cold comfort in the fact that the old man standing before him would be the first line of defence, allowing him to – hopefully – quickly scoot up the ladder...

The old man before him was turning round, his face a grimace, or a look of deep – it's-all-up, kind of – disappointment. Christopher was sure he'd seen a roll of the eyes.

A figure, Christopher could now see, was emerging from the shadows… and it wasn't a wild animal at all, but another human, a man, but a very, very, very old man, with a few straggly grey hairs up top, hardly able to walk, grasping a stick in one hand and seemingly taking gasps of air every few seconds. He called out, wheezily, and Christopher's interlocutor rushed to his aid, issuing words of solicitation and advice, his hands gently reaching out and helping the very, very, very old man. This released the curtain, blocking Christopher's view somewhat. He was unsure what to do – reach forward and pull back the curtain, or just remain where he was? Both had the potential to give shock. He didn't fancy doing something precipitous, some action that might be interpreted wrongly, and give the old fellow a heart attack. So, he reached forward very delicately and slowly, and only very gradually pulled back the hanging thing, at least partially, so as to be able to view things better.

It was a little strange – understatement of the century – to be standing there witnessing all this, but Christopher had now become convinced that he had a right to be here, and a right to find out what the hell was going on. But he was also glad to let the first man take care of the second one, as he now did, leading him to what looked like a folding wooden chair next to a small wooden table. 'I'll get you a drink, Professor, please just wait,' said the solicitous fellow. '…And, oh, terribly sorry to tell you, but we have… a little visitor. He's just popped in for a chat.' Hearing this cheered Christopher somewhat, but it also confused him slightly, as it appeared to attribute him a motive or a reason he hadn't even thought of before this. He had just come here by accident, after all. Was that humouring language? Whatever it was, it gave him the cue to step in a little further, letting the curtain drop behind him.

'Visitor?' said the very, very, very old man, with, Christopher thought he could hear, a little tinge of an accent. 'Did you give

301

him some tea?' he asked, his eyes closed, and with his face so encased in wrinkles it was hard to say where they might be. Definite accent, thought Christopher – European, for sure. The first old man was dancing about looking for items and doing his best to issue nice-sounding ripostes to whatever the ancient one was saying. He clearly felt it important to offer only sweetness and light to the older man. They formed a curious pair, thought Christopher, who continued to just stand where he was, observing the scene inside the cave no-one knew about. The light from the standing gas lamps was warm, but it created innumerable shadows. Some of these shadows criss-crossed each other; others occasionally transformed faces into scary masks. The ceiling above them, as curvy and natural-looking as the walls, was about three metres above the floor; there seemed to be little makeshift metal grilles over holes in that ceiling at a few points here and there. The air was a little damp and cold, but it seemed to be fresh enough. He knew there were supposed to be five caves at Cave Hill. Word of this new one would make headlines by itself. But, still, his curiosity insisted: 'What is it that those funny old guys are up to? That's what I want to know.'

Now the first old man, who was remarkably perky for his age, and flexible within that enormous overcoat, was lifting over another wooden table from out of the murk behind them and stationing it next to that of the ancient one's. He then dipped into a box at the side of the cave and pulled out what looked like three plastic bottles of water, plopping them down on the top of the second table. From nowhere Christopher could see he then produced three small glasses and placed them daintily next to the bottles. His final action was to drag two folded wooden chair contraptions from out of the dark area behind and place them at either side of the new table, opening them both. Lastly, he turned round to his visitor and, to said visitor's amazement, smiled broadly and radiantly. This also struck Chris as a little curious, given the fact that by this stage the old codger must have been knackered. With his hands making a bit of sweeping flourish, the silvery-haired gent indicated the arrangements he had just made and said, very posh-like: 'Won't you join us for a quiet libation, good sir?' It was the best invitation he'd had all day, and shaking off the feeling that he'd just walked onto the set of the Twilight Zone, Christopher took advantage of the courtesy, walked over as he was bid and sat down on one of the wooden chairs. The lights around them lent a warmth to compensate for the slightly damp air. They also, Chris now noted, gave off a tiny sound, somewhere between a humming and a hissing. He guessed they were gas-operated. Memories of sessions in The Crown Bar surfaced briefly.

The first old man – the host! – opened his elderly fellow's plastic bottle, poured some water ('Ballygowan', Christopher noted – 'nice!') into his glass, did the same for himself, and motioned for Christopher to do the same for himself. And then, with all glasses now containing water, offered an impromptu toast: 'To Belfast City Council!' he said. Christopher threw a quizzical look at the host, but then thought it best to keep things simple and echo the sentiment, if haltingly: '…To Belfast… City…Coun…' But his host wouldn't let him finish. 'Up their bloody arses!' he suddenly shouted out, which, Christopher gathered, was signal enough to knock back. Just before he did, Christopher managed to throw in a tiny echo of his host's words, getting out at least the first two: 'Up… their…' ('When in Rome…' after all.) They supped, Christopher and his host at least, as the Methuselah figure, with his heavily wrinkled face, the odd tuft of scraggly hair on the top of his pate, and eyes still closed, had seemingly nodded off to sleep. His ancient hand only appeared to hold the standing bottle. 'Drink, Professor, drink!' encouraged the host, adding, jocularly (Christopher hoped): 'For tomorrow we die!' The ancient one, a few strands of his grey hair suddenly catching the light, grudgingly shuddered out of his slumber and cupped his bony right hand round his glass and slowly raised it to his now vaguely trembling lips. Christopher was still reeling from the weirdness of all this, but the impulse to ask questions was growing stronger by the second. He thought he might start with the easy stuff: 'So... what's the problem with the Belfast City Council, if I may?'

This seemed to enervate his host. His eyes became steely and his face flushed a tad. 'The problem?' he threw back. 'The problem? Because they're...' And here he started in on what could only be described as a rant, listing not one but many, many issues which had led him to the conclusion that the council was not simply bad, but had been bad for a long time. 'Indeed,' he exploded, 'the Council has been destroying this city for the last hundred years and more! The bastards! Just look at CastleCourt! Look at Victoria Bloody Square!' Christopher knew these as huge shopping developments which had transformed, respectively, Royal Avenue and the area near Cornmarket – and even in his own opinion – in the worst possible way. His wife and kids had loved wandering through both, to dally and dawdle in clothes shops and record stores or shops selling the latest smartphone accessories, but he knew these malls had come at a cost. Their establishment had destroyed the historic buildings already occupying those spaces, their bricks and mortar sold out for the ugliest constructions of steel-girding and glass, all done in the newest way, so that a visitor would find absolutely no difference between visiting one of these faceless collections of shops selling high-priced fare made in China whether it be in Belfast or in Leeds, or in Tokyo. Gone was the Avenue Cinema where he'd seen films like *The Jungle Book* and *Rollerball* – and *Thunderball!* – with his Da of a Saturday afternoon, and gone was the Kitchen Bar, where he'd enjoyed innumerable pints and beef pies... a few years later.

'And don't mention Donegall Place!' the host then shouted, this time seemingly distraught. 'Those stupid bloody...' and here he seemed lost for words, as he sought about for the best word, or words, '...giant ugly metal... stakes... ruining the street...' Christopher knew what he was referring to. It was a very recent architectural tweak, if you might call it that, of perhaps the most prominent street in Belfast, the one which led up to the City Hall. A row of eight huge vertical curving shafts done in bronze had been pile-driven into the pavement on the Robinson & Cleaver's side of the street, each of which was supposed to represent one of the famous ships of yore built in the city. The most famous, of course, was the Titanic, and that graced the final position, closest to City Hall. He had seen this on a visit one time back to Belfast a few short years previous, and had been unprepared for the experience, which had immediately depressed him. Why had Belfast City Council fallen in love with a ship that had gone down so spectacularly in the freezing waters of the Atlantic Ocean? James Cameron had a lot to answer for, thought Christopher (even if he did enjoy his film and the fancy new Titanic Centre...) Meanwhile, his host was now virtually sobbing: '...the masts, the masts... ah, what about the Venetian masts...!' Christopher had no idea what he was referencing there, but he could see that his host was not well pleased with the town fathers, and what they had done to his beloved city. He also wondered why they were even talking about this, and how much light it would shed on why they were all sitting here in an unknown under-forest cave drinking Ballygowan spring water and crying about Belfast.

As the host seemed to be coming out of his despondency, Christopher thought it best just to wait until he recovered himself and got back on track. He didn't have long to wait. 'We wanted to do research here, you see,' said the old man with the silvery hair. Christopher noted it was only he who would do any speaking, with Methuselah content to just loll there in his chair, sometimes nodding off, sometimes watching what was going on. He was a harmless old character; Christopher wondered about the rigidity of his clothes, which consisted of what might be called field-outfit gear, heavily padded. He guessed this sartorial arrangement helped to keep his body warm and protected, and in possession of some sort of shape. It held him up. His face may have been intensely leathery, but it was no less warm for all that, in the sense that it seemed to radiate something like enjoyment at what was going on. Christopher could imagine he was listening to every word. This take seemed to be confirmed by the occasional flash or twinkle of his eyes, which would uncover themselves from the leathery folds, making the occasional appearance like moles poking their noses out of the ground. He noticed pince-nez glasses peeping out of a breast pocket... The host continued: 'People have been asking to do research up here for years, generations even! Do you know that now, in 2019, there hasn't been even one serious scientific study done on the caves here?' He spoke with forcefulness, but the forcefulness of a very old man, a bit throaty or wheezy now and again. 'Maybe that's why they never found this one!' He said the last sentence with a bit of a flourish, stabbing the table with his finger.

'I had no idea,' consoled Christopher. 'So, did they reject your application or something like that?' 'Yes!' struck back the finger-wielding one, 'yes! In a manner of speaking... Yes!' Christopher's eyes asked what *that* meant. 'It means that they said, officially,' and here he adopted a parodic Malone Road accent, with emphasis placed on particularly annoying phrases, a few mocking facial gestures thrown in for good measure, 'We will take it *under consideration*. We will debate it in due course, according to *the schedule we have,* and we will *report back to you* once we have *made our decision*.' That's what they said!' With this, the host stabbed the table so hard that he seemed to have hurt his own finger. It went sideways with the force of it and he was reduced to grabbing it with his other hand and whispering sibilant words to it for it to be well again.

'And what kind of research were you... are you doing...?' asked Christopher, and, seeing the host still fiddling with his sore finger, added: 'So, you just went ahead anyway?' To which his old interlocutor nodded, very demonstratively, as though hoping to communicate their bold initiative and their sense of mission. 'I see...' said Christopher, 'I see...' He didn't see, not really, but he could see that his queries had been addressed and that was probably that. He had maybe disturbed them enough, he could also see that. Their research obviously concerned surveying this cave —what else did he need to ask? He thought it might be a good time to retreat, with dignity, and not overstay his welcome. 'Well, as they say in Japan,' said Christopher, starting to stand up, 'Soro, soro, shitsurei-shimasu, or Thank you very much, but I must be going...' As he said so he felt he was being too polite to not press for a proper answer to his query about the nature of their research, but maybe it was the patterns of behaviour he had somehow become accustomed to in his adopted country. It was not good to over-expect from your host, and he had understood, basically, what was what, making it time to exit. His immediate interlocutor seemed impressed and happy at this development, and beamed a smile in his direction, issuing forth a few well-chosen words of praise for having 'listened to two old men' as well as asking, 'please don't tell the authorities, at least for a few days... then we'll be finished our survey...' 'Very well,' answered Christopher, 'very well', even as curiosity burned in him all the stronger now. *Who were they and how goddamned old was that other feller? And what was their research anyway? Just to check out this cave?*

It was the old, old, old feller who saved the day. Much to the chagrin of his slightly younger -or less elderly- fellow, he suddenly woke up and pitched his gaze directly at Christopher, saying, with force: 'We found them! By Gott! We found them!' To which Christopher began to answer, 'What…?' but was cut off by the host. 'No! He's fatigued…' he pleaded to Christopher, 'he needs his medication… he's becoming delirious…' To which the old, old, old man countered, in a voice of -wheezy- thunder: 'Don't! Don't! Don't!' This seemed to have an effect on the host, who threw up his hands and seemed to become distraught once again. Methuselah continued, speaking only (and…in a heavily German-sounding accent) for the benefit of the man he didn't knew from Adam: 'Leeettle dinosaurs! Here! Zeere fossils! *Leeetle, leeetle* dinosaurs! Here, I tell you! I tell you! HERE!' And with this last dramatically-pronounced word, up he got, shakily, maybe very shakily, using both stick and chair. Christopher could see that the man, when younger, had likely been tall and handsome, with a full shock of hair. Age had made him stoop, reducing his stature considerably. And yet, there was something magnificent about him, too. He was making it clear to his guest that he wouldn't be cowed by age, or by anything. He fumbled momentarily at his breast pocket until he could pull out, and then attach to his upper nose, his pince-nez glasses. Somehow, with these on, he looked already much younger. That, or the determination on his face was making age irrelevant.

Using his walking stick, he stepped, slowly, but determinedly, over to a smaller tabletop to his left and picked up some stone-like object. With difficulty, but with the enthusiasm of a person determined to convince another of the significance of what he had in his hand, he ambled/staggered over to where Christopher stood, again making good use of his stick. By this stage, Christopher was trembling with the excitement of the moment, unsure what he was hearing and what he was about to see… 'Look!' commanded a near breathless, if not quite toothless, Methuselah: 'Look!' So Christopher looked.

At first Christopher noticed the leathery hand holding the piece, lines feeding off like tributaries on a map of some lost world… then he concentrated on the flat rock at the centre of that unknown territory… a yellowed, somewhat crumbly-looking rock, about four inches long, at the centre of which dwelt a shape like a shadow, faint but discernible… as some fossilized organism, the trace of some creature with a bulbous head, a slightly curving backbone which developed into a longish tail. Where the legs or arms might have been the lines of their imprint had become fuzzy and indistinct… it was incredible to behold and he said so to the ancient fellow who held it in the palm of his ancient hand… adding: 'What is it?'

'A dinosaur! Zat's vat it is, my boy, a dinosaur! Likely a teropod, too!' said the excited man, his eyes, behind the pince-nez, twinkling with a joy that further melted his age. 'But it's only a few *inches* long!' countered Christopher, who hadn't quite understood 'teropod'. 'Zat is ze magic of it!' the man exclaimed, continuing: 'Nanism! Nanism! They all became pygmies! Ha, ha, ha! A four-inch T. Rex! Ha!' He turned around, and replaced his treasure, very reverently, on a tabletop behind him and started ambling about in a state of apparent elation, his steps at times perky enough to suggest he was going to break into a dance. 'Think of Homo Floresiensis!' he shouted once, but Christopher didn't know what that meant. He was still reeling from the idea of it all, and that maybe that fossil had been of a tiny, tiny T. Rex. *What a discovery,* he thought. The host approached, looking older than a few moments ago, and launched into an explanation that Christopher couldn't quite take in, but which concerned the special conditions of Cave Hill, with its limestone recesses and caves which had created a kind of island territory a few million years before the comet hit, allowing a variety of dinosaurs to subsist here in seclusion from the rest of the continent, and had encouraged a nanism, or extreme dwarfism.

'No! No! NO!' piped up Methuselah, gesturing with his suddenly very animated fingers. 'Don't simplify it, you klutz! Zei did all zis in different place! Zis place was all under vater, or it was exploding with lava! Mein Gott! Tectonic plates, Tweedy, tectonic plates! Moving, mein Gott!' The old, old, old man was showing no patience with his 'underling', causing said underling untold stress, as the latter then wailed away at the 'iniquity' of his 'station', and why had he tied his 'fate' to 'this albatross'. It was becoming all a little too much for Christopher who thought that maybe he should try again to extricate himself from this situation, and the craziness it was becoming. Meanwhile, old and very, very, very old were now arguing it out face to face, with the host, who Christopher could now discover was named 'Tweedy' —'appropriate, considering what he's wearing' he thought- arguing his corner valiantly. 'Yes, but, this area *became* their sanctuary, OK?' It was a tactic, or a tone, that seemed overly forthright, and only helped to inflame his even more elderly interlocutor: 'Mein Gott! You make it sound like one of zeez romance novels you read! Vat do you sink zei ver doing? Hiding in ze caves and praying to Jesus?'

Things were looking bad, thought Christopher, and he felt partly responsible for it, too, having dropped in here unannounced and, by whatever means, caused them to fight. So, he had to say something and say it fast. Then a lightbulb went on. The distant past flashed on, briefly, in the most forgotten room of Christopher's mind, a room covered in cobwebs and dust, as neglected as the novels of Rafael Sabatini by modern readership. (Yes, he once sold books by the millions!) Maybe it had been the name 'Tweedy', or the German accent of the ancient one, but whatever had been the spark, it opened up a portal -his second of the day- to a story from so long ago it was practically pre-historic. He thought about it a little, watching the two old codgers go at it hammer and tongs. He had it: 'Terribly sorry to interrupt,' he stammered, 'but didn't you… [he almost said 'guys']…find the first dinosaurs in Ireland, or something like that?' He smiled sheepishly, adding: 'They were found fighting together…?' Now Christopher suppressed the urge to develop his smile into a laugh, only now realizing the resonance that this had with the present situation – two old dinosaurs fighting it out and all… His words certainly had an effect: the two old men stopped their bickering immediately and looked straight at Christopher, neither of them with a particularly happy demeanour. Methuselah spoke first, if you could call it 'speaking'. It was more like a rising crescendo of angry-sounding words: 'Vatsa…vasta… Kalumbatsa… Der unfug nonsens… Der Quatsch. . . Scheissekopf… Dummendorfenheisse!' Or something like that. He had now become distraught, at his wit's end, and was swinging his walking stick for added effect. Tweedy now joined in with the histrionics, arms aflail and proceeded to walk around like a man in grief, uttering imprecations. They both continued this for about a minute, with Christopher now convinced he should just get the hell out, when, in tandem, they stopped and turned to look at Christopher. The strangeness of witnessing of this was only increased, significantly, when the two opened their mouths at the same time and said, accusingly: 'And WHO are you?'

Christopher stared back at them, his mouth agape, the most agape it had ever been in his fifty-six years of life.

Chapter Five: Weird scenes, pt.2

It was a fair question. Christopher had come to their secret
den without invitation after all. And he had found out all
their secrets, if in somewhat garbled fashion. This was
certainly enough to answer whatever question he might have had
on why he had come to Cave Hill in the first place – obviously
finding such an incredible thing as this was answer to that. He
had found a secret! A mystery! An adventure! He could go home
a satisfied man, and yet, he wasn't happy about causing these two
old, or very, very, very old, gentlemen any stress. And, compared
to them, with their intensely fascinating discoveries, the ancient
prehistoric past at their fingertips, WHO was *he* indeed?
Somehow his thoughts went back to that poem by Seamus
Heaney where he gives his family name to the priest but his first
name to the policeman holding the sten-gun. This prompted him
to answer, merely, and desperately unsatisfyingly: 'Christopher...'

Before his interrogators could press for a family name they
all took note of the sudden sound of a loud thump above where
they were. Then another thump, even louder. 'Animal?' asked
Tweedy. No-one answered. There was another thumping sound.
The reason he'd thought it was animal was likely because the
thumping sound had been hard and fast, suggesting fast
movement. What human would be doing that up above? There
it was again, and now there was another sound, like a scream!
That could only be human... Again, again, the thumping sounds
rained down, the majority, it seemed, on the wooden portal that
had been rigged up as the secret entrance. Christopher was
beginning to feel a little freaked out. How much stranger was
this day to get? Hadn't he satisfied the gods of adventure already?
He didn't really need this. As though in answer to his pagan
prayers, the sounds stopped, diminished at least, then went away.

Christopher had a sudden thought, which he could pass off

as levity, even if he didn't mean it entirely as such: 'Are you sure,' addressing his captive audience, 'your dinosaurs are all dead?'

Instead of garnering smiles, this idea seemed to infuse the older of the two with renewed sobriety. It was as though he was actually contemplating it. But Tweedy laughed, rudely and contemptuously: 'Oh, sure, next we'll be visited by Steven Spielberg!' He continued to mock, employing a parody American accent: 'Oh golly, is that a little old T. Rex up there or are you just pleased to see me?' He followed this up with a mock chortle. 'What do you think this is… *Christopher?*' Tweedy lambasted his visitor, almost spitting out his name. 'Fantasy world? Giant behemoths plodding about eating people up on Napoleon's Nose?' Christopher didn't enjoy being talked to like that. He could just ignore it, or, now having become somewhat accustomed to being here, and perhaps affected by the madness of the whole experience, he could strike back, as the old, old, old man had. He was tempted: 'OK, OK. I was just saying… But…' 'Yes?' said Tweedy in his haughtiest, and wheeziest, tone. Christopher thought about his response. Egged on to counter the idea that he bought into fantasy, he would throw out another thread entirely, one with more bite.

'Well, sir,' he explained, 'OK. Those sounds might not have been produced by T. Rex out for a quick hike up the hill, but rather…' and here shifting into a somewhat more dramatic-sounding tone, '…the fellow I saw not so long ago, up there…' Christopher pointed up. 'Yes, he looked a bit crazy, I am sorry to say… He was acting very erratically…' 'Yes, and?' snapped an unimpressed Tweedy. 'Well,' continued Christopher, 'I can't be sure, but he seemed to be attacking birds!' 'Attacking birds? Whatever do you mean?' asked Tweedy testily. Christopher then did his best to explain what he thought he had seen, when in fact he hadn't actually seen what he said he had seen, all in an effort to push his new theory about what was happening above their heads. 'I think he's attacking them... and mutilating them! He's a crazy guy! I saw what he did to one poor chick! Oh my God... the blood and guts...' Methuselah was looking confused, asking his fellow what the visitor was saying, but Tweedy was not answering. Tweedy was looking more serious than before, serious and unconvinced of what he was hearing. He confirmed this with: 'You see... you say you saw this and that, but you didn't actually see him do any of that, did you? Did you? You do live in fantasy! You live *for* fantasy! Don't you, Christopher Whateveryournameis?' This was laying down the gauntlet. Christopher came close to uttering a swearword in response, half because he didn't like to be accused of lying, and half because Tweedy was absolutely correct.

Suddenly, Methuselah spoke up, his eyes excited: 'Maybe it's Fritz!'

Christopher and Tweedy looked at him, Christopher, at least, wondering *'Who the bloody hell is Fritz?'*

The thumping resumed. Thump! Thump! Scream! Thump! Until... Crash! Nay, CRASH! Behind them sounded the most almighty scare-the-bejaysus-out-of-ye sound of wood breakage and screaming and a thudding off the walls and onto the ground, with no end even then: the screaming continued. Against all the fear coursing through his veins, Christopher reached out and pulled at the black curtain, tugging it so hard it detached from where it had been clinging to the roof of the cave entrance, revealing...a furious creature, legs and arms pumping away, its mouth open and from it issuing screams and sounds that no-one could hear without fright. The three inside the cave jumped back a few paces, making it even harder to discern what had entered, the dust flying up in a torrent of clouds.

It was only when Christopher heard the word 'Help!', and, once, garbled, 'Fuck!' in the midst of all this that he realized what had fallen in had not been an animal, or a prehistoric one for

314

that matter, but a human. A decidedly prehysteric one. And though it was likely *that* human, the crazy one who attacked birds, an impulse within him forced him to go forward and answer the call. 'Help' the figure called, 'Help! They're biting me! Monsters!'

Monsters? He was crazy! To what he might be alluding was unsure, but once Christopher had reached down to help, he felt the most important thing was to show him that help was at hand. 'You're safe here, don't worry…' Christopher recognized the face from his experience above, and yet, here he looked helpless and harmless, and even quite scared. Perhaps, as Tweedy had implied, he was too quick to attribute bad intentions. All he wanted to do now was to help, so he grabbed at the man's lapels and somehow pulled him up from the heap he had been in. Considering his size and weight, though, that was easier said than done. Dust and soil and bits of broken wood covered his entire body, with even a few scrapes on his skin, hands and face, where blood trickled out. He was still babbling on about 'monsters', though.

'What are you talking about? Make sense, man, make sense!' commanded Christopher. 'And what are you doing?' Methuselah turned to Tweedy and said in a tone of disappointment: 'That sure doesn't look like Fritz…' Tweedy nodded to his elderly companion and then looked back to see what would be the next madness to occur.

'The birds! The birds! Up there, they're monsters, I tell you!' said the fallen one. Instead of indulging the unexpected guest, Christopher felt he should bring things down a pitch or two, inquiring: 'Look, who are you and what are you doing here?' To which entreaty the fallen man suddenly seemed to warm, reaching into the inner pocket of his cream-coloured mac-like coat and pulling out ID. As he showed it to Christopher, he pronounced the following words: 'Ivan Stacks, Reporter for the *Belfast News Letter*… Retired.'

Ivan Stacks? It was a name that Christopher had kept in his mind for decades, and not in the dingy backrooms of memory. Why, he wasn't sure, but on hearing it now, the past came rushing back in a torrent. He thought he had received enough wonders for one day, but to learn that the man beside him now was the same person he had met all those years and years ago, randomly on a Belfast street, instigating a phase when all he could think about was dinosaurs, dinosaurs and even more dinosaurs, well... he could now call himself well and truly flabbergasted. 'Ivan Stacks! Wow! Hisashiburi!' exclaimed Christopher, realizing immediately he had to translate that unconscious slip into Japanese, with: 'Long time no see!' Ivan Stacks had no idea why this fellow would say that and just looked at him in something like total confusion. Christopher felt the need to explain, and went madly into a summary of how they'd met on the street and he had given him the newspaper with his article about finding fighting dinosaurs, '...back in '77? '78?'

'Nineteen seventy-nine!' thundered Methuselah, throatily anyway, and as if that statement hadn't gotten the attention of his two unexpected guests, he repeated it, with even more – somewhat breathy, wheezy – thunder in his voice: 'Nineteen Seventy-Nine! It is inscribed on my brain! As is your name, Ivan Stacks! Du!' The very, very, very old man launched out his right arm and hand, an accusatory index finger pointing directly at the large, dishevelled figure who had just fallen in. His second 'Du!' was like a sonic projectile aimed at the point right between Ivan Stack's piggy eyes. 'You ruined me! Your stupid article in that stupid newspaper ruined our mission! It ended in ignominy! Ignominy! Za university pulled the plug a few weeks later, and all credit was given to that damn amateur who just found the fossils. *Nothing* for us! *Nothing for me!*' At this point, Tweedy seemed to feel the need to interject: 'But Professor Heinkle...' To which Professor Heinkle, formerly Methuselah, and formerly something at Heidelberg University, too, replied with the swiftness of a Megalosaur confronted with a puny Scelidosaur: 'Don't! Don't! Don't!' And Tweedy fell silent, cowed, defeated.

Heinkle continued, the same index finger now in the air, as though he would deliver the most devastating blow of all, because he was indeed Professor Heinkle, Professor Heinkle of the Palaeontology Department of Heidelberg University, Retired, Grand Emeritus, a pioneer in the field, a man destined to be remembered as legendary, now that he had discovered the world's first example of dwarf dinosaur fossils, and in Ireland! The place of his greatest defeat -to paraphrase what was actually quite a garbled and hard to follow rant- would be re-staged as the place of his greatest victory! 'I vill overcome! I vill conquer! I, Janek Heinkle, a hundred and five years old, *vill never die!*'

'Sorry to burst yer wee bubble, there, fella,' now said Ivan Stacks in response. But I've discovered something even better. Or...' he smiled, mischievously, 'a hell of a lot worse! *How about living dinosaurs?* At this point, he turned round, looked down and retrieved what looked like a notebook. He opened up the pages. Look!' He dusted things off a little and then opened up and showed page after page of hand-drawn pencil images of little birds, with copious notes scribbled in below each and generously filling the margins, too. He explained: 'I know a thing or two about birds.' Here, Ivan leaned forward and then pointed at the badge of his lapel: 'RSPB member, don't you know?' All looked, but no-one reacted. 'And,' he continued, 'I know about dinosaurs, too! [But no badge, this time.] And according to my research, these little sods are descended directly from dinosaurs! Birds don't have gnashers!'

This had Heinkle smiling, then laughing: 'Ha, ha, ha! Birds?' he exploded. '*All birds are descended from dinosaurs*, you klutz!' He continued laughing, looking genuinely happy with himself. Ivan was not to be undone: 'Aye, but these boyos don't exist on the Grand Register of Known Species, Professor! And...' 'Yes?'

asked a slightly mollified Heinkle. 'And… they're dangerous! They will attack hu…' Ivan stopped speaking and started pointing… to an area on the ground halfway between where he and Christopher were standing and where the two retired Professors stood. What it was was moving, walking, hopping even, a bird, or a bird-like creature, a proto-curlew, perhaps, but with a long beak that opened and revealed a row of serrated teeth. Then it started pecking at the ground and pecking with force. It was hopping again, getting closer to Tweedy and Heinkle. 'Move!' shouted Ivan, 'it'll bite!' And, whether it was the tone of panic behind those words, belief that their second visitor's 'research' was correct, or observation of the thing's seemingly violent behaviour that did it, Tweedy and Heinkle did move, and precipitously so. You might even say they jumped. Then they retreated step by step, a little, then a little more, almost into the shadows behind them, as though in the grip of an entirely irrational fear. And yet, as it now became clear to everyone, the little hopping creature was not a solitary hopping creature, but just one of many! They seemed to be hopping out of the shadows or from behind tables and chairs. Christopher and Ivan looked round in panic and saw dozens of them now, right behind where they had been standing, now hopping and snapping and coming toward them…

'What should we do?' shouted Tweedy. Instead of responding with words, Ivan decided to try something. He looked down at the one closest to him, as did Christopher, noticing the fine feathering upon its taut body, its hard black eyes, its longish neck, which would stretch forth every moment to snap and the teethy mouth that, if you listened, issued a nasty hiss like a snake. It looked like a bird, but also not like a bird. The legs were sturdier than you'd usually see on anything local. But it was the movements and the confidence of those movements which cloaked it in an aura of being not just any old bird. Even if it was only half a foot tall, it walked like it was much taller, and was much less inclined to skedaddle at the approach of a human. Humans were not frightening for it. It was frightening for humans! 'I think we'll try this,' called out Ivan, and with that drew back his right foot and gave it a thundering kick. 'George Best, eat yer heart out!' exclaimed Ivan. The creature flew. Hit the wall of the cave with a dull thump and fell in a heap on the ground. It was still moving, but its pride had certainly taken a hit.

This now became the strategy adopted by all, all except Heinkle, who had gone into a paroxysm of grief at the wantonness of his fellows in their infliction of violence. 'Stop, oh, stop! I implore you! Ich flehe dich an!' he cried, but Ivan and Christopher and even retired Professor Tweedy, who at one point let it be known that, by the by, he was no spring chicken, but eighty-eight years old himself, got the boot in.

Abandonment of the cave was adjudged the best next strategy, with most of the effort being expended on trying to push and pull the screaming Heinkle up and out. It was made even more difficult by the fact that he'd crammed his pockets with all manner of stone fragments and the fact that they had to break up one of the wooden chairs to use a wooden leg to smack at the offending creatures which seemed to think they could block the way of the puny humans. 'Take that, you wee shites!' shouted an invigorated Tweedy, much to the dismay not merely of Heinkle, but of Christopher and Ivan, too. 'One expects a higher standard of behaviour from academics, after all,' whispered Christopher to a beaming Ivan.

Up the rope ladder they clambered, Tweedy first, Christopher and Ivan pushing Heinkle up, Tweedy then lending a hand as the first one up. It was hardly a surprise to see that many people had gathered at the path below. They had been looking up with great concern, and only when figures started to emerge from the cave's entrance, with the remains of the great, but shattered, wooden portal now pushed over and back, did they think of clambering up the bank of the forest. They were just day hikers, a collection of ordinary, likely mostly local people who had heard a great commotion and had wanted to find out what was going on. Now, they were helping, making a great fuss over the two men of extremely advanced years, treating them like royalty, even, proffering drinks and wiping their foreheads with cloths and whathaveyou. No-one paid much attention to the little birds that were walking and hopping about nearby, whether they on the Grand Register of Known Species or not. All that mattered was just getting everyone down to the path.

Only one of the impromptu group looked less than local; this was perhaps because he had a large, professional-looking camera round his neck, with a rucksack seemingly filled with camera gear, and he was holding a large tripod. How had a reporter managed to know something like this was going to happen, many wondered? The other salient feature of the man with the camera gear was his moustache, which was large, and like something you'd see in old photographs. The bushy eyebrows enhanced this impression.

'Fritz!' called out Professor Heinkle excitedly, who had now been gently brought down to the forest path by the random helpers. 'Fritz! Was für ein Tag! Was für ein Tag!' and, fetching out one of the stone fragments from his pockets and holding it at chest height, 'Mach ein Foto davon! Schnell! Schnell!' No-one likely understood his words, but it was clear what he wanted done. Christopher looked at Tweedy and said: 'Yer man's not from the *Belfast Telegraph*, by any chance?' Tweedy looked a little uneasy, hesitating before he could answer: 'Mmmm....' he emmmed, 'bit of a German operation all this...' To which Christopher raised an eyebrow, which Tweedy noted, saying: 'Belfast Bloody Council... Belfast Bloody Council... Just think of the glory we could have had! The glory of a local find...'

'Well,' said Christopher, in consolation, 'don't worry, someone very local has maybe found something even more exciting!' This drew a joyless smile from Tweedy, who then kicked, rather viciously, at a bird hopping near him.

Meanwhile, that very local person was still feeling all a bit over-excited by the day's events; he still looked fearful of those little hopping creatures, hoping they'd keep their distance for a while – a sure case of hopping and hoping... It was not them he had to fight off now, but an old and not particularly attractive aul' bird who was wiping his face and telling him what a state he was in, poor thing. He didn't want to hear it, thank you very much. He could hear someone shouting. It was Heinkle, barking out his commands in German, sounding, to Ivan's ears, distinctly Führer-like. What a pain that man was, he concluded. He looked over, then walked over to where the German was standing, holding his ancient treasures in his hand over his chest and looking as professorial as he could in his ancientness. The flash went off once, twice, three times and Ivan felt blinded, momentarily, even if he had been looking from the same vantage point as the cameraman.

What with the flashes and the mad excitement of just now, not to mention the awkwardness of having to navigate his way through all these bystanders and well-wishers, Ivan's mind was in a very delicate state. This, some might suggest, was why, when he eventually caught sight of the cameraman standing beside him, Fritz – with his giant Walrus-style moustache and his evilly bushy eyebrows – he suddenly felt faint. The world seemed to swim before his eyes. A repressed nightmare of his past life had suddenly surfaced, like a whale. He could see again the business-end of a gun barrel...

He thought he was going to die. But he wasn't. Life didn't work quite like that. You had to go through the ringer first, with embarrassment after embarrassment, shock after shock, knock after knock, joy after joy, pint after pint, ad infinitum or ad nauseam, and of the two it was the latter which seemed the most apt right now.

For it was then that Ivan Stacks, Ace Reporter for the *Belfast News Letter* (Retired), proud member of the Royal Society for the Protection of Birds, loving husband to Masie and father to three fine sons, *and* author of the famous 'Belfast, the Troubles, and Me', then succumbed to his fate. Unceremoniously, and with a bit of an audible sigh, he fell smartly and squarely on his arse once again – his right royal sixty-three-year-old roundly Belfast (in both senses) arse.

BOOK THREE

Finale, 2019-20

Embarrassment could be a mighty engine for change. So Christopher had decided long ago – at least in *his* life. After his debacle in Kelly's Cellars, long, long ago, he had determined that the next time he spoke with a beautiful girl, he'd know his onions and be able to indulge in the witty repartee his slightly-elders seemed well versed in. This would take confidence-building, image-training and to study his onions like bejaysus.

The embarrassment he had felt in Glengormley Library that time, confronted with his childish attempts at describing fossils, had been even more emboldening. He hadn't waited around, feeling sorry for himself – he had stabbed back right there and then. He had hit back – against his lesser self! He had subsumed the shame of his rubbish efforts, regrouped, counter-attacked… and won! The resultant re-written description shone all the more radiantly for it. He could go home and feel good about his victory against the page.

Sometimes, though, embarrassment could be excruciating, with no discernible lesson to be learnt… If his bowels had metaphorically tapped him gently on the shoulder as he struggled with the English language in Glengormley Library, another time they had virtually blown him up with gelignite. The human body is a wonder, but it can also be a curse, and on one day in his very early years at Barrack Street, circa 1975, poor Christopher Maguire had suffered a treacherous and unprovoked assault from his internal plumbing. Where had it come from? What was it doing? Why me? How can I stop it? How can I make others think I'm not responsible for this growing stink? These were the questions which surfaced in his twelve-year-old panicked mind at lunchtime. Even now, forty-four years on, he could see himself pathetically trail a line of excrement, which was dribbling down the inside of his school kecks towards the unoccupied chair of a fellow student (during lunchtime) in an underhand attempt to point the blame at someone else. It didn't work. It couldn't work. It was clear to all what he had become, with the slowly building cries of 'Unclean!' 'Unclean!', or what passed for that in a 70s Belfast argot. This was followed by a bus journey home, riding past the beautiful bay-window residences of the Antrim Road, and the glorious sun-drenched Cave Hill with its profile of a sleeping giant, and… a carriage-full of passengers staring in absolute horror at the incarnation of all their worst olfactory nightmares... Then, at home, a showering away by his mother of all the (brown) woes of the world as he stood half-naked in the bath. A day to remember, indeed, if for all the wrong reasons.

What Christopher had learnt, or had been inspired to do, from this experience, was not entirely clear. It hadn't brought about much in the way of lifestyle change, even if he had told his mother, 'No more Bemax for me!' – 'Bemax' being the health-grain his mother had insisted one day that all her kids had to sprinkle on their cereals, despite the fact that it tasted like dried boke. Who cared if it was good for you? Christopher was now equipped with the knowledge of an experience he'd rather not have had, to proclaim that Bemax was in fact *not good* for one's health at all, but bad, *very bad*, as it had unleashed forces from the bowels which should happily remain relatively dormant, at least most of the time. Whether he really did proclaim this or not, however, is lost to history.

Lost to history! – what a dreadful phrase, and a dreadfully common one, at that. All those gaps in memory… What day did Christopher suffer his Waterloo? From what day in time did his mother begin the Bemax experiment, and until when? If he had kept a diary and taken copious notes, and not just spent half his time doodling in the margins of textbooks, Christopher might very well have been in possession of such knowledge. He would, of course, have needed to hold onto said diary for decades, carrying it -or all the ones thereafter, 1976, 1977, 1978 etc.- around with him to whatever location he happened to move to. Would he indeed have wanted to record his indisposition for the sake of dear posterity, or even posteriority? Imagine that entry: 'Today. Oh, what a day! Well, I was the victim of an assault by my treacherous bowels. Yes. They ganged up on me and beat the living shit out of me!' This to be followed by a graphic account of what had occurred, drip by drip, horror by horror. Not very likely. No, young Christopher would likely have hoped to put it behind him, pardon the pun, and gone to bed after a glass of warm milk or even hot Ovaltine, prepared by his caring, loving mother. He would have luxuriated in the cleanliness of the sheets and blankets and his warm jammies and slipped happily into sleep. Or… possibly not! He may have appreciated the cosiness of his prepared surroundings and felt the loving care of his mother, but he knew that the next day might be one of the worst he could ever possibly imagine – *The Return of the Leper!* (Starring Christopher Maguire, Directed by Michael Winner. Rated X.) Imagine the slagging he'd get. Imagine, also, the potential for absolute shame he might face at the highlighting of his panicked ploy to incriminate a fellow student. Imagine all that and you could picture the poor sod crying into his pillow, having spent the last hour screaming at his mother that he wouldn't go to school the next day. *No way, José!*

What all this meant was anybody's guess. Perhaps it showed the problematic aspects involved in looking back through the mists of time: to what extent did memory preserve and to what extent distort? Or hide? Christopher's memory of the next day's school remained a total blank. Ah, the embarrassment of youth was sometimes best forgotten. Now, however, at the age of fifty-six, a man of standing, respected professor and all that, Christopher had a different reason for potential embarrassment.

It had nothing to do with social inhibitions before the fairer sex or his body playing nasty tricks on him, but rather on how to relate his recent experience to all and sundry, or anyone still left – those not dead, or 'fallen away'. *The adventure on the hill.* Where would he begin? With his encounter with the apparent bird mutilator, or after having entered the secret sixth cave and met the squabbling superannuated professors? What should he say about dwarf dinosaurs, or those scary hopping proto-curlews with their penchant for biting? People might just think him crazy. They might look at him askance and think he'd had a nervous breakdown, that Japan had not agreed with him, that he was drunk (again), or had fallen prey to premature dementia. Or they'd humour him with 'Dear, dear, dear' and 'Get away now, isn't that a story now?' and 'Well, I never, boys a dear, boys a dear…'

He could tell his brother Jim, of course, to whose house he had wended his weary way immediately after the madness at the hill. And Jim was all ears, even if they weren't quite working, and lapped up every detail -for the first fifteen minutes at least. The amount of detail Christopher could go into with hastily written notes, the most effective way to communicate with someone who'd lost their hearing, was measly, though, and he ended up just giving a basic outline, which, at the end of the day, Jim likely thought was an extended joke, or the plotline for his latest projected novel. After twenty minutes, it seemed preferable for both to just sit back and watch *John Wick II*. Halfway through it, after Keanu Reeves had blown away about fifty people with a variety of guns, blood splattering a variety of walls, Christopher realized the only way he'd be able to convince his brother of the truth of what had happened would be to find corroboration on the Internet or on the TV news. But things had changed. Where was Larry McCoubrey or Barry Cowan when you needed them? (His sojourn in Japan had had the effect of preserving his old life and TV habits in temporal amber.) Every hour, on the hour, the BBC TV from London would broadcast their news, and what they broadcast at 6pm didn't look a whole lot different from what they had put out at 5 o'clock, or 4 o'clock, or 3 or 2pm either. Where was the local stuff? Surely, they had a story on events up on Cave Hill? Not having Wi-Fi, Christopher's iPhone couldn't connect to the internet and so he was left to keep asking his brother to see if there was a 21st century equivalent to BBC's *Scene Around Six* with Sean Rafferty, or Ulster Television's *Good Evening Ulster* with (G.L.O.R.I.A!) Gloria Hunniford. That strategy soon became a bore, however, and so Christopher desisted and was happy to keep the chat on all the other stuff they'd spent the last fifty plus years talking about -music, books and films. As they watched Keanu blow away another dozen or so really, really bad guys, blood all over the shop.

By the end of his stay with Jim, Christopher was beginning to wonder if he'd dreamed the whole thing up himself or had suffered a delayed hallucinogenic trip after smoking Michael's weed two days previous. After returning to his hotel room, Wi-Fi restored, he spent an hour and more desperately searching on the little screen of his smartphone, not looking very smart, his eyelids closing autonomically every few moments. But nothing, zilcho, diddly squat appeared. Christopher's story was beginning to look decidedly lost to history. And so it was the following day, despite repeated searches. By Saturday, when his wife and kids came, there hardly seemed much point in mentioning his 'adventure', especially with all the chat they had to get through and meeting peeps and all the things they'd planned to do from now. In light of this, and the complete absence of news on the mysterious goings-on at Cave Hill, the urgency of the story dissolved, and, happily, its potential for embarrassment, too.

It wouldn't be until long after they had returned to Japan that Christopher would instigate his searches once again, and even then, almost as an afterthought. After one day, in early 2020, as the world started to take stock of the terrible pandemic beginning to take hold, he spent a whole evening screen-bound, becoming progressively more and more bored and mindless by doing so. After dabbling with his latest poetic attempt, net surfing for a not particularly necessary new watch and doing actual work in the shape of prep for a more than likely online teaching future, a flash of inspiration edged him into typing out the word 'Heinkel' and dropping it into the Yahoo search engine. This led to multiple entries for the German airplane company and another which manufactured, as far as Christopher could tell, centrifuges… It took a fair bit of scrolling down, but eventually he was able to find listings for the man, spelt 'Hein*kle*' not 'Hein*kel*'. He could scan the impressive achievements in palaeontology of Professor Janek Heinkle, born in Munich in 1914 – but, about his time in Belfast, nothing whatever was written. It was at least a good first step toward unravelling the mystery.

'Tweedy' brought up investment bankers, a musician, and lots of links to clothes shops selling woolly mohair coats -oh, and, something Christopher might have expected, a very minor character in Joyce's *Ulysses*. With a few more clicks, though, he did come across the Tweedy in question, skimming through details like 'Emeritus Professor of Archaeology at Queen's University, Belfast', 'President of Belfast-Venice Friendship Association' and, on a slightly less glossy note, 'twice divorced'. 'Irish dinosaurs' brought up a few sites which mentioned about a find of dinosaur fossils. Interestingly, one was from the Belfast *News Letter*, but it certainly wasn't penned by Ivan Stacks. This mentioned a place called Ballystrudder in Country Antrim and suggested that evidence of two different kinds of dinosaur had been found there, a 'Thyreophora' and a 'Theropoda'. Abandoning the idea of trying to say these words five times in rapid succession, or even once, Christopher simply checked what they meant, and then wondered if those were the chaps who had caused the whole ruckus. Alas, after forty years, he couldn't remember. The names didn't ring any bells, that's for sure.

In coming days, balancing his screen time between work-related activities and those which were clearly not, he was able to peer through the clouds of history, and prehistory. One website, from 2008, and entitled 'When Dinosaurs Ruled in Northern Ireland', focused on a special exhibition and TV programme which BBC Northern Ireland had run at a time when the Ulster Museum had been undergoing a redevelopment. The Blueprint Exhibition, he discovered, was designed to encourage young people's interest in the ancient past, displaying exhibits of fossils and bits and pieces of Mesolithic artefacts. Interestingly, part of the exhibition seemed designed to allay the worries of 'Creationists'. 'I was expecting a little bit more controversy,' the presenter was quoted as saying, noting that 'Northern Ireland... is quite religious still.' Adopting a rather soft approach, he brought the Belfast-born CS Lewis into his discourse as an example of someone who could believe in both the Creation *myth* and the Evolution *fact* at the same time. 'There should be no contradiction,' he said, equivocating slightly: 'I don't think there's a contradiction.' This had Christopher, safely ensconced in his faraway world of happily pagan atheism, where people visited shrines only to pray for good fortune and absolutely no-one walked around traumatized by hell or painted their kerbstones in tribal colours, sighing and smiling. It felt like he'd done a Joyce, that by coming to Japan he'd flown right by the prehistoric nets of Norn Iron Presbyterian thinking, the kind that that had resulted in the locking up of children's play parks of a Sunday because it was the 'Sabbath', a 'day of rest'. It was the same mind-set which continued to promote the 'idea' that the world, according to Church of Ireland Archbishop of

Armagh James Usher (1581-1656), had begun at precisely 6pm on October 23, 4004 B.C.! To Christopher's ears, Ballystrudder was beginning to sound as exotic and also as *prehistoric* as Thyreophora and Theropoda. He could also breathe a sigh of relief to have detached himself, from Catholic thinking, too, having by now safely consigned 'Transubstantiation', 'Hell' and 'Jesus, Son of God' (and his big Da, up in the clouds) to the rubbish bin of the mind.

It was only upon re-reading the article that Christopher noticed reference to the fossilized bones of two dinosaurs, the only found in Ireland. And these were slightly easier to pronounce than the ones in Ballystrudder: a scelidosaur and a megalosaur. Surely these were the ones that had started all the ruckus? Found by a man called Roger Byrne, this had to be, Christopher punningly told himself, a major find indeed. A subsequently-dug-up web-listed note, this time from a proper palaeontological journal, dated to 2001, also identified Byrne, calling him 'an amateur collector', who had discovered the fossils 'more than 20 years ago'. This, Christopher recalled, would be the 'damned amateur' Heinkle had complained about! He also vaguely recalled the ancient one saying something about the university pulling funds and giving all the credit to this guy... 'Nothing for us! Nothing for me!' What a scene that had been! thought Christopher, what a bloody scene. Memories surfaced also of the scene which took place immediately after, when a huge dark blue helicopter had appeared out of nowhere and had then proceeded to lift up Heinkle, Tweedy, and Fritz, in special harnesses, to fight – not die – another day. That, Christopher noted, was his second close encounter with a swooping, aerial mechanical beast...

A few clicks later, and Christopher could see that these Byrne fossils were actually on display in the Ulster Museum, and he could view a video about this from two years previous with the curator Mike Simms, putting all this into a nutshell -because it was a very short video! These online discoveries were opening a door into the dark for Christopher. If embarrassment could prompt one to action, so too could ignorance, and Christopher had that in bucketfuls. Ignorance of Heinkle, and his life, beyond what meagre pickings he could rummage from the net, that is. He had ignorance aplenty in regard to dinosaurs, too. Despite his teenage interest in them, spurred by his chance meeting with ole Ivan Stacks way back when, Christopher had never really given them much thought thereafter. Like everybody else, he'd been thrilled to see them come alive in the early 1990s, thanks to Spielberg and Stan Winston in *Jurassic Park*, read the Michael Crichton book, too, Conan Doyle's *Lost World* an ancient echo... He'd flipped through coffee table books of the behemoths but skipped the captions largely and just drank in image after image of the dreadful beasts. Rather he'd been taken more with what was going on in the world of poetry and prose, of Heaney and the rest, of Lorca, Dylan Thomas and the world of Joyce, not to mention long forays into the world of literary medievalism. *Not many dinos stamping across their hallowed pages!* Now, at fifty-seven years old, he wondered if he could drum up the energy sufficient to explore a world he didn't know, a lost world beyond anything Professor Challenger had ever found.

He could. He'd certainly give it a go, he told himself. It would be his new niche line of inquiry into a world best kept secret for now, an exploration of a past so far removed from what he knew that he'd need all the chisels, tweezers and tongs he could get his hands on. It was also the beginning – something initially his conscious mind failed to pick up on – of a process to explore, or at least tantalizingly recall, an entirely other lost world, one in which giant lumbering forms patrolled the streets not on scaly pachyderm legs, but on wheels, and paperboys stood on street corners yodelling out near unintelligible calls for punters to buy the late edition of the *Telegraph*, '*Siiiiiiiiiiiiiiixxxxxxxxx Teeeeeeeeeeeelllllllllleeeeeee!*' Never mind the hawkers yelling out, '6 lighters for a pownnnnnn!' and old ones ambling about with signboards advertising the end of the world…

Little by little, Christopher began to rummage through the threads of ancient history in regard to Professor Janek Heinkle, ordering books and articles on his university budget -anything to help flesh out his background. It didn't come easy. The biggest clue came from a sober-looking biography of the man, *Janek Heinkle: Legendäres Leben* – penned of course in German. Yet again, Christopher was saved by his handy 21st Century Swiss Army-knife, the iPhone, as he employed Google Translate to scan selected pages throughout the massive tome. He learned about Heinkle's Luftwaffe experiences and there was a paragraph or two about his rather liberal incarceration in the Republic of Ireland. He also learned about his work as a palaeontologist, digging with some bigwig in the quarries of Germany, where they uncovered fossils of some weird bird thingys, but singularly not resembling curlews. It seemed that the ole earth digger had also given his name to a small mammal that had co-existed with the dinosaurs in the Upper Jurassic – the Heinkleodon, no less. From the accompanying illustration he could see it was not unlike a duck-billed platypus, but with fierce-looking horns on its bonce. He learned that Heinkle had a knack of intuiting fossilized bones, that after a short examination he could usually identify what animal it came from and what part of the body it belonged in; this, it was stated, took an extraordinarily encyclopaedic knowledge of dinosaurs to be able to accomplish, and gave a touch of the legendary to his already gilded name - hence the book's title.

The last chapter seemed to suggest Heinkle had mysteriously 'retired' from the world in 1979 and had then taken up residence in the Peruvian Andes. That, or that was where he'd carried out the next stage of his research. This had Christopher checking out precisely where he might have gone and what he might have done, and as he did, he learnt about Peru. He discovered that Peruvians were famous for extended longevity. All that goat milk, beans, potatoes and high altitude was just the trick, it seemed. With a little extra digging, dredging through German-language journals, Christopher uncovered that Heinkle, after a gap of about ten years, seemed to have been still active at the ole palaeontology lark. A few obscure academic notes kept surfacing from time to time, from 1990 onwards. One was about the Titanosaurus, one of the largest dinos ever known. Strangely, although they could be over twenty metres long and weigh a colossal sixty tons or more, Heinkle had seemingly discovered one an eighth that size and weight, and termed it 'verkümmert', for 'stunted growth', if against the opinion of a few others who argued it was just a smaller, different dinosaur in the first place. Upon learning these snippets, Christopher soon became convinced that he'd unravelled (a) how the Professor had endured so long and (b) where his dino-hunter instincts were directing him. 'Eureka! Progress!' he told himself, keeping things vague at the dinner table. 'Open up the Moët!' It helped that they were selling them at extreme cut-price at the nearby OK Supermarket. (Japan's answer to Crazy Prices.)

Then darkness. No more gems from latter years, a trail gone cold and damp. Until, that is, Twenty First Century Tech -yet again- came to his aid, this time in the form of Twitter, and a chance search therein, after inputting twenty cross-referenced terms or so... *Bingo!* Somehow, Christopher had navigated to what he was to discover was a 'Deep Web' site, a site not listed on the standard www. His computer, however, threw up barriers to stop him accessing it, suggesting it was dangerous to proceed, that, in other words, if he did go ahead, his files and software would become infected and maybe even destroyed. Christopher was feeling all the more isolated now, on a mission to seek knowledge beyond knowledge, against the odds and even beyond reason. It was time to open something else (from 'OK Super') and think about it.

Meanwhile, he thought about other stuff, or rather, other stuff just tended to rise to the surface of his over-worked consciousness. As would happen from time to time, in chat with Eri about this and that, he once found himself talking nine to the dozen about that other lost world, the one he'd left behind thirty years before. It had nothing to do with quadrupedal creatures, and everything to do with bipedal ones – former teachers, classmates, friends who'd died or 'fallen away', or his neighbours, like Michael, of course, and his lovely mother Ina and sometimes overly strict father Jim, or the fiercely Presbyterian McAllisters next-door to them, their son Stephen with the thick glasses and more than a bit of the righteous Christian about him, who'd then grown up to be an RUC man... Then there was Shirley Gorman, with her always welcoming smile, except when her next-door neighbour Mrs Trewin was involved. They'd been locked in a neighbourly Cold War since the day they'd unhappily met, decades previous, the reason for which no-one really knew. And yet, individually, they'd throw out the warmest welcome mat for Christopher and family on every visit. Norn Irish hospitality at its best. There was also the staunchly Scottish Presbyterian Mrs McGregor who'd lived down the street, looking not terribly unlike Whistler's Mother's sister. Christopher shuddered to think what a visit to her house would have been like. Of course, it could never have been as bad as a visit to his Aunt Theresa, with her desperately gaunt and joyless poker face, who used to hold Christopher in his toddler years on her lap, stroking him with her skeletal hand and calling him 'My wee chicken, my wee chicken...' Christopher had had nightmares about such times, from when he was very young, half-convinced that she might one day slip a sharp knife down her sleeve and go for his helpless child's throat...

The more he thought about all this, and them, the more he realized there existed a cast of lively characters still going strong within his memory. They weren't going anywhere. They hadn't gone anywhere. His digging in the soil for Heinkle, perhaps, somehow, had him looking back on what and where he'd come from himself. Consciousness of Belfast -and its environs- long ago was growing, and given added edge by distance, made all the worse by the growing pandemic that forbade all global travel. Only digging down into his mind was possible. Or on a page... But of course, he had a job to do! Beyond what his cyber students demanded of him, he had to find out what had happened that day on Cave Hill and confirm to himself he wasn't going crazy. So, reeling from his latest hangover, the potent residue of Campo Viejo Rioja Reserva 2014, two iterations of Punk IPA, and that last wee snifter of Jameson's still coursing through his Irish veins, Christopher threw caution to the wind. He'd enter the 'Deep Web' and bedamned the consequences. So, he brought out his older laptop, a Windows 7 job, and cracked his aging knuckles. Click, click, crack, and click, and then another click, and he was through – to...

Aži Dahāka's Chicks

...all done in red text over a black background. This added a layer of mystery, as did the more than vaguely religious but irreverent title, and a layer of difficulty in terms of legibility. In contrast to the flowery (spidery?) font of the title, the script was neutral and legible enough, once the eye became accustomed to the nasty colour scheme. Staccato entries proliferated, on this crazy topic and that, and it took a bit of tiring eye-work to scan the page and all connected ones for scraps of info, but the hungover Christopher wasn't going to go away empty-handed, oh no! All of it was fascinating, but he had to keep on track.

He didn't want to know about the 'Rendlesham Forest UFO Incident' and how the victims couldn't have their medical records released, even with Senator John McCain (now deceased) having done his best to petition the US government, *whatever that was all about*. He also didn't want to know about the Navy's patent for a UFO-type craft that allegedly had the ability to 'engineer the fabric of our reality at the most fundamental level' by 'seemingly bending the laws of physics as we know them.' What he was looking for was something about Belfast! And… marvel of marvels… he found it!

'Update on the Heinkle story. April 1 2020'

Unspecified 'authorities' in Northern Ireland have successfully addressed the leaks about the August 8th 2019 Belfast Cavehill Incident. Witnesses' stories discredited and all traces covered up. Doctor Dino [Heinkle], a fellow 'academic' and a personal assistant taken away aboard a German-registered helicopter. Heinkle said to be close to releasing photo evidence of the discovery of 'new taxon of dinosaur'. Stay tuned.

'Dynamite!' shouted Christopher, to no-one in particular, just at the screen, 'this is the biz!'

It certainly was. He scanned the pages for more, feverishly, now having raided the fridge for a hair of the dog that kicked his teeth in. The Mahou, souvenir of Madrid airport, certainly had bite! But he was biting back now, at the awning gaps of darkness he'd been straining under. Weeks and months of keeping to himself what he knew had happened, now here in black and white – or black and red. Or red and black! Another story he came across concerned one of Heinkle's other theories, about dinosaurs, incredibly, having been blasted out into space by the Chicxulub asteroid 66 million years ago and which, he'd postulated, *were still flying around in suspended animation!* The flash-frozen dinos, according to his 'secret knowledge', had been locked into orbital loops called 'Lagrange Points' (whatever they were)! There were five of these Lagrange Points circling the Earth and it was '99% certain' that some 'organic material' had been 'captured for eternity'. 'Imagine that!' said a beery Christopher, again to no-one in particular, or maybe to the refrigerator door, which he now spied thirstily. 'Hey, fellow astronauts, you won't believe what I just saw flying past the window! Yes, that's right: a Brontosaurus!' (Then he re-said that as 'Hey Cap, I think a Bronto saw us!') This guy Heinkle, Christopher was learning fast, was way beyond the bounds of legend -a deity among researchers, perhaps. 'Doctor Dino! That'll do it!' he spluttered as he supped another beer (prize *Newcastle Brown Ale* at that). He was certainly having fun, but... what about Belfast?

There was a backstory, he now read, going way back a few pages, involving a lot of scrolling, and it concerned events said to have happened in 1979. Yes, it stated, the Byrne fellow had found the fossils, and they'd been given to a certain 'Prof Thompson' for checking up at Queen's. Then, the university had brought the big guns in, in the form of visiting Professor Janek Heinkle, of the Palaeontology Department of Heidelberg University, no less. He was to be ably assisted by Professor Ronald J Tweedy of the Archaeology Department at Queen's, and the whole operation was to become a 'glorious illustration of the importance of Queen's University as an institution of topflight scientific research', a strategic move at a time of government cuts, and as a demonstration of the institution's 'advanced and globalized thinking'. The dream, however, Christopher read, had turned a sudden paler shade of white upon the publication in the newspapers of a story concerning the nature of the fossils, which stated, completely incorrectly, that the two fossils showed evidence of a dinosaur battle -

between the two bodies they had come from. What should have been a simple case of exposing this falsehood was complicated by apparent internal squabbling, a focus on the fact that Heinkle's team had also been given the wrong the location by Thompson (who was, unbeknownst to himself and others at that time, suffering from dementia) and the fact that the bogus story had generated so much general ridicule. The university authorities had then stepped in and drawn a veil over operations, contacted Byrne, and swept the entire episode under the carpet. Subsequent reports, in later years, would state that the fossils had been found from the year 1980, and no-one, but no-one, wanted to quarrel with that.

Christopher sat back. It was all coming back to him, as it had begun to inside Cave Hill's sixth and unknown cave. That would explain a lot, he sighed, mulling over what he'd just read. He saw poor Professor Heinkle in his mind's eye, reeling from the debacle… and from the professional embarrassment of it all. Embarrassment! Christopher reflected on that. Be it in Kelly's Cellars, Glengormley Library or a classroom at Barrack Street, he knew a thing or two about embarrassment himself! And how it might empower you, if it didn't crush you to a pulp. He saw Professor Heinkle's flight now to the Peruvian Andes for what it was – escape! And who could blame him? And yet, *it hadn't crushed him;* it had made him… gifted him with incredible longevity and re-focused him onto pathways new and even more exciting! Oh, and then to return to the land he knew so well, the very place of his defeat, and to… make his newest, greatest discovery there? Christopher felt awe as he contemplated this, an awe which only a 350 ml can of Heineken could hope to sate (well, it was the only beer can left). 'Oh, Heineken!' slurred a half-cut Christopher to the shining green tin can, 'How much closer you bring me to Doctor Dino! Oh, Heineken! Are you Heink*len*?' He then tried that again, in varied drunken dog-

German forms: 'Heine*klen*? Heinekellen?! Heinkellassen! Heinekellegötterdämmerung!' Et cetera, supping all the while, and saying 'I'll raise a glass to ye, Janek!'

Things, however, were suddenly and precipitously taking a turn for the worse. *'Oh, no!'* exclaimed a suddenly alert Christopher Maguire. Something was happening to the screen. The script on the page he'd been peering into for all those joyful minutes and hours, can after can, was now turning fuzzy. He wondered if it was because he'd drunk so much. And yet, he could see it wasn't that - the script was actually dissolving! The red would shimmer and dim for a sec and then appear to sink into the black, occasionally reappearing, then sinking back again, until... it was just a screen of black, ugly and pulsating with the hum of the mindless energy which empowered it. Was this a sign that his computer would be infected from now on? He didn't care, because, not having anticipated this, and not having written anything down, Christopher began to feel he only now had seconds to learn everything he could before the whole site, and maybe even his computer, blew up. Suddenly, the Heineken didn't taste so good.

The next page, still accessible due to an enduring screen button, was no less stable than the first, the red words fuzzing far beyond legibility. But Page Two, he knew, had nothing on Belfast or Heinkle, so he clicked ahead to Three and then to Four, witnessing the same disastrous dissolution of the text. Knowing that Five had some material he hadn't had the time to check properly before, he now clicked on that and scanned it like he'd never scanned any text before in his life, speed-reading, cross-reading, then vertically scanning for scraps, until in the last line he found something on, to his surprise, the one and only Ivan Stacks! He had to click on Six to the get the rest and, as the text began to shimmer and to dim, Christopher Maguire, Professor of English at Tsurumi University, Yokohama, man of standing, had his beery, flustered face right up at the screen drinking in the few precious red-text on black words he could just make out, before it went... **KAPUT!**

The screen went blank, or rather, it went black -deathly black, like a funereal shroud.

'Quick!' he said to no-one in particular, again, and scoured the tabletop for pen and paper. As he did, he dislodged things that would otherwise be deemed precious, including a paperweight he'd picked up in Barcelona, a fossil-imprinted rock, 'Muy raro! the guy had said.' He couldn't care less about it or the books he'd stacked for easy consultation. They could go on the goddamned floor for all he cared -only pen and paper were needed now! As is the way when one panics, the eye can miss the obvious, and so it was with stunned relief and not a little annoyance when Christopher saw the pencil and the memo pad and grabbed them, writing feverishly for all his worth, and other idioms that might suggest a mixture of haste and undignified desperation.

Rather like the way one might hope to latch onto the contents of a fast-receding dream, Christopher's efforts to record all he'd seen on Page Six resulted in a series of patchy, fragmentary, and disjointed sketches. He'd captured something about Ivan Stacks' statements about 'living dinosaur birds' from the Cavehill Incident, and, intriguingly, suggestions that Bellevue Zoo might have played a part in all this. It was something about a mishap years ago when a few chicks of the strain of a flightless bird from the Russian Steppes had apparently escaped their assigned perimeters at the Zoo. The report had prefaced this with a short rundown on Mr Stacks' life, mentioning his career as a journalist, and a bomb explosion he'd survived, along with a man now well known as 'firebrand D.U.P. MP David Wilson'. With his long-term residence in Japan, the Wilson name didn't ring any bells with Christopher, but he could always look that up. And, then, finally, the last smidgeon of information Christopher had extracted from the fast dissolving scene was the name of the person responsible for the majority of these articles: 'Electra'. That, he soon decided, was clearly just a nickname, to add to the mystery of the site. Obviously a nom-de-plume.

And the site? What was its name again? This more than anything now was what he craved to recall. The 'Chicks' part he remembered. It was the exotic religion-infused name he couldn't quite picture correctly. He sat there at the dining-room table he used as his impromptu office when at home, trying out a few combinations: 'Avi Dala's Chicks?' / 'Avi Dakota's Chicks?' / 'Azi Dalakota's Chicks?' / 'Azi Dada's Chicks?' It was getting nowhere, and even he was beginning to think he was wasting his time, sat there mumbling rubbish at the dead screen. Indeed, time had flown. He'd started the session about one o'clock, after lunch (of cheese on toast – old habits die hard and all that), but now it was well past three thirty. How the time had gone! And how many beers he'd had, too! What a crazy thing to do in the middle of the day, he realized. He wasn't prone to such behaviour, unless he'd visited some restaurant or British style pub with Eri, and usually on the weekend. What madness had possessed him here, today?

He'd be ok. He'd have a coffee. He'd then go out for a walk before the daylight weakened, buy some groceries, take a bath, set the rice… And then, as he contemplated doing that, he had one last idea he thought he'd try. He put away the old Fujitsu computer, worrying about it and wondering if it would ever revive, and then retrieved his trusty -newer- Panasonic. Opening up Yahoo, he typed in 'Electra' and one combination after another of the title as he thought it might be. The Internet, he had realized, is user-friendly after all. It knows illiteracy is rife, illiteracy and general ignorance of English, or that we all have such busy lives that no-one cares too much anymore about the small stuff, typing 'it's' to mean 'its' and vice versa, or slightly bigger typos like 'scientits' for 'scientists' (harf, harf). 'Don't worry, sir, we'll take care of that,' the Internet might say. 'We have predicative autocorrect in all our latest devices, too. Just type in some rubbish and we'll make sure it looks like gold, or if you've only half the name, throw it in and we will set our bots on it.' And so, Christopher threw his fragmentary bits and bobs to the super-efficient bots of the search engine, linking them each time with the name 'Electra' and did so for longer than even he realized, as the day's light did weaken, if almost imperceptibly… until… click, click, click… he had it: 'Aži Dahāka's Chicks'! There was no portal to the site, alas, but a different, safer, site had mention of its (or it's?) contents, and the name 'Electra'. By clicking on it and scrolling down a tad, Christopher at last laid eyes upon the mystery name, and, as a bonus, what seemed to be her family name, unless that was likely bogus, too – 'Electra Jal-Williamson.'

It didn't mean a thing. Nothing, zero, zilcho, diddly squat. (Did anything on this site? In the age of 'fake news'…) But he wrote it down anyway. Time for that walk, he saw. Time to leave the world of the computer screen and use his legs and lungs and breathe in deeply – if through a mask- and look around at the world in three dimensions. He had so many questions to ask, so much ignorance, and yet so little time to see the last of that day's simple beauty.

He thought of Heinkle, as he ambled, thought of Ivan Stacks, and thought of Belfast, too. If he were on board the starship Enterprise, perhaps, or in the seat of H G Wells's Time Machine, he could engineer a return visit to that time and place, to Belfast, Nineteen Seventy-Nine. Or earlier, much earlier, to the Jurassic Period -why not? See the behemoths lumbering about in paradise before the Chicxulub Impactor slammed into their world. A slingshot round the sun would do it, or just by

pulling back that crystal-headed lever, delicately, but firmly...
He'd get there, easy enough. But, then again, that was science-fiction. No-one travelled through time. It defied the laws of physics. Yes, but so did Transubstantiation...

Time was a funny substance altogether, however you looked at it. Time was fluid. It stretched or contracted whatever it was you happened to be doing *at that time*. Writing and concentrating intensely contracted it, or obliterated awareness of it, as had happened just today; meetings at work, especially ones conducted in a language he hadn't yet come to terms with, and probably never would, stretched it out like a black hole might stretch out an unfortunate astronaut falling into one.

Time was bridgeable. This was the really interesting part, he felt. Just ask any palaeontologist, or archaeologist, pro or amateur. All you needed were some mallets, chisels, trowels and a few brushes. Down on your knees, not before the altar to pray to some invisible Being, but to get into the dirt and muck of what time had wrought upon the surface of the planet. Well, you needed knowledge, too, or you'd likely break the precious things and then not have a clue what anything meant. A hundred thousand people would see just another basalt rock upon the beach; it took someone special, someone who had made the effort to learn, to see the jewels amidst the bric-a-brac. Thereafter, the detective work would start, the rigorous checking, calibrating and recording, and the networking with fellow souls. Eventually the past would be unlocked, and one once ignominious dead organic body, or fossilized bit thereof, would shine pristine and glorious, to take up new residence in human knowledge and human consciousness. Time need not always mean an end. The past existed still; it just needed a little dusting off.

Christopher reflected on that. He'd been doing his own explorations of the past for the last twenty years or so, picking up the stones of words dropped on papery shores, peering at their hard surfaces, and trying to figure out how they came to be there. Doing so took time, patience and a fair bit of cunning. Ten years on a single poem, Christopher winced, but what gems he'd discovered in the process. He had opened a door into the world of the twenty-something-year-old James Joyce, taken fragments of *this* calcified artefact of words and *that* and fitted them together in a hundred different ways, or at least until they had begun to tell a *half* decent tale of what was going on in Joyce's head at the time of composition. And it was generally always a half decent tale, too, never quite completely fixed, something for others to argue about. This interpretative thing increased as time lengthened. He'd peered back at literature produced a half millennium before, too, brushing lightly – endlessly, it sometimes seemed- at the accumulated dust and muck of centuries, before a jewel began to shine. And in doing so, he'd entered into the world it came from, seeing with the virtual eyes of those who ate the altar rails for breakfast five, six hundred years ago, and those who had only one book in the house and that a giant handwritten thing on vellum composed of three parts religious tracts and one part stories about knights, fair maidens and dragons... He'd seen a heaven-dwelling mother in one of those religious tracts, led by angels down to Hell. He'd seen her laugh with delight at the sight of her own daughter being tortured by devils for her sins, safe in her conviction that Justice, even if it meant inflicting pain and injury on her own flesh and blood, was a thing Divine...

He'd seen much worse, mind, on the TV, his mother's dinner on his lap. Nine years old, spooning the Ma's ham soup into his mouth as he watched a balding, kindly-looking man, waving a white hanky, leading a group of men carrying the inert body of a young man down some street in Derry. Chaos everywhere. Weapon-wielding soldiers running here and there, townsfolk gathering, their faces wretched amidst the smoke and screams, a sense of all-pervasive fear... 'Mammy, what's happening there?' he'd innocently asked. Yes, the fifty-seven-year-old version of that same being now had to admit, his consciousness of things past was slowly being stoked – from Bloody Sunday to Bloody Friday, just six months on. Headline news on *Scene Around Six*, the usually quietly ebullient Barry Cowan looking seriously grim. Who wouldn't, mind, having to tell his audience about all the ordinary people who been killed in Belfast that day, pedestrians and shoppers, ambling round the town. Oxford Street bus station, the remnants of a person having to be shovelled into a black plastic bag. Later on, the Shankill Butchers would get their knives out, and search for random Taigs. The regular UVF, of course, could do sectarian assassinations just as well. Christopher's family had to keep a camán [Irish hockey stick] propped against the front doorjamb, in case they came at night... 'Daddy, what's that for?'

He shuddered at the memory of those times -especially now, as he sat on stone steps looking out into a tranquil early-dusk Japanese scene of farmsteads, a quiet road beyond, a temple and a cemetery to his left. He could see a solitary crow flapping through the cloudless sky... *So far away, so far away... in place... in time...* he told himself. *Perhaps... but reachable.* It only took a little thought, a jiggling about with this half-calcified recollection and that. Or deeper down the memories may have been, beneath all consciousness, untouched and still as painful, or as fresh, as the day they were formed. Imprinted on hard, undying surfaces, the trace of some wild, violent monster running away after a quick kill...

The longer Christopher sat, looking out on that serene vista, the more he felt the need to walk that bridge of time... it helped he hadn't been directly traumatized by all that... 'stuff', for want of a better word. Not knee-capped, not had his legs blown off, not left for dead in a ditch, or been beaten senseless because he wore the wrong school tie. Just the usual stuff of growing up, if against a background of a society gone mad. He could live with that. He had, quite happily (unless you quizzed that poor sheep on the hill), diving into worlds beyond the one he lived in, feeling every moment vital, fresh, alive, peopled by a cast of characters you couldn't make up if you tried. And now that cast list had been added to. Who was Heinkle? Tweedy? Who was Ivan Stacks? Who Electra? *Who… 'Christopher'?*

He could almost see them all… See Belfast City, too. He'd maybe need his Da's Tasco binocs, or Janek Heinkle's chisel and brush set, but very definitely he could just make out the outlines of *that vast skeleton of then*. Hear the sound it made, too… the thundering of feet, the three-toed ten-ton sort *and* the size-13 clodhoppers on sale at McManus's of Ann Street, just the ticket for a dander round the town, kicking up a bit 'o dust. He'd get down upon his writerly knees in all that dust and dirt and dig a bit. He'd walk through Donegall Place again, shorn of all its giant ugly metal stakes, and through the not-so-giant but just as ugly metal Ring-of-Steel… He'd skit up the steps of the Linenhall Library and spend a few idle hours perusing all the shelves, plonk down at a free ancient wooden desk and open up Hardy's *Tess of the D'Urbervilles*, or have a shufties through the *The Northern Whig*. Or, you never know, he might try the Central… He'd meet up with Michael again, Michael, whose memory of times past was way better than Christopher's, able as he was to replay all the things they'd gotten up to in fine detail, and to relate all the neighbours' intrigues. He'd ask him about the Gorman-Trewin quarrel, and whatever happened to Stephen with the glasses and the attitude… He'd go back there… It wasn't lost, that world. He'd lived in it, and it in him. All the shite he'd gone through growing up… and all the shite that gone through him, too – and down his bloody school kecks!

Christopher then closed his eyes and waited a wee bit. Time and patience, cunning, too, were needed. Awareness of the interpretative thing helped, too. Looking back could always change, contingent on what new finding had been made. The dinosaurs of way back when, when way back when was only forty years ago, were naked scaly beasts. Now, apparently, they weren't; they'd sprouted feathers and were multicoloured, according to the latest research, like over-sized Barry Manilows with banana-sized teeth. ('At the Copa! Copa Banana!') Of course, their outer appearance needn't necessarily be what made them shaggy…

Soon enough, emerging from the dark, Christopher could see a form appear… It was not that of a dinosaur, or even a fellow in 'saurian relapse', but that of a tallish, impressive-looking gent, wearing dainty circular glasses… He was striding into an auditorium somewhere, some paper in his hand and boy did he look livid? About to blow a gasket. Boys a dear, boys a dear, as the Da was wont to say. *And what has got his goat and what'll be the first words out of his beak [pronounced 'bae-ek']? That I'd like to know. That I'd like to know!* mused Christopher.

But that would do for now. He could play with things a bit. Or a lot! Sure, at this stage nothing was set in stone… nathin'!… until, of course, it was. Preserved in time's preservative of words upon the page. (Who the feck wrote that? © Ivan Stacks?) *How to make a fossil, Step One!*

Christopher opened his eyes. The light had noticeably dimmed. That crow had returned, too, and had sat itself on the top of a telegraph pole. It was looking at him.